It was supposed to be a simple tag

One of Ibarra's dealers was down for the count, a couple of his watchdogs wasted in the process, and there seemed to be no problem with the first stage of the action.

Not until he tried to disengage.

The hit was streamlined, nearly perfect. The Executioner was pulling back and had reached the street before he realized he had a problem.

Spotters, four of them, emerged from a black sedan across the street, shouting at him, showing hardware, two more staying with the car. His own wheels one block down and well beyond his reach. Even if he beat them to the car, he stood a chance of taking hits before he got the vehicle in motion, and a spray of bullet holes would stop him short at customs, when he tried to cross the Rio Grande.

A choice, then. Bolan made it on the move, a sharp left turn into the nearest alley, running for his life until he reached a rusty garbage Dumpster and crouched in its shadow, the Beretta ready in his hand, set for three-round automatic bursts. He braced the weapon in a firm two-handed grip and sighted down the slide toward the neon afterglow.

Accolades for America's greatest hero Mack Bolan

DON PENDLETON's
MACK BOLAN®
HELLGROUND

A GOLD EAGLE BOOK FROM
WORLDWIDE®

TORONTO • NEW YORK • LONDON
AMSTERDAM • PARIS • SYDNEY • HAMBURG
STOCKHOLM • ATHENS • TOKYO • MILAN
MADRID • WARSAW • BUDAPEST • AUCKLAND

First edition June 1994

ISBN 0-373-61436-5

Special thanks and acknowledgment to
Mike Newton for his contribution to this work.

HELLGROUND

All spirits are enslaved which serve things evil.
                                    —Percy Bysshe Shelley

Dark religions may cloak evil deeds, but
there's no way they can stand before the
cleansing fire. It's time for captive spirits to
be freed . . . or to go up in smoke.
                                    —Mack Bolan

Two guards were waiting for them at the ranch, tired-looking men in wilted khaki uniforms. They rose reluctantly from simple wooden chairs and stiffened to attention as the first of half a dozen vehicles pulled in. The lone American immediately noted that they did not leave the shade provided by a squat adobe house.

He couldn't blame them. Even with the hat and mirrored aviator's shades, he felt like he was baking under the relentless sun. Two hours driving, and he wondered now if it was even worth the trip.

Around them, visible through the settling dust, stood a weathered shed and an empty split-rail corral. An ancient pump near the house. Outbuildings lay hidden from where the American stood, beside a military jeep, but he had seen them coming in. The house would have no running water, no electric power. Lamps or candles served as illumination after sundown, and a black wood-burning stove.

It seemed ridiculous to even use the term ranch, impossible to picture crops or livestock being raised on barren, sunbaked soil like this. Still, they would have to call it something, and the former tenants had named this godforsaken piece of desert Rancho Santa Maria.

He savored the irony for a moment, trying to picture the original inhabitants, coming up with vague peasant caricatures. They would have been religious, in the way of poorly educated, hungry men and women, looking forward to a better afterlife than they would ever find on earth. With sweat and luck, they might have scratched a living from the desert, barely hanging on, but something had displaced them. Illness, economics—it was unimportant why they left. The point was that the ranch had passed to other hands and other uses.

And the evil came.

He caught a whiff of it from where he stood, but he was in no hurry. He stood and watched the *federales* forming sloppy ranks, manhandling their prisoner as they removed him from the van.

In other circumstances, the American would probably have raised objections to their treatment of the prisoner. Experience had taught him that brutality was ineffective, but the *federales* had their own approach. A love tap here and there. A soda bottle shaken long and hard before its contents were released inside the nostrils of a stubborn prisoner. Sometimes, he had no doubt, the statements they obtained were slanted to appease the officers, more wishful thinking than intelligence.

But he was a guest here, nothing but a lowly gringo with no official standing, and he would not risk expulsion from the scene by raising abstract points of human rights. Besides, the prisoner deserved worse.

Rancho Santa Maria. If the stories were true, they should have renamed it Rancho Diablo, but the predators he sought were not world-famous for their sense of humor.

They started with the shed, Commander Garza following the prisoner, a dozen sweat-stained uniforms strung out behind him, slouching in the heat. Their automatic weapons seemed incongruous in the surroundings, and the American could draw no comfort from them.

There was evil here, but it could not be killed with guns.

The sixteenth member of their party was a priest from Ciudad Acuna, drafted for the mission when Commander Garza finished listening to the confession of his prisoner. It would be difficult to guess the padre's age within a decade, but his hair was gray, his face as brown and brittle as the desert. Even broiling in his cassock he did not appear to sweat, as if his vital fluids had been baked out years ago.

The smell grew stronger as they neared the shed. At twenty paces, it was enough to turn the stomach, conjuring the mental image of a slaughterhouse where he had worked one summer, after high school. Blood and pain and death distilled into a fragrance that could never be forgotten, once sampled.

Commander Garza gave the prisoner a shove in the direction of the shed, all eyes upon him as the small man shuffled forward, awkward in his leg irons, reaching for the simple wood-and-leather latch. He did not hesitate, but pulled the door wide open, breathing deeply of the foul aroma emanating from the shack. It seemed to give him strength, his posture straightening, the narrow shoulders squared. He turned and smiled at Garza, beckoning to the commander.

Step into my parlor...

The American pushed forward, swallowing the urge to vomit, breathing through his mouth in an attempt to overcome the stench. He saw the padre cross himself and brought his eyes back to the shed.

Commander Garza shoved the prisoner inside, and followed with his right hand covering the nickel-plated automatic pistol on his hip. It was a rule of thumb that *federales* liked their pistols shiny and their rifles automatic, part of the machismo trip that came with pinning on a badge in Mexico.

The shack was stifling, almost hot enough to stupefy the swarming flies. It did not matter how he tried to breathe, or even hold his breath. The stench filled the eyes and ears and clothing. It would take a dozen showers to expunge the reek of death, and even then the smell would linger in the mind.

Behind him, the American could hear a couple of the *federales* vomiting, a sound that caused the prisoner to smile. Commander Garza slapped him hard across the face and cursed him, gutter Spanish interspersed with threats.

The lone American ignored them, studying the contents of the shed while he had time. A makeshift altar stood against one wall, crowded with candles, statuettes, a human skull that tried in vain to smile without its lower jaw. He recognized a number of the saints in residence, black rooster feathers on the earthen floor. The rusty stains of blood were everywhere—upon the altar, spattered on the walls and soaked into the dirt, stray droplets on the ceiling.

Pushing past Commander Garza and the prisoner, he crouched before a blackened metal caldron bristling with sticks. He did not need to count them—there were always twenty-eight—and so he concentrated on the other contents of the pot. A grisly stew of sorts, with some of the ingredients already decomposed beyond a cursory analysis. He picked out strands of something that resembled hair, a turtle's shell, the shriveled husks of several scorpions, and jagged splinters that he took for bits of bone. A rusty railroad spike protruded from the mess, and flies had laid their eggs within, the pot aswarm with maggots.

This was where the evil lay, its earthly root. The gardener had slipped away from them this time, but they had found his crop.

How long had he been waiting for this moment? Miami seemed a world away, but flashbacks to another life still troubled him. He had a score to settle, but it seemed that he had missed his chance today.

A rough hand on his shoulder dragged him away as the commander of the *federales* shouted orders to his men. One of the uniforms came in and swept the altar with his rifle butt, then turned and kicked the caldron over, scattering its contents.

So much for the rules of evidence.

The priest was waiting as they left the shed. He had a vial of holy water in his right hand and a prayer book in his left, a bland expression on his face. This man had seen it all before, and he was only waiting for the order to begin his cleansing ritual.

Commander Garza gave the word, and the American hung back a moment, watching as the padre disappeared inside the shed. His prayers were muffled, even with the door wide open, but a couple of the *federales* crossed themselves, soft voices answering the padre in a kind of chorus.

Exorcism.

It was worth a shot, but the American was more concerned with those who brought the evil here. He did not know or care if there were evil spirits lingering around the ranch. His answer lay in tracking the progenitors of evil, running them to earth. While they remained at large, a thousand exorcisms would be fruitless. They could always find a new place, set the evil free once more...unless he stopped them.

Turning, the American found Garza and the others moving past the dry corral. He fell in step behind them, catching up as they approached a ratty garden plot. No peppers or tomatoes growing here. Some straggly weeds had taken over for a while, but even they could not endure the relentless sun.

These days, the garden plot was sprouting foot-long stalks of wire.

He counted thirteen separate wires, arranged in three short rows. The prisoner stood to one side, examining the plot with a crooked smile before he spoke.

"Esta aqui."

Commander Garza gave the prisoner another shove, but the small man did not seem to mind. He was showing off now, albeit for a hostile audience, and he enjoyed his place at center stage.

The American watched as their guide shuffled forward, bending to grasp one of the wire stalks with both manacled hands. He put his back into it, straining against gravity, working up a sweat for the first time since they had arrived. The sandy earth heaved up as if a giant mole were burrowing between his feet. Another mighty tug and he lurched backward, sprawling on his backside, with a bulky, serpentine object draped across his legs.

A human spinal column, with the pelvis still attached.

One of the *federales* lunged forward, aiming a kick at the prisoner's face. The small man raised his arms in self-defense and took it on the biceps, rolling away before another boot could find his ribs. Despite the dust and sudden pain, he came up grinning, staring at the bony relic, proud of his achievement.

Twelve more stalks protruded from the earth like grave markers. A garden of the damned.

Commander Garza barked an order to the ranks, and someone tossed a shovel forward, clattering against the bones. Another order to the prisoner, and he struggled to his feet, using the shovel as a crutch. He started digging, hampered by the shackles, but no one offered to remove the irons. At last, he found a kind of rhythm and began to excavate the grave.

The first of thirteen graves.

From behind them came an explosive whoosh of sound. The American turned in time to see the shed erupt in flames, dark smoke pouring from the open doorway, seeping through cracks in the walls and from under the eaves. The priest stood near enough to feel the heat against his face, sprinkling holy water on one of the plywood walls like an ineffectual fireman.

Purification by fire.

The American grimaced, wondering if it would help.

At least, he thought, it couldn't hurt.

The evidence of evil could be excavated, exorcised, incinerated, but its soul had slipped away. His quest would not end here. Not yet, not after all he had gone through.

Resigned to settle for the bird in hand, he turned back toward the garden patch and watched the prisoner as he turned up a femur, scraping carefully around the bone.

Unmindful of the sun, he settled in to wait.

CHAPTER ONE

The worst thing about Texas, Mack Bolan decided, was trying to cross it by car. The Lone Star state lived up to its reputation for size, devouring four whole pages in his Rand McNally road atlas, when most states were satisfied with one.

On paper, Texas seemed as crowded as Brooklyn or Queens—each city, town or village labeled, creeks and parks and mountains tagged with names in a variety of colors, filling up the map—but there were no such visual diversions on the open highway. You could drive for hours through the open flatlands, meeting no one, watching out in vain for anything that might resemble human habitation. Much of it was desert, stark and primitive, where rugged men—red, white and brown—had spilled their blood for centuries, defending what they took to be their home.

In retrospect, the Executioner believed that all of them were wrong. No man could truly claim the desert for his own until his bones were bleaching in the sun, picked clean by scavengers, the elements and time. The desert cared no more for man, his buildings and machines, than for the scrabbling of an insect in the sand.

Hard land, but not without a simple and compelling logic of its own. The fittest would survive by cunning, strength or speed, and those who fell below the standards of the land were meat. No one to mourn the passing of the losers, whether they were snapped up by a lizard, flattened by an eighteen-wheeler on the interstate, or snapped up by a lean coyote on the run.

The desert was not hostile, Bolan realized. It was a neutral zone that played no favorites. A perfect killing ground.

From Amarillo he took Highway 27 south of Lubbock, switching onto Highway 87 south of town and thus continuing his journey southward. Some two hundred miles of open, sunbaked land before he reached San Angelo and found his interchange, Highway 277, running due south to Del Rio on the Mexican border.

Texas conjured grim memories for Bolan, keeping him alert while he drove, the speedometer needle hovering just under sixty miles per hour. His bogus paperwork would pass inspection by a traffic cop, but he would just as soon avoid the test. No point in pushing it unless he had to, and the soldier did not even have a mission yet.

He had been caged in Texas once, an effort by his enemies to pin him down, and pure dumb luck had played a major role in his survival. He had no desire to go back and recapture the experience for old time's sake, and while his situation vis-à-vis the government had been revised since then, he had no way of knowing when some rural sheriff might be thumbing through his dusty Wanted posters, watching out for a familiar face or set of fingerprints.

It was supposed to be a simple meeting in Del Rio, in and out, no strings attached. He meant to keep it that way, if he could. Brognola had not briefed him on the job, preferring to let Bolan size up the facts on his own and make his choice without official pressure. If he chose to pass, Hal said, there would be no hard feelings, no recriminations down the line.

Which had to mean Brognola thought it was a job worth doing...if it could be done. Outside his jurisdiction, from the sound of things, and possibly beyond the scope of Bolan's talents.

But he would have to wait and find out for himself.

Just yesterday, he had been wrapping up a job in Kansas City, stepping on a wing of the DiCarlo family that had begun importing crack cocaine in major quantities. The local Mafia, embodied in the person of one Rico Balderone, was sick and tired of showing red ink on the books while youngbloods from the ghetto drove around in limousines and thumbed their snotty noses at the family. The K.C. capo, Jake DiCarlo, was a doddering antique, incapable of reining in his own subordinates— assuming that they even briefed him on their plans. He drew a pension that would make the U.S. President's look minuscule and issued vague directives that were generally ignored. When Rico Balderone consulted him at all— less frequently with every passing month—the old man heard that everything was great, no problems on the street. If Jake suggested any course of action to his first lieutenant, Balderone would smile and nod, toss in a compliment or two about the old man's vision, and proceed to override the orders with his own.

It was a situation ripe for exploitation, and the real heat started coming down when members of the Crips had flown in from Los Angeles last year, recruiting local teenage gangsters to expand their web of drugs and death. There was a fortune to be made in crack—from ghetto residents at first, infecting whitey with the virus over time—and when the locals heard how easy it could be, they started signing on in droves.

Their only obstacle—aside from the police, who did their best but had no more success than any other agency

from coast to coast—was Rico Balderone. The would-be
capo knew that he would have to turn his failing family
around before he could demand respect from *La Com-
missione,* and there was no way that could ever happen
if he let a bunch of teenage dipshits raid his territory
anytime they got the urge. A lesson was in order, and if
Rico managed to corner the crack market in the process,
so much the better.

Then Mack Bolan dropped into the scene, with the war
drums already rumbling in K.C. He had no sympathy for
either side, but experience had taught him that a drug
war, unrestrained, inevitably claimed civilian lives. The
Crips were no great marksmen, and they made up for
their technical deficiencies with firepower, strafing res-
taurants, shopping malls, whole residential neighbor-
hoods in the hope of tagging a single target. The stage
was set for a bloodbath, but Bolan had in mind a deviation from the script.

It was a classic razzle-dazzle, two days of playing one
side off against the other, manipulating the troops
through selective strikes and taunting phone calls, setting up a showdown between Balderone's finest and two
dozen hard-core Crips near the K.C. stockyards. The FBI
and locals were alerted in advance, but Bolan still had
time to stage a personal appearance on the killing ground,
before he slipped away.

They would be counting bodies and discussing charges
for the next few days at least, while the surviving repre-
sentatives of either side were held in lieu of bond. From
that point, it was no concern of Bolan's if the trials
dragged on for months or years. His work was done—
one job, at least.

The call to Wonderland had been a routine check-in,
touching base with Hal before he took some downtime,

catching up on sleep, perhaps a decent meal or two. But apparently it wasn't in the books yet.

Brognola had been cagey, playing down the sense of urgency when he suggested Bolan might relax en route to Texas, more specifically Del Rio, where an old associate of Hal's from the Miami drug wars would be stopping over for a day or two. It would be nice, Brognola thought, if Bolan and his friend—Doyle Mitchum, late of Metro-Dade—could have a little chat. No details on the phone, but it was something Bolan ought to hear. Doyle Mitchum had a problem on his hands, and if the Executioner could help, so be it. If he couldn't... well, of course, no obligation was implied.

Like hell.

He almost had to smile when Hal resorted to psychology, except that Hal's concern was always genuine. They had an understanding from the start that Bolan was at liberty to pass on missions where he thought his talents would be wasted or where he believed there was no reasonable prospect for success. In practice, Bolan almost never turned a mission down, but he relied upon their understanding, just in case. And Hal refrained from mentioning the obvious... unless his own concerns were such that he felt honor-bound to warn a friend of special danger in the air.

Point taken, then, but he would meet Doyle Mitchum all the same, hear what the ex-cop from Miami had to say. It was the least that he could do, and if he thought the guy was chasing ghosts—or looking for a fancy way to kill himself—the Executioner would pass.

He had not questioned Hal about the mission, knowing it would do no good, but he was free to speculate while driving south from Kansas City, through the heart of Oklahoma, jogging east to Amarillo for a change of scene. The odds against an interception of his call to Hal were astronomical, but Bolan liked to cover all his bets. A deviation from the most direct approach would cost him several hours, but he had no rigid schedule to observe. Avoiding Dallas and the capital at Austin put his mind at ease, the open desert giving Bolan ample opportunity to check his rearview mirror for potential tails.

He thought about the chosen meeting place and pondered its significance. The proximity of Mexico could mean that they were talking weapons, drugs or wetbacks—maybe all of the above. With crackdowns in Miami and in Southern California, Texas had become a major corridor for heroin, cocaine and marijuana in the past few years. A good five hundred miles of border, not including ports and islands on the Gulf, made Texas ripe for smugglers of every sort, and while the traffic flowed both ways—with weapons, Anglo prostitutes and kidnapped children moving south—the vast majority of merchandise was northward bound. Customs, DEA, and the Border Patrol did their best against impossible odds, hopelessly outnumbered, ill-equipped, and underfinanced, but they had a losing battle on their hands. Pronouncements of "cooperation" from the *federales* issued annually from Washington, but they were blowing smoke. Across the border, where the payoffs dubbed *mordida* were established practice, it was hazardous to place your trust in anyone who wore a badge.

Some years ago, an agent of the DEA had tried to infiltrate a major ring of narco traffickers in Tamaulipas, operating out of Nuevo Laredo. His cover was blown, and the agent was tortured to death, along with one of his informants, their bodies dumped like so much garbage in the desert. Even so, it had not been the style of execution that produced such outrage in the States, but rather

documented evidence suggesting that a ranking leader of
the *federales* was responsible for setting up the hit, arranging the abduction and participating personally in the
carnage afterward. Dismissed from service with a wrist-
slap prison sentence and parole after serving six months
easy time, the human slime was reportedly back in business at the same old stand, taking advantage of government contacts to coordinate drug shipments across the
Rio Grande.

Perhaps, Bolan thought, while he was in the neighborhood...

But he would have to concentrate on first things, first.

With less than thirty miles to go, Bolan reviewed his
superficial knowledge of the meeting site. Del Rio was the
seat of Val Verde County, some 3,200 official residents
within the city limits, for roughly ten percent of the
overall county population. Laughlin Air Force Base lay
due east, encroaching on the county line, and the huge
International Amistad Reservoir flanked Del Rio on the
northwest, drawing sportsmen and tourists from both
sides of the border.

Val Verde County—and specifically the town of
Langtry, forty miles northwest of Del Rio—was Wild
West territory, famous for rough justice in the nine-
teenth century, when Judge Roy Bean's gallows repre-
sented "the only law west of the Pecos." While not
strictly true, the image was too colorful to die, rein-
forced by popular fiction and films through the years,
until Bean's legend took on a life of its own.

In some ways, Bolan thought, Texas still embodied the
Old West. Vast, open spaces, inhospitable desert and
great cattle ranches with no end in sight. The kind of land
where rugged men still settled quarrels with their fists, or
knives and pistols, and the lawmen still wore rolled-brim

Stetsons on the job. Of course, the Indians had been confined to reservations—arid slums with a view—but if you listened closely in the wasteland, you could almost hear the war cries echoing across a century and more.

There would be ghosts here, Bolan knew, if he took time to seek them out. Gunfighters who gambled their lives on the luck of the draw. Horse soldiers and Indian braves who had christened the plains with their blood. Rugged settlers who put down roots and dared the elements or savage man to drive them out.

Men shaped the land, but they were also shaped and altered in return. No man who took on the desert would ever be the same again, no matter if he won or lost. There was a price for progress, Bolan realized, and sometimes it was paid in blood.

He found a truck stop three miles north of town and used the rest room, taking time inside the stall to double-check his side arm. The Beretta 93-R was a selective-fire model, capable of 3-round bursts at need, and his was fitted with a custom silencer that did not interfere with Bolan's draw. The weapon's magazine held twenty parabellum rounds, and he had two spares hanging in a double pouch under his right armpit. If there was unexpected trouble waiting for him in Del Rio, Bolan had a mini-Uzi tucked away beneath the driver's seat of his sedan.

All things considered, he felt confident about the meet, but he would take his time on the approach, observing the precautions that had helped him stay alive this long.

His destination was a motel called the Desert Star. Its neon was already burning as he made a drive-by, checking the straightforward layout and noting the bright No Vacancy sign. A Friday night in Del Rio, and business was good.

The motel parking lot had several empty spaces showing, but he concentrated on the cars. All empty, as far as he could tell, though he would have to make a walking search, check each in turn to look for gunners huddled on the floorboards. It was probably a waste of time, but Bolan drove around the block, alert for any overt signs of treachery. No lookouts posted on the sidewalks, seeming out of place. No cars with passengers who sat and smoked, when they should logically have gone inside the nearest restaurant or tavern. Shops had begun to close down for the evening. Rooftops appeared deserted—though, again, he could not say for sure without a personal examination.

For now, he'd let it go. A town this size, in spite of tourist traffic, any stakeout would be spotted by the locals and reported to the sheriff's office in about two minutes flat. The border's proximity demanded vigilance, with lawless scum of every race and creed attracted to the Tex-Mex netherworld. If local residents did not look out for one another in the circumstances, who else could they count on for support?

Approaching the Desert Star on his second pass, Bolan pulled into the parking lot, cruised past the manager's office and found himself an open slot at the far end of the north wing. His destination was Room 17, but he was in no hurry to get there. Caution came with his lifestyle, a sort of occupational paranoia that had kept him alive since Vietnam, through all his wars.

Room 17 was three doors down, beyond a stairwell where an outdoor ice machine was tucked away, its motor humming in the dusk. Fluorescent lighting on the wall attracted moths, and he could see a gecko waiting on the sidelines for its evening meal.

A slender blonde emerged from Room 19, a few steps distant, moving toward the car immediately next to Bolan's. She retrieved a shopping bag, made sure to lock the car, and paused to favor Bolan with a smile before she made her way inside. An older couple moved along the balcony above him, coming down the stairs and moving off in the direction of the motel coffee shop.

He left the mini-Uzi where it was and primed the vehicle alarm before he crossed the twenty feet of sidewalk leading to his destination. There were muffled voices inside the room, loud enough to register, the words still indistinct. He could have made them out by standing with his ear against the door, but there was too much traffic on the street and in the parking lot for spies to go about their business undisturbed.

He knocked and listened to a sudden silence from behind the door. A moment later, footsteps, and a rattling as the chain was disengaged. The door eased open to reveal a man of roughly Bolan's height and age, dark hair trimmed close enough to satisfy a military purist, features that were tan without the desert's standard dried-out look.

"Mike Belasko," Bolan told the stranger. "You're expecting me, I think."

"That's right. Doyle Mitchum."

There was power in the handshake, but it stopped short of being a challenge. Bolan gave back as good as he got, easing past Mitchum and noting his host's furtive glance toward the parking lot, checking things out.

The voices had prepared him for the fact that they were not alone. A slender Latino stood beside the double bed, appraising Bolan with frank interest, his lightweight jacket failing to conceal the pistol slung beneath his arm. On Bolan's right, a tall, broad-shouldered Anglo studied him with something more like curiosity, blue eyes and sandy hair a perfect complement to the sprinkling of freckles on his face.

"I'm glad you found the time to meet us," Mitchum told him, as he closed and double-locked the door.

"Who's 'us'?"

"Of course, you weren't expecting company." He introduced the Anglo first, as if adhering to a point of protocol. "Brock Hargis, from the Texas Rangers, and Emilio Sanchez, of the Mexican Federal Judicial Police."

Sanchez must have picked up something in the warrior's eyes, reacting with a swift, defensive frown. "My business here is unofficial, for the moment," he declared. "If you have any doubts..."

"Relax, Emilio." Doyle Mitchum moved between them, acting like a referee. "I'm sure Mr. Belasko doesn't prejudge anybody, am I right?"

"I'm here to listen," Bolan said. "I'll save my judgments for the wrap-up."

"Fair enough. Sit down, please. We're a little short on luxury, but I can offer you a Lone Star."

"Maybe later."

"Shall we get down to business, then?"

"We might as well."

"Okay," said Mitchum. "For a start, what do you know about black magic?"

CHAPTER TWO

"Black magic?"

The question caught Bolan off guard, taking him back to another place and time, another mission in the hellgrounds. He flashed on a band called Apocalypse, and a satanic cult that called itself the Children of the Flame. His mind's eye saw a cemetery in the dead of night, robed figures chanting, muzzle-flashes in the darkness.

Mitchum cracked a beer and sipped it, frowning as he spoke again.

"Relax, okay? It's not as crazy as it sounds."

"I'm listening."

"All right. I don't know how much you were told about my background."

"Metro-Dade narcotics," Bolan said. "Retired."

"They sugarcoated it a little," Mitchum told him, smiling. "I'm retired, all right, but I was asked to leave. It got embarrassing for some of my superiors, just having me around. They thought my brain was on a permanent vacation in the Twilight Zone. It isn't, though. I promise you."

"Still listening."

"Okay. Before we get to me, a little background. When I say black magic, I'm not talking witches on a broomstick or some kid in high school listening to heavy-metal songs. Are you familiar with the history of voodoo, *santeria,* anything like that?"

"Bad movies on the late show," Bolan answered. Neither one of Mitchum's friends was smiling now. If anything, they looked uneasy, wishing they were somewhere else.

That's three of us, thought Bolan, but he kept his seat and listened as the ex-cop from Miami forged ahead.

"It all goes back to slavery days, before the Civil War," said Mitchum. "When the slaves came over here in chains, they brought their own religions with them, tucked away up here." A finger tapped against his skull. "Historically, you've got two basic groups. Yoruba tribesmen practiced something they call juju, and the Bantus mostly followed a religion called *mayombe.* In the New World, now, they're forced to swallow Christianity, but there's resistance all the way. In time, they figure out a simple name game, covering their native gods—what they call *orishas*—with the names of Catholic saints. That way, if any of the masters stumble on their icons, they can pass it off as evidence of what good Christians they've become. Before you know it, some are borrowing the parts they like from two or three religions, playing mix-and-match. They've got one kind of ceremony while the white man's watching, and another when he's not around. In Haiti, juju became voodoo—sometimes bastardized as 'hoodoo' in the States. The Brazilians have variations like *macumba* and *candomble.* In Cuba, you've got *santeria*—literally 'the path of the saints'—or *palo mayombe,* all using the same basic guidelines."

"Makes sense," the Executioner put in. "About these *orisha...*"

"Right. There's probably a couple dozen of them, maybe more, depending on who you ask. Each god or goddess has a corresponding saint, a special list of pow-

ers and responsibilities, right down the line. The top
seven are Babalu-aye, Chango, Eleggua, Obatala, Oggun, Oshun, and Yemaya."

"Babalu-aye?" asked Bolan, frowning.

"Rings a bell, I bet. Think 'I Love Lucy.' Desi beating
on his conga drum and singing at the Copa."

"Right, okay."

"Nobody thought about it at the time, but what's the
big surprise? Arnaz was Cuban, and the whole damn is-
land's rife with *santeria* witchcraft."

"You mentioned powers and responsibilities."

"That's right. Take Babalu-aye, for instance. He's
synonymous with Saint Lazarus, patron saint of the sick.
For sacrifices, he prefers cigars and pennies, sometimes
just a glass of water. When he's pissed, his enemies get
him with leprosy or gangrene."

"Nice."

"The gods are like that," Mitchum answered, sipping
at his beer. "They all have special weapons, and they
don't mind kicking butt from time to time. Of course, it
helps if you provide incentive, something in the way of a
nice sacrifice. It may be rum, some coins and feathers...or, it may require a living sacrifice. Goats, chickens, lambs...whatever. The Humane Society's been
getting after some of these practitioners the past few
years, but nothing really slows them down."

"The other gods?"

"Let's see. Chango hides behind Saint Barbara, controlling thunder, lightning and fire. Eleggua switch-hits
as Saint Anthony or the Christ child, depending. He
controls gates and crossroads, both physical and emotional. Obatala's peculiar. They call him the father of all
saints, but his Christian cover is Our Lady of Mercy. Go
figure. Oggun is the warrior god, in charge of all weap-

ons and metals. That's probably why they match him with Saint Peter, checking all those soldiers through the pearly gates. Oshun is a matchmaker, controlling money and sex. Practitioners link her to the patron saint of Cuba, Our Lady of La Caridad. Yemaya is the mother of all saints, Obatala's wife, in effect. She looks out for women and fertility, controlling the seas in her spare time. Her symbol is the Virgin Mary, usually portrayed as a black woman.''

"That's a lot to remember," said Bolan.

"You're getting the short form. For every one of the major gods, there are two or three small fry, at least. *Santeros* and *paleros* pick their favorites, arrange their prayers and sacrifices to appease the gods they need for special tasks. Let's say you're bringing in a load of coke by speedboat. You'd be checking in with Oshun, to protect your bankroll, and you'd also want Yemaya on your side, for smooth sailing.''

"Where do the drugs come in?" Bolan asked.

"Wherever you want," Mitchum said. "That's the great part about all the Afro-Caribbean cults. They're completely amoral, just like the *orishas*. You can pray to heal the sick or strike your neighbor dead. It's all the same to Chango and his buddies as long as you follow all the proper ceremonies. The *orishas* don't care how you make your living, selling ice cream cones or crack, as long as you remember them with sacrificial offerings on time.''

"I get the picture.''

"In the old days," Mitchum said, "we used to see some voodoo in Louisiana, and here and there among the blacks in other states. Along the border, there were scattered pockets where the Mexicans still practiced *brujeria*—native witchcraft—but we've seen an absolute explosion in the field since 1980.''

"Mariel?"

"You hit it on the head," said Mitchum. "Castro gets it in his head to score some headline points and get one up on Uncle Sam at the same time, unloading a bunch of political dissidents in Florida . . . with the provision that every voluntary emigrant must be accompanied by four or five of the government's choice. Next thing you know, we're hip-deep in convicts and mental defectives, not to mention a shitload of cultists. The last official count identified 100,000 practicing *santeros* in Miami, with an estimate of some five million nationwide."

"You're not suggesting all of them run drugs."

"No way. But let's suppose it's ten percent. We're looking at a crime wave like we've never seen before. These characters believe they're bulletproof, invisible, you name it. If they go to trial, the courthouse janitors start finding chickens slaughtered in the hallways overnight. Two years ago, we found three dealers floating facedown in the Miami River, shot execution-style. One of them was handcuffed to the body of a sacrificial goat. Check out the haul on drug busts in Miami, L.A., San Francisco, Dallas, New York City, and you'll find religious shit you won't believe. Everything from idols and altars to human remains."

"All *santeria.*"

"That's the problem. Like I said, these bozos like to mix and match. Some of them hit on *santeria* for a start, throw in some voodoo for a little native color, maybe try some satanism on the side. And then, you've got *palo mayombe.*"

"Go on."

"I told you that voodoo and *santeria* were strictly amoral, but *palo mayombe* goes them one better. We're talking black magic all the way, though some of the practitioners masquerade as *santeros,* claiming to follow the teachings of 'Christian *santeria.*' In fact, *paleros* call upon the same *orishas* in their ceremonies, but the rituals are something else. The central object is a metal caldron, the *nganga.*"

As he spoke, Mitchum rose to fetch a briefcase from the bed. Returning to his chair, he placed it on his lap and opened it, withdrawing a slim manila folder. From the file, he took a glossy eight-by-ten photograph and handed it to Bolan.

The photo was simple enough. A black, cast-iron caldron was the centerpiece, bristling with sticks of varied lengths. Aside from what appeared to be a set of antlers, Bolan could not recognize the other contents. They were lumpy, dark, further disguised by the black-and-white film.

"Your basic *nganga,*" Mitchum said. "The ingredients are a matter of taste, so to speak, but they generally include coins, spices, various small animals, spiders and poisonous insects, pieces of bone, along with human blood and organs. There are twenty-eight sticks in the cauldron, used to stir the contents and wake up the spirits inside. The Spanish word for stick is *palo,* which gives us *palo mayombe*—'stick magic,' more or less."

"The human remains?" Bolan prompted.

"That's the ticket to the whole damn thing," said Mitchum. "The *nganga* is supposed to be a kind of mini-universe where souls are held imprisoned, subject to the master's will. With proper incantations, captive souls communicate with the *orishas,* striking bargains to protect a business enterprise, strike down a chosen enemy, whatever. Now, you can't nab souls by robbing graves or picking up cadavers from the morgue. Too late, you follow? Living victims are required to feed the caldron."

"Human sacrifice?"

"In spades. Before a spirit qualifies for service on the other side, it has to be 'charged up' with fear and pain. *Paleros* torture their victims to death as a matter of course. Sometimes they drink the blood or chow down on the heart. Selected organs like the brain and tongue go into the *nganga,* where they're left to rot. The more corruption and decay involved, the better. It's a sick scene, any way you run it down."

"And these *paleros* are involved in dealing drugs?"

"From coast to coast," said Mitchum. "If they don't run shipments on their own, the dealers put them on retainer for insurance. If you buy their rap, these guys can read the future, tell you when the time's right for a run across the border or a move against the competition. For a price, you can arrange a death spell on your enemies or break a curse from someone else's witch. Your basic superstitious hit man likes to think the gods are on his side, police can't see him, bullets bounce right off...you name it."

"What's the answer when it doesn't work?" asked Bolan.

"Simple. It's the client's fault, whatever happens. Maybe he was short on faith, or there's a new curse on him. The *palero* can't lose, either way."

"Neat trick."

"A classic con," said Mitchum. "Gypsies have been working variations of the scheme, removing 'evil eyes' and whatnot, for a hundred years. The difference is, they don't kill anybody in the process. For *paleros,* death is what it's all about."

"How widespread is this *palo mayombe?*"

"Nobody knows for sure, the way it mixes up with *santeria,* but most *santeros* don't trust the *paleros.* I've talked to some who claim we've got two thousand practicing *paleros* in Miami, but I'd have to guess for the United States and Mexico at large."

"You seem to have a fairly decent handle on the problem," Bolan said. "Why don't you work it out with Metro-Dade, ring in the FBI and DEA."

"I wish." There was a note of bitterness in Mitchum's tone. "I told you my retirement wasn't strictly voluntary. Even with the evidence in hand, my stock's not worth a lot around Miami. Metro-Dade and DEA would rather make it on their own, or try to. Never mind the Bureau. They're afraid of getting tagged with any kind of witch-hunts since the Hoover days, much less *real* witches."

"Even so, you got in touch with Washington."

"Our mutual acquaintance," Mitchum said. "Call that a last-ditch effort, if you like. We have a history, some operations in Miami and around the Keys. No guarantee he'd buy my story, even so, but here we are."

"I need to know what soured you with Metro-Dade."

"Why not? Two years ago, my partner and I were working a low-life dealer named Raoul Escalante. He was moving up the ladder in a major way around Miami, stepping on the competition where he could. The more information we gathered, the more peculiar he seemed. Consorting with magicians, shit like that. I had him figured for a psycho when I heard he had a death curse riding on my partner and myself."

"But something changed your mind."

It did not come out sounding like a question. Mitchum stared at Bolan for a moment, finally nodded.

"Right again. The night they hit my partner, Danny Bridges, they left feathers scattered on his body, with some scribbling on the wall in Danny's blood. It was a drawing of a bow and arrow, the symbol of Ochosi, the hunter."

"One of the *orishas?*" Bolan asked.

"A second-stringer, but he's popular with the *paleros* when they throw a death spell. Anyway, I figured it was time I had a word with Escalante on my own."

"What happened?"

"Let's just say he had an accident. It came back borderline from the commissioner's review board, self-defense on the shooting, bad judgment and unprofessional conduct for going in without warrants and backup. You know the legalese. I had a choice to make. Suspension and a desk job while I finished out my twenty years, or hit the road with partial benefits. I took a walk."

"That's not the same as letting go, I guess."

"Hell no. I squared accounts for Danny, but we've still got hundreds—maybe thousands—of *paleros* working for the drug rings, sacrificing victims anytime they have a gang war brewing or a shipment to protect. I've made some progress, talking to the rangers, local agencies, the *federales* down in Mexico, but we're a long way from the finish line."

"I'm not sure what you have in mind," said Bolan, "but I frankly don't have time for any long-term projects."

"Understood. We're working on a special case, right now." He nodded to include his two companions. "We were close last week, across the border in Coahuila, but the big fish wriggled through our net."

Another photograph changed hands. The subject was a handsome male, Hispanic, smiling for the camera. His shirt was silk, the collar open to reveal a thick gold chain around his neck. It was a posed shot, nothing a police photographer would handle.

"Meet Fernando de Leon Martinez," Mitchum said. "Age thirty-one, Miami-born of Cuban parents. No line on his old man since the boy was born. Fernando's mother is a stone *palero,* telling fortunes, selling potions to the lovesick, breaking evil spells . . . the whole nine yards. She sent Fernando off to study with the big boys early on. The past ten years, he's been a full-time *curandero,* performing ritual 'cleansings' and reading the cards for anyone who can afford his services. And he doesn't come cheap."

A photograph in color this time, showing four men from a distance. An arrow drawn in felt pen marked a tall man on the left. Broad shoulders in a tailored suit, thick brows, a bristling mustache. He looked like money on the hoof, with danger running close behind.

"Ramon Ibarra," Mitchum said. "These days, he runs the biggest drug ring in Coahuila, slopping over into Tamaulipas. He's got something like a hundred soldiers on his payroll, and he still relies on witchcraft to protect his merchandise. Last year he shelled out half a million dollars to Fernando, that we know of, for communications with the spirit world."

Another photograph, this time a man and woman standing side by side, apparently caught up in conversation. Both were young, the male Hispanic and the woman Anglo.

"On the left," said Mitchum, "one Marcella Grant. A college student out of Brownsville, Texas, when she met Fernando, roughly eighteen months ago. My information is, they're lovers, and she also doubles as *madrina* for Fernando's cult. That's like a priestess, or a mother figure. On the right, a part-time dealer out of Ciudad Acuna, one Gregorio Ruiz. Fernando hits the sack with him as well, from time to time. The big guy swings both ways.''

"That makes it interesting."

"And then some."

Mitchum's next three snapshots showed a barren sprawl of desert with a burned-out shack. In one shot, thirteen body bags were lined up, baking in the sun.

"Those shots were taken at Rancho Santa Maria," said Mitchum. "West of Ciudad Acuna, in the desert. The *federales* were running a drug interdiction campaign last week, roadblocks and all, when this pickup blows past them like a bat out of hell. They ran it down and collared the driver after a couple of miles. Crazy bastard was laughing his head off. He didn't believe they could see him. Around the time that sank in, he started promising they'd never hold him in a cell. Strike two. By the time they finished negotiating, he led them to the ranch where Fernando carried out his rituals. We've got thirteen bodies to start, along with his *nganga,* but we missed Fernando and the in-crowd."

One more photograph. A human spinal column with the pelvis still attached, a wire noose wrapped around the upper vertebrae.

"One of Fernando's trinkets," Mitchum said. "He buries them like that to let the meat rot off the bones, then drags them out again for use in rituals. We've got IDs on seven of the victims—one of them a college freshman missing out of San Antonio. I doubt we'll ever name the other six."

"So, what's the plan?" asked Bolan.

"I've been working on a liaison with the Rangers and the *federales,* sort of a package deal to bring Fernando down. It's unofficial at the moment—just the three of us, in fact—and it occurred to me that we could use some reinforcements."

"That's a compliment, I take it."

"Not at all. Our friend in Washington said he was sending out his best."

"I wasn't sent," the Executioner corrected him. "I heard you might have something interesting to tell me."

"And?"

"Okay, I'm interested."

"All right. Here's what I had in mind."

Before he could continue, Bolan's ears picked up a sound of footsteps on the outer pavement, slowing as they neared Room 17. He half turned toward the door, ears cocked, in time to see the broad front window shattered by a burst of automatic fire.

CHAPTER THREE

Eduardo Rojas thought the hit should be a piece of cake, as gringos always say. Three targets in a cheap motel, like goddamn sitting ducks. They couldn't miss, for Christ's sake, and the targets weren't expecting any trouble.

He wondered where the gringos came by their expressions, but he let it go. It was a waste of time to try and understand the Anglo mind, where black was white and up was down. Too damned confusing for a man who took his business seriously, knowing any fuck-up that he made could cost his life.

Eduardo did not think of it that way, if he could help it. Picturing his own death made him nervous, and a case of nerves could get you wasted, hesitating when you ought to draw your piece and let some other bastard have it right between the eyes. Besides, he had no reason to be nervous these days.

Eduardo Rojas was protected from his enemies by magic.

El padrino told him so.

The Anglos would not understand, of course, with all their science and philosophy, but growing up dirt-poor in Mexico, closer to the soil and Mother Nature than a gringo ever gets, Eduardo knew that there were forces in the universe a man cannot explain. If you aligned yourself correctly with the spirits, managed to appease them somehow with the proper offering, their blessing kept you safe, no matter what. He had observed the power of healing in his native village, watched as men grew sick and died from curses or the evil eye. It did not matter what the gringos thought, with all their college education. Rojas knew the truth, and he felt better going up against his enemies with Chango on his side.

He did not know what these three men had done to merit death, nor was he interested in finding out. When *el padrino* gave an order, it was carried out. No foolish questions or debate. If anybody argued with a man of power, they were asking to get burned.

Like Rubio, for instance.

Rojas thought about the last time any member of the family had challenged *el padrino*'s orders, and the vengeance that had followed. Just remembering the ceremony made his stomach churn, but there was also something like exhilaration in the feeling. Joining in the slaughter, Rojas had been reassured that he belonged to something greater than himself, that his obedience would be rewarded over time.

And he was following his orders to the letter now, regardless of the risk involved.

He did not fear the men he was assigned to kill. If anything, he pitied them for crossing *el padrino*'s path, but there were other risks involved. The border crossing to begin with, driving up from Ciudad Acuna to Del Rio on the toll bridge, knowing they could easily be challenged by the Customs men and searched for contraband. They had no drugs, of course, but automatic weapons were the next best thing. All four of them would go to jail if they were searched, and there were dangers also after they were finished with the hit.

He stopped himself. He trusted *el padrino*'s magic to protect them, shield them from their enemies in combat and provide immunity against arrest. If anything betrayed them, it would be their own misgivings, weakening the master's spell with doubt. As long as they believed, they were secure.

His three companions had been handpicked for the mission. All of them were skilled assassins, fearless in a shoot-out, ready for anything. Paco was driving, a cool hand with cars. Ricardo and Juan were the shock troops, each armed with an Uzi and spare magazines. Eduardo was packing a Streetsweeper shotgun, twelve rounds in the cylinder, ready to rock, and he had more Magnum shells in his pocket.

Del Rio was the kind of town where gringos looked at you with fish eyes when you came across the border, half suspecting every Mexican they saw of criminal intent. Well, they would have it right this time, and any cowboy who was fool enough to try and interfere could kiss his Anglo ass goodbye. A few more dead would make no difference to Eduardo Rojas.

If the truth were known, he might enjoy it all the more.

The Desert Star Motel was marked by garish neon, bright stars flashing off and on around the name. They had a number for the room, and Paco drove directly to it, double-parking two doors down for safety's sake.

The targets weren't expecting trouble, but they could be armed. No point in taking chances, when a lucky shot might nail their driver at the wheel.

Eduardo left the vehicle, his door wide open, with the backup gunners on his heels. The dome light had a switch to disconnect it, so that Paco was protected from the prying eyes of any witnesses. You could never tell, with gunfire, who might stick his head outside or risk a peek between drawn curtains.

Walking back to number 17, Eduardo felt the old familiar tension building in his gut. A pleasant feeling, like a hunter sighting down on game, before he makes a trophy kill. No trophies this time, but a job well done would be its own reward.

Along with *el padrino*'s promised payoff of an extra thousand dollars each.

Eduardo and the others would have done the job for nothing, but it helped to know they were appreciated, that their skills had value. It was good to keep things on a business footing, everything professional, despite the common bond of faith.

"Right here."

Eduardo took his stand between the others, with Ricardo on his left, Juan on his right. He braced the stubby riot shotgun tight against his hip and heard the others cock their Uzis, taking aim.

A piece of cake, he told himself again.

And fired.

THE FIRST ROUNDS came in high, but not by much. As Bolan hit the floor and scrambled toward the bed, he knew the drapes had saved them. If the enemy had seen what they were aiming at...

He glanced around and saw his three companions still alive, apparently unharmed by the initial burst of fire. All three were on the floor and seeking cover, Hargis and the *federale* drawing pistols to defend themselves. Doyle Mitchum seemed to be unarmed, a dazed expression on his face as he lay next to Bolan, covered by the bed.

"Goddamn it, I was sure nobody trailed us here. You checked for shadows?"

"Every way I know," the Executioner replied. "Could be you have a leak."

"Well, shit!"

"Let's talk about it later, shall we? We've got work to do right now."

"Damn right," snapped Hargis, crawling up beside them with a big Colt Python in his fist. He risked a glance above the mattress, squeezing off two thunderclaps in the direction of the shattered window.

Another burst of fire came back in response, shotgun blasts thumping in counterpoint to the rattle of automatic weapons. The stucco walls were taking hits and bleeding streams of dust, cheap reproduction artwork shot to hell and crashing to the floor. A wild round struck the bathroom sink, and Bolan heard the brittle sound of cracking porcelain.

"Did anybody check the bathroom window?" Bolan asked.

"Too small to do us any good," said Hargis. "It's the front or nothing."

"Just as well," said Mitchum. "We're not going anywhere on foot. Our playmates have us cut off from the cars."

"So far," said Bolan, edging past the Texas Ranger as he spoke.

"Why don't we just sit tight?" asked Hargis. "All this racket, someone's bound to ring up 911."

"No good," Mitchum reminded him. "If we wanted this official, we'd be meeting at the sheriff's office to begin with."

"Yeah, okay. So, what's the action?"

"Start with a diversion," Bolan told him, moving toward the open floor. "If we don't make a move, they're bound to come in looking for survivors."

"Want to clue us in?" asked Hargis.

"Just be ready with the mattress when it's time to rush the window. Make it fast and keep your heads down when you go."

The motel carpet had a musty smell about it, coupled with the dust that leaked from several dozen bullet holes in walls and ceiling. Breathing through his mouth to keep from sneezing, Bolan crept across the floor in the direction of a flimsy vanity and chest of drawers. He needed something, anything, to put the enemy off guard, however briefly, setting them up for a swift counterstrike.

A shotgun blast ripped through the door and left a foot-wide hole. It missed the locking mechanism, and the door held fast, but Bolan knew that it would only take another round or two to clear the way for an invasion of the room. His time was running short. A few more seconds, and the enemy could be inside.

He had no fix on numbers yet, but they were certainly outclassed in terms of hardware. He thought about the mini-Uzi in his car and understood that it was useless fretting over past mistakes. Surprise was half the battle, and he had to strip their enemies of the initiative at once, before the home team started taking casualties.

The Zenith nineteen-inch TV was bolted down to frustrate thieves, the picture tube already shattered by a bullet, and he wasted no time trying to unseat it from the vanity. Instead he pulled the bottom drawer completely free and found a year-old telephone directory inside. A sudden inspiration blossomed in his mind.

"A pillow, quick!" he called to Mitchum, then reached up to catch it as the ex-cop from Miami made his pitch.

The pillow had already taken several hits, and it was leaking feathers as he stuffed it down inside the drawer. A brisk tug ripped the slender telephone directory in half, along its spine, and Bolan shoved the rumpled pages underneath the pillow, so that paper was exposed on either end. He palmed his lighter, flicked it into life, and lighted the rolls of paper, waiting for a steady flame to show.

It took another moment for the pillowcase to catch, and then it started smoking. Bolan pushed the drawer ahead of him, smoke getting in his eyes, his right hand clutching the Beretta 93-R as he crept across the room. Above him, a fresh spray of bullets swept the room, their adversaries having taken the time to reload.

"On me," he called to Mitchum and the others, hoping they could pull it off. It was a poor diversion, but the only one they had. And if they did not move against their enemies within the next few moments, they were finished.

Hargis flashed a thumbs-up signal from behind the bed, already pushing on the far side of the mattress, hoisting it to serve himself and Mitchum as a shield. Behind the bullet-scarred vanity, Emilio Sanchez waited with a nickel-plated automatic in his fist, a look of grim determination on his face.

No time to think about the leak, whoever might have set them up. The question would be moot if they were penned and slaughtered here. There would be time enough to think it through and look for those responsible when they were free and clear.

Assuming that they ever got that far.

The outer walls of the motel were built of cinder blocks, providing greater insulation than the flimsy walls between adjoining rooms. He reached a point between the door and window, dragged the smoking drawer against his knees and gripped it with his left hand, gripping the Beretta in his right.

A backhand toss with all his strength sailed it directly through the shattered window, taking shredded curtains with it on the way. One of the gunners barked a curse in Spanish, firing at the object hurtling across his line of sight, and Bolan heard it strike the sidewalk with a crack.

The rest of it was chaos, up and moving toward the door, as Mitchum and the Texas Ranger followed, charging toward the window. Gunfire rang in his ears as Bolan wrenched the door wide open, braced himself and charged outside.

THE WHOLE DAMNED THING was going sour, Mitchum thought, and they were barely getting started. He had no idea what brought the gunners to their doorstep, and he did not even want to think about it now, when all their lives were hanging by a thread.

The mattress seemed to weigh a ton, and Mitchum's arms were trembling as he helped the Texas Ranger hoist it upright, worming underneath. The box spring scraped against his knees, and Mitchum cursed the sudden pain. He felt the mattress taking hits and grimaced, waiting for the first bullet to penetrate, slamming into his flesh.

A stupid goddamn time to leave his pistol in the car, but he had felt confident in their security precautions. No one should have had a clue that they were meeting Hal Brognola's agent, much less where to find them with a hit team.

He was short on friendly contacts as it was. The prospect of a traitor in that company was chilling. If he could not even trust the handful of selected friends he still had left . . .

Another scrape, against his shins this time. At least the pain meant he was still alive. His arms were trembling, and he told himself it was the deadweight of the mattress in his grip, but there was also fear involved.

"Okay!" Brock Hargis snapped. "Let's go!"

A sudden rush, high-stepping as they charged across the box spring, no time to maneuver. Mitchum felt his heel rip through the flimsy covering, springs snagging at his shoes. He stumbled, almost falling, but momentum kept him upright, bouncing like a schoolboy on a trampoline.

He tried to keep his head down, knowing that if it popped up above the mattress it would be an easy target for the gunners on the walk outside.

He risked a glance behind him, to his left, and saw Sanchez on his feet, advancing toward the window in a combat crouch, his automatic spitting flame. The *federale*'s teeth were clenched in an expression that could just as easily have been a smile or a snarl.

And Mitchum stumbled once more, coming off the box spring, going down on one knee with a curse. Pain shuddered through his leg and hip. He almost lost his grip on the mattress, but determination drove him to his feet a step behind the Texas Ranger, hobbling to keep up. The rapid blows against the mattress seemed more powerful, but they were also slacking off, somehow.

Outside, more guns exploded, followed by curses from the enemy in gutter Spanish, and a startled cry of pain. Huddled below the window ledge, the mattress curling backward over him, the ex-cop from Miami knew that he should join the fight. At least dredge up the guts to watch, if he could not participate.

Cheeks burning with embarrassment, his bowels ice-cold with fear, Doyle Mitchum struggled to his knees and risked a glance outside.

EMERGING FROM Room 17, the first thing Bolan did was count his enemies. Three gunners pouring lead in through the window, and he registered a dark sedan downrange, double-parked on his left with the engine running. Possibly a wheelman, but he could not rule out reinforcements.

The nearest gunner held an Uzi submachine gun, pivoting to meet the Executioner's advance. He looked a bit surprised, perhaps pissed off, but there was nothing that resembled fear or worry on the shooter's face.

The 93-R had been set for 3-round bursts, and Bolan stroked the trigger as his adversary swiveled into target acquisition. Parabellum shockers ripped through the gunman's chest and neck. Instead of pain, the dying shooter's face reflected stark amazement, something close to incredulity, as if he couldn't make himself believe that he was hit, much less about to die. Slumping to his knees, he triggered off a burst at Bolan, but it came in high and wide, exploding through the window of the room next door. A woman started screaming as the gunner toppled over on his face.

One down.

The middle gunner had a riot shotgun, one of the repeaters patterned after a revolver. Bolan was already moving, sliding in between parked cars, when buckshot rattled off the pavement, ripping through a fender of the family station wagon on his left.

He was shifting to a new position, looking for an angle, when Sanchez popped up in the doorway, blasting at the nearest standing gunner from a range or fifteen feet. His weapon sounded like a .45 and had the knockdown power to match. The weasel with the shotgun staggered backward, reeling, sprawled across the hood of an Isuzu compact, slowly melting to the pavement.

Two for two.

The Executioner was waiting when the final gunner broke and ran. A shot from Hargis, in the window, grazed the runner but it did not knock him down. He sprinted for the double-parked sedan, heels clacking on the pavement, features frozen in a grimace that was two parts shock and one part fear.

He never made it.

Bolan caught him on the run and hit him with a 3-round burst that spun the gunner like a top. His Uzi clattered on the pavement, saved from accidental discharge by the grip safety, as Bolan gave his man three more to die on. The parabellum manglers slammed his human target backward, going over in a lifeless sprawl, his shoulders touching down before his buttocks struck the pavement.

That made three, and Bolan swiveled toward the idling vehicle. Before he took two steps, the wheelman recognized the danger, knowing that he had lost his passengers. He stood on the accelerator, burning rubber as a burst from the Beretta stitched three tidy holes across the trunk of the sedan. Brock Hargis got a Magnum round off from the door of number 17 and took the right rear window out with an explosive crash.

The frightened wheelman did not bother with the exit signs. He jumped the curb instead, knocked down a newspaper vending machine and scattered copies of the evening edition across two lanes of traffic. Horns sounded as he cut off a semi, and then the giant truck was skidding, going over with a squeal of tortured metal, covering the black sedan's retreat.

"Goddamn it!" Hargis swore.

"We're out of time," said Bolan. "If you want to miss the boys in blue, we need to leave right now."

"Let's do it!" Mitchum snapped, emerging from the empty window frame and jogging toward a nearby car.

Brock Hargis followed on his heels, Emilio Sanchez bringing up the rear.

"I'll follow you," said Bolan, knowing he could break off in an instant if it looked like Mitchum had a trap in mind. It did not feel that way, but you could never tell.

They drove due north until they reached the outskirts of Del Rio—Bolan with the mini-Uzi on the seat beside him—then pulled over by some lighted tennis courts. Young women, playing doubles underneath the lights, did not appear to notice them at all. He took the little submachine gun with him when he walked around to Mitchum's car and got in back, beside the Texas Ranger.

"Jesus, that was grim," said Mitchum. "I still don't know how they found us."

"I watched my back the whole way down," Bolan informed them for the record. "If they had a tail on me, it was invisible."

"They damn sure didn't follow us," the ex-cop from Miami said.

"Okay, unless you buy coincidence, that means a leak."

Brock Hargis glared at Sanchez, half-turned in the shotgun seat. "I wonder where the leak could be?" he said, sarcastically.

An angry flush of color stained the *federale*'s cheeks. "I don't need lessons from a gringo in the problems of my own department," he replied. "We have maintained the strictest possible security. Besides myself, my captain is the only other person who has knowledge of our plans."

"That's two more than we need, in my book," Hargis said.

"And what about the famous Rangers, gringo? Are they suddenly above corruption? Your attorney general does not seem convinced, from his investigations in the past few months."

"You want to talk about corruption, boy? Let's talk about—"

"We're getting nowhere," Bolan interrupted. "If you don't trust each other, you've got no damn business on the job."

"I trust them both," said Mitchum. "And I don't trust easy. What you're seeing is the classic jurisdictional antagonism. On the border, everything boils down to race and nationality, no matter how you try to sort it out."

"So, are we finished here, or what?" the Executioner inquired.

"I'm not a quitter," Hargis told him, glaring at the *federale*.

"Nor am I," the Mexican cop said, a bit reluctantly.

"Okay," said Bolan, "then we need a plan the four of us can bank on. If you have to get in touch with your superiors, you keep it short and sweet, no more specifics than are absolutely necessary. Can you live with that?"

"A new plan, right?" said Hargis.

Sanchez settled for a simple *"Sí."*

Behind the wheel, Doyle Mitchum had a wide grin on his face. "A new plan, eh? It's funny you should ask."

CHAPTER FOUR

The new plan called for a division of labor. Rolling into Ciudad Acuna in a rented car, Doyle Mitchum kept a sharp eye on the rearview mirror, wondering if he could even spot a tail in the congested border traffic. Half the vehicles around him on the toll bridge were driven by Hispanics, and while none of them appeared to notice Mitchum, he could not be sure. They had not seen the wheelman, back at the motel, and it would be a simple matter for Martinez to select another shadow for the job.

At that, he could not even prove Martinez was involved. Ramon Ibarra had as much to lose as anyone, if they succeeded with their plan, and the Coahuila drug king was not known for taking losses gracefully. Ibarra's enemies were prone to fatal "accidents" and sudden disappearances. Whole families had been slaughtered as insurance, to forestall vendettas, and authorities were still no closer to a bust than they had been last year, or the year before.

It was a long way from Miami to Coahuila, more than the miles warranted. Pursuing the *paleros*, Mitchum felt as if he had stepped through a time warp, flashing back a century or more to an age when witchcraft and magic overshadowed psychiatry and the physical sciences. In many parts of Mexico and South America, he realized, native shamans still competed with priests and local officials for the hearts and minds of peasant villagers. In some districts, most of them remote, human sacrifice was still regarded as a useful method for insuring crop fertility, preventing storms and earthquakes, or eradicating plague.

Even with the circumstances of his partner's death, it had required some time for Mitchum to accept the grisly facts of cult-related crime. Ostracized by his old colleagues at Metro-Dade, he had gradually made contact with other lawmen in a similar position, some retired and others hanging tough despite the jokes and gibes of those who called them "ghost busters," leaving strings of garlic and the odd crucifix on their lockers or desks.

It was an uphill fight, but Mitchum had discovered a nationwide network of cops who were waking up to the dark side of organized crime. At the New Jersey Port Authority, two officers pursuing a child pornography ring came up with evidence of snuff films depicting infant sacrifice. In Denver, satanists and self-styled witches dabbled in juvenile prostitution. Bikers in California and Nevada, sporting pentagram and "666" tattoos, ran automatic weapons to suspected members of the cultic underground.

And everywhere, the spread of drugs.

It ran both ways with the occult practitioners. Some dabblers snorted coke or swallowed LSD to fuel hallucinations, conjuring the demons of their own subconscious minds. The flip side of the coin was what troubled Mitchum most, however: mercenary dealers moving drugs in massive quantities, accepting satanism, *santeria,* and a host of other offbeat creeds to justify their own behavior and provide "insurance" for illicit schemes. In Mexico and South America, the lure of "witchy" cults was second nature for countless Indios with one foot firmly planted in the faith of their ancestors. Some still believed, for others it was wishful thinking or a way to rationalize their own behavior on the wrong side of the law.

The trick was breaking through a wall of silence that surrounded many of the old beliefs. In part, the silence was a product of respect for tradition, but there was also a substantial element of fear involved. He still remembered the Constanzo cult in Matamoros, three years back. An estimated twenty dead, and the reluctant *federales* were still trying to identify half of the victims, speculating on others yet undiscovered. Nor had Constanzo been the only warlock practicing in the vicinity. Police in Mexico City still had the unsolved ritual murders of sixteen infants on their hands from the same period, and each new year brought a fresh crop of mutilated victims, written off for the most part as victims of "persons unknown."

Not this time.

Mitchum knew the bastards he was stalking, and he did not mean to let them slip away. He could not put his finger on Martinez or his cronies at the moment, but he had a plan in mind, if he could only pull it off.

He would begin with the bodegas, special shops that catered to the needs of witches, sorcerers and such. They specialized in herbs and amulets, ingredients for spells and potions, "magic" literature... but if he played his cards right, Mitchum reckoned he could also strike a bargain for the kind of information he required to track Martinez down.

The first shop on his list was situated near the central marketplace of Ciudad Acuna. Parking halfway down the block, he spent another moment sitting in his car, considering the move. It would be tricky, Mitchum knew. The wrong word now—or the right word in the wrong ear—and he could tip Martinez off. Mitchum was treading on the enemy's territory now, and any intersection of their paths spelled danger.

Information flowed both ways, and while he would not mind drawing Martinez out of hiding, even if he had to use himself as bait, Mitchum had no desire to wind up dead.

Not yet, before he had a chance to score against the opposition.

Mitchum locked the car and pocketed the keys, merging with the foot traffic under the glare of neon from shops and cantinas, moving toward the small bodega down the block. He felt suddenly vulnerable, naked, but at least he had his side arm with him, nestled in a high-ride holster on his hip.

He reached the front door of the shop, glanced back along the sidewalk in his wake, and stepped inside.

"I DON'T THINK this is gonna work," Brock Hargis muttered, switching off the engine of his four-door Chevrolet and stepping on the parking brake.

"It will, unless you blow it," Sanchez told him, sitting in the shotgun seat.

Their drive across the river from Del Rio into Ciudad Acuna had been made in stony silence. Hargis figured Sanchez must be pissed at his remarks about the *federales,* which concerned the Texas Ranger not at all. For his part, Hargis reckoned that the less he told his "partner," the less he stood to lose.

It was not as if he had to manufacture any slurs about the quality of law enforcement here in Mexico. The whole world knew that cops—including *federales*—made a bare subsistence wage, the government expecting them to pick up tips and bribes when and where they could. It was a standard practice, recognized at every level of society and universally accepted in the absence of a scandal that would shake things up.

From time to time, the Mexican police went over-board, even by their own peculiar standards. Every time Brock Hargis turned around, it seemed more local cops and *federales* were indicted for cooperating with the drug cartels, supplying services that ranged from passing information to harassment—even pure, cold-blooded murder—of American drug-enforcement agents operating south of the borderline.

He understood about the little things like fixing traffic tickets, letting gringo tourists slide on minor raps when there was money to be made. The same damn thing went on in various departments all across America. But running drugs and killing brother cops for money was beyond the pale, as far as Hargis was concerned. It may have been his rural Texas background, or the sense of duty he had picked up in the army, followed by his service with the Rangers, but he looked on cops like that as traitors to their oath of office, no damned cops at all.

No punishment was too extreme, in his book, for an officer who sold out his brothers and watched them die, in order to help a scumbag narco dealer stay in business. If he ever found out that Emilio Sanchez was the one who set them up back there, at the motel...

Relax, he thought. You don't know anything for sure. Not yet. It could as easily have been the new guy, this Belasko. He was something with the feds, but that was all they knew from Mitchum. Some big troubleshooter out of Washington, supposed to make their problems go away.

Doyle Mitchum was a kind of riddle. Ex-cop, for starters, with a forced retirement in Miami over his pre-occupation with this voodoo shit. Brock Hargis could not

argue with him there, for he had seen the evidence all over
Texas, drugs and death and witchcraft intertwined like
rattlers in their winter den. The man himself remained a
mystery, however, and you had to wonder if he might not
have some enemies behind him, breathing down his neck.

Whatever, Brock's superiors in Austin were impressed
enough with Mitchum that they bought his plan and de-
tailed Hargis to cooperate, reporting back as things
shaped up. At that, the Rangers had been Mitchum's
second choice, once he was stonewalled by the mighty
FBI. The feebees saw no evil, when it came to cult-related
crime, and they were keeping it that way.

Their problem, Hargis told himself. *His* problem
would be working with a *federale* whom he did not fully
trust, on soil where he had neither expertise nor jurisdiction. Great. If Sanchez decided to rat him out, he was
screwed.

The least he could do, Hargis thought, was play along
for a bit and see what happened. Sanchez might surprise
him, after all, and every man deserved a chance to prove
himself before you cut him off at the knees.

"You're sure about this place?"

"I'm sure," the *federale* answered, reaching underneath his tailored jacket to adjust the shoulder holster he
was wearing. "Are you ready?"

"Ready as I'll ever be," said Hargis, taking care to
lock the car when he got out. Border towns crawled with
thieves, and Hargis had no intention of finding himself
on foot when they were finished.

The cantina had been labeled El Inferno, with a giant
neon devil stationed near the entrance, and from what the
Ranger saw on his approach, it seemed to go for truth in
advertising. Half a dozen patrons were emerging from the
club as Hargis and the *federale* crossed the parking lot,

two men who looked like sleazy pimps or dealers, and four women who had to be whores or the next best thing. The hulking bouncer was dressed in black from head to toe, including the patch that covered his left eye, the one he had left regarding Hargis and Sanchez with frank suspicion before he passed them inside.

It was an inferno, all right, and nothing like the country-western bars that Hargis favored back in Austin. He could smell the marijuana mingled with cigar and cigarette smoke as he entered, "hostesses" on hand to greet the new arrivals and convey them to an empty table. Sanchez waved the women off and Hargis watched them pout, but once the *federale* spoke to them, Brock noticed that the ladies did not give him any lip.

Their part of Mitchum's strategy, as cooked up with Belasko following their rout at the motel, had Hargis and the *federale* cast as dealers looking for a solid contact, someone who could fix them up with steady shipments of cocaine to be delivered in Del Rio, or perhaps in Brownsville, where the nonexistent syndicate they claimed to represent would be on hand to pay the tab. They were prepared to offer half a million down, in earnest money, for a meeting with the main supplier, and it seemed to bother Mitchum not at all that they had barely seven thousand dollars cash between them.

Hargis figured they could deal with that one if and when the need arose. So far, he had not managed to convince himself the plan was viable, much less that they could actually arrange a meeting with Ramon Ibarra or his number two. Ibarra had not reached his present state by being careless, and it stood to reason he would run a check on any strangers who came sniffing after him, regardless of the cash they claimed to have on hand.

And if Ibarra dug too deeply—or if Sanchez had a leak on his end—they were both as good as dead.

Assuming Sanchez was not playing Hargis for a sucker all the way.

The Ranger knew that he was getting paranoid, but that was how an undercover lawman stayed alive. Trust no one. Double-check your friends and triple-check your enemies. Be ready for a double cross at every turn, and from the most unlikely quarter.

It had burned him, hearing Sanchez cast aspersions on the Rangers earlier, but Hargis knew no agency could be above suspicion, not where drugs and the unending flow of tax-free dollars were concerned. It would defy all logic if there weren't a few bad apples on the force, but Hargis trusted his immediate superiors as much as he had trusted anyone since he pinned on the badge.

If Sanchez played it straight, they just might have a chance, regardless of the odds. Brock Hargis was not counting on success, by any means, but he was ready to admit the possibility.

And if the *federale* tried to screw him . . . well, he understood that Mexico was overpopulated, as it was. They would not miss one crooked lawman, more or less.

They found two empty bar stools, ordered drinks, and Sanchez started dropping names. The scar-faced bartender feigned innocence, shrugging off the questions as he mopped the bar with a dingy towel.

Strike one.

But making waves and leaving tracks were part of the assignment, even if they never got an answer face-to-face. You could not ask about Ibarra in Del Rio more than once or twice, without the word of your inquiries getting back to someone in the family.

And that could be enough, thought Hargis, to arrange a meet . . . or get them killed.

Say fifty-fifty, either way.

He settled in and sipped his beer, prepared to watch the night unfold and meet his enemies head-on, when they arrived.

THE EXECUTIONER HAD KEPT his plans deliberately vague in the conversation with Mitchum and company, leaving his options wide open. Collecting information on the cult scene would be Mitchum's job, while Sanchez and the Texas Ranger did their best to pose as dealers looking for a source. It might not work, but even if they blew it, there was still a chance of contact with the enemy, if only in the form of an assault.

At this point, Bolan knew that they were damn near flying blind, and any leads at all could only help.

For his part, Bolan had obtained a sketchy list of targets from Mitchum, including known associates of the Martinez cult and members of Ramon Ibarra's narco syndicate. Confirmed addresses were hard to come by, but he had enough to get him started, with a handful in Del Rio and a couple more outside.

Enough to put the ball in play, at any rate.

Before he started rattling cages, though, he had to get in touch with Hal Brognola, find out something more about this ex-cop from Miami and his personal crusade. He made the phone call from a public booth before he crossed the border, using the unlisted number for Brognola's home. It was not late enough for Hal to be in bed—in fact, he might still be at work—but it was worth a shot.

Brognola answered on the second ring, a note of caution in his voice.

"Hello?"

"It's Striker, calling on an open line."

"Hang on." There was a heartbeat's hesitation while Brognola hooked up the scrambler at home, and Bolan used a portable device at his end, clipped on to the public phone. "Okay," Hal said at last, "we're on the box."

"I'm down here at the meeting site," said Bolan. "We've already had a problem."

"Oh?" The caution in Brognola's voice had been replaced by obvious concern.

"You're bound to hear about it soon. Three shooters at the meet. Their wheelman got away."

"The other three?"

"We didn't have a chance to talk."

"Okay, I'll keep an eye out for transmissions, maybe ask around. You think it was Ibarra?"

"From the story Mitchum tells, it's hard to say. It could have been this guy Martinez, just as easily. Did Mitchum fill you in?"

"The basics. It reminded me a lot of that satanic gig you handled, some time back."

"If Mitchum has it straight, we're looking at a whole new game," said Bolan. "These guys have a tap into the narco trade, big time. For all I know, they're dealing on their own, aside from any help they give Ibarra. There's no reason to believe it's localized."

"I got that feeling, too. That's why I thought you might be interested."

"Right now, I'm interested in Mitchum. What's your reading?"

Hal delayed his answer for a moment, wanting it just right. "I checked him out, of course. The bit about his semi-forced retirement was confirmed. A couple of his old superiors went off the record, telling me they wished they had him back. I guess he said some things before he left, predictions like, and now they're coming true around Miami. More involvement of the *santeria* cults and whatnot with the dealers, homicides with evidence of ritual, you name it."

"So, why don't they take him back?"

"You know the way it works with office politics. Somebody gets pissed off, they take a stand, and then it's all their credibility is worth to change their minds. Besides, I told you *some* of his superiors were having second thoughts. The ones who count still think he ought to have his head examined. What I'm hearing, you could have a voodoo priest performing rituals at city hall, and half those guys from Metro-Dade would make believe they didn't see a thing. It's like admitting you believe in ghosts or UFOs."

"Okay. We've got a plan, of sorts. I don't know how we'll manage, but I'll try to keep you posted as we go along."

"You'd better," Hal replied. "There isn't much that I can do for you officially, across the line, but if you hit a major snag, at least I may be able to arrange some kind of smoke screen."

Bolan smiled and said, "I'll make a note."

"Note this." Brognola hesitated for a moment, then he said, "Stay frosty, huh?"

"I feel a chill already."

"Yeah. I guess that means somebody else is in for frostbite, pretty soon."

"I wouldn't be surprised."

"Good hunting, Striker. Try to stay in touch."

"Affirmative."

The line went dead on Hal's end, Bolan dropping the receiver in its cradle, disconnecting the mini-scrambler before he walked back to his waiting rental car.

Across the bridge, Del Rio waited for him like a glowing jewel, her neon helping to cover up the rot and running sores. Beyond Del Rio, there was all of Mexico, a land where Aztec rituals and shamanism jostled for breathing room with 21st-century technology.

A dicey battleground, replete with challenges.

The Executioner would not have had it any other way.

CHAPTER FIVE

Jesus Dominguez checked his Rolex watch and found that he was running late. Not that it mattered terribly. Considering the large amounts of cash at stake, his contact was certain to wait at the rendezvous point. Dominguez hoped that it would be the gringo *señorita*—they had hit it off spectacularly, last time, and Jesus was looking forward to a rematch—but he was resigned to deal with anyone Martinez sent.

Business was business, after all, and it should not be muddled with emotion if such complications were avoidable.

Ideally Dominguez would have preferred to conduct negotiations on his home turf, in Nuevo Laredo, but Martinez was insistent that they meet on neutral ground. It was a matter of security, of course, and if Martinez did not trust him fully, neither was Dominguez ready to place all his faith in *el padrino*.

But there were stories circulating on the border, tales of how Martinez held fantastic powers in his hands. He could predict the future, change the course of history by calling on his contacts in the spirit world. A man to reckon with, by all accounts.

Security worked both ways, of course. A man of Dominguez's stature, ranking in the top-ten narco dealers operating out of northern Mexico, could not afford to travel unprotected, even to a meeting with reputed friends on neutral ground.

This evening, Dominguez had settled for two bodyguards, including his driver. Both carried machine pistols under their expensive tailored jackets, and both knew how to use their weapons. Dominguez could only estimate the number of victims they had claimed, between them, but he counted them among his most proficient soldiers.

Still, if things went well, their skill would not be utilized this evening. He was hoping for an amiable chat, perhaps some wine, to culminate in an agreement that would make him rich—or richer than he was already.

The initial contact by Martinez had surprised him, coming—as the Anglos said—out of the clear blue sky. It was a well-known fact that *el padrino* worked his magic for Ramon Ibarra, on retainer, making certain that Ibarra's border shipments met with no misfortune. He had done his work extremely well so far, according to the various reports Jesus received from his selected spies inside Ibarra's family, and while Dominguez never would have called himself a superstitious man, he knew the value of insurance when his life and liberty were riding on the line.

If he could seal a bargain with Martinez—and why else would *el padrino* have dispatched his woman to Dominguez in the first place?—it would be a double coup. For a percentage of the profits on cooperative ventures, he would gain the magical protection that Martinez could provide...and at the same time, he would gain a whole new insight into the Ibarra syndicate. Martinez had been working with Ibarra for the past two years or so, and he had doubtlessly picked up many secrets that Dominguez could employ to tip the scales against Ramon.

There would be risks involved. Ibarra was not one to take such a maneuver lying down. Retaliation was a certainty, but with Martinez on his side, Dominguez was convinced that he would finally prevail.

It was a masterstroke on *el padrino*'s part, using the woman. Martinez obviously knew Jesus's reputation as a cocksman, counting on the woman to entice him... which she certainly had done. But if Martinez thought Dominguez could be swayed by sex where business was concerned, the shaman had already made one critical mistake.

Dominguez sat back in his limousine and conjured up a picture of the woman in his mind. Blond hair, with just a touch of red that danced like tiny flames by candlelight. Her smile was dazzling, and her body...

Dominguez stopped himself. He knew that he would have to keep his wits about him in the next few hours. Even if Martinez sent the woman, he could not allow himself to think with his *cojones,* risking everything. He was a businessman first and foremost; the rest of it, his private life, would always take a back seat to pursuit of the almighty dollar.

Approaching Piedras Negras on Highway 67, Dominguez lighted a fat cigar and filled the passenger compartment of the limousine with fragrant smoke. In front of him, his driver and the shotgun rider watched the highway, flicking frequent glances at the rearview mirror to make certain they had not acquired a tail along the way. So far, they seemed to be secure.

Piedras Negras lay midway between Nuevo Laredo and Ciudad Acuna, technically within the territory dominated by Ramon Ibarra, but Dominguez was willing to risk an excursion beyond his own stronghold in the adjoining state of Nuevo León. It stood to reason that

Martinez was conducting the negotiations secretly, because he had as much to lose from premature disclosure as Dominguez himself.

Ibarra might rely on *el padrino* for advice and magical protection, but the spirits alone would not be enough to protect Martinez from the wrath of his employer if Ibarra recognized the shaman's treachery.

Dominguez had a hole card now. If he could not negotiate a suitable agreement with Martinez, then he could always make a phone call, let Ibarra know the kind of viper he was dealing with.

And it was something for Jesus to keep in mind, at that. A man who stabbed one master in the back would stab another, when the time was right. Dominguez would be forced to watch his back in any future business with Martinez, but he *always* watched his back, no matter whether he was dealing with a friend or foe.

In the drug trade, he had learned, the difference between a "friend" and "enemy" depended on the moment. Friends were faithful as long as you were helping them make money. When they found an opportunity to earn more elsewhere, they were gone—but not before they looted every peso they could get their hands on in a rush.

Dominguez had experience at dealing with all sorts of enemies, and with the persons who disguised themselves as friends. He could not say what prompted *el padrino* to forsake Ibarra, and he did not care. It was enough to have Martinez make the move and let Dominguez profit by association with a man of power.

Wait and see.

He still hoped it would be the woman, warm and willing to pick up where they had let it rest the last time.

He drew on his cigar and concentrated on the open highway leading to Piedras Negras. Leading to a brand-new fortune that was now within his grasp.

GREGORIO RUIZ WAS TIRED of waiting, but he would not let it show. He would not need to touch the compact walkie-talkie on the seat beside him. Checking on his men would be a waste of time. They were exactly where he left them, following their orders to the letter. They would wait all night, if necessary, and be waiting when the desert sun rose in the morning, glaring hot enough to fry their brains.

Not *his* men, though, Ruiz corrected himself. The men belonged to *el padrino,* and they always would. As *he* did, bound to a dynamic leader heart and soul, for all eternity. Of course, in his case there was more than simple loyalty involved, but that made their cooperation all the sweeter. *El padrino* was the center, the dynamic focus of his life.

Ruiz had spent the first nineteen years of his life alone, or nearly so, before he met Francisco de Leon Martinez. He would not relive those wasted years for all the gold that drugs could bring him in a thousand years. Before Martinez, there had been no magic in his life. No hope. No love.

It was a point of pride that *el padrino* had selected him to meet Jesus Dominguez, rather than the bitch. Of course, his absence meant the two of them could be together now, rutting like a pair of desert rabbits, but his jealousy extended only to the woman. Somehow, in complete defiance of logic, Ruiz found he could not get angry at Martinez. It was one more mark of their relationship.

The real thing.

Love.

He still remembered their initial meeting in Mexico City. Lord, how could he ever forget? Fernando had been telling fortunes with the cards, a simple parlor trick...or so Ruiz had reckoned at the time. Attracted to the stranger, he had laid his money down and smiled appropriately when Martinez told him to be vigilant for the appearance of a dark man in his life. A force that he could not control, but one which he would follow gladly, reaping glory for himself as the reward.

It was a standard reading, up to that point, but Fernando was not finished. He began to read the past, unbidden, studying the cards at first, and then Ruiz's face, as he described a barren childhood with a father who would rather curse than praise, preferring violence to affection every time. Martinez saw Ruiz emerging from an affluent but loveless home to play at education, wasting time in college, pulling down indifferent grades. The scandal in his junior sophomore year, discovered in the shower with an upperclassman. Driven out of school, disgraced.

By then, of course, it hardly mattered. With his father's death, Ruiz had access to a fair supply of money. It would last a year of two, if he was lucky, and he would defer consideration of employment to a later time. Meanwhile the capital of Mexico was filled with young, attractive men and nightclubs where a meeting could be easily arranged. The Mexican police still frowned on homosexuality, but they went blind where bribes were paid on time. Ruiz soon learned which clubs to patronize, and while he outwardly enjoyed himself from one night to the next, he felt that he was drifting aimlessly, without a goal in life.

Fernando saw right through him at a glance, like magic. Only later, talking over drinks, did he reveal a portion of his secret. While Ruiz was speaking figuratively, he hit upon the truth.

It *was* magic.

Not the simple tricks that children learn from books and television shows, but something else again. A mystic link between Fernando and a world beyond the visible. Beyond the reach of normal men.

Gregorio was skeptical at first, but he had listened to the story of Fernando's childhood, raised in the tradition of occult knowledge, handed down from his ancestors in Cuba. An American by birth, Fernando shunned the gringo doctrine of assimilation, clinging to his roots with stubborn pride. Of course, he still loved luxury, and by the time Gregorio first met Martinez, he was on his way to building up a fortune of his own.

Their affair had been spontaneous, completely unanticipated—at least on Gregorio's part. In time, as jealous rages came and went, he would suspect Fernando of deliberately seducing him to tap his family inheritance, but when his anger cooled, the accusations always seemed absurd. Fernando loved him. It was simply fate, a fact of life, that he was also drawn to other men—and women— on the side.

He thought about the bitch again, and scowled. She served her purpose, drawing new recruits and sponsors to the family, but it was still beyond Ruiz to understand exactly what Fernando saw in her. Of course, she was attractive in her way, but you could never really trust a woman with your heart. The rift between Ruiz's parents had been all the schooling he required on that score, and he learned his lesson well. At school, he watched the little bitches scheming on their boyfriends, cheating every chance they got, and the charade repulsed him.

Men could do the same, of course, but even when they let you down, the situation had a different feel about it. You could always tell yourself that it was simply physical attraction, something casual, and never meant to last.

Until Fernando.

His induction into magic had been gradual, beginning with a simple ritual or two, some after-hours reading, nights of listening with rapt attention while Fernando spun the story of his childhood, adolescence, and the powers he attained through study, concentration and the power of his will. When it was time to sacrifice a cock, Gregorio was ready. He had nearly gagged on his first mouthful of fresh, warm blood, but he had kept it down somehow.

A goat, next time, and other animals of varied breed and size, to meet the paying patron's needs. Fernando had a "menu" for his customers to choose from, the exotic, larger beasts reserved for those with ample cash on hand, who needed special magic worked on their behalf. For six dollars, they could get a chicken. Thirty dollars bought a nice young goat. A boa constrictor or python, for those more inclined toward voodoo or *macumba,* ran nearly five hundred dollars at the current rate of exchange. An adult zebra could be obtained and sacrificed for twenty-five hundred dollars, plus expenses. The ultimate, an African lion cub, would set the patron back a cool four grand, paid up front.

It was a business for Fernando, but the magic worked. How many times within the past two years had Ruiz seen his lover's predictions come true, in precise and meticulous detail? Too often for his memory to count, offhand. His spells were potent, and his reputation soon spread beyond Mexico City, into the hinterlands, where *narcotrafficantes* lived in their fortified ranchos, directing empires with a wave of their finely manicured, diamond-studded hands.

The ritual of human sacrifice came later, first described by Fernando as a matter of necessity. The tiny souls of animals no longer served his purpose as emissaries to the world beyond. He needed more coherent messengers to make his magic strong and satisfy his new, important—and demanding—customers. For such rituals, he would need to construct a *nganga,* using relics from the animal that eats salt.

Relics of man.

The transition seemed easy, even welcome, to Fernando, but Ruiz had faltered during the first ritual, losing his supper as he watched from the sidelines. The second time was easier, the third easier still, and eventually he began to crave the experience, sharing Fernando's rapture as the cuts were made and blood was spilled. The blood had power, he could tell, and most especially when you drank it from a heart still warm and throbbing in your hands.

"*Aqui,*" his driver said, and now Gregorio could see the limo running dark, Dominguez being cautious as he neared the rendezvous. As if his petty schemes and strategy could help him now.

Ruiz picked up his two-way radio and held down the transmission button with his thumb. "Be ready," he commanded. "Wait until they show themselves. Make no mistakes."

His driver flashed the headlights and received an answer from the limousine. Dominguez had his wheelman park some thirty feet in front of them, a neutral zone between the vehicles. His shotgun rider stepped out of the limo, circled back to open up the door for his patrón, the dome lights showing only two men left inside the car. Gregorio Ruiz was smiling as he left his vehicle, watching Dominguez exit the limo, dark eyes scanning the street for any sign of danger.

It was too late for that.

The first shot, from a rifle on a roof across the street, struck Dominguez's bodyguard in the chest, spinning him around and dropping him facedown in the street. Before the echoes of the first shot died away, two more rang out, the limo's windshield starred with cracks in an intricate spiderweb pattern. The driver was killed instantly, slumping over in his seat before Dominguez had a chance to react.

The dealer turned to run, but there was nowhere left to go. Two of Gregorio's soldiers had emerged from the darkness, brandishing automatic weapons, cutting off their captive's retreat.

Ruiz stepped forward, smiling.

"*Ola,* Jesus," he said. "You're right on time."

THE SMELL OF DEATH was like an aphrodisiac for Fernando de Leon Martinez, sending shivers of anticipation up his spine. He never drank before a ritual, because he did not wish to dull his senses for the feast and spectacle ahead.

Tonight it would be sweet, a comeback from the momentary setback at Rancho Santa Maria. He was building up a new *nganga,* and he needed help. Who better to assist him that Jesus Dominguez, who had been competing with Ibarra in the border drug trade from Coahuila for the past few months?

Two birds with one stone, Martinez thought. Elimination of a rash competitor, while furthering his own cause with a worthy contribution to the pot. Dominguez was a pig, but he was full of fear and energy, a perfect emissary to the demon spirits on the other side. Once his brain and other vital organs had been added to the new *nganga,* they would be in business, ready to begin anew, stronger than ever.

A fresh start, indeed. Martinez wondered if he ought to thank the *federales* for doing him an unintentional favor, but he decided to let it go. The bribes he paid each week were thanks enough—and maybe more than the police deserved, considering the fact that no one had forewarned him of the raid.

Miguel Calzada was to blame for that, a so-called honest cop, but every badge in Mexico had its price. Martinez simply had not found the proper method of negotiating with Calzada yet. And if he failed...well, there was always room in the *nganga* for another donor's contribution.

Yes, he liked that notion very much.

Gregorio Ruiz was on his right, the blond Marcella Grant immediately on his left as he approached the sacrificial altar. Naked, stretched out on his back with arms and legs securely bound, Jesus Dominguez was reduced to something in the nature of a giant slug. His chest and abdomen were almost hairless, and his genitals were shriveled by the fear that he could not control.

"How kind of you to join us here, Jesus."

The others chuckled at his little joke, Martinez solemn and respectful for the moment, addressing the goat without horns.

"For mercy's sake, Fernando, I implore you. If I have offended you, accept my most sincere apology...with payment, naturally...and let me go."

"Your life is an offense to me," Martinez answered. "Your apology is useless, but there is a way that you can serve me."

"Anything!" Dominguez blurted, grasping at the slender reed of hope.

"Your cooperation is appreciated."

Turning to Ruiz, Fernando drew the ceremonial knife from its scabbard, lifting it up to let the blade catch candlelight, reflecting dozens of tiny flames from the polished, double-edged surface.

"You are about to make a priceless contribution, Jesus. Consider it the first step of a grand adventure."

Stepping closer to the altar, he let Dominguez see the knife, the blade no sharper than Fernando's hungry smile.

"We call this method 'the two hundred cuts,' " he explained, ignoring the blubbering pleas from Dominguez, nearly incoherent now. "Your attitude must be improved, you see, before we can make use of you to full advantage."

He bent close to whisper in the dealer's ear before he went to work.

"Feel free to scream. The spirits like a little music with their meal."

CHAPTER SIX

The Golden Ram, in Ciudad Acuna, had a reputation as one of the sleaziest dives in Coahuila, catering to what the manager described as an "exotic" clientele. In practice, that meant that the in-house prostitutes were five or six years younger than the local average, the nightly sex shows more explicit and depraved, illicit drugs more readily available to paying customers. It was a matter of degree, as such things go, but water seeks its own level . . . and so does slime.

Few Anglo tourists patronized the Golden Ram, aside from horny servicemen and border trash who eked out their living along the fringes of the law. The normal clientele ran heavily toward smugglers, dealers, pimps and thieves. It came as no surprise, therefore, to learn that one Ramon Ibarra held a controlling interest in the club.

Bolan parked his rental in an alley two blocks down and locked it up. The night was warm for his trench coat, but he needed it for cover, to conceal the mini-Uzi he was wearing in a shoulder sling beneath his right arm. Spare magazines were slotted into narrow inside pockets of the trench coat, the outer pockets heavy with incendiary sticks and tear-gas canisters.

All set to party down.

The club was crowded when he got there, music blasting from a four-piece salsa band while several teenage strippers worked the narrow runway. A tired-looking "hostess" took Bolan's hand, but he shrugged her off, moving toward the bar while she glared daggers at his back.

The bartender wore slicked-down hair and a pencil-thin mustache, resembling a pirate from a 1930s movie. Bolan shouldered in and propped one elbow on the bar, beckoning the weasel closer.

"¿Habla usted Ingles?"

"I do."

"Good deal. I've got a message for your customers."

"¿Señor?"

"You're closing for repairs."

"Say what?"

"Let's put it this way."

Bolan palmed a tear-gas canister and yanked the safety pin, seeing the bartender's eyes go wide as he lobbed it overhand, toward the band. It missed the lead guitarist, rolled behind the pounding bass drum, and erupted seconds later in a hissing cloud of gas. The music faltered, dying with a screech of amplifiers as the four musicians beat a swift path toward the nearest exit.

All around Bolan, patrons were breaking for the street, men cursing, women crying out in alarm. One of the nearest drinkers turned on Bolan with a snarl and cocked his arm to strike, staggering backward and sprawling on his back as Bolan smashed a beer mug in his face.

Behind him, the bartender was doubled over, reaching for something out of sight beneath the counter. He came up with a revolver, but the mini-Uzi got there first, ripping out a 3-round burst that slammed him backward, dropping bottles in a shower of glass and liquor as he toppled to the floor.

The sound of gunfire accelerated the stampede for safety, more screams than curses now as boozy patrons jostled one another aside, racing for the safety of the outer darkness. Chairs and tables scattered, shoes losing traction in puddles of beer and tequila.

Bolan headed for the stairs and started climbing toward the second floor. En route, he dropped an incendiary stick behind the bar, leaving it to sputter while he mounted the steps. Above him, women screamed as the first fumes of tear gas began curling through the floorboards. Heavy footsteps rushed toward him down the corridor immediately on his left.

He turned to meet the gunners head-on, two of them rushing into the gap belatedly, brandishing shiny automatic pistols. Bolan hit them with a parabellum figure-eight and dropped them in their tracks, one squeezing off a wild round toward the ceiling as he fell. Behind them, moving cautiously, three naked girls and their equally nude customers crowded into the hallway, driven from cramped bedrooms by the encroaching gas.

"Outside!" Bolan shouted at them, gesturing with his weapon for emphasis. *"¡Pronto!"*

They moved past him in single file, one of the girls crying out as she saw flames leaping up behind the bar. Bolan followed them in his own time, first making sure the other bedrooms were empty, dropping incendiary sticks behind him as he went.

Downstairs, tear gas and smoke combined to make the atmosphere impossible. Bolan held his breath until he reached the street, quickly merging with pedestrian traffic and working his way back to the alley where he had left his car. He passed police in khaki uniforms along the way, all headed for the fire, but no one gave the tall American a second glance. They were preoccupied with a mixture of excitement and alarm, anxious to share in the excitement, even if it only meant counting bodies on the sidewalk.

Bolan left them to it, reaching his car and finding it undisturbed. He slid behind the wheel and turned his key in the ignition, smiling as the engine caught and came to life.

One down.

Mack Bolan was on a roll. And before he finished up his game, he meant to roll right over Ibarra, Martinez and the whole damned pack of savages.

The Executioner had only just begun to fight.

ON HIS THIRD STOP in Ciudad Acuna, Doyle Mitchum reckoned his luck was due for a change. He had gone down swinging at the first two bodegas, conversing with the clerks in Spanish perfected over years of working Miami's "Little Havana," but he was still a gringo, and a stranger besides. The clerks—both women—had been cautious, shrugging off some of his questions, answering others with cautious negatives or vague generalities.

At least it wasn't his technique, thought Mitchum. He was fairly positive of that. In close to twenty years with Metro-Dade, and all his travels since, he had perfected his discreet interrogation methods to an art form. All false modesty aside, Doyle Mitchum knew he had the knack.

But there was something wrong in Ciudad Acuna. All along the Tex-Mex border, when it came to that. The two bodega clerks were frightened, Mitchum realized, and not by any prospect of arrest. A glance was all it took for them to know he had no jurisdiction in Coahuila, and the questions he had asked them would not have supported an arrest, in any case. He did not stroll in off the street inquiring whether anyone could tell him where to find Fernando de Leon Martinez and his gang of killer cultists. There had been no reference to human sacrifice or any other kind of criminal activity. You start with generalities, expressing interest in the shop and working up to the specifics of ingredients required by a *palero* to conduct his special ceremonies.

If you got that far.

And Mitchum had not, on his first two stops. The general questions were enough to put his subjects off, insisting they knew nothing of black magic in general or *palo mayombe* in particular. They specialized in "Christian" *santeria,* which the gringo was at liberty to verify by checking out the statuettes of Catholic saints lined up for sale in glass showcases. He could see the Virgin Mary, Saint Lazarus, Saint Barbara—the whole roster of saints, in fact. The clerks were ignorant of any magic used for evil's sake, and they were happy to remain that way.

At Mitchum's second stop, he asked about the fat black candles on display, the nervous clerk responding with a shrug and threadbare explanation of their use in an obscure "fertility" ritual. By that time, Mitchum knew the tools of a black mass when he saw them, and he also knew that browbeating the clerk would be fruitless, resulting in an ugly scene that took him nowhere…except, perhaps, to the local jail if things got out of hand.

That made it two down and three to go. They had a late start from Del Rio, thanks to the fiasco at the Desert Star, and he was surprised to find the third bodega still open. Flexible hours, perhaps, for witches on the night shift. Pushing through the door, he heard a small bell chiming somewhere in the back, announcing his arrival to the staff.

A man, this time, as tall as Mitchum, hair slicked back like something from an inner-city street gang in the States. He wore a baggy peasant shirt and trousers, some embroidery on the breast pocket featuring flowers and vines intertwined. His face was deadpan, showing no expression whatsoever as he waited for Mitchum to approach the register.

"Can I help you, *señor?*"

"I hope so." Mitchum was relieved to hear the man speak English. Thinking in one language and speaking another had begun to make him feel a bit schizoid. "Basically I'm looking for some information."

"Ah. With proper tools and practice, we can learn about the future or the past. It's all the same."

"I wouldn't be surprised." He palmed a roll of bills and held it in his hand, just visible, to whet the salesclerk's appetite. No offer yet, but he would set the tone. "Specifically, I'm interested in learning all I can about *palo mayombe* as practiced in Mexico . . . for a series of articles I'm writing back home."

The salesclerk frowned and crossed himself at mention of the cult. "Good luck," he said. "Unfortunately there is no way I can help. *Paleros* do not shop at the bodegas, *comprende?* They prefer their relics . . . how you say it . . . fresh."

Or crawling with flies and maggots, Mitchum thought, like at Rancho Santa Maria. Instead of saying it, he plastered a smile on his face and replied, "It occurs to me that a man of your knowledge and experience must hear things, now and then. Reports of certain rituals, for instance. Possibly the name of a *palero* I could speak to. Anything at all."

As he spoke, Mitchum idly fingered the roll of cash, seeing the clerk's eyes dart back to his hand time and again. The man was weighing his priorities and making up his mind.

"It happens that I do know a *palero,* but he's very . . . bashful with Americans."

"But for a price?"

"Perhaps. He may not be available tonight."

"But if he is . . ."

"A phone call is required."

Doyle Mitchum peeled the top bill from his roll and laid it on the countertop. "At my expense, of course," he said.

The sales clerk smiled. "If you insist."

"I do."

The clerk retreated through a beaded curtain, out of sight. When he began to speak into the telephone, his voice was muffled, pitched too low for Mitchum to decipher any of the words. He had a sudden urge to move around the counter, eavesdrop more conveniently, but it would blow his act if he was caught.

He tried to relax, but it wouldn't come easy. He knew the kind of trouble he could face, blundering into a meeting arranged by a total stranger on hostile turf. There might not even *be* a meeting, when you thought about it. Make a call to Juan and Pablo, maybe have them waiting when he left the shop. Relieve the gringo of his bankroll, and perhaps his life while they were at it.

Mitchum smiled. He might be off the job with Metro-Dade, but he remembered all the moves, and he was packing heat this time. If someone tried to take him down, he had a rude surprise in store for his attackers.

Moments later he could hear the beaded curtain rattle softly, and the clerk approached his register. The bland expression on his face was noncommittal, making Mitchum glad they did not have to face each other in a poker game.

"My friend will speak to you," the clerk informed him, sliding a small piece of paper across the glass countertop. "Here is the address where he will meet you in one hour. You may call him Franco if you like, but that is not his name."

"Of course." Mitchum pocketed the slip of paper without reading it, peeling another bill from the roll. "And for your trouble."

"Ah."

The clerk made his bill disappear, perhaps the only magic he would see tonight. Outside, Doyle Mitchum breathed the desert air—complete with car exhaust, stale beer, perfume, and urine in the gutters—to relieve the cloying smell of herbs and spices from the shop.

He had a date with a *palero* coming up, and it had only cost him twenty dollars to arrange. With any luck at all, the meeting would not wind up costing him his life.

THE RURAL WHOREHOUSE known as Rancho Margarita was, in fact, a kind of trailer camp, not unlike certain establishments plying their trade in the state of Nevada. Instead of more expensive mobile homes, however, the proprietor had settled for small two-wheel trailers, their interiors roughly the size of a gas station's rest room. Any one of them could easily be towed behind a car or pickup truck, their only nod toward permanence the cinder block supporting each trailer's hitch, to keep the tiny "bedrooms" from rocking while their occupants performed at an average rate of twenty dollars for fifteen minutes.

Drawn up in a semicircle on the open desert, a mile outside of Ciudad Acuna, the trailers reminded Bolan of a wagon train braced for attack by marauding Apaches. He pulled off the highway, nosed his rental car in toward the manager's office—another trailer, slightly larger than the rest—and counted half a dozen other vehicles on hand. Most would belong to customers, but one or two inevitably came with the place, representing personnel or muscle in residence.

He left the car unlocked this time, no street waifs or winos to rip him off out here in the middle of nowhere, and he carried the Beretta 93-R in his right hand, pressed against his thigh as he approached the manager's trailer. The OD satchel Bolan wore across his other shoulder was heavy with frag grenades, their bulk hard and knobby against his ribs.

A chunky bouncer was emerging from the "office," roused by Bolan's headlights, and a quick glance told him that the new arrival was no ordinary customer. He snapped a warning back to someone else inside the trailer, groping for a pistol in his waistband even as he spoke.

He wasn't in time.

A parabellum round impacted on the bridge of his nose, snapping the bouncer's head backward against the trailer's aluminum side wall. He left a crimson smear behind as he slid to the ground, winding up in a seated position, his thick shoulders wedged into the wheel well.

A second gunner filled the doorway, like a pop-up target in a shooting gallery. He had a sawed-off double-barreled shotgun in his hands, but there was no time to use it as Bolan squeezed off another round from his Beretta, slamming the man over on his back. A reflex clenched dead meat around the shotgun's double triggers, and both barrels erupted toward the ceiling, blowing a jagged hole in the thin aluminum.

Bolan checked the office briefly, found signs of life remaining, and moved on to the next one in line. Faint light was showing through the windows, muffled voices speaking rapidly, showing signs of strain after the sudden burst of gunfire. Standing well to one side, he ham-

mered on the door and called out for the occupants to
show themselves.

A heartbeat later, the small door swung open and a
slender young woman emerged, pulling a terry robe over
her nakedness. The man who followed her was heavyset
and middle-aged, an Anglo whose tan was confined to his
face, neck and forearms. His chest and sagging gut
looked unnaturally white in the desert moonlight, reminding Bolan of something he might find beneath a
rock.

"Clear out," he told them in English, glancing inside
the trailer to make sure it was empty. A rumpled bed took
up most of the floor space, with a single chair and night-
stand. The latter supported a Coleman lamp, providing
light for the party in the absence of electricity.

He palmed a frag grenade, removed the pin, and
lobbed it to the far side of the bed, already moving on to
the next trailer in line before it blew. The blast took out
a ragged section of one wall, leaving the whole trailer
twisted beyond repair. A write-off, any way you looked
at it.

Moving down the line, he repeated the process six
times. At his next to last stop, two women emerged with
a white-haired old man, and the last trailer in line was
empty, its normal occupant doubtless tied up with the
threesome next door. Each trailer received a grenade as
Bolan made his rounds, and there was no interference
from the women or their johns. By the time Bolan finished, the parking lot was empty of cars, except for his
own, and all but two of the girls had vanished with their
frightened customers.

He backtracked to the office, found a field telephone,
and dragged it out where the two whores could see it,
leaving it beside the body of the first man he had shot.

"You want to talk," he told them, "you've got ample time before the sun comes up. Or, you can call your boss and tell him what went down. If you decide to make the call—or even if you don't—I have a message for Ibarra. Do you understand? ¿Comprende?"

"Sí," one answered for them both, the other nodding like a puppet.

"Tell him this is just beginning. He's got trouble that he hasn't dreamed of yet. Okay?"

"Okay," they said in unison. Surrender in stereo.

He walked back to his car and left them, driving toward the city lights that marked his destination in the desert like a fiery beacon in the night.

CHAPTER SEVEN

Three cantinas in a row, and Hargis was beginning to feel the effects of tequila and beer. The mild buzz failed to mellow his disappointment at their failure to turn up a single lead on Ramon Ibarra so far. It stood to reason that the locals would be tight-lipped, but the operating budget was not inexhaustible, and the two cops had spent more than two hundred dollars already, between overpriced, watered-down drinks and their vain bids to pry information out of poker-faced Mexican bartenders.

Number four was the Yankee Rose, named for no particular reason beyond the neon display out front. There was no rose motif inside, and the bloom had long since vanished from the hostesses who led them to a corner booth, facing a smallish dance floor.

This time, Hargis and the *federale* had agreed, they would pace themselves better, drinking with the girls for a while before they dropped an inquisitional bomb on the waiter. It was worth noting, thought Hargis, how the canteens they had visited so far did not employ cocktail waitresses in the American tradition, preferring to let their female employees fill the "hostess" role, keeping the customers lubricated in more ways than one.

The system seemed to work, but it would mean three sets of ears when Sanchez got around to popping the question this time. No problem, if their cover held, since Hargis knew most border dealers had a fine disdain for cloak-and-dagger bullshit. They preferred to strut their stuff, unless they were arrested, whereupon they suddenly became the meekest of the meek, acting as if butter wouldn't melt in their collective mouths.

And then, of course, there were the handful who were so damned tough—or thought they were—that they insulted everyone, including gringo cops, with big talk, threats of dire reprisals if they were not set at liberty without delay.

Those kind had accidents from time to time, in Texas jails. More than one had carelessly fallen down stairs or slipped off his chair during an interrogation, bruising his face and losing some teeth in the process. The gringo technique didn't always measure up to seltzer water in the sinuses, but it had a kind of hands-on gratification the good old boys dearly loved.

Payback time for some smart ass who should have kept his mouth shut and his business on the far side of the border.

Well, Hargis was on the far side of the border now, another world, and he was feeling none too happy with the move. If anything went wrong, he was without official sanction for the move, cut off from any kind of meaningful assistance from the Rangers or the U.S. government in general.

In short, if they got burned, his ass was grass.

The hostess on his left was smiling at him, massaging Brock's thigh and working her way upward an inch at a time. He was starting to enjoy it when a shadow fell across their table, and he knew the waiter was not due yet with another round.

Glancing up, Hargis found himself face-to-face with two of the sleaziest hoodlums he had ever seen. Sleazy and *big*, their hulking size especially startling in relation to the stature of their average countryman. An easy six foot each, and maybe more. Their bulk reminded Hargis of the way some cons work out in prison, pumping iron.

"You gringos have our table," said the older of the two, a scar-faced specimen with salt-and-pepper hair.

"I'm not a gringo," said Sanchez, taking immediate exception to the insult.

Hargis felt angry color seeping into his face, remembering an old joke about the Lone Ranger and Tonto. What you mean "we," white man? He took a firm grip on his beer mug, waiting.

"Sit and drink with gringos, you become a gringo," said the younger hoodlum, sneering at Sanchez to reveal rotting teeth.

"You have our women, too," the first one said.

"The ladies didn't seem to know that, when they picked us," Hargis told him. At his side, the hostess had withdrawn her hand and wiped the coy smile from her face.

"You're calling me a liar, then." The older one smiled. If he was irritated by the thought, it didn't show.

"I'm saying that there must be some mistake."

"You made it, gringo pig."

He glanced at Sanchez, caught the *federale*'s nod, and he was ready when the table vaulted toward their challengers, propelled by a mighty kick from Sanchez. Hargis kept his grip on the beer mug, spilling most of its contents on the floor as he rose, ready with a roundhouse as the hoodlums scrambled backward.

The older one was digging in the pocket of his denim jacket for a weapon, but he never got there. Hargis swung the mug with everything he had and saw it detonate against the slugger's cheek. Blood spurted from a ragged wound between his adversary's eye and jawline, impact driving the thug backward with a startled howl of pain.

Beside him, Sanchez had the younger hoodlum by his throat and balls, propelling him backward against the bar, slamming him into the woodwork with force enough to numb his spine. A sharp right cross finished it, and his assailant crumpled to the floor in an unconscious heap.

It was a good beginning, but they were not exactly finished yet.

Behind Sanchez, another punk was moving in, a bottle cocked to swing against the *federale*'s skull. Hargis shouted a warning, half turning to protect his own back as Sanchez did the same . . . and just in time.

Two of them rushed toward him like a pair of tackles on a high-school football team. He booted one directly in the face, feeling bone and cartilage collapse, and then the other had him, bony fists driving into Brock's midsection and forcing the air from his lungs. For an instant, he felt as if he were suffocating, drowning, and then he found the will to fight back without breathing, slamming big fists into his assailant's face and scalp.

At least it wasn't all one-sided, Hargis thought, watching men pair off in slugging matches all around the dimly lighted cantina. Having dropped his second man, he risked a glance at Sanchez, just in time to see the *federale* finishing his adversary with a hard chop to the neck.

"I think we've done this joint," he said to Sanchez, clenching his right hand to work the bruised knuckles.

"I think you're right, this time."

"What say we hit the bricks, before the cops show up?"

"I'm right behind you."

Putting a myriad of jumbled questions on hold for the moment, Hargis turned and moved in the direction of the open doors, the street beyond. For once, the neon night looked welcome, like a waiting friend.

CONSIDERING the neighborhood, Doyle Mitchum was relieved that he had brought his pistol with him. Slums in the United States were one thing, but in Mexico and farther south, you saw a whole new meaning to the word. The living quarters were not merely old, run-down and ready for the wrecking ball; they were constructed, literally, out of trash. The patchwork shacks were everywhere, cardboard and corrugated metal, splintered plywood and tar paper held together with tape, tacks or nothing at all. Windows, where they existed, were carved with a knife. Doors were larger, lopsided holes, covered with cardboard or hanging sheets at night to keep the dogs out and the chickens in.

The smell was something else, a combination of raw sewage, unwashed bodies, poultry and domestic animals at large, all overlaid with a mixture of dust and smog for seasoning. It crept inside the car, though Mitchum kept the windows tightly closed and ran the air conditioner to keep himself from sweltering.

The slums of Ciudad Acuna are a dead end for the hopeless. Peasants driven from their farming land by drought and debts. Industrial workers and day laborers rendered jobless by recession or drink. Unwed mothers and widows with children to feed and no income to feed them on. Petty criminals too lazy to work if a job was offered to them on a silver platter. Alcoholics, drug addicts, the mentally ill without fortunes or families to pay the rent on a stylish padded room in some executive asylum.

And the children.

They were everywhere, despite the hour, running wild and dodging through his headlight beams like desert rabbits scurrying across a highway. Mitchum finally gave it up, when he was close enough to find the address that he sought on foot. He locked the car, gave twenty pesos to a pair of sleazy-looking punks to watch it for him, and departed praying it would be there when he returned.

If he returned.

It was an exaggeration to speak of addresses, per se, in the heart of this slum, but he had followed the directions he was given, and he knew that he was getting close. With his experience of hunting men around Miami and environs, he could feel it in his gut.

The shack was somewhat larger than its neighbors, and more solidly constructed. Mitchum had the feeling that its tenant might have been a carpenter before he gave it up to dabble in the spirit world. In any case, the place looked sturdy underneath the mandatory layer of soot and grime that covered everything within his line of sight. It even had a door of sorts, a plywood sheet on hinges lifted from a decorative cabinet, old and rusty now. No knob, but the designer had contrived a latch of wood and rawhide, like you sometimes find on garden gates in the American Southwest.

He knocked, afraid of shaking something loose inside the shack or beating down the door. No answer, and he waited for a moment, wondering if he should try again, when a voice at his elbow scared him out of ten years' growth.

"What is it that you seek?"

Mitchum turned on his heel, hoping the sudden fright would not show in his face. The new arrival was a slender Mexican, somewhere between forty and sixty years old, stringy hair showing gray beneath the brim of a ratty straw hat. His clothes were old and threadbare, but he seemed to keep them clean. The leather sandals on his dusty feet looked almost new.

"Excuse me?" Mitchum knew it sounded lame, but he was at a sudden loss for words.

"What is it that you seek?" the man repeated, frowning slightly as he spoke.

"I'm looking for an Esteban Montoya," Mitchum said.

"You've found one. Who has sent you here?"

He gave the name of the bodega and described its clerk, watching Montoya's face as he spoke. The man did not appear surprised or irritated by the news, and it occurred to Mitchum that a great deal of his business probably arrived this way, by word of mouth.

"Let's step inside."

Mitchum let his host lead the way, noting that no special lock was affixed to the door. A tug on the rawhide, and they were in. Montoya struck a match and crossed the room to light a kerosene lamp. Its flame cast eerie shadows around the cluttered interior of the one-room shack.

There was an altar on his left as Mitchum entered, but no sign or smell of the *nganga*. Visibly relieved, he looked around for somewhere to sit, finally following Montoya's example and parking himself on an upturned packing crate.

"What business do you have with me?" Montoya asked. "Has someone cursed you? Are you interested in knowing what tomorrow may bring?"

"Not quite. I'm looking for another member of your faith, a strong *palero*, and I've had no luck at all with the bodegas. It occurred to me that someone with a knowledge of the arts, like you, might know where I can find this man."

"Perhaps. Why is it that you want to see him?"

"This is personal."

"But you expect my help to carry out your private business," said Montoya, frowning. "Who am I to point a finger, when for all I know you may intend great harm."

"I understand. Perhaps I should have said, the business that I would discuss with this *palero* is a private matter. I can tell you that he has not wronged me, nor I him. I bear him no ill will, but rather have a plan to make him wealthy."

"Ah." A crafty smile replaced the frown. "And I should help you find him, so that you and he can both grow rich together, while Montoya lingers here."

He spread his hands to indicate the hovel with its shabby, makeshift furnishings. The lamplight made his dark eyes glimmer like obsidian.

"Of course," said Mitchum, "I would not expect the information free of charge."

As Mitchum spoke, he palmed the shrinking roll of bills and let Montoya have a glimpse. The shaman's eyes narrowed, but the corners of his mouth inched upward.

"If I knew the name, perhaps..."

"Fernando de Leon Martinez."

"Ah."

Montoya lost his smile. It had to be a trick of lighting, Mitchum thought, but for a moment there, the shadows underneath the shaman's eyes appeared to deepen.

"This is not a name to play with," said Montoya.

"If you'd rather not do business," Mitchum said, "I won't waste any more of your time."

He was putting the money away when Montoya leaned forward, stretching out a hand to stop him.

"For a price."

"How's fifty dollars sound?"

"A hundred would sound better."

"Sold."

The bills changed hands, Montoya staring back at Mitchum as he made them disappear.

"Before you seek this man, be certain that you know what you are doing."

"I'm as sure as I can be."

"In that case..."

THE WAREHOUSE north of Ciudad Acuna, on the Rio Grande, was used primarily for storing furniture, appliances and other household items manufactured stateside and imported into Mexico for sale. It also handled exports, of the pharmaceutical variety, but merchandise from Bogotá was stored and shipped without a record being kept for Customs.

It was half-past ten o'clock when Bolan parked his car downrange and walked back toward the warehouse, carrying the mini-Uzi and a C-4 satchel charge. He had no way of knowing whether there were drugs inside the place tonight, but it would make no difference in the long run. While Ramon Ibarra owned the warehouse and the land it sat on, it remained fair game.

He climbed a flight of concrete steps to reach the loading dock, no sentries showing yet. The access door was locked, but Bolan spent a moment with his pick and felt the tumblers clicking into place. Across the threshold, darkness, with a faint light showing at the far end of a narrow corridor. He moved in that direction, treading softly to avoid unnecessary noise.

The warehouse was about half-empty at the moment, crates and cartons piled up at the farther end, with yards of open floor in front of Bolan. On his right, an office cubicle had been constructed from glass and plywood, with an open view on three sides. Two Mexicans were standing in the office, looking over something on the desk between them, and they did not seem to notice Bolan as he approached.

They registered the new arrival as he filled the doorway, Bolan noting piles of greenbacks on the desk. The stout man on his left appeared to be unarmed, but the taller one on his right was wearing a shoulder holster, exposed with his jacket off, and he went for the gun at his first glimpse of Bolan.

The Uzi stuttered briefly, spitting out a 4-round burst that punched the *pistolero* over backward, slamming him against a file cabinet before he slithered to the floor. Bolan swiveled to cover the survivor, pinning him where he stood, hands trembling as he raised them shoulder-high.

"*¿Habla Ingles?*" Bolan asked.

"*Sí.* I mean, yes."

"Step back."

The fat man did as he was told, shuffling two steps back from the desk and stopping when his thighs collided with a swivel chair.

"You work for Ibarra?" Bolan asked.

"*¿Quien?*"

The Uzi rose to lock on target acquisition, level with the fat man's nose.

"Ibarra," Bolan said again.

"I work for heem, tha's right."

"You want to keep on working for him," Bolan asked, "or would you rather die right now?"

"I'm please to stay alive."

"We'll make a trade," said Bolan, setting his OD satchel down on the desk and lifting out the C-4 charge with its timer attached. "You keep this, I'll take the cash."

As Bolan spoke, he began scooping up the green-backs, dropping them into the satchel until it was full and the desktop was bare. Almost as an afterthought, he set the timer for five minutes and lifted his hand clear, listening to it tick in the ringing silence.

"Time to go," said Bolan. "Unless you'd rather stay and watch the fireworks."

"No!" the fat man blurted out. "I go."

"And take a message to Ibarra while you're at it."

"*¿Sí?*"

"Tell him he's going out of business soon. His days are numbered. Have you got that?"

"Going out of beezness. Numbered days."

"So, move it!"

Bolan let his hostage lead the way, hanging back to make sure the man did not hide out in the parking lot or try to double back and disable the timer. He read the fat man as a coward, and his first impression was confirmed as he watched the runner disappear up the street, covering ground with an awkward, waddling stride.

Bolan was pulling away in his car when the warehouse blew, a mushroom of fire blasting through the sheet-metal roof and lighting the block like an artificial sun. Somewhere inside, a secondary blast crumpled the giant doors on the loading dock and sent one of them spinning across the parking lot.

All right.

The night was not precisely young, but there was still time left to make another stop or two before he headed back across the border. Time to rattle Ibarra's cage a bit more and let the dealer stew, before he took a breather.

Bolan wondered how the other members of the team were doing, and he wished them well.

The war was heating up, and it was only a matter of time until someone got burned.

CHAPTER EIGHT

Ramon Ibarra lighted a Cuban cigar, drawing deeply before he shook out the match and dropped it into a ceramic ashtray sculpted to resemble a rattlesnake. The ersatz reptile studied him with eyes like chips of flint, unblinking, seeming to bore through his skull. At last the dealer turned his high-backed swivel chair away, facing toward the window and the light of early morning on his garden.

The telephone was silent on his desk, a blessed relief from the past few hours. The Anglos said no news was good news, and Ibarra thought they had a point, but he could use some good news for a change.

Beginning with the names and number of his enemies.

Five raids against his property in Ciudad Acuna overnight, with half a dozen soldiers dead, and he had no idea what the hell was happening, or who would dare to challenge him this way. Ibarra was accustomed to the violence of his trade, but this was different. To the best of his knowledge, there were no competitors between Tijuana and Matamoros who could mount this kind of blitz... and none who hated him enough to try.

Of course, Ibarra had his share of enemies. No dealer came this far, this fast, without incurring the wrath of others who craved the money, the power, but he had always made a point of eliminating his worst enemies along the way. It was a simple, economic form of life insurance...much like his negotiations with Fernando de Leon Martinez.

Magic, *sí*.

Ibarra did not regard himself as a superstitious peasant, but he had grown up hearing stories of the *brujas* who could blight crops with a glance or cure a dying man with a touch of their withered hands. The dealer had no faith in God, per se, but he had seen things he could not explain—including some of the magic practiced by Martinez.

One ceremony in particular, *sí*, where Ibarra had been summoned as the guest of honor, watching while Martinez and his ghouls dismantled a peasant. Ibarra was a violent man, and he had killed at least two dozen enemies with his own hands...but this was something else. The screams still came to him at night sometimes, in dreams of blood and pain that woke him with a start, his bedding drenched with sweat.

There came a knocking on his study door. Ibarra swiveled back to face his houseman, waiting as the *pistolero* spoke.

"Esta aqui."

"I'll see him now."

The houseman disappeared, returning moments later with Fernando Martinez in tow. The smile on *el padrino*'s face stopped short of mockery, but there was no concealing the gargantuan ego that powered the man. Sometimes Ibarra thought that he was dealing with a lunatic, but there was genius in the man, as well. A twisted genius, granted, but a genius all the same.

Martinez crossed the room and took a seat without waiting for an invitation. The houseman left them, closing the study door behind himself. Ibarra knew he would

be waiting in the corridor, one hand on his pistol, ready
to act if Ibarra pressed the alarm button under his desk.

Insurance.

"Your summons sounded urgent, Ramon."

"Speak to me about last night," the dealer said.

"Your difficulties in Ciudad Acuna?"

"*Our* difficulties," Ibarra corrected, frowning through
cigar smoke at the *palero.*

"As I meant to say."

"I want this problem dealt with quickly. We cannot
afford these kinds of losses or allow ourselves to be insulted in the public eye."

"I understand, Ramon."

"I hope so. If you cannot help me . . ."

Ibarra left the statement there, unfinished. There was
no need to verbalize the threat with Martinez. The *palero*
was too sharp for that, and an ugly scene at this point
would be counterproductive.

"The problem shall be dealt with. Trust me."

"And your own difficulty, at Rancho Santa Maria?"

The *palero* shrugged and smiled. "A minor setback.
Nothing has been lost which cannot be replaced. In
fact . . ."

"Go on."

"I had a visitor last night. Jesus Dominguez, from
Nuevo Laredo."

"That pig?"

"I have persuaded him to join us," said Martinez.

"What?"

"In the *nganga.*"

"Ah."

The screams came back to him again. Ibarra saw Martinez with the bloody knife clutched in his fist, raising a

heart to his lips, the muscle pumping jets of crimson through the reeking air.

"And your employee?"

"Serafino," said Martinez. "He was foolish. He must pay the price."

"He may be talking now."

"Forget him," said Fernando. "By this time tomorrow, he will be a memory. In the meantime, I will be working on *our* problem."

"I wish you luck," Ibarra said.

Martinez was already on his feet, moving toward the door, as he said, "Luck has nothing to do with it, Ramon."

"You'll be in touch?"

"Of course."

Of course, Ibarra thought, as the door swung shut behind Martinez.

Or *I* will.

The last thing that Ibarra wanted, at the moment, was a war against Martinez and his magic, but no one—the *palero* included—could make a fool of Ibarra and live to boast about it. If it seemed to him that his good friend Martinez was about to let him down...well, then Ramon Ibarra had a few tricks up his sleeve that even magic might not counteract.

He felt a little chill race down his spine, and frowned at the sensation, still remembering the blood and screams at Rancho Santa Maria. Gone now, but Martinez was reconstructing the *nganga* somewhere else. Beginning fresh, with contributions going into the pot from Jesus Dominguez and God knows who else.

It was enough to make the blood run cold.

But it would not prevent Ibarra lashing out against his court magician if he had to, somewhere down the road.

Cold blood ran in Ibarra's family, as it was, and it would help him bear the chill.

MARCELLA GRANT could not acknowledge she was nervous, but Fernando's early-morning meeting with Ramon Ibarra had to mean bad news. She knew about the violence overnight in Ciudad Acuna, but she had continued hoping that it would not touch their lives...until the phone rang, and Ibarra's man was on the other end, demanding that Fernando meet *el jefe* to discuss the problem.

Still, she knew Fernando could manipulate Ibarra when he wanted to. She had observed him time and time again, exuding charm, sincerity, charisma, winning hearts and minds.

The same way he had won her heart and mind, not long ago.

She was a simple college student, in her junior year of study, when she met Fernando de Leon Martinez. Quite by accident, or so she thought. A weekend trip to Brownsville, Texas, with some friends, and they had run into each other—almost literally—on the street, a traffic altercation shifting gears somehow, becoming lunch, then dinner, finally a drive to his apartment with the heated water bed. She knew that there was something different about this man, beyond the gift of gab, but she could not explain the instant, animal attraction that she felt.

It took some time before Fernando told her of his magic, the *orishas* who advised him on the great decisions of his life. His background was exotic, and it turned her on when she began to realize that he was dealing the with underworld on a daily basis, just like in the movies.

Well, not quite.

The product of a Catholic home, Marcella went to church on Easter Sunday and at Christmastime, filing her childhood catechism away during the rest of the year. Religion seemed like useless, excess baggage, and if anyone had asked her opinion on witchcraft, she would surely have laughed in their faces.

But that was before Fernando.

Slowly, deftly, he had taken her in hand, educating her to the *other* realities of life. She watched him work and saw the solid, physical results of his endeavors. Money in the hand, a prophecy come true. Marcella could not deny the evidence of her own eyes . . . her own heart.

Her parents were beside themselves, of course, when she did not return to college for her senior year. So be it. If they chose to cut her off without a dime, she now had other sources of support. Fernando de Leon Martinez was her man, a man of power, and he would not let her down.

At first, when she discovered that he sometimes shared his bed with other women—and with men, dear God— she had been heartsick, feeling like a wounded animal. Fernando understood her gut reaction, and he counseled her with loving patience, helping her to understand how rigid guidelines of morality could have no bearing on a man of mystic power like himself. He was above the petty rules and regulations of society, so far removed from common men that few of them could even recognize his greatness when confronted with the fact made flesh.

It was amazing, thought Marcella, how a little faith and self-control could vanquish jealousy and foolish pride. Weeks later, when Fernando had suggested that she sleep with other men, to lure new recruits or please important allies of the family, she had resisted only briefly, understanding that her duties as a *bruja* must be different from the tasks that *el padrino* took upon himself. She was not soiled by opening her legs for strangers; rather, by contributing to the advancement of Fernando and their family, she was exalted, sanctified.

A matter of perspective, yes, as such things always are.

The strangest thing of all had been how quickly she adapted to the sacrificial ceremonies. Anyone who knew Marcella as a child would be amazed to see her now. She still amazed herself, in fact, with her ability—indeed, her eagerness—to see the sacrifices carried out. There was a lesson to be learned from that, but she could not have said exactly what it was.

Except that for the first time in her life, she truly felt that she belonged.

Ten days ago, she thought her world was crumbling, about to shatter while she stood and watched. A foolish acolyte, one Serafino Escobar, had let himself be bullied by the *federales,* leading them to Rancho Santa Maria and exposing its secrets to the world at large. Marcella had been terrified at first, but she had learned another precious lesson from Fernando. Any small adversity could be endured, perhaps reversed and turned into a positive advantage.

Magic.

She could only hope the same was true with this Ibarra business, all the bloodshed overnight. The thought of losing Fernando somehow was too hard to even contemplate.

Suddenly she heard a car outside. Her heart was pounding, but she kept her seat, projecting calm. A moment later there were footsteps in the corridor outside, and Fernando entered the study, smiling with his normal boyish charm.

Marcella felt her bright smile slipping as she saw Gregorio Ruiz behind him, but she caught it before the smile disappeared entirely. She thought of Ruiz as a weasel, unworthy of trust, but she knew Fernando would regard such feelings as a sign of simple jealousy, and thus unworthy of concern.

"How did it go?" she asked.

"Ibarra was upset, of course," Fernando said. "I calmed him."

"Did he threaten you?"

Fernando chuckled to himself and poured a glass of wine. "He's not that foolish, little one."

"What did he want, then?"

"Guidance. Help against his enemies. I told him we would deal with those who have disturbed him."

"Ah."

"And he is frightened that the *federales* may get something more from Serafino."

"I will deal with that one," said Gregorio Ruiz.

Fernando smiled again. "Remember to be subtle, eh, Gregorio? No fireworks."

"As you say."

"I need to meditate just now," Fernando said. "If you would leave me, both of you...."

Marcella felt a sudden pang of disappointment, but she swallowed it and rose to leave the room. Gregorio Ruiz stepped out in front of her—no gentleman, this weasel—and left her to close the door behind herself. His back looked so inviting, like the perfect place to plant a blade.

Someday, perhaps, but not without approval from Fernando.

She would have to work on that, when they had private time together. If they were not heading for a war that could destroy them all.

She felt unworthy, harboring such doubts, but the *orishas* would forgive her. All they needed was a little blood to put them in the mood.

ALONE ONCE MORE, Fernando de Leon Martinez finished off his wine and took his favorite seat, within a short reach of the telephone. His "meditation" would consist primarily of phone calls, but he did not need to share that information with Marcella or Gregorio. It would be just as well, for all concerned, if they assumed he was communicating with the spirit world directly, one on one.

Martinez was a true believer in his craft, raised from childhood in the proud traditions of *santeria* and *palo mayombe,* apprenticed at age nine to a powerful *palero* in Miami, but his lessons had included certain notes on practicality. He knew, for instance, that the gods most frequently help those who help themselves.

When a client shelled out thousands for a cleansing or a reading of the future, he or she expected prompt results, with no mistakes. It would not boost Fernando's reputation if he counseled smugglers to move their product on a certain night, and they were intercepted by police. In fact, such errors would be fatal if the narco dealers thought that he was double-crossing them somehow.

Insurance was the key, for the *palero* as for all his clients, and Martinez found his own with the police. As he acquired more cash, Martinez spread the wealth around, participating in the grand tradition of *mordida* from the local level to the highest-ranking *federales* in the land.

One of his sometime clients was the second in command of Interpol's Mexican branch, an invaluable source of information when it came to checking out the FBI or DEA.

A simple phone call, in addition to his work with the *nganga,* could insure that no surprises overtook his clients. They remained impressed with his ability to see the future, predict police raids and direct border shipments with remarkable efficiency, never guessing—or caring— that the gods had been assisted by men in uniform.

In truth, Martinez was disturbed by the reports of violence overnight in Ciudad Acuna and environs. Normally he should have been alerted in advance to an impending war for territory. Now it appeared that one or more of Ibarra's enemies had found a weak spot in the dealer's stout defenses, slipping through to raise some hell before disappearing back into the woodwork.

Admiration for the raiders' tactics would not help Martinez track them down, however, and he knew that rescuing Ibarra from further damage was his top priority. It had been true, his statement to Marcella that the dealer had not threatened him directly, but Martinez understood Ibarra, and he knew that failure always had a price. He had been paid, repeatedly and handsomely, for helping the Ibarra empire run without a hitch, and if he failed to keep it running smoothly, he could always be replaced.

At least, Ramon could try.

Eliminating a *palero* of Fernando's strength and reputation could be difficult and costly, but Ibarra was an animal when anger took control and overrode logic in his mind. He might act first and think about the consequences only later, when it was too late to call his soldiers back.

Insurance.

While Martinez stalked Ibarra's enemies, employing every ally he could find in both the physical and spirit worlds, he would also have to think in terms of self-defense. In case, against all odds, he failed to satisfy Ibarra this time. There were preparations to be made, against the marginal, unlikely possibility of war.

A stab of apprehension brought a frown to the *palero's* face. It would not do for him to dwell on fear, the thought of failure. Attitude was everything, whether dealing with men or demons. If he could not project a solid air of confidence, he would be beaten at the start, before he made a move.

Still, he was made uneasy. So many troubles, all at once, the raid on Rancho Santa Maria for starters, thanks to clumsy Serafino and his flapping mouth. He was soon to be silenced forever, if Gregorio made good on his promise. Now, there were troubles with Ibarra, which could easily expand to threaten Martinez and his family if they were not controlled. An enemy who moved against Ibarra might not readily discriminate between the dealer and his spiritual advisers when the guns went off.

Fernando de Leon Martinez breathed and bled like any other mortal man, but he was not prepared to bleed today.

Not while another could be found to bleed in his place.

CHAPTER NINE

Emilio Sanchez listened to the distant ringing of the telephone, three cycles grating on his nerves before a secretary picked it up. He recognized the woman's voice but could not place her name.

"Hello."

"Emilio Sanchez calling for the captain."

"Un momento, por favor."

He waited in the sweltering motel room, wishing that the air conditioner would do its job, until another voice came on the line. Captain Miguel Calzada had a voice like gravel, from his years of barking orders in the military and the cheap cigars he smoked throughout the day. When he was angry, the gravel voice acquired a cutting edge. At other times, like now, it merely sounded gruff and tired.

"Sanchez?"

"Good morning, sir."

"Forget about good morning. What have you been up to, there in Ciudad Acuna?"

Sanchez frowned. He did not think that he was being watched, and it surprised him that Calzada would already know about the brawl in the cantina.

"The fight was not our fault, Captain."

"Fight?" Calzada seemed confused. "What fight?"

"Sir?"

"I want to hear about Ibarra and the trouble he's been having since last night."

Sanchez was confused. "Ibarra, sir?"

"Five of his establishments around the city were destroyed or badly damaged overnight. At least five of Ibarra's men are dead, perhaps more. You sound surprised, Sergeant."

At a loss for words, Sanchez had no choice but to tell the plain, unvarnished truth. "Sir, I had no idea."

"Somehow, that does not give me confidence," Calzada said. "Perhaps if you were more attentive to your duties..."

"Sir, I feel that we are making progress." He had already decided to dispense with the brawl, unless Calzada pressed him. It was time to make some points, without delay. "Last night, we were approached by one who represents Ibarra's interests in the city."

"Oh?"

"Yes, sir. A front man named Ricardo Obregon. We have another meeting scheduled with him for tonight. With luck, we may be able to arrange a meeting with Ibarra for ourselves."

"I do not place my faith in luck, Sergeant...and neither should you. We may be running out of time, if Ramon is on the verge of going to war. I don't want to lose this *cabrón* or his playmates to a cut-rate triggerman."

Sanchez frowned to himself, thinking that at least it would be a solution of sorts. The removal of Ibarra from the scene, by force or otherwise, would give them all some breathing room, an opportunity to thin the herd as Ramon's hungry subordinates scrambled to fill his shoes. Still, Emilio knew that it would be a kind of failure, allowing the scum of the earth to do his job, when he should be working overtime to bring Ibarra down.

"You won't be disappointed, sir."

"I hope not, Sergeant. Disappointment always makes me angry. I insist that those around me share my feelings, if you understand."

"Of course, sir."

"Good. I will be waiting for your next report. I trust that you won't keep me waiting long."

"No, sir."

As if against his better judgment, Captain Calzada softened his tone a fraction, adding a reluctant "Good luck" before he cradled the telephone receiver.

Sanchez hung up on the dial tone, his frown deepening as he regarded the empty motel room. Five attacks on Ibarra's operations overnight, all in the neighborhood of Ciudad Acuna? It had the feeling of an all-out war, but it had blown up out of nowhere. Sanchez cringed at the idea of running a lap behind unknown competitors, eating their dust and muddling along in the rear echelon while events raced ahead and left him hopelessly behind.

He swore aloud in the silent motel room, frustration closing in on him.

Sanchez had been working in Mexico City for the past two years. He had no street informants in Ciudad Acuna for starters, and while he had visited the city half a dozen times, it was more or less virgin territory. Otherwise he would never have been chosen by Calzada to take the undercover assignment...but his very strangeness to the territory imposed new problems. He was starting from zero in the scramble for information, and if he did not make up the deficit soon—very soon—Sanchez knew that it might be too late.

He thought about Ricardo Obregon, the way he sought them out last night in the wake of the cantina brawl, almost as if he had been trailing them around the town. The notion was not inherently implausible, Sanchez knew. They had dropped Ibarra's name in three cantinas before the fight broke out in number four, and some news spreads faster than others on the street. It would not be out of character for Ibarra to hear of their interest and dispatch an emissary. Not impossible by any means.

The sudden violence troubled him. From out of nowhere, Sanchez thought about the stranger—this Belasko—and wondered what he had been up to overnight. The gringo had been deliberately vague about his plans, letting it go with the remark that he planned to "shake things up" a little while the others carried out their more specific schemes.

There was much about Belasko that remained unclear, but he was obviously able to handle himself in combat situations. The kind of man Americans referred to as a "special operative," and Sanchez knew they sometimes worked outside the law, especially when they were not on U.S. soil.

Belasko would bear watching, one of the potential problems Sanchez had to scrutinize and control, before he could bring the present case to a satisfactory conclusion.

A war was the last thing he needed right now.

The problem was that Sanchez did not know if he could head it off.

It might already be too late, he realized. For everyone.

THEY HAD AGREED, reluctantly at first, to let Mack Bolan choose their second meeting place. In fact, he had made the selection before crossing over the toll bridge to Mexico, bypassing the motels in Del Rio proper and selecting one two miles north, near Amistad Reservoir. The others were not informed of his selection, scheduled simply to meet him in the parking lot of Del Rio's largest supermarket and follow Bolan's car from there.

The plan had built-in safeguards, starting with the fact that he would not be trapped inside another motel room if one of his supposed allies blew the whistle to their enemies. The parking lot gave Bolan ample time to see the gunners coming, if they came, and he would have the necessary combat stretch to run them ragged before he disengaged. Likewise, if one or more of his companions picked up a tail—voluntarily or otherwise—there would be ample time to spot it on the drive to their selected rendezvous.

Bolan was first to arrive, by design, checking the lot for watchers before he parked his car in shadow, near a set of Dumpsters on the east. Moments later, Doyle Mitchum arrived, flashing his headlights in the prearranged signal as he approached Bolan's position. Both men remained in their own vehicles, separated by several yards, waiting for Hargis and Sanchez, each troubled by the possibility that they might be delayed... or not show up at all.

In fact, the mismatched partners were only two minutes late, falling into line as Bolan led them out of town. There was a possibility that one of them would have a two-way radio, he knew, perhaps alerting enemies to their destination, but that would have to make it Mitchum, since the Texas Ranger and the *federale* did not get along well enough for one to risk a fatal indiscretion in the other's presence. And, at the moment, Bolan had no reason to believe that Mitchum would deliberately sabotage his own campaign.

They reached the motel without incident, trooping into Room 23 while Bolan stood guard outside. Two chairs and two single beds comprised the seating arrangements, with Mitchum drawing the blinds before he sat down. Outside, the early-morning sun was already heating up the blacktop, shooting for another record high.

"You get the number of that truck, Emilio?"

Sanchez frowned at Mitchum's joke, raising one hand to gingerly probe the bruise below his left eye. "Better than that," he replied, "I trashed the gringo who was driving."

"We had some trouble at one of the cantinas," Hargis explained. "No big deal."

"A set up?" Mitchum asked.

The Texas Ranger shrugged. "No way to tell, off-hand."

"Okay, who wants to start?" asked Bolan as he took his seat.

"I will," said Mitchum, glancing quickly at the Ranger and the *federale*. "That is, unless . . ."

"Feel free," Brock Hargis said, reclining on one of the beds and resting his Colt Python beside him, within easy reach.

"All right. I had to pay through the nose," Mitchum told them, "but I finally made contact with a *palero* who knows Martinez. Knows *of* him, at least. Word gets around, you understand, among the people involved in these kinds of rituals."

"You get an address?" Hargis asked him.

"Next best thing," the ex-cop from Miami answered. "Seems Martinez and his people have relocated. They're hanging out around Piedras Negras now."

"That's not much of a move," Sanchez said.

"It doesn't have to be. The way it was explained to me, they've got some friendly lawmen there who mostly look the other way, no matter what goes down. Ibarra helps defray the cost, in return for services rendered. Besides,

if Martinez made himself too scarce, it would look like
he was running, and he can't have that. Bad for the old
macho image, you know?''

"Piedras Negras," Bolan said.

"Means 'black rocks,'" Hargis told him. "Wish I had
a chance to drop one of them on his pointy little head."

Mitchum forged ahead, ignoring the interruption.
"The good news is, we hurt him with the raid on Rancho
Santa Maria. He lost his *nganga* and he had to start from
scratch. That's the equivalent of a gypsy fortune-teller
losing her crystal ball, whatever. In the meantime, his
power's at low ebb. He can't intercede with the spirit
world or read the future for his clients in any meaningful
way."

"And the bad news?" Bolan asked.

"He isn't wasting any time recouping his losses. Word
is, he's already putting a new *nganga* together . . . if he
hasn't got it done by now."

"Which means another human sacrifice?"

"Or several, if he wants the stew pot to have its former potency. The more the merrier, with these *paleros.*"

"Jesus Christ," the Ranger muttered to himself, "I
hate these goddamn psychos."

"This one's crazy like a fox," said Mitchum. "Never
mind if he believes the magic part or not. Assume that
everything he does is geared toward self-preservation and
making more money. Martinez never takes a break from
looking out for number one."

"What about his entourage?" Bolan asked.

"From what I was told, Gregorio Ruiz and Marcella
Grant are with him all the time, unless he packs them off
on errands somewhere. Count on several gunners for
backup, though most of the muscle technically belongs
to Ibarra."

"That's it?"

"For now. I'll have to ask around Piedras Negras if we want to pin him down, and that gets dicey. You never really know who you're talking to."

"Alternatives?" asked Bolan.

"None that I can think of," Mitchum answered. "I was thinking I'd go in today and get a start."

"Okay, let's hear about this fight."

"The fight's no biggie," Hargis answered, "but we got lucky afterward."

"A couple of the hostesses?" asked Mitchum.

"Bite your tongue and pass the penicillin. How about a contact with Ibarra's mob?"

"If that's supposed to be a joke..." There was a warning tone in Mitchum's voice.

"You see me smiling?"

"It's no joke," said Sanchez, taking over from the Ranger. "We were on our way to the fourth cantina when we were approached by a dealer on the street. Ricardo Obregon by name. Apparently he heard that we were looking for Ibarra, and he tracked us down somehow."

"Convenient," Bolan said.

"I thought so, too," said Hargis.

Sanchez frowned. "At least we have a contact, and another meeting scheduled for tonight."

"In Ciudad Acuna?" Mitchum asked.

"That's right."

"It splits us up," said Hargis.

"We were split last night," said Bolan. "Nothing we can do about it now but follow through. With caution."

"There is something else," said Sanchez, shifting his gaze from one face to another, making a circuit of the room. "Ibarra's operation was attacked last night in Ciudad Acuna, several times. We need to understand what's happening before we wind up in the middle of a border war.''

"No war," the Executioner assured him. "Not yet, anyway."

"You sound pretty sure of that," Hargis remarked.

"Sure enough. I'm the one who was hitting Ibarra last night."

"Say *what?*"

The exclamation came from Mitchum, but all three of Bolan's companions were staring at him now, incredulous expressions on their faces.

"Maybe you should run that down," said Mitchum, "before we go any further."

"It's what I do," said Bolan. "Details aren't important. I've been rattling Ibarra's cage to see which way he jumps. No comebacks, so far, but it's early in the game."

"I thought you said this joker came from Washington," said Hargis, addressing himself to Doyle Mitchum.

"Once removed," Bolan answered for himself. "I'm a free agent, so to speak, but I take jobs for Justice now and then."

"They know about the way you work?" asked Mitchum.

"Let's just say that we respect each other's privacy," the Executioner replied. "I don't tell them how to prosecute cases, and they don't tell me how to clean house."

"Can't say I like the sound of this," the Texas Ranger grumbled.

Bolan had foreseen the objection, and he did not hesitate with his reply. "We can play this one of two ways," he said. "If you're uneasy with the tactics, we can split right now and no harm done. You go your way, and I go mine."

"And the alternative?"

"We stick together and continue as we are, pursuing separate paths to the same end. Your call. Somebody want to take a vote?"

Doyle Mitchum glanced around the room, taking a moment to register the nods of his companions.

"The vote's taken," he said at last. "We'll stick...for now."

"Fair enough," Bolan said. "Here's the plan."

HE HAD ANTICIPATED reservations, even strenuous objections, from the lawmen when they caught on to his methods. Hal Brognola would not have briefed Mitchum up front, telling him what to expect, and it was a lot for any cop—or ex-cop—to swallow on short notice. Some officers, perhaps the majority, would have bailed out at once, but it seemed the three that he was working with were members of a different breed.

He knew the type from long experience, of course. Battered and disillusioned by the system's many failures, chafing at the rules that bound their hands in confrontations with the underworld. The *federales* were less constrained by liberal court rulings than American authorities, and it was possible that Sanchez was disgusted by the rampant corruption within his own department. But there could be other motivations.

It crossed Bolan's mind to check back with Hal and find out whether there was any feedback on his queries about Hargis and Sanchez, but he told himself that it could wait. He had a list of targets waiting for his personal attention, and the day was getting on.

The others had their work cut out for them on different levels, each with danger waiting in the shadows. If there was a traitor among them—and Bolan had not

ruled out the possibility as yet—they would be exposed
as the game unfolded.

And he would be waiting to deal with any treachery in
the ranks, if and when the problem arose.

Meanwhile the Executioner had work to do.

Beginning now.

CHAPTER TEN

Salvador Vidal Fragosa was accustomed to giving orders and having them obeyed on the spot, without question. Receiving orders, and obeying them himself, was something else. His rank of colonel with the Mexican Federal Judicial Police meant that Fragosa had few superiors, and his distinguished record made them treat him with respect.

Fragosa had been serving with the *federales* for the past two decades, tracking narco dealers in the hinterlands and grilling would-be revolutionaries for the names of their supporters and accomplices. He had killed six men in the line of duty—five of them armed—and his troops were well known for their ability to produce confessions from the toughest, most recalcitrant of suspects. Their conviction rate was well above the average in Coahuila, despite the fact of Fragosa's friendly relations with Ramon Ibarra and other major dealers in the territory.

It was the perfect symbiotic relationship. Fragosa turned a blind eye to the operations of his paying customers, while running down their small-fry competitors, boosting his own conviction statistics while he cleared the field for Ibarra and a handful of others to earn greater profits with less risk.

On the side, there were appearances to be preserved, in dealings with the American FBI and DEA, but Fragosa dealt with the gringos from strength. They had no authority in Coahuila, could accomplish nothing without his assistance, and the Americans knew it. They catered to Fragosa, courted him with compliments and federal grants, thanking him effusively when he delivered some two-bit piece of border trash into their hands. When they inquired about Ibarra, though, the well ran dry. Fragosa promised to investigate all leads the gringos could supply, but he predictably came up with nothing in the end.

Success was sweet for a peasant boy from Tamaulipas, and Fragosa made the most of his newfound affluence. His system was foolproof, or so it had seemed... until he met Fernando de Leon Martinez.

Things were different now, a subtle change at first, the tenor of activities shifting gradually away from the standards of business that Fragosa understood. In place of the normal hit-and-run street shootings he was accustomed to, Fragosa came to recognize the savaged remains of ritual victims, used up and spat out in the rituals Martinez practiced with his clique of disciples.

A whole new game.

Fragosa recognized the signs. He had not grown up poor and rural without encountering the signs of *brujeria* in his youth. He knew that peasants sometimes felt a need to "pay the earth" with human blood before they planted crops, or when the weather turned against them with a vengeance. Ancient crones cracked eggs and juggled chicken bones to chart the future, casting or removing spells on the basis of who paid them first—or best.

This was different, however, a vicious new twist on the old rules of play, no quarter asked or given. Fragosa would have gladly turned his back—or taken steps to crush the new savages—but greed had taken precedence once more. Fragosa had struck a bargain with Martinez... and the rest was history.

Today, when Martinez called, Fragosa was compelled to answer with alacrity. If he refused, who knew what might befall him next?

They met outside Piedras Negras, at a small cantina patronized by border scum and no one whom Fragosa should expect to recognize. The colonel drove himself, in an official car, and he was waiting when the sleek Mercedes pulled in next to him, a nameless *pistolero* at the wheel, Martinez seated in the back.

Fernando waited for Fragosa to join him, a small indignity, but one the colonel was prepared to bear. He knew Martinez would not risk a daylight meeting if the matter were not urgent, and he had a hunch that last night's violence in Ciudad Acuna was the key.

The car was cool and dark inside, with tinted windows, air-conditioning that shaved twenty degrees from the outside temperature. A glass partition separated them from the driver, and Fragosa left a yard of empty air between them, half turning to face Martinez directly.

"What is so urgent, Fernando?"

"You know what happened last night?"

"With Ibarra? *Sí.* He has made someone very angry, has Ramon."

"The question is who?"

"If I knew that..."

"It is your business to know, Salvador. You are paid to know these things."

"You don't need to remind me—"

"Paid extremely well," said the *palero,* no trace of a smile on his face as he spoke.

"I'm working on it," said Fragosa, hoping that the anger did not show on his face.

"Work harder," the *palero* said.

"Perhaps, if I knew a bit more about Ramon's enemies. Someone new to the territory, possibly from Mexico City or farther south."

"I'll see what I can learn. Meanwhile..."

"Your *compadre* from the rancho is talking."

"For now."

"You have a plan?"

"Do not concern yourself with trivia. We have more important matters to deal with at the moment."

"I expect results, Salvador."

"It may be expensive, Fernando."

"Do the job, and let me worry about the expenses."

"*Sí.*"

He closed the door behind him, instantly perspiring in the desert heat as he stalked back to his car. The Mercedes pulled away, and Fragosa stared after it with stony eyes.

Someday, he thought, an opportunity will present itself. A chance to settle accounts at no great cost to himself.

He would be ready when it came, and the sooner the better.

Meanwhile Fragosa had work to do. For himself, if no one else.

IT FELT WRONG, traveling to meet a new *palero* who would certainly be weaker than Fernando, but Marcella had her orders. It was something that Fernando thought important, and she would not let him down. A small thing, but it raised unpleasant questions in her mind.

If *el padrino* really knew so much, with the *orishas* speaking in his ear, why should he have to ask another shaman for advice?

It was not quite that way, of course. This new *palero*, one Esteban Montoya, had approached Fernando, sending word through intermediaries that he had some information *el padrino* would be interested to hear. No threats or ultimatums hidden in the message, but it still disturbed Marcella, dealing with a peasant some might call Fernando's competition, now that they had pulled up stakes in Ciudad Acuna for the most part.

Going back to the city just now was dangerous. With Serafino talking to his jailers, local officers and *federales* would be watching out for any of Fernando's followers. They were sure to have Marcella's name, perhaps a likeness they could use to spot her on the street, though she did not remember any photographs offhand.

Her family might be a source, but there was nothing she could do about that now. A call to warn them would arouse suspicion, at the very least, and it might even send her father to the law. He had mistrusted and despised Fernando from the start, some sort of jealousy directed toward a younger man—a Mexican, at that—and Marcella could simply not trust him where such matters were concerned. There might be phone taps on the line at home, by now. For all she knew, the FBI could be involved.

A sudden chill raced down Marcella's spine, and she responded with a smile. She should be frightened now, or worried at the very least, but she was actually enjoying the experience of living on the dodge. It was a measure of her growth since she had joined Fernando that she did not panic in the face of danger. Rather, it excited her. A part of her felt just like she was acting in a play or movie, filled with dark intrigue. Another part was conscious of the risks involved but simply did not care. Her basic fear was smothered by bravado and a kind of self-reliance she had never felt before.

Reliance on Fernando might have been more accurate. Fernando and the various *orishas* who controlled man's fate.

It had been shocking to discover that her priest and parents were mistaken, all these years, but she had seen the evidence for herself, etched in blood. Fernando's magic worked, unlike the prayers of Father Patrick back in Brownsville. It would be amusing, she supposed, to watch the two of them confront each other, faith confronting faith, but from Fernando's viewpoint it would surely be a waste of time.

And he was always right.

If Fernando said a trip to Ciudad Acuna was safe, Marcella would not argue. To be on the safe side, though, she had driven herself in a secondhand car, shunning the limousine and driver she would normally have used for such an errand. The older car would help her fit in with the neighborhood, and she would not incite comment or draw attention to herself with a chauffeur.

At that, Fernando had refused Montoya's first suggestion that the meeting take place at his home. A neutral site had been arranged, Marcella understanding that it would be easier for her to slip away if anything went wrong. In case of trouble, she was carrying a loaded .38 revolver in her handbag, with a sawed-off shotgun hidden underneath the driver's seat.

The neutral site was a botanica in the heart of Ciudad Acuna. Once Marcella parked the car and started walking toward the shop, she felt exposed, imagining a host of enemies around her, spying on her, but she kept her chin up, her expression treading on the line between resolve and grim defiance. She would carry out the task Fernando had assigned, or she would die in the attempt.

And if it came to death, she would not go alone.

Montoya must have seen her coming, for he met her on the sidewalk, giving her a start before she understood his errand. He was short, stoop-shouldered, wiry strands of graying hair protruding from beneath the straw hat that he wore. His face was brown and seamed with wrinkles, weathered like the desert and equally timeless. She could not have guessed his age within a decade if her life depended on the answer.

She mistook him for a beggar when he first approached her, sandals shuffling on the pavement, smiling with a twinkle in his eye.

"Forgive me, *señorita*..."

"I have nothing for you," she replied, prepared to step around him when he spoke again and captured her attention.

"*I* have something for *you*," the old man said. "And for the one you serve."

"Montoya?"

"*Sí*. The very same."

She led him to an open newsstand on the corner, where they made a show of browsing through the magazines while they were talking. The proprietor ignored them, though he surely would have run Montoya off without a gringo in attendance to suggest the prospect of a sale.

"What is it that you want?" she asked Montoya, coming swiftly to the point.

"There is a gringo searching for your master," said Montoya. "He pays well for information on the street."

"He paid you well, I take it?"

"I am poor, but not a fool," Montoya answered. "I informed him he should try Piedras Negras. Anything he learns beyond that point will not have come from me."

"Describe this gringo."

"Ah, my memory..."

"Will be improved by cash, no doubt." She palmed a bill and passed it to him, frowning in response to Montoya's satisfied smile. "Go on now, quickly."

"Tall, perhaps six feet. Dark hair and eyes. Clean-shaved. I would guess his age as forty years, no more than forty-five. He speaks Spanish and knows which questions to ask."

"Explain."

"He is no stranger to the art," Montoya said. "He knows of the *nganga* and its uses, maybe other things that make him dangerous."

"If he returns..."

"You will be notified, of course."

"Beforehand," she insisted. "It is no good to me, after he has gone."

Montoya frowned. "Unfortunately, *señorita,* I do not control his movements. He was unexpected when he came to me last night, referred by one who operates the shop, just there."

"Your friends should learn to hold their tongues," Marcella said. "It is a valuable lesson for us all."

"Agreed. In this case, though, I feel that I have done a service for your master."

"How?"

"By sending him the gringo," said Montoya. "It should be no problem for a man of *el padrino*'s skill to intercept a stranger in Piedras Negras. This way, he will not be forced to wait and scour the countryside at large."

"No favor, if the gringo brings an army with him."

"Ah, the troubles." And the smile returned to taunt her as he spoke.

"You know too much, old man. It isn't healthy."

"Knowledge equals power, *señorita*. He who would reject it leaves himself unarmed against the world."

"It's not the world you need to fear," she told him, "if you toy with *el padrino*."

It was pleasant, then, to see the color draining from his cheeks. His pink tongue flickered out to moisten nervous lips.

"Believe me, *señorita*, I have nothing of the sort in mind. I only wish to help your master in his time of trouble."

"And to help yourself."

"If *el padrino* feels that I am worthy of a small reward..."

"Your life is the reward," Marcella answered, speaking through clenched teeth. "Remember gluttony and greed are mortal sins."

She turned away and left him at the newsstand, moving briskly toward her car. Marcella felt the old man staring after her, suspected he was angry, but his feelings stood for less than nothing in the scheme of things. An order from Fernando could destroy the peasant shaman, if she urged it, but her instinct told her that Montoya might be useful to the family alive for a while.

There would be time enough to silence him if he became a nuisance. At the moment, she had other problems to contend with, chief among them a determined gringo, name unknown, who would be looking for Fernando in Piedras Negras. Soon, perhaps today.

Impatience made her hurry leaving town, but she was not about to trust the telephones in Ciudad Acuna. Not this time.

She would report her findings to Fernando in the flesh, and take a lesson from his face, the way that he responded. There was always something to be learned from *el padrino*, most particularly in the midst of crisis.

She would live and learn.

Some others, though, would not be quite so fortunate.

"A GRINGO, EH?"

Marcella nodded, frowning, and Fernando de Leon Martinez shared her evident concern, though he could not afford to let it show. A gringo asking questions could mean any one of several things, but all spelled trouble for the family, for him.

One of their sacrificial donors back at Rancho Santa Maria had been American—a Texan, more precisely— who had crossed the border for some whoring and remained forever, offering his heart and soul to the *nganga*. By appearances, the man had been a drifter, possibly a cowboy, but Martinez knew how sharply the Americans reacted when a gringo got in trouble on the wrong side of the borderline. No matter that the man had come prepared to wallow in depravity; it was the color of his skin that mattered to the gringo press, and nothing else.

In truth, it was the gringo's race—the risk involved— that had encouraged the selection of an Anglo sacrifice. The gringos made a show of bold machismo when they roamed in packs, but when the shoe was on the other foot they wept and whined like children, pleading for their worthless lives.

Too late for mercy now, but there was always payback, and he wondered if the gringo FBI might be involved. In theory, they could not investigate a crime in Mexico, but if the *federales* played along...

No good. Fragosa would have warned him in advance, which meant the gringo working Ciudad Acuna was a private agent, possibly alone, more likely working for a sponsor in the States.

But why?

Fernando did not read the papers, so he had no way of knowing if the gringo donor had a family, or whether they were saddened by his death. It was conceivable that someone could have hired a detective—what the Anglos called a "private eye"—to check for leads and try to solve the case. Again, he thought Fragosa would have warned him, but the Anglos might avoid cooperation with the *federales*, fearing such a leak if they revealed their plans.

An alternative scenario involved competing traffickers, someone who longed to see Ramon Ibarra damaged, even dead. The sudden rash of violence aimed at Ibarra overnight could hardly be coincidental, but the supposition of a link brought Martinez no closer to an answer.

He needed names, and quickly, to resolve the puzzle for himself and satisfy Ibarra in the bargain. Failure had a price that he was not prepared to pay.

Not yet.

He would consult the spirits for assistance, but they would not have to work alone. While he was at it, *el padrino* had fresh orders for his lookouts on the street.

He turned the full strength of his smile on for Marcella as he told her, "Here's what we must do..."

CHAPTER ELEVEN

Piedras Negras lay sixty miles south of Ciudad Acuna, separated from Eagle Pass, Texas, by a toll bridge spanning the Rio Grande. The normal clientele was little different from that enjoyed by other border towns, from Tijuana on the far west, to Matamoros on the Gulf. The border was more than an international boundary line; for many, it was a demarcation line between fantasy and their nine-to-five weekday world. Across the border lay cheap whiskey and willing women, saloons where age was not an issue, the opportunity to cut loose and raise hell without repercussions at home.

In any such atmosphere, predators dominate, and Piedras Negras was no exception to the rule. It did not have the national reputation of Tijuana or Nuevo Laredo, but its dives and sex shows were every bit as coarse, its prostitutes and nightclub "hostesses" as readily available to anyone with cash on hand. If it was drugs a visitor desired, they could be purchased on the street at slightly lower rates than those prevailing in El Norte. When it came to major shipments, though, the standard cutthroat jungle rules applied.

It came as no surprise to Bolan when Doyle Mitchum told him Fernando Martinez had run to Piedras Negras, fleeing the exposure of his ranch outside Ciudad Acuna. The *palero*'s patron, Ramon Ibarra, had strongholds in both towns, but he spent more time in Piedras Negras, with its access to the flow of merchandise on Highway 57,

running north from Monterrey. The highway was a life-
line, connecting Ibarra's border operation to the hub of
Mexico City, and DEA sources could only guess at the
number of trucks rolling northward each day, cocaine
and heroin concealed in shipments of "novelties" or
"household items" coming from the nation's capital.

It was a modern gold rush, growing richer for the
Mexican distributors since pressure in Miami and Los
Angeles had put a crimp in more direct deliveries from
Bogotá. Coke still got through the major ports, of
course, sometimes in massive quantities, but every
headline seizure prompted South American suppliers to
consider the alternatives. A new route here, a fresh drop
there. It added up to more security and higher profit
margins in the end. The Mexican police were generally
amenable to bribes, and when a bust was necessary for
appearances, the seizure could be scheduled and negoti-
ated in advance.

Smart business, all the way around.

By noon on Bolan's first full day of stalking the Martinez operation, he was still without a solid lead to the
location of his target or the cult. Ramon Ibarra remained his most direct connection, and as such, he was
about to feel the heat again.

Between Doyle Mitchum and a contact in the DEA,
Bolan had learned the schedule of deliveries to a warehouse Ibarra maintained on the southern outskirts of
Piedras Negras. He was running well ahead of time when
he arrived, and Bolan's drive-by at the warehouse found
it bristling with guns, no doubt convened in a response to
last night's shake-up in Ciudad Acuna.

If he could not afford a daylight raid against the warehouse, he would take the shipment out before it got there,

on the road. In fact, the more he thought about it, the more Bolan liked the idea.

He started calculating risks and odds, deciding they were bound to have a point car, probably some kind of radio communication with the troops in town. His timing would be crucial, hit-and-git before the reinforcements could be summoned to surround him in the desert wasteland.

He chose a spot five miles due south of town, where open highway cut across the desert like an ancient scar. He parked his rental in a gully, out of sight and covered from the highway, nothing in the way to block him if he had to cut and run.

The two LAW rockets were a bonus, something in reserve from the previous night's action, held for an occasion such as this. He found himself a stand of Joshua trees and tall saguaro cacti, laying out his weapons in the shade and settling back to wait.

Beside the two disposal bazookas, both their fiberglass tubes extended and ready now, he would be using the standard GI M-16A1. He left his jacket in the car, for easy access to the Beretta 93-R in its shoulder rig, and wore the Desert Eagle .44 Magnum automatic on his right hip, clipped to military webbing.

He had been in place for fifteen minutes, not a car in sight, when Bolan's ears picked up the sound of tires on heated asphalt, humming as they closed the gap, approaching from the south. He squinted in the heat haze, picking out a black crew wagon in the lead, two canvas-covered trucks behind it, no sign of a tail car bringing up the rear.

He shouldered one of the LAW rockets, sighting as the fingers of his right hand closed around the firing lever. From his present angle, he would barely be required to lead the point car at all. A perfect shot in perfect weather, all that he could ask for in a daylight ambush.

That, and getting out alive.

He fired, no recoil to speak of as the rocket whooshed away toward impact, plowing through the grille of the sedan. There was a smoky thunderclap, immediately followed by a burst of flame, consuming half of the sedan before the driver knew what hit him. He was dead by that time, anyway, the mangled engine resting in his lap, the crew wagon swerving hard left and plummeting into a roadside drainage ditch.

The lead trucker slammed on his brakes, tires smoking on the pavement, trying to shift as Bolan raised the second launcher into target acquisition. He sighted past the lead truck, on its number two, and slammed his second missile home to close the back door with a cloud of oily smoke and flying shrapnel. Someone screamed from the wounded truck, before the fuel tank went up in a secondary blast and turned the screamer's vocal cords to ash.

The driver of the lead truck saw a chance to break for daylight, charging straight ahead, but Bolan beat him to it with the M-16A1. A burst of 5.56 mm tumblers took out the windshield first, and then the driver's face behind it, ripping through the shotgun rider almost as an afterthought. The truck rolled on for several yards before its motor stalled, and Bolan cautiously approached on foot.

No gunners were positioned in the back to guard the Spanish-labeled crates of merchandise. He did not need to read the labels, knowing in advance that one or more of them contained the payload. He would not have time to sort it out, nor was he so inclined.

He backed away and fired a long burst from the M-16A1, searching for a hot spot and finding it with his last rounds, watching as flames began to lick along the underside of the vehicle. Bolan, leaving the LAW tubes behind for whoever came looking, was moving toward his car when the fuel tank blew.

It was hot as hell already in the desert, a relentless sun beating down on Bolan as he reached the highway, driving north. A hundred in the shade perhaps, and climbing by the hour.

It would be a damned sight hotter for Ramon Ibarra in Piedras Negras, but the dealer didn't know it yet. The Executioner had one hand on Ibarra's thermostat, and he was turning up the heat.

MIGUEL CALZADA knew it must be trouble when he got the summons from his *commandante*'s office to report without delay. No mention of the subject matter, nothing that would help him to prepare himself for the interrogation that was sure to come.

Commander Salvador Vidal Fragosa had a reputation in the FJP. He never praised his officers, expecting them to do their very best at all times, without expectation of rewards or special favors. When he spoke to his subordinates in normal circumstances, it could only be to issue orders. Any extraordinary contact, then, meant trouble. It was inescapable, and so Miguel Calzada searched his memory to figure out what he had done that would arouse the *commandante*'s wrath.

The only possibility that came to mind involved the recent violence in Ciudad Acuna. It was worse than usual, but at least no tourists were involved, and it seemed unlikely that Fragosa was concerned about the body count, in itself. Unless it had to do with Ibarra.

It was widely rumored in the service that Fragosa now acknowledged two superiors. One wore a uniform and occupied an office in Mexico City, headquarters of the Federal Judicial Police. The other dressed in custom-tailored, thousand-dollar suits and made his home outside Piedras Negras, the better to supervise his booming narcotics trade.

Ramon Ibarra spent his money freely when it came to buying badges, taking out insurance to protect himself from trouble with the law. In three years' time, he had established bold new standards for political corruption in Coahuila, paying off police and officeholders from the local level to the state capital... and, some said, reaching beyond Coahuila itself, to share the wealth with influential men in Mexico City. In return for his largesse, Ibarra had effectively become untouchable, though no one ever spelled it out in words, much less on paper. When his runners were arrested, judges threw the cases out, and the arresting officers were often reprimanded for wasting their time and the taxpayers' money on futile pursuits. Miguel Calzada had been cautioned twice himself concerning the career risks that accompanied "harassment" of "respected businessmen" renowned for sterling "service to the state."

Calzada never knew exactly what that service was, though it was rumored that Ibarra helped finance a public clinic in San Carlos—using it, upon completion, as a front and sometime storehouse in the transport of illegal drugs. There were reports of periodic contributions to the church, as well, Ibarra covering his bets with an attempt to place salvation on the auction block.

It turned Calzada's stomach, thinking of the way his service had been prostituted by the dealers, officers in uniform converted into spies and contract killers for the drug cartels, their honor sacrificed for cash in hand. It had been different in the "old days," ten or fifteen years ago, when the *mordida* came from after-hours bars, a pimp or two, perhaps coyotes running wets across the border to El Norte. Even then, Calzada had resisted the temptation, but he understood why many officers had not. Their families needed sustenance beyond the limit of a poor policeman's salary. The system made allowances for "innocent" bribery, treating lawmen more like waitresses who work for tips to supplement a bare subsistence salary. Miguel Calzada struggled by because he never married, lived alone, and nurtured no expensive vices. Even so, he was an object of suspicion—sometimes ridicule—among his fellow officers who made a living with their hands out, taking payoffs from the scum they should have locked away.

And overnight, it seemed, the drugs changed everything. There was no such thing as "innocent" graft anymore. Policemen did not simply look the other way when minor violations of the law occurred. Instead they had become participants—informants for the drug lords, spies inside their own departments, torturers and triggermen. Hopelessly compromised the first time a bribe was accepted, the corrupt *federales* and local policemen were hooked like fish on a line, unable to refuse their masters anything without subjecting themselves to disgrace and dismissal... or worse.

In the "old days," Calzada recalled, Mexican criminals had cringed at the thought of killing a policeman, certain of the grisly retribution that would follow. Only homicidal lunatics or mindless border trash would risk interrogation followed by a firing squad, or summary disposal in a dry arroyo somewhere, with a bullet through the head and no account of the arrest.

Today, by contrast, narco traffickers shot first and never got around to asking questions. They insulted the police in public with impunity, aware that payoffs at the highest levels would protect them from retaliation on the street. In many parts of Mexico, the law meant less than nothing now. It had become a sorry joke.

It had to do with Ibarra, then, but Calzada still could not think what he had done to set Fragosa off. The raid on Rancho Santa Maria had been well executed, but it was leading them nowhere, their handful of named suspects having vanished like a dust devil in the wasteland.

Fragosa's young receptionist let Calzada wait ten minutes before she passed him through to the commander's office, a technique Calzada recognized and sometimes used himself with his subordinates. It gave the subject of interrogation time to worry, pick himself apart, and it was still effective, even when he knew exactly what was happening.

Frogosa met him with a frown and waved him to a straight-backed chair that stood before his desk. Calzada sat and waited, meeting the commander's gaze, childishly pleased with himself when Fragosa was the first to blink and turn away.

"The murders at Rancho Santa Maria," said Fragosa without preamble. "How is your investigation proceeding?"

"As explained in my last report, sir, the suspect Serafino Escobar has named participants in the crimes. Fernando de Leon Martinez, a Gregorio Ruiz, the American Marcella—"

"Yes," Fragosa cut him off, "I read his statements. What I need from you is a report on any progress made toward bringing in these criminals."

"As yet, sir, we have been unable to discover where they are. If we assume the cult was subsidized by *narco-trafficantes,* then—"

"Assume? Is it our business to *assume?*" Fragosa's voice was tight with sudden anger. "I need evidence before you make an accusation such as this."

"The statements from our prisoner—"

"Are vague, self-serving, and perhaps a web of lies. Without corroboration and substantial evidence, his word is worthless, Captain."

"Sir—"

"What have you done about the troubles in Ciudad Acuna?"

"I'm investigating, sir, but it is difficult without co-operation from the victims. If Señor Ibarra would agree—"

"You are not paid to wait for victims to arrest their own assailants, Captain. It is *your* job to protect the public—most especially respected businessmen—from such harassment and attack."

Calzada knew it was a losing battle, and he settled for a curt "Yes, sir."

Fragosa shifted gears. "I'm told you have an under-cover operative working the Martinez case."

Miguel Calzada blinked. He felt a sour churning in his stomach, trying desperately to figure out who had betrayed him. Not Sanchez, by any means. And that left...

"That information is confidential, sir."

"From your commander?" Fragosa's bushy eyebrows formed an angry vee, almost meeting in the space above his nose.

"Sir—"

Fragosa's open hand struck the desktop with the sound of a pistol shot. His face was livid, lips drawn back from yellow teeth in a snarl.

"I will not tolerate your insubordination, Captain. Covert operations are subject to approval from this office. Violation of the rule subjects the guilty parties to suspension or dismissal, without benefits. You understand, Calzada? I want names and details. Now."

Miguel Calzada's shoulders slumped, the gesture of a beaten man. He had no choice, but there might still be time to warn Emilio Sanchez of the danger, if only he had some way to get in touch.

"Yes sir," Calzada answered, feeling totally disgusted with himself.

And told Fragosa everything.

FERNANDO DE LEON MARTINEZ cradled the telephone receiver, frowning as he swept his eyes around the empty room. Fragosa's report was troubling, but at least it put some measure of his recent troubles in perspective.

An honest policeman, of all things. There was irony here, considering the amount of money Martinez and Ibarra had spent between them on protection from the law. It was a sorry state when some self-righteous renegade could buck the system and impose his own morality on others, undermining years of work and sacrifice.

Martinez smiled.

Perhaps another sacrifice would help. If nothing else, it would improve the spirit of his followers, encourage them to keep the faith and persevere through troubled times. They had been getting soft, he realized, accustomed to the easy life, but that would have to change. He needed hardened warriors for the days ahead, prepared to give their all in confrontation with the enemy. They must divorce themselves from fear and stand united, fearless.

With the information from Fragosa, he might still prevent the enemy from doing too much damage, if he struck back swiftly, with determination and resolve.

Martinez left the study, moved along a paneled corridor and slipped out of the house unseen. He did not need an audience for what he had to do.

The shack stood eighty meters from the house, concealed within a grove of dry mesquite, but he could smell it from a distance, even so. The reek of the *nganga* beckoning, commanding him to call upon the spirit world for counsel in his time of need.

Inside the shack, the heat and stench were stifling, fat bluebottle flies buzzing about insanely at his approach. They rose and settled, swirled about his head in greeting, lighting on his hair and shoulders, crawling on his face. Their offspring wriggled in the caldron, feasting on the stew that Martinez had provided for their pleasure.

Crouching by the blackened pot, he curled his hands around a pair of the protruding sticks and worked them slowly back and forth, stirring the pot, manipulating the *palos* as if they were the gearshifts on a piece of heavy equipment. Fernando's eyes were closed, flies squatting on his eyelids, tickling his lips as he began to chant. He called upon Ochosi, Oggun, Chango and the rest, imploring them to hear his voice and answer their obedient servant.

In the pot, a tortoiseshell surfaced briefly, turned belly-up, and went down for the count. A cat's skull, shreds of flesh still clinging to the bone, bobbed up to grimace at Fernando, staring at him with hollow eyes. The husks of scorpions, tarantulas and centipedes were stirred up from the bottom, tangled up with bits of human viscera and stringy hair with pieces of the scalp attached.

Fernando prayed.

And in due time, received the answer he was waiting for.

CHAPTER TWELVE

Emilio Sanchez drew the magazine from his nickel-plated Llama automatic, counting seven rounds before he slipped it back inside the pistol grip. With one round in the firing chamber, that made eight, and if he could not do the job with that, he still had two more magazines in pouches on his belt.

Brock Hargis sat behind the steering wheel, spinning the cylinder of his big Colt Python before he tucked it out of sight. The Ranger's mouth was set in a frown, his eyes hidden behind the mirrored lenses of his aviator's shades.

"This don't feel right," said Hargis. "Coming down too easy, what I say."

"You think last night was easy, gringo?"

"What's this 'gringo' shit?" the Ranger asked. "You think this operation ever would've gotten off the ground if we were waiting for your people to call the shots?"

Sanchez felt the angry color rising in his cheeks. "What are you implying, Hargis?"

"I'm implying nothin'," Hargis said. "I'm tellin' you straight out, Em-ee-lio. The FJP is so damn crooked I could use it for a corkscrew."

Sanchez glowered at the Texas Ranger, wishing that he could refute the comment. It was true, though. From his first year as a rookie, Sanchez had been embarrassed by rampant corruption among his brother *federales*. Even so, he felt a sense of loyalty to the force, a strong desire

to help reform the system, even if it proved to be a hopeless task.

The Federal Judicial Police had elevated Sanchez from
his status as a lowly farm boy to a figure of respect,
however marginal or undeserved. He wished sometimes
that he could pay that debt by helping win some vestige
of the force's rightful honor back, but there had never
been a decent opportunity before this case.

"I have a chance to change this for the better," Sanchez said. "If we can beat Ibarra and his *narco-
trafficantes,* it will be a start."

"You think so?"

"*Sí.* I think so."

"What the hell," said Hargis, one corner of his mouth
twisting upward in a crooked smile. "Let's give it a shot."

The meeting had been fixed on neutral ground, considering the violence that had shaken Ciudad Acuna
overnight. Driving into San Carlos, they kept the air
conditioner turned on full blast, competing with the desert sun that baked the soil on each side of the highway,
leaching every trace of moisture from the earth, leaving
it dry and cracked as old leather.

At a glance, the desert seemed to be a lifeless place.
You had to live there for a time to understand the truth.
Beneath the hardpan surface there was wildlife in pro-
fusion—insects, birds and reptiles, even fish that sprang
to life in dry lakes on the rare occasions when it rained.
They lived a day or two, just long enough to mate, lay
eggs and wait for the relentless sun to steal their lives
away.

No quarter asked or given in the desert, and Emilio
Sanchez liked it that way. There was never any doubt on
where you stood with Mother Nature.

You were strictly on your own.

They entered San Carlos from the southeast, following directions that Ricardo Obregon had given them the night before. Sanchez watched the sun-bleached shop fronts slipping past his window, nothing in the nature of a border town's flamboyant advertising here. Traffic was thin, but their dusty rental was plain enough to pass unnoticed.

"Left turn," the *federale* said.

"I see it, man."

Hargis made the turn, braking for a gaggle of pedestrians, nosing into the alley behind a cantina when they had cleared the way. He parked beside a rusty garbage receptacle, killed the engine, slipping one hand under his jacket to double-check the big Colt in its shoulder rig.

"Let's do it, man."

Outside the car, the heat was waiting for them, beating down on Sanchez, bringing instant beads of perspiration to his forehead. Half a dozen steps, and he could feel the shirt sticking to his back and chest, sweat crawling underneath his arms.

The back door of the tavern was unlocked, as Obregon had promised it would be. Brock Hargis led the way, Sanchez close behind him. Darkness in the entryway, with a swamp cooler laboring somewhere overhead, vents spitting moisture and air that was barely an improvement on the heat outside. The rest room, on their left as they entered, smelled as if it hadn't seen a mop or disinfectant for at least a year.

"Nice place," said Hargis.

"*Sí.*"

A narrow, murky hallway led them into the cantina proper, past the bar. No customers in evidence, but Sanchez saw Ricardo Obregon waiting at a corner booth, smoking a thin cigar.

He was not alone.

A woman sat beside him, blond, her face in shadow from where Sanchez stood. Still, there was something...

"He didn't say anything about company," Hargis muttered, a frown carving lines on his face.

"Relax. A girlfriend, maybe."

"Goddamned unprofessional, is what I call it."

"Smile, *compadre*. Strictly business."

"Right."

They moved across the open dance floor toward the corner booth, boot heels clicking on the faded linoleum. Obregon raised a slim hand in greeting, gold and diamonds glinting on his fingers, blue smoke curling from his cheroot.

Beside him, the blonde turned to face them directly, lifting her chin and putting on a smile of her own.

"Well, shit," Brock Hargis whispered.

"*Sí,*" said Sanchez, smiling back into the blue eyes of Marcella Grant.

HARGIS FIGURED they had trouble from the moment when he recognized the woman. Here they were, expecting to cut a deal with one of Ibarra's front men, and he showed up with the number-two witch in Fernando's crazy coven at his side.

Even so, she wasn't hard to look at, if you found a way to tune out on reality. The hair was something else, a perfect frame for what he might have called an angel face, in other circumstances. Eyes so blue they made you think of mountain lakes in summertime. Brock caught himself wondering what her full, moist lips would taste like, and he pulled the reins in on his scrutiny before he got around to checking out her body.

Well, almost.

The Texas Ranger did not bother with a smile as he confronted Obregon. "Who's this?"

"A close associate. Please, won't you both sit down?"

Obregon and the woman scooted closer together, making space on each end of the semicircular booth. Emilio Sanchez slid in next to Obregon, which left the Ranger with Marcella Grant.

"You didn't tell us you were bringing company," Hargis said.

"Is there a problem?" Obregon inquired.

"Depends. We've never worked with women, up to now."

Marcella smiled. "How quaint. Don't tell me you're a sexist, Mr...."

"Drake. Joe Drake," he answered, giving her his alias. "I keep up with the times, all right. It's just the business that we're in, you understand. I've never met a woman who was interested . . . or who could pull her weight."

"Times change."

"I guess that's right."

Sanchez broke into their dialogue. "Speaking of business," he said, "why don't we get to it?"

"As you wish," said Obregon. His voice reminded Hargis of a reptile gliding over sand.

"We're interested in major weight," said Hargis, "but before we cut a deal, we'd like to meet the man in charge."

"This is . . . irregular."

"It's how we play the game. I don't mind buying peanuts from a stranger, but you start in talking six or seven hundred thousand at a shot, I want to know exactly who I'm dealing with."

"Of course, I understand," Ricardo Obregon replied. "Arranging such a meeting may take time."

"Take all the time you need," Sanchez interjected. "But you won't mind if we shop around some while you're stalling, maybe try to find ourselves a better deal."

"I can assure you, gentlemen, you will not find a larger, safer operation in Coahuila."

Hargis shrugged. "So, maybe we'll try Tamaulipas or Chihuahua. We started shopping here because we heard Ramon Ibarra does good work. Now, if he'd rather hit us with some kind of song-and-dance routine, I don't mind looking elsewhere. Señor Vargas?"

Sanchez took his cue and nodded. "*Sí.* We've heard about your recent trouble. If Señor Ibarra does not feel that he can cope..."

"Señor Ibarra copes quite nicely, thank you." Obregon seemed irritated, maybe nervous, but he tried to cover with a smile. "The meeting you request can be arranged, of course. Perhaps tonight...."

"Tonight would suit me fine," said Hargis. "Any later, though, I'd have to think your boss would rather have us take our money somewhere else."

"I can assure you, that is not the case."

"So, let's talk product, shall we?"

"As you wish." The dealer drew on his cheroot and sent an acrid cloud of smoke across the table, making Hargis wonder how a sane man smoked the goddamn things. "You mentioned major weight?"

"Our clients like the best, and plenty of it," Hargis said. "We've been importing through Miami and New Orleans for the past three years, but there's a lot of extra heat around these days. This crap about a 'drug czar' and the rest of it."

"Of course."

"We're looking for a new approach without a sacrifice in quantity or quality," said Sanchez, picking up the spiel. "We are prepared to pay a reasonable price to get the merchandise we need."

"When you say reasonable..."

"In Miami," Hargis told him, "we were paying forty, forty-five per kilo. That was straight from Bogotá, delivered to the Keys. We handled ten to fifteen kilos every month."

"You dealt with the Colombians directly?"

"Right."

"Of course, they have no overhead to speak of. They produce the merchandise themselves, and transportation is a small thing, up until they reach the U.S. border."

"So?"

"Señor Ibarra would be dealing with the source on your behalf. For this, he would expect the payment of a service charge."

"How much?"

Obregon pretended to think about it, making believe that the price was not fixed in advance. "Another five thousand per kilo," he said at last, "above the base price you were paying in Miami."

"So we're talking somewhere in the range of fifty, fifty-five?"

"For quantity," said Obregon. "If you are only interested in one or two..."

"I told you we need major weight," the Ranger snapped. "I didn't drive out here to jerk your chain."

"In that case, gentlemen, a glass of wine to celebrate our bargain."

"You want to celebrate, that's fine. But nothing's sealed until we meet the man."

"Of course," said Obregon, all smiles. "Of course."

Brock Hargis stiffened as he felt a warm hand on his thigh, beneath the table. Turning toward Marcella Grant, he found her smiling at him, with a hint of invitation in her eyes.

Well now, he thought.

IT WAS A SHAME, Marcella thought, that both these men would have to die. The Mexican who called himself Ernesto Vargas had the dark eyes of a fox, but he was not her type. The rugged Texan, on the other hand—"Joe Drake" he chose to call himself—was something else again. Of course, her heart and soul belonged to Fernando...but her body sometimes had a mind of its own.

Obregon had been clever, making contact with the would-be cocaine buyers on his own, when he learned they had been asking around for Ibarra in Ciudad Acuna. Risky business, that, but sometimes it paid off.

And sometimes, the payoff was entirely unexpected.

Thanks to Commander Fragosa of the Federal Judicial Police, they knew both men were really undercover agents. One of them, the Mexican, was named Emilio Sanchez. He had been selected for the mission by a fool whose days were numbered on the force, his fabled honesty a quaint anachronism in the world of modern Mexico. He would not be dismissed immediately, since appearances must be preserved, but he had seen the last of his promotions, and a transfer to Quintana Roo was in the works. Once he was out of sight and out of mind, a fatal "accident" could be arranged.

As for Emilio Sanchez, he would never live to hear his *commandante*'s tale of woe.

The Anglo was a Texas Ranger, they had learned that much, but the commander who selected Sanchez for his acting role had never learned the Ranger's name. If he wanted to be called Joe Drake, she would oblige him. One name served as well as another, taking up space on a headstone.

Still, it seemed a waste. If she could find some time alone with the American, before he had to die...

She did not bother concentrating on their conversation, price and kilos, all the rest of it. A poor charade, with none of them intending that the deal should ever come to pass. It was enough to make her laugh, but she controlled herself, surreptitiously examining the Ranger, studying his face, the tenor of his voice.

If this man understood the power, how to speak with the *orishas*...

She caught herself, a little flustered by the thought, which came uncomfortably close to treason. No one could replace Fernando, and the Ranger would not if he could. He was a lawman, with the antiquated moral values of a "hero" from a John Wayne movie on the late show.

Nevertheless, she found she could not quite let it go. Marcella placed her left hand on his thigh, a move so casual that she was ready to award herself the Oscar for a star performance. Drake was staring at her now, surprise and something like confusion showing on his face, which suited her just fine. She liked to keep her men off balance. All except Fernando, who was always in control.

Before the Texan had a chance to speak, she gave his leg a little squeeze and flashed her brightest, most alluring smile. Her hand was inching higher on his thigh, as if by accident, when she was suddenly distracted.

On her left, three men had entered the cantina, pausing long enough to let their eyes become accustomed to the shadows. Two were relatively short, a tall man standing in between them, all three wearing jackets that were out of place in summer heat.

Except to cover guns.

BROCK HARGIS did not recognize the new arrivals, no good reason why he should, but he could spot their type a block away. Cheap *pistoleros,* plenty of them in the border towns, prepared to execute a contract for as little as a hundred dollars if the rent was overdue. All three of them had greasy hair and pockmarked faces, resembling stereotypical Mexican thugs from Hollywood Central Casting.

Except that these thugs were for real.

They started toward the corner booth, and Hargis spied a shadow hanging back in the corridor through which he had entered the tavern with Sanchez. Someone covering the back door, just in case. More than one someone, perhaps.

His eyes flicked rapidly from Sanchez to Ricardo Obregon, and then Marcella Grant. The *federale* made their opposition, right enough, and Obregon looked startled, but he could not read the blonde's expression in the split second available. She had removed her hand, at least, as if anticipating that one or both of them would have to make a sudden move.

If it had been a set up, Hargis would have looked for Obregon to start gloating about now. Instead the dealer gulped his wine and set the empty glass down on the table almost hard enough to crack its slender stem. He muttered something to himself, but Hargis could not make it out, and he was busy concentrating on the gunners now.

When they were something like a dozen paces from the booth, the trio stopped. Nobody had to give the signal, they just froze, like actors on a stage who recognize their mark. The tall one made his move a split second before the others, flipping back the right side of his jacket to reveal some kind of stubby automatic weapon in a swivel rig... and then the whole thing went to hell.

First thing, somebody kicked the table over. Hargis thought it might have been Marcella Grant, but there was no way he could tell for sure. All four of them were scrambling for the meager cover it provided, Hargis feeling better with the big Colt Python in his hand, despite the fact that they were clearly up Shit Creek.

Somehow, the gunners all fired high at first, a storm of bullets peppering the wall and raining brick dust, with a few rounds ripping through vinyl upholstery with flat, smacking sounds. Marcella Grant cried out, a breathless kind of scream, before she bit her lip and managed to control herself. A curse from Obregon, and that was all Hargis had time for, knowing he had something like a sliver of a second left before the shooters found their mark.

The table would not save them, and that knowledge made him feel a little better when he wriggled out from under cover, shoving with his feet and scooting on his side, the Python braced in both hands as he sighted down the vent-ribbed barrel, squeezing off two thunderclaps in rapid fire.

His target was the gunner on his left. The big .357 Magnum rounds punched through him with sufficient force to drop the *pistolero* on his backside, slouching over with his weapon spraying hot rounds at the ceiling as he died.

Sanchez took the stubby bookend on the right, his Llama automatic putting one round in the bull's-eye and another one to die on as the shooter staggered backward, going down. The middleman was smart enough to run, but too slow to save himself as Hargis and the *federale* fired together. Spouts of crimson oozed from between the runner's shoulder blades as he made a long dive forward on his face.

It wasn't finished yet.

The shadow from the hallway poked a riot gun around the corner, squeezing off a blast of shot that ripped a bullfight poster off the wall nearby and blew a potted cactus all to hell. Hargis pegged a shot at the sniper, then Marcella Grant was up and running, right across his line of fire, hesitating long enough to grab his jacket sleeve and give a mighty tug.

"Come on!"

He didn't know where she was going, but both of them were exposed now, and Hargis scrambled to his feet, wasting another Magnum round on the dark corridor, hoping to keep his enemy pinned down. Behind him, Sanchez was firing, prodding Obregon to his feet.

"Where the hell—"

"This way!" Marcella snapped, and led him toward the exit facing on the street.

It seemed a bad idea, no matter how you sliced it, but the only viable alternative was clearing out the hallway leading to the back door and the alley where their car was parked.

The car.

"We're parked out back," he told Marcella, running on her heels and holding one round in reserve, afraid that he would never get a moment to reload.

"I have a car outside," she told him, at the door now, reaching for the handle.

"Wait!"

He pushed in front of her, heard Sanchez firing at the gunner near the bar, an aimless shotgun blast responding, smashing glassware. Hargis cursed his own stupidity and shouldered through the door, bright sunlight lancing at his eyes, the sudden heat oppressive, like a suffocating blanket thrown across his head and shoulders.

Hargis heard the sound of shots before he made their source, another *pistolero* sitting in a black sedan and plinking at them with a .38. He gave one back, rewarded by the sound of impact on the door or fender, dragging Marcella into cover behind a parked vehicle.

He fumbled a speed-loader out of his pocket, dumped the six empties and replaced them in two seconds flat. Okay. At least they had a fighting chance.

He looked around for Sanchez or Ricardo Obregon, but neither of them had emerged from the cantina.

"Where?"

"My car," Marcella told him, reaching up to stroke the fender of the vehicle that was providing cover at the moment. "I can reach the driver's door from here."

"Okay, I'll cover."

Hargis waited for the blonde to make her move, then came up firing. One round wasted, while he found his mark, and he was on the money with the next two, one slug punching through the gunner's door, the last one drilling through his jaw and snapping his head over sideways, spraying the driver with crimson and gray.

It was enough to get the wheelman moving, rubber smoking as he burned out from a standing start, jumping the curb and rolling west along a nearly empty street.

Hargis hesitated, watching him go, glancing back at the cantina where gunfire continued.

Marcella leaned on the horn, throwing his door open and beckoning frantically for Hargis to get in the car. He was about to let it go, duck back inside and see if he could help Emilio, when a shooter with an automatic rifle came around the corner of the building, firing as he ran. Hargis gave one back, saw his bullet strike sparks on the pavement, and then he was scrambling into the car, Marcella peeling out and covering the first block in reverse, before she whipped the wheel around and put the pedal on the floor.

"Your friend, back there?" he asked.

"I don't know who they were," she told him, speaking with a tone of something like exhilaration in her voice.

"The others?"

"We can't help them if we're dead," she snapped. "Your friend seemed competent enough, and Obregon still knows a trick or two."

"I hope so."

"Think about yourself," she said. "You're still alive."

So far, he thought. And said, "Okay, what now?"

"A safehouse. Somewhere we can wait and rest."

"Sounds good," the Texas Ranger said. "Your place or mine?"

CHAPTER THIRTEEN

Emilio Sanchez saw Brock Hargis disappear through the swinging door of the cantina, following Marcella Grant, and cursed his luck at being left behind. The gunner in the shadows of the murky corridor had missed them, thanks primarily to Emilio's cover fire, but there was no one left to cover his retreat with Obregon. Incredibly, the dealer was unarmed, a quirk that spoke volumes about his personal confidence but did nothing to help them out of their bind at the moment.

Sanchez ejected the spent magazine from his Llama, slipping a fresh one in place and working the slide to chamber a live .45 round. He had no way of telling if the shotgunner was on his own or supported by backup, but they were swiftly running out of time in either case. Their cover was inadequate, and with the gunfire he had heard outside, Sanchez knew police would soon be on their way.

He would have to make a break, and live or die with the consequences. Sitting still and waiting for the gunner to blast him out of cover was a dead-end proposition, for himself and Obregon.

It crossed Emilio's mind that Obregon might have some hand in the attack, but their assailants seemed indiscriminate, blasting away without regard to specific targets. It was always possible, he thought, that they had walked into the middle of a gang war in the making. Stranger things had happened, and he had to slip away, alive and functional, before he would be able to evaluate the evidence.

"We're getting out of here," he hissed at Obregon.

"But how?"

"Stay here. Don't show yourself or make a move unless you absolutely have to. Got it?"

"Sí."

If Obregon was acting, he deserved some kind of an award. His eyes were saucer-sized and showing white all the way around, lips quivering as he spoke. Sanchez had seen enough abject fear in his time to recognize the real thing, and he was looking at it now.

"Okay, sit tight."

He made his move without further thought, fully aware that he could talk himself out of it if he stalled long enough. Breaking from cover, he winged two shots at the hidden gunner to buy himself some time, sprinting straight across the open door floor toward the bar. From eight feet out, he launched into a headlong dive, sliding across the polished surface of the bar and dropping out of sight behind it, landing painfully on hands and knees just as the shotgunner came back with a near miss, shattering several beer mugs and a bottle of tequila.

Close, but no cigar.

Sanchez found the bartender staring at him, huddled in a corner, trembling. This was heavy action, even for a bar which had undoubtedly seen its share of knife fights and brawls in the past.

Taking his chances, Sanchez lunged toward the lowest shelf of liquor bottles he could reach, snaring a half-full bottle of rum and clutching it to his chest as he dropped back into the safety of cover. Another shotgun blast swept overhead, exploding bottles, showering the *federale* with liquor and fractured glass. It would have been an alcoholic's dream, drowning in booze, but he was busy, trying not to cut himself on broken bottles as he prepared his surprise for the enemy.

Tugging a handkerchief from his pocket, Sanchez uncapped the bottle of rum, poured enough on the clean cloth to soak it through, then stuffed his handkerchief into the open mouth of the bottle, poking it deep with his finger to insure a tight fit. It would not do for him to lose the wick when it came time to make his pitch.

He palmed a plastic cigarette lighter, flicked it twice before he got a spark, and held its flame beneath the wick. His handkerchief caught at once, and Sanchez reckoned he had ten or fifteen seconds if he chose to hold the makeshift Molotov cocktail in his lap.

No, thank you.

Rising to a crouch, he held the Llama .45 in his left hand, the sputtering bottle of rum in his right. When he made his move, Sanchez was braced and ready, squeezing off two quick rounds to cover himself and pitching the cocktail overhand, with all the accuracy he could manage in a rush.

It struck the far wall of the corridor, shattered on impact, and his wick did the rest. A ball of flame erupted in the corridor, followed heartbeats later by a scream of panic and an aimless shotgun blast, as if the hidden gunner thought that he could murder fire itself.

Sanchez was braced and waiting when the shooter erupted from cover, dancing a frantic jig and slapping with both hands at his burning clothes. No sign of the shotgun, and that was fine. Sanchez shot him twice in the chest and left him twitching on the floor, dead or well on the way, as he raced to check the corridor for any stragglers.

Clear.

"Come on!" he snapped to Obregon. "We're out of time."

The dealer staggered to his feet, staring briefly at the dead men around him, going pale before he followed Sanchez out the back door, to the waiting car.

"We need to have a talk," the *federale* told him, when he had the vehicle in motion, putting blocks between them and the shooting scene.

"Of course," said Obregon, attempting to regain a measure of his self-control. "Of course."

SERAFINO ESCOBAR was sick and tired of jail. He realized that he had made a grave mistake, but there were ways for him to compensate and earn forgiveness. *El padrino* would be understanding, if they only had the chance to speak like men.

Of course, that would be difficult, with Serafino locked up in a cell.

His faith was weak. That had to be the root of all his problems, since the *federales* never would have seen him, otherwise. The magic was supposed to render him invisible, and since Fernando never failed, that had to mean that Serafino was deficient in his own resolve. He *did* believe, but maybe not enough. If he could only have another chance....

Confessing, now that raised another problem. Once he understood that the police could see him, that they meant to lock him up, he had begun to panic. Even so, he had not spilled his guts immediately. It had taken diet soda up the nose and threats of worse to come before he cracked and led them to the ranch, explaining what had happened there.

Revealing names.

The worst of it would be the fact that he had cost Fernando his *nganga*. Serafino was not worried that the *federales* would succeed in capturing Martinez or the others. All of them had faith to spare. If need be, they could walk into the very cell block here and set him free, unseen, untouched by human hands or bullets from the *federales'* guns.

It gave him something to look forward to, besides the thirteen counts of murder he was facing at the moment. There could be no bargain with the prosecutor while the others were at large, and if the *federales* never found Fernando, all the weight would fall on Serafino's shoulders. He would certainly be locked away for life, at least. He could not rule out death by firing squad.

But he understood that it did no good for him to worry and upset himself. Fernando had decided he should cool his heels in jail awhile for being weak. It was a fitting punishment, but he did not believe the master would allow him to be shot or jailed for life. It had been Serafino whom Martinez sent to fetch a special sacrifice—a gringo—on a night not long ago, when he was working special magic to protect a heavy shipment of cocaine. When Escobar returned with the intended prey, he had been welcomed like a long-lost son.

His service to the family would not escape the master's notice now, in time of need.

He thought of doing penance, but the family was not prepared for moments such as this, and Serafino did not know what he should do, which prayers to the *orishas* he should use. Without an altar, prayers would probably be wasted, anyway. But once he was released, he would present the master with a sacrifice unrivaled in the family's experience. Perhaps a gringo infant, lifted from a cradle in Del Rio or the trailer park outside of Eagle Pass.

He smiled at the idea, was caught up in the mental image, when the jailer brought his tray for lunch. Tamales again, goddamn it, but his stomach was growling, and it would be another six or seven hours before supper came around. Escobar wolfed down the food, chasing it with a cup of lukewarm coffee, no refills available to help him clear his palate of the pasty corn meal.

Sometimes he thought the food in jail was worse than being stripped of freedom. It was one thing, being locked up in a cell and counting off the days, but when your meals were all the same, or nearly so, the time began to drag more slowly, monotony taking shape as part of the punishment.

No doubt, it was exactly what the *federale* bastards had in mind. They tried to break a man any way they could, all the way from forcing soda water up his nose or beating him to cutting meat out of his diet and lacing his food with saltpeter to suppress his natural desires.

Come to think of it, the tamales *did* taste slightly different today, as if they might have been dusted with something. He scowled, pushing the empty plate away, telling himself that it had to be his imagination. Why would his jailers worry about Serafino's sex drive now, when he had no cellmates, no prospects of coming in contact with another human being before his trial.

Two weeks, they thought, before his day in court. Not long, but when he thought about the months and years beyond the trial he wondered—

Sudden pain, like someone jabbing ice picks in his stomach. Serafino doubled over, tipping his tray with the plastic plate and coffee cup as he slumped to the floor. The pain was crippling, overwhelming, radiating from his gut in waves like fire.

He tried to scream but could not find his voice. His throat felt constricted, parched beyond what he expected from the corn meal. He had spilled his dregs of coffee on the floor and could not wet his lips now, even if the wracking pain had let him drink.

A sudden twist of nausea, and even through the haze that clouded his vision he could see that he was puking blood, along with the tamales. So much blood, as if . . .

At once Serafino understood. A flash of insight that accompanied the pain with terror, sending icy tremors through his muscles as they spasmed, locking tight.

It was.

It had to be.

The master's will.

More blood, more pain beyond imagining, and Serafino Escobar was dead before the jailer came to fetch his tray.

THE HIGHWAY AMBUSH was a hard act to follow, but Bolan had plenty of targets to choose from. Piedras Negras was an open sewer, something like a third of all the bars and sex clubs owned by or heavily indebted to Ramon Ibarra. In the old days, back in Vietnam, an air strike or artillery barrage would do the trick, scorched earth, but Bolan's private war required more discretion, greater selectivity.

He had to hit Ibarra where it hurt, without annihilating stray civilians in the process or attracting the police before he had a chance to flee. The warrior was required to pick and choose for maximum advantage, and to minimize the snafu factor in advance.

The gambling was a sideline for Ibarra, but it still made money for his syndicate, and that was good enough for Bolan. He had scouted out the place—a back-room layout, tucked away behind a tavern called the Flame Club—and decided he could take it down without extraordinary risk.

Though he might still be shot and killed at any moment, the risk of death was not new for the Executioner, by any means.

He came in looking like a tourist, shortly after one o'clock. Loud shirt, a size too large and worn untucked to hide the pistol in the waistband of his slacks. A jacket would have made him stand out in the crowd, and Bolan knew he had to travel light if he was going to pull it off. The slim incendiary sticks that filled his left-hand pocket did not make a noticeable bulge.

He found an empty bar stool, drank two beers before he got around to asking the bartender where he could find some action. A five-dollar bill and a glimpse of the roll it came from bought Bolan a pass to the back-room casino, the doorman smiling at him with a bright gold tooth in front.

The quarters were cramped and smoky, but they had enough equipment crowded in to do a decent job of separating suckers from their money. Bolan counted off two dozen slot machines, a crap table and roulette wheel, three tables devoted to poker and blackjack. All the comforts of Las Vegas—except for air-conditioning, plush carpets, pretty women, free drinks and a nice hotel room for the night.

The gamblers at the Flame Club seemed determined, working the machines and tables with a kind of missionary zeal. Four-fifths of them were Anglo border-hoppers, some of them undoubtedly compulsive gamblers who could not afford Nevada or Atlantic City on their current budgets. Anyway, Piedras Negras fit the bill: It gave them one more opportunity to throw their hard-earned cash away.

Bolan thought about playing a few hands of poker, finally decided not to waste the time. He had a clear fix on the cashier's cage and moved in that direction, spotting bouncers near the men's room and against the nearest wall. Three goons, aside from Gold Tooth, and it looked like all of them were armed.

Poor odds, but he had dealt with worse and walked away.

The cashier was a woman, old beyond her years, with pancake makeup trying unsuccessfully to cover up the deep lines in her face. Instead of changing cash for chips, as she expected, Bolan reached beneath his shirt in back and handed her a folded paper shopping bag. He let her see the gun and left no doubt about the purpose of the bag.

And he was ready when she dropped below the counter, screaming like a banshee. As it happened, he was counting on the woman to react exactly as she had.

Her screams would serve his purpose admirably, as an early-warning fire alarm.

He spun to meet the goons, saw one advancing on his immediate left, digging for a shiny pistol underneath his jacket. Bolan shot the gunner once, between the eyes, and swiveled toward the second-closest threat.

The other bouncers had been hanging out together, near the men's room, when the screaming started. They were slower to react than their associate, but both of them were drawing hardware when a parabellum mangler caught the taller one in the throat and slammed him back against the wall. A chunky gambler lurched across Mack Bolan's line of fire and spoiled the second shot, but he was ready when his third mark broke for cover, lunging toward the men's room door.

A bullet helped him get there, crimson spouting from between his shoulder blades, the momentum slamming him face-first against the swinging door. He went down with a crash, the door wedged open by his bulk, exposing two men at the urinals, so startled they were hosing down their shoes.

And that left Gold Tooth.

Bolan's target had been caught in the stampede and shoved aside, prevented from escaping in the rush. He had a snub-nosed .38 in hand and got a shot off while the Executioner was turning back to face him, but a luckless gambler stopped the bullet, dropping in his tracks.

Before Gold Tooth could fire again, the sleek Beretta 93-R sent a parabellum messenger of death to close the gap between them, punching Bolan's target backward, off his feet, the last round from his snubby boring through the ceiling overhead.

No other guns in evidence, and Bolan turned his full attention back to the cashier's cage, slamming two sharp kicks against the flimsy door before it gave and the cashier rushed past him, still screaming for all she was worth. He let her go, filling the paper bag with all the cash it would comfortably hold—a new war chest for his Mexican campaign—and dropping one of his incendiary sticks to take care of the rest.

The crowd was gone when Bolan emerged from the cage, jostling drinkers in the cantina as they raced for the street, jabbering excited, confused descriptions of the attack. The gunshots had interrupted happy hour, and Bolan found the bartender staring at him as he emerged from the back room, one hand gliding out of sight and reaching for a hidden weapon.

Bolan let him show it, saw it was a leaded baseball bat, and raised the ante with a clear look at the pistol in his hand. The bartender blanched, shook his head, and dropped the bat in a heartbeat.

"You're out of work," said Bolan, trusting the bartender's smattering of English to work it out. "The place is on fire."

As he spoke, Bolan rested his sack of cash on a table cluttered with beer bottles, drew two more incendiary sticks from his pocket and lighted them up, tossing one behind the bar and its mate across the room.

The bartender had his meaning now, leading the handful of stragglers in a headlong rush for the street. Bolan was the last man out, smoke already curling around him as he reached the sidewalk, his pistol safely out of sight, the heavy sack tucked underneath one arm.

The action would not break Ramon Ibarra's bank, but it would give him further food for thought.

A few more meals like that, the Executioner decided, and a man could choke to death.

FERNANDO DE LEON MARTINEZ slammed the telephone receiver down, then caught himself and took a few deep breaths to check his anger. He needed all his wits about him in the next few hours, if he was to salvage something from the morning's disaster.

The highway ambush was a new and unexpected twist. It hit Ibarra where he lived, three million dollars' worth of drugs at wholesale rates, and eight of Ramon's *pistoleros* rotting in the sun. Beyond the loss of merchandise and personnel, it was a loss of face for someone of Ibarra's stature to be treated so, embarrassed in the public eye. Machismo demanded an immediate response, but Ibarra could not put his hands on the man or men responsible.

For that, he turned to *el padrino* and the family to solve his problem. He had paid Martinez well, but he was never satisfied with the results. The dealer's greed demanded more and more, new visions of the future, iron-clad assurances that he would be protected from the law and his competitors.

So far, Martinez had been equal to the challenge, calling on his law-enforcement sources when he needed special information, spreading bribes around where they would do the most good for himself and Ibarra. And it had always done the trick... until now.

His eyes and ears on both sides of the border seemed useless in the present crisis, no matter how he pressed them for current information. Fragosa had uncovered the name of a *federale* assigned to Ibarra's case, unraveling part of the puzzle, but Martinez knew no lawman was responsible for the assaults Ibarra had suffered over the past twelve hours. No police agency in the free world operated in this fashion, and the agents of various dictatorships had no need to conceal their activities in such a way.

That left business competitors, and Martinez knew how dangerous they could be, where drugs and money were concerned. His problem still remained, however, since his spies in half a dozen border syndicates reported no unusual activity against Ibarra or incursions on the dealer's territory.

An unknown factor, then... and that made *el padrino* nervous.

He was used to dealing with the dark side, unseen spirits from the other side, but it was different when his unseen enemies took solid form and started wreaking havoc with his best-laid plans.

At least the traitor Serafino had been dealt with. He would trouble them no more, but his elimination was a small thing in comparison with the continuing attacks against Ibarra. If Martinez did not find a swift solution, he could count on trouble from the dealer, and he did not have the troops to win a shooting war.

Not yet, he thought.

Two avenues of pursuit, then. One to pacify his patron, and the other to protect himself. Whichever seemed more likely to bear fruit, Martinez would have a viable choice.

And when the time was right, he would attack decisively.

He only needed to decide on who would be his chosen target, when the moment came.

CHAPTER FOURTEEN

It was Marcella's place, or one of them at any rate, a small house on the outskirts of Piedras Negras. Hargis had one hand on his Colt as they pulled into the covered carport, Marcella switching off the engine and favoring him with a smile.

"We're safe here," she told him, resting a hand on his leg once more in a way that almost, but not quite, made Hargis lose sight of his mission.

Almost.

"You say so."

He didn't sound convinced, and Marcella picked up on his skepticism. "Are you frightened of me, Mr. Drake?"

The Ranger frowned. "Not hardly," he assured her, "but I'd like to know how those boys back at the cantina found out we were meeting there."

"Coincidence, perhaps," the blonde replied. "Ricardo Obregon has many enemies."

"But you're one of his friends?"

"Indeed."

"I never did hear why you happened to be with him."

"Can we talk about the rest of this inside?"

"Sure thing."

He covered the street while Marcella unlocked the front door, and then they were inside. Cool and dark in the house, until she found the light switch and brought some muted illumination into the small but comfortably furnished living room. The kitchen was separated from the parlor by a kind of breakfast bar, in the style of an American apartment or condominium, and a hallway led off to the left, toward the bedrooms.

Hargis found himself thinking about bedrooms a lot, with the foxy blonde standing close enough that he could smell her perfume and something else, the feminine essence of the woman herself. Give Hargis a choice, and he would take that essence over perfume, every time.

"A drink, perhaps?" Marcella asked.

"I wouldn't turn it down."

"Please, have a seat."

He picked the sofa and sat at one end, adjusting the Colt so it would not dig too deeply into his armpit. Marcella returned in a moment with tall glasses of red wine and handed one to Hargis, keeping the other for herself as she settled in beside him, close enough that their thighs were touching, her warmth communicating itself to him.

"Wine's all I have. I'm sorry."

"Don't be."

"You were asking me . . ."

"About Obregon, right. What's the story on that? We were expecting old Ricardo by himself."

"I hope I did not disappoint you."

"Not at all. I said you came as a surprise. That doesn't mean it was unpleasant."

"So."

"Speaking of Obregon, I need to get in touch with him pronto, and find out where he's gone to with my partner."

"They'll be fine, I'm sure. Obregon has many contacts in Coahuila. Many places he can hide, if need be."

"Hiding's not exactly what I had in mind, this afternoon."

"You had your mind on business, yes?"

"That's right."

"Still, hiding out can have advantages, I think."

Her hand was on his leg again, massaging, and Hargis had begun to think about the benefits of undercover work. Sometimes it happened that you had to play a role up to the hilt, and that was sounding better all the time.

"Advantages?"

"I wouldn't be surprised." Her smile was magic, making Hargis wonder if this witch might not have cast a spell on him when he was busy concentrating on the downside of his job. It was ridiculous, of course, and yet...

"You go for being shot at in cantinas? That's a new one, when it comes to turn-ons."

"Not the shooting," she replied. "But now, we have this time together. Privacy. A chance to know each other better, if it doesn't slip away."

"Ricardo didn't even get around to telling us your name," said Hargis. "I feel funny sitting here and thinking of you as an 'Obregon associate.'"

She laughed at that and said, "My name's Marcella."

"What's a—"

"Girl like me doing with a character like Ricardo?" she finished for him, smiling over the lip of her wineglass.

"You read my mind," the Ranger said.

"I like money, and the things it can buy. Sometimes, you have to seize the opportunities as they become available."

"Amen to that."

"So, how about it?"

"How about what?" Hargis asked.

She took his hand and brought it to her breast, leaning forward, letting him feel the firm weight of her flesh in his palm. It felt as if electric current had begun to flow along his arm, directly to a flash point in his groin.

"How about seizing the opportunity, cowboy?"

Hargis left his hand where it was, covered with hers, and set his glass of wine aside to free the other one. He smiled and said, "I don't mind if I do."

PIEDRAS NEGRAS was new territory for Doyle Mitchum, and he took his time getting acquainted with the streets. The border town had a familiar feel to it, after his time spent in Matamoros and Ciudad Acuna, but no two towns were exactly the same. Each harbored secrets and potential dangers of its own for the unwary, traps that might be sprung without a hint of warning.

Mitchum started out with the botanicas again. Esteban Montoya had informed him that Martinez and his cronies might be in Piedras Negras, but he did not have—or would not yield—specific information on their whereabouts. Beyond the generalities, his statements had been limited to cryptic warnings that a gringo should not interfere with things he did not understand.

Mitchum did not mind the legwork, having done enough of it around Miami in his time with Metro-Dade. It came with the territory, and he recognized the inherent danger of turning over rocks on unfamiliar turf. The creatures living underneath might be as deadly as they were repulsive, and he had no plans to end his days in Mexico.

Not yet, at any rate.

Once upon a time, before his marriage fell apart, Mitchum had dreamed of retiring to a little village on the Gulf, living like a gringo king on his pension and cautious investments built up through the years, fishing when he cared to and baking himself in the sun every day.

If he closed his eyes, he could still see the cottage, surrounded by cacti and Marjorie's roses, ceramic wind chimes plucking music from a soft breeze off the water.

What the hell, times change and dreams go belly-up without a moment's notice. Here he was, retired from Metro-Dade ahead of schedule, chasing dealers and their henchmen on the wrong side of the border, maybe gambling his life.

So what?

His wife had bailed out years ago, disgusted with his hours and the company he kept, a nervous wreck from close-call shootings and the times he stayed out late without remembering to let her know that he was still alive. Nobody's fault, perhaps, but Mitchum took the blame upon himself without complaint. He missed their life together, woke up reaching for her sometimes in the middle of the night, but there was no such thing as gambling for free. You took your shot and did your best to stand the losses like a man.

The game went on, no matter who dropped out along the way, and Mitchum could not think of anyone off-hand who had a prayer of getting out of life alive.

Still, there was something unappealing to the thought of dying in Piedras Negras. If he had a choice, the ex-cop from Miami thought that he would rather make his final stand in Omaha or Bakersfield. At least the heavies there stopped short of carving up their opposition for the cooking pot.

Five years ago—or even one—he would have viewed the quest as an adventure, poking into murky corners, looking for the baddest mother in the neighborhood and scoping ways to take him down. Today, it was a chore that he had taken on himself, and there were times when he regretted it.

Like now.

The same ingredients were there, of course—the danger and excitement, good and evil in the flesh—and Mitchum understood the change had taken place inside himself. It was not age, since Mitchum felt as vital as he ever had. Well, nearly so. Nor was it, he decided, the repulsive nature of his quarry and the crimes involved. Around Miami he had dealt with torture, mutilation, murder on a daily basis, and it never got him down this way.

I'm tired, he thought. That was it, in a nutshell. Doyle Mitchum was fed up with wading through shit and handling trash every day of his life.

Which did not mean he was prepared to stop.

Not yet.

When he was done with this one, maybe. In the meantime...

The first two botanicas were dry holes, the proprietors staring at Mitchum as if he had egg on his face, shaking their heads and replying in firm negatives when he asked about *palo mayombe* in general or Fernando Martinez in particular. That left two shops in town that advertised their wares, and he would have to try them both before he gave it up. As for the other dealers, amateur *brujos* and herb doctors selling potions out of their homes or back rooms, he would not have a hope in hell of tracing them without a local guide to point the way.

The owner of the third botanica was a thin, almost-cadaverous man, with sunken cheeks to match his deep-set eyes, and hair slicked back to hide a bald spot showing near his crown. The most expressive thing about him was his lips, which reminded Mitchum of raw liver come to life.

Approaching the counter, Mitchum smiled and launched into his patented spiel: an interest in *palo mayombe,* some experience with rituals around Miami, and a burning desire to meet the young *palero* who was making a name for himself in Coahuila. Granted, it was less than totally convincing from a gringo's lips, but when you put a hundred dollars in the pot, credibility sometimes improved dramatically.

The thin man heard him out, considered Mitchum's story for a moment, and began to nod. At first the movement of his head was almost imperceptible, but in another moment it was clear that he had something on his mind.

"I may be able to assist you," he said at last, his voice so soft that Mitchum had to strain his ears to catch the words.

"Outstanding. If you know where I can reach Señor Martinez—"

The proprietor held up a warning hand and glanced around his empty shop. "We must not speak of this in public. Come this way."

Doyle Mitchum frowned. He was the only customer in the botanica, but he was not about to argue with the owner at the risk of losing a potential source. He trailed the thin man to a combination storage room and office in the rear, behind a beaded curtain that appeared to be the standard issue for occult supply stores everywhere. His nostrils crinkled at the smell of something musty, gone to mold, but Mitchum caught himself, determined not to offend his new contact prematurely.

The thin man kept his back to Mitchum for a moment, shuffling papers on his cluttered desk. "You mentioned some *dinero,*" he remarked.

"That's right."

"I need two hundred dollars cash, American."

"That would depend upon the information," Mitchum said, folding one hand around the roll of bills in his pocket. The amount was not exorbitant, but he was not about to pay up front for what might prove to be another runaround.

"Of course," the thin man said, turning back to face him. He took a step toward Mitchum, bringing up his right hand with a flash of stainless steel, the dagger aimed at Mitchum's throat.

Mitchum threw himself backward, sweeping one arm across the top of a nearby filing cabinet, pelting his assailant with empty bottles and jars. The thin man raised an arm to shield his eyes and kept on coming, boring in to the attack. Mitchum's boot to the groin was off target, striking his assailant's thigh, but it was enough to stagger the thin man, driving him backward a pace while Mitchum clutched at his pistol. He drew the Browning double-action from its shoulder rig and thrust it out in front of him, drawing a bead on the knife wielder's chest.

"Think twice," he cautioned, tightening his finger on the Browning's trigger as he spoke.

The Mexican thought twice...and charged directly toward him with a snarl, lips drawn back from his teeth, the dagger raised to strike. Mitchum's first round struck him in the chest and knocked him back a pace, the second drilling through his open mouth to explode from the back of his skull.

"Well, shit."

Despite the shock, his mind was working fast enough to make him stop and find his brass, the cartridge cases going in his pocket as he stowed his automatic out of sight and left the shop.

Somebody had anticipated Mitchum's movements in Piedras Negras, and they meant to stop him cold. As in dead. The second move against him in as many days.

The game was heating up, and Mitchum had begun to understand that he was still unclear about the rules, except that it was going into sudden death overtime.

Doyle Mitchum only hoped the sudden death would not turn out to be his own.

MARCELLA GRANT, still naked, sat beside the prostrate lawman, studying his face. He had been adequate in bed, perhaps a cut above the average, but she felt nothing in the nature of affection for him now. Seducing him had been a job, and she had done it well, as always.

He was breathing slowly, regularly in his sleep. The sedative had taken its toll, administered in a fresh glass of wine when they finished making love the second time. His face looked peaceful, almost childlike, but she was not fooled by the illusion.

It would be a simple thing to kill him now, but that was not the plan. Fernando wanted this one alive—both of them, if possible—and she was prepared to deliver on her part of the bargain. It would be a new experience, observing the destruction of a man who had lately shared her bed and body, but Marcella knew that she was equal to the challenge. It would be a good experience, a chance to prove herself before Fernando and the other members of the family.

Ten minutes since she had placed the call, and it would be at least another quarter hour before Ruiz arrived with the collection team. Marcella did not mind the wait. If anything, it gave her time to savor that which was to come.

It was an honor, when she thought about it, being trusted by Fernando with the task of bringing down his enemy. He had advised her to expect some kind of a diversion at the cantina, but the shooting had taken Marcella off guard. It had seemed so terribly real—doubly so for the men who were killed—but it had all worked out exactly as Fernando had predicted.

Which was no surprise at all.

She wondered how Ricardo Obregon was handling the *federale,* but she pushed the problem out of mind, concentrating on the task at hand. Rising from the bed, she began retrieving her hastily discarded clothes, dressing at a leisurely pace while she kept an eye on the unconscious lawman.

A Texas Ranger, she was told. One of the cocky elite who thrived on laudatory publicity and specialized in manhandling minorities on the side. Marcella knew their reputation, and she had no doubt Fernando would be able to outwit such adversaries. She would help him all she could, and in return...

It was unlike the new Marcella to consider personal advancement. Since her union with Fernando de Leon Martinez, she had felt a change within herself, defying ego in its normal sense. But lately, when she thought about the future, she began to see herself as Fernando's second-in-command, outstripping Gregorio Ruiz in *el padrino*'s trust and affections.

Soon, now. When Fernando had seen what she could do on her own, for the benefit of himself and their family.

Marcella poured herself another glass of wine, without the heavy sedative, and settled back to wait.

THE TELEPHONE RANG half a dozen times in Washington before Brognola answered in his deep, gruff voice.

"Hello?"

"It's Striker. Open line."

"Hang on."

Bolan attached his portable scrambler to the pay phone while Hal was punching buttons at the other end. Another moment passed before the man from Justice said, "Okay, we're set."

"Any feedback on those queries?"

"Yeah, there was." He heard Brognola shuffling papers, coming up with a report or two. "Who do you want first?"

"Take your pick."

"Okay. Doyle Mitchum we've already discussed. Hargis, first name Brock. He's got eleven years behind the badge, two commendations, wounded once in the line of duty, about two years ago. That was in a shoot-out in Waco. He planted three bank robbers by himself that day."

"Connections?"

"Not the kind you're looking for. I ran him past the FBI and DEA this morning. He looks clean across the board."

"That leaves the *federale*."

"Right. Emilio Sanchez," Hal replied. "I've got a couple contacts down that way, but then again, you never know exactly what to think about the FJP. We've all been burned from time to time on dealings with the *federales*. What I hear, he's as clean as they come south of the border, but..."

"You could be wrong," Bolan finished for him.

"Damn it, I just can't be sure."

"Okay, I'll make a note. How many of his people are involved in this?"

"Supposedly, immediate superiors only for Hargis and Sanchez both. That narrows down the field, unless somebody's holding out."

Translated, that meant Bolan still had to watch his back where all of his allies were concerned. Any one of them could have arranged the ambush at the Desert Star Motel last night.

Any one of them might try again.

The Executioner would have to watch his back. Business as usual in the hellgrounds, right.

"Okay," he said, "I'll keep in touch."

"You do that, Striker. If you need some kind of help . . ."

"We're set, so far."

"All right. Just let me know."

"Will do."

But were they set?

He broke the connection, moving back toward his car with long strides. And set for what?

It could turn out to be a massacre.

The only question left in Bolan's mind was who would die, and when.

CHAPTER FIFTEEN

Gregorio Ruiz scrambled out of the Mercedes as soon as it parked in Marcella Grant's driveway. The others fell in step behind him, playing catch-up as he moved directly to the porch and hammered on her door. Another moment passed before Marcella answered, smiling at him, with a half-full wineglass in her hand.

"Gregorio."

She stood aside and let him in, the others following.

"Where is he?" asked Ruiz.

"The bedroom. That way."

Gregorio followed her pointing finger, moving along a short hallway toward the bedroom. He stepped across the threshold, stopping short when he saw the naked gringo sprawled across Marcella's bed, eyes closed, his flaccid penis plainly visible.

He turned back to Marcella with a twisted smile. "I see you've had a party," sneered Ruiz.

"I followed my instructions, Gregorio. If you have any questions or complaints, I would suggest that you consult Fernando."

The cocky smile froze on Gregorio's face, taking on the aspect of a grimace. "As you say."

He snapped his fingers at the members of his pickup crew, issuing curt instructions, watching as they rolled the hulking gringo in a sheet from head to toe. He resembled a mummy, or perhaps a giant moth's cocoon, and

Ruiz wondered briefly if their man could breathe through the sheet.

"His face," Ruiz snapped. "Leave an opening."

"Take care," Marcella warned them. "If he dies, Fernando won't be pleased."

"I know what I'm doing," Gregorio told her, repulsed by the thought of taking orders from a woman. His personal predilection did not reduce the inbred sense of machismo that underlay his personality, determining the way he felt and reacted in any given situation.

"Is Fernando at the ranch?" Marcella asked.

"He will be, by the time we get there."

"And the *federale?*"

Ruiz hesitated, cleared his throat, feeling a twinge of embarrassment. It went against his grain, confessing defeat to the Anglo bitch, but she would find out anyway, before much longer.

"Gone," he said, hoping she would let it go at that.

"Gone?" There was an incredulous tone to her voice. "You lost him?"

"Obregon lost him," Ruiz snapped. "We were supposed to take delivery from the dealer, but his nerves...the shooting frightened Obregon too much. He lost sight of priorities and made us look like fools."

"Whose idea was the shooting, anyway?" Marcella asked.

Gregorio felt color rising in his cheeks, uncertain whether it was anger or embarrassment. Again, he knew that any lie he told would be found out within an hour, two at most.

"The plan was mine," he said, watching the sly smile spread over her face and hating her for it, wishing he could rush across the room and kill her where she stood.

"Your plan. Of course, it was. How foolish of me."

"None of you were harmed," Ruiz reminded her.

"And your men?"

"Free-lance peasants," he informed her. "They were paid to do a job, and it was done. Such people are expendable."

"Are you expendable, Gregorio?"

"The family comes first," he answered, finding strength to return her smile, hoping that some of his anger and contempt showed through. "For *el padrino,* we are all expendable."

"You may be right, at that."

The bitch was scheming, but he could not read her mind, and so Ruiz busied himself with the task at hand, directing his men as they hoisted the Texan between them, supporting him like a roll of carpeting. They were not athletes, and the Ranger's weight was telling on them, causing them to grit their teeth against the strain.

One of them stubbed his toe against a dresser, cursed and almost dropped their bundle, but he caught it in the nick of time. Ruiz snapped out an order, brushing past them to lead the way outside. It would be risky, carrying the lawman to their car, but residents of the neighborhood were known for their discretion when it came to sharing observations with police. Still, the less that anybody saw, the better.

He could not afford mistakes at this point in the game, with Sanchez running free and Obregon inexplicably out of touch. Gregorio had enough to answer for already, and he only hoped Marcella's success with the Ranger would momentarily satisfy Fernando, perhaps even place him in a forgiving mood.

If not, Ruiz would try to find a way of turning that success against the woman, and to his own advantage. It would not be easy, but it still might work.

There would be time to think about it on the drive.

This time, the short *palero* was determined not to fail.

MARCELLA DROVE her own car, following the gray Mercedes east from Piedras Negras, through the desert waste and toward Fernando's latest hideaway. The radio was on, an undercurrent of the latest salsa music making no impression on her as she drove. Her mind was fixed upon Gregorio Ruiz and plans to counter what she felt was sure to be a sneak attack upon herself.

It was Ruiz's style, and she expected nothing less. The trick would be to counter him before he had a chance to harm her in Fernando's eyes.

Something had gone wrong with Gregorio's end of the plan, for starters. They were supposed to separate the *federale*, Sanchez, from his Anglo crony, and that much had been achieved despite the surprise fireworks in the cantina. Marcella had taken her man home and sedated him as ordered. The sex was strictly optional, a pleasant means to an end.

Ruiz, meanwhile, had been assigned to collar Sanchez, but the man had slipped away somehow. Not only that, but they were out of touch with Obregon, an inexcusable mistake. It told her both men had escaped from the cantina shooting gallery, but they were lost beyond that point.

Gregorio would have to put a brave face on his failure, and the quickest way to do that was to cast aspersions on Marcella, challenge her techniques, perhaps try to elicit some jealousy from Fernando. Marcella wished him luck in that regard, convinced that it would be a waste of time. Still, there were ways Ruiz could harm her, by casting doubt upon her loyalty.

She reminded herself that Fernando was the one who had instructed her to use her sex against their enemies a dozen times or more, in other situations. And she was delivering her man on schedule—unlike Ruiz, who came home empty-handed once again.

She felt secure, for now, but she would have to keep her eyes wide open for the next few days, and watch her back at every turn. Ruiz was nothing if not persistent. Failing in one approach, he would try another and another, until he ran out of ideas...or until somebody squashed him like a cockroach on the sidewalk.

The image made her smile, but only for a moment. It was there and gone, replaced by images of the impending ceremony at the ranch. A rally of the family, to summon Chango and the rest of the *orishas,* calling up the power of the *nganga* to defend them in their time of trial.

She thought about the tall American who called himself Joe Drake, and felt no pity for him. He had brought this trouble on himself, by meddling in the affairs of others. Now he would be punished and rewarded, all at once. For punishment, a death that he could not imagine and would not wish on his worst enemy. His reward, an opportunity to serve Fernando de Leon Martinez on the other side.

There had been times, more recently, when Marcella Grant wondered what it must be like to endure the pains of sacrifice to enter the *nganga*. More specifically, she wondered what came afterward, the details of a journey into death and darkness from which no one ever returned.

Or did they?

She had seen things during ceremonies, heard strange sounds that she could not explain. Marcella didn't know if they were echoes or hallucinations, but Fernando called them voices from the other side. A universe of pain and pleasure lay just beyond the reach of mortal men. Its magic could be tapped and utilized by those with skill and knowledge. If an upstart poseur tried to work the magic, demons from beyond the pale would turn upon him, deaf to pleas for mercy, greedily devouring his soul.

The tall American was hers, by right. Fernando would perform the main part of the ceremony, as he always did, but she had made the catch alone, without another family member to assist her. It would be her blood right to devour the Texan's heart, absorb whatever strength and cunning he possessed.

With that in mind, she could defy Ruiz, perhaps force his hand prematurely, while he was yet unprepared. Defeat him that way, by taking advantage of the little *palero*'s weakness.

She would have to do her best today, be ready when the throbbing heart was offered up. The first time, she was hesitant, her bite too tentative. The sacrificial victim's fear and anger flooded through her all at once, like the rush of some powerful new drug. Her body and soul were on fire, ripped apart. Marcella had glanced toward the earthen floor of the shack, terrified, expecting to see scraps of her own flesh and vital organs littering the squalid hovel.

But she had survived, and she was stronger now, better prepared for the next stage of her becoming. The first man whose heart she had sampled was a peasant farmer, powerless within society, although his passions were extreme. The Texan would be different—used to giving orders in his line of work and seeing them obeyed, a man of violence who would pass his courage on to her in blood.

Another fifteen minutes to the ranch, if they were not delayed. Fernando would inspect the catch and listen while she gave him her account of the capture. Gregorio, in contrast, would be busy explaining his failure, no doubt trying to shift the game, make it seem as if Marcella was to blame somehow, because she did her job efficiently.

Just let him try.

She did not fully understand the bond between Fernando and Gregorio, this macho thing they shared in bed and out, but she would bet her life against Ruiz once it was seen that he had let the *federale* slip away, losing Ricardo Obregon in the process.

Poor Gregorio. His failures would come back to haunt him someday. They might even spell his death.

Marcella smiled and raised the volume on the radio. A new song just beginning, and her own reflection in the rearview mirror was aglow as she began to sing along.

BROCK HARGIS CAME AROUND by slow degrees, a painful throbbing in his skull, concentrated behind his eyes. Hangover? His memory came back in bits and pieces, images of Marcella Grant, the two of them together in her bed. A glass of wine when they were finished with the second time around.

Sweet Jesus!

Hargis tried to rise, and two things happened simultaneously. He discovered he was bound securely to some kind of rigid surface, like a table, and a putrid stench assailed his nose, the churning in his stomach blooming into full-scale nausea. He turned his head, a last-ditch bid to keep from puking on himself and only got a little on the bare skin of his shoulder.

Naked.

They had been together, naked in her bed, and now the Texas Ranger understood that he was *still* buck naked, even though the room had changed. That stench, Christ's sake, it was enough to gag a maggot, but he could not spot the source from where he lay.

Another moment, clarity of consciousness returning, and he did not have to.

Overhead, long strips of corrugated metal formed the ceiling, dusty cobwebs hanging from the two-by-four braces, a black widow spinning in one corner, surrounded by its milky egg sacs. On his left, a wooden plank was laid over cinder blocks and cluttered with the effigies of saints, some chicken feathers, candles and a silver chalice. On his right, he saw a plywood door without a knob or latch.

The sudden fear took Hargis by surprise, and anger followed swiftly after. Damn it, he would not allow these two-bit voodoo artists to intimidate him, even if he seemed to be their prisoner just now.

Every trap had an exit, it was all a matter of finding your way out while there was time, before the hunter came around to finish off his prey. Like now, with Hargis safely on his own and no one watching.

He began by testing his bonds. Some kind of rawhide looped around his wrists and ankles, holding them fast to a long, low table. There were leather straps, like belts, around his chest, waist, thighs and calves. No matter how he tried, he could not seem to shift the straps and thongs. If anything, his struggles only made the bonds cut deeper into his flesh.

"Goddamn it!"

The stench of putrefaction was working on his nostrils and stomach again, making Hargis feel dizzy. There was nothing left in his stomach, and he clenched his teeth against the dry heaves, swallowing hard to keep his gut under control. He might not be able to escape, but Hargis was damned if he would let his captors see him moaning and whining like some punk kid.

The trick was scoping out exactly what his adversary had in mind and being ready when the shit came down. A trade, perhaps, although it seemed unlikely on the face of things. No telling how these freaks had blown his cover, but at least there was a possibility that Sanchez had escaped.

That is, assuming Sanchez had not blown the whistle on him to begin with.

Interrogation was the next most likely option. If Martinez and his crowd were short on information, wondering exactly who was on their track, it stood to reason they would try to make him talk. The prospect sent a cold chill down the Ranger's spine, but he determined to resist as long as possible. Anyone could be broken, he knew, but at least he could slow the bastards down, make them work for everything they got.

With luck, he might even come out on the other side of the meat grinder alive.

His ears picked up the sound of footsteps on gravel, drawing closer. Hargis took a deep breath, holding it a moment to help calm his nerves and the rolling of his stomach.

The plywood door scraped open, dragging tracks in the sand, fairly blinding Hargis with the sudden glare of sunlight. Shadows circled the table where he lay, some half a dozen, but he closed his eyes against the light and waited for the door to close.

The shack seemed stifling now, sweat beading on his skin. He told himself that it was nothing but the temperature, no fear involved, but Hargis knew it was a lie.

He was scared shitless, not so much of dying, but of what would come before. The notion that he might be glad to die, before they finished with him.

He tried to steel himself. A Texas Ranger did not beg for mercy under any circumstances. Hanging tough was a tradition with the Rangers, almost a religion. Tough it out and show no fear to anyone, regardless of the circumstances.

It sounded fine, until his eyes snapped open and he saw the knife.

THE SESSION with Marcella and Gregorio had been infuriating, Fernando listening to Gregorio's lame excuses for losing Sanchez *and* Obregon, while trying to lay the blame off on Marcella. Fernando had cut him short, demanding that Ruiz get back to work and try to salvage something from the situation while they had a chance. Gregorio was banished from the ceremony, like a child sent off to bed without his supper, and Martinez had not missed the glint of triumph in Marcella's eyes as they were left alone.

He did not mind a certain strain between his chief lieutenants, competition for his favor that would keep them on their toes. The only danger came when they grew too preoccupied with undercutting each other and forgot their broad objectives. Worse, if they lost track of who was actually in charge.

No fear of that, so far.

Ruiz would sulk awhile, but it would do him good. A reminder of his subordinate position, to keep him in his place. Martinez could always make it up to Gregorio, soothe him in other ways.

Marcella had earned her reward, but he was not about to rush the sacrifice for her sake. It was more than a ritual this time, with so much still unknown about their enemies. Martinez needed information first, before he sent this gringo on to the other side and offered his heart to Marcella as payment for a job well done.

The sun was blazing hot outside, and Martinez was sweating through his cotton shirt and slacks before they reached the shed where the *nganga* and the prisoner were waiting. Marcella walked behind him, four of his privileged disciples trailing out behind. The others would be standing guard or carrying out their duties around the house and grounds.

This sacrifice was not designed to be a family spectacle. Martinez had more practical concerns in mind.

A blast of stench met Fernando as he opened the door to the shed, stepping across the threshold into stifling semidarkness. The Ranger lay before him on the sacrificial altar, naked and securely bound. A fine specimen, by all appearances. Some flies from the *nganga* had settled on his pale legs, crawling on his flesh and tasting the salty perspiration there. They lifted off as Martinez and his disciples ringed the table, settling once more when their insect brains determined no immediate threat.

Martinez drew the dagger from a belt sheath. Its blade was double-edged, razor-sharp, bright stainless steel. With this tool, he could administer a single killing thrust or make the torment last for hours, even days.

Somewhere between the two, perhaps. Enough to wring the Texan dry of necessary information and charge his spirit up for the journey, before Martinez opened his chest and removed the gringo's still-beating heart.

A moment to savor.

The Ranger's eyes came open, fastening briefly on the dagger before they rose to Fernando's face.

"Nice place you've got here," said the Anglo.

Fernando smiled in appreciation of the Texan's machismo. It would soon desert him, once the dagger went to work.

"I'm glad you like it, gringo. Make yourself at home."

"How about I slip into something a little more comfortable?"

"You're fine as you are."

"I wouldn't want to shock the lady."

"Have no fear."

"I guess you're right, at that. It's pretty hard to shock a whore."

"Such language." Martinez brought the dagger's edge to rest against the Texan's groin.

The Ranger clenched his teeth as Martinez applied more pressure, not quite breaking the skin.

"I reckon I could use a shave, at that."

"We need to have a talk," Martinez said.

"Suits me. You start."

Martinez gave the blade a sudden twist and saw the Ranger grimace. Good. He had the subject's full attention now.

"I think we'll start with you."

"Fuck off."

"Of course."

Steel gliding over flesh and leaving blood behind. And when the Ranger started screaming, it was music to Fernando's ears.

CHAPTER SIXTEEN

The meet had been arranged before they separated last time, a new motel outside of Eagle Pass. The Executioner showed up ahead of time to scout it out and check for any indications of an ambush in the making.

He parked three doors down from the appointed room, entered with one hand on the Beretta, and checked out the bathroom at once, even searching the closet before he began to relax. All clear, as far as he could see, but there were still a hundred different ways for it to blow up in his face. He cracked the blinds and drew a chair up near the window, where he could watch the parking lot and highway without exposing himself to hostile eyes.

His last stop in Piedras Negras had been a tiny hole-in-the-wall gift shop, utilized by Ramon Ibarra as a drop and pickup point for shipments of cocaine. The shit went out in paper bags, piñatas, plaster statuettes—you name it—for the customers assuming the responsibility of border crossings on their own. The rules were simple: cash and carry, with a rider that anyone who took a fall did his own time and kept his mouth shut. Exposure of the source and drop was tantamount to suicide, and no one had been dumb enough to blow the whistle yet.

They would not have to, now.

It had been relatively simple, in and out. A look at Bolan's mini-Uzi cleared the shop of browsing tourists, but he had to waste a pair of goons Ibarra hired as muscle to protect the place. Small loss. The register was almost empty, hardly worth his time, and he was more concerned about the stock in back. Specifically, four kilos stashed in plaster busts of Pancho Villa, waiting for a pickup that would take them north.

Not this time.

Two of his incendiary sticks had done the job, and he had left the manager alive, to take a message home. Another warning that Ibarra should consider going out of business on his own, while he was still alive to make the move.

Of course, the Executioner had no intention of letting the dealer off that easy, but it helped to stir the pot, plant seeds of doubt where they would sprout and put down roots inside Ibarra's mind. Every moment that the dealer spent examining his known competitors along the border, wondering which one of them would dare to make a move against his empire, bought Mack Bolan that much time to undermine Ibarra's action in Coahuila, chipping away at the foundation of his evil family.

As for Martinez and the other cultists, he was waiting for some word from Mitchum, anything that would direct him toward a target he could recognize. So far, the ex-cop in Miami was feeling his way through the dark, playing it by ear and coming back with vague impressions, nothing they could use to mount a blitz.

By now, it was a race of sorts. Doyle Mitchum had been drawn to the fight by evidence of cult activity among the dealers, while Bolan would be reasonably satisfied to break Ibarra's back and let it go at that. If he could take down the *paleros* in the process, that was fine, but his crusade was not about religion, voodoo, atheism or the rest of it. He hunted savages, and if he saw a chance to waste Martinez, he would take it. Not because Martinez worshipped different, unfamiliar gods, but rather on the basis of the way he treated men and women. Using them like slaves or sacrificial goats to satisfy his own warped view of life and death.

The Executioner espoused no recognizable religious doctrine of his own. His long experience with evil had been too extensive to allow for a belief that God—Jehovah, Allah, Christ, whatever—took a daily interest in the personal affairs of men. He *did* believe in some intelligence or power greater than himself, beyond the grasp of humankind, but he was not prepared to name it or denounce the views of those who saw things differently. The sects or cults that he despised were those who took advantage of their followers for money, sex or twisted power trips, and Bolan cut no slack for any self-styled "holy man" because of his affiliation with a given creed. It made no difference, in the long run, if a thief or pervert called himself a Christian, Buddhist, Moslem, Jew or satanist. The predators who robbed old people of their hard-earned money or molested children in the choir loft were as guilty and corrupt, in Bolan's eyes, as those who toppled headstones in the dead of night or sacrificed their pleading victims in conjunction with the vernal equinox.

This time around, the cancer had a Spanish name, but evil was a universal concept, known in every culture, every language and religion of the world. If Bolan got a chance to stop Fernando de Leon Martinez—stop the bastard dead—he would not hesitate.

But first, he had to find himself a target.

A dusty sedan pulled into the parking lot outside, nosing up to the curb next door. He recognized Emilio Sanchez at the wheel, and felt a momentary tremor of concern at seeing that the *federale* was alone.

Relax.

There had to be an explanation, and the only thing you got from worrying was premature gray hair.

He watched the *federale* lock his car and scan the lot with nervous eyes. Behind him, pulling off the street, Doyle Mitchum drove a German compact, nodding to Emilio before he parked and left his vehicle. They walked up to the door together, Bolan there before them.

"Looks like we're one short," he said, by way of greeting.

Sanchez scowled and shook his head. *"Madre de dios,"* he said, "I was afraid of this."

EMILIO SANCHEZ HAD BEGUN to understand what gringos meant when they made reference to the "hot seat." The heat was real, and all the more uncomfortable because he still felt he had brought a measure of it on himself.

"We recognized the woman right away," he said to Mitchum and Bolan. "She looks better than her pictures, but there was no doubt."

"Marcella Grant," Doyle Mitchum said, not asking, more like he was talking to himself.

"With Obregon," said Sanchez, repeating himself. "Martinez sent her, I suppose, to check us out."

"These shooters," said Bolan, seated on the nearest bed. "You said that there were four of them?"

"Four men inside," the *federale* answered. "More out front, I think. At least, we heard more shooting after Hargis and the woman left that way."

"You got cut off." It did not come out sounding like a question.

"Sí. The *pistolero* who came in the back way had us trapped. I flushed him out and killed him, but by then . . ."

"You don't know where the others went?"

Sanchez shook his head. "We had no chance to plan a meeting. Hargis knew that he should be here, though, if he was able."

The words hung between them, cold and lifeless. If he was able, Hargis should have joined them by now. If he was still alive and capable of acting on his own initiative.

"He may still be all right," said Mitchum. "Hell, for all we know, the woman's taken him to see Martinez."

"I'm not sure I like the sound of that," Bolan said. "This business with the ambush smells."

"To throw away his shooters, though . . ."

"That may have been a fluke. Could be Martinez thought his men were better at their jobs. Then again, he could have picked cheap talent off the street to make it seem more realistic."

"Damn!"

"What happened after, when you got outside?"

"We left in my car," Sanchez told them. "Obregon was shaking like an addict in withdrawal pains. I think he wet himself."

"Tough luck."

"He thinks Ibarra or Martinez tried to have him killed. I did my best to keep him thinking that, in case it helps us later on."

"Good thinking. Can you get in touch with him again, if necessary?"

"*Sí.* He has a small apartment in Piedras Negras. Secret even from Ibarra and Martinez, so he says."

"I hope he's right," Mitchum said. "If Obregon is spooked enough, he just might be the key to busting up Ibarra's network."

"If he stays scared, anyway," Bolan added. "And he has to keep believing that Emilio here's a friend that he can trust."

"I think that I can handle him." The *federale* swallowed hard, prepared to spill the rest of it. "But there is more," he said.

"Okay."

"I tried to reach my captain, to report."

A pained expression twisted Mitchum's face. "Emilio—"

Sanchez raised a hand for silence, forging ahead despite the interruption. "I have known Miguel Calzada long enough to tell you he is not involved with drugs or bribes. I trust him with my life."

"You've done exactly that," Bolan said.

"Not this time," Sanchez countered. "He was not available."

"Which means?"

"Officially he came to work this morning, took a private call and left the office. The police in Ciudad Acuna have his car, discovered in an alley on the outskirts of the city. No one answers at his home."

"You think somebody picked him off?" Bolan asked.

Sanchez shrugged. "If so, we run a deadly risk of being compromised. Calzada personally picked me for this job. He knows the Texas Rangers are involved, although I never told him Hargis's name. If he is questioned, tortured..."

"Christ," Mitchum groaned, "we're screwed."

"Not yet," Bolan said. "Assuming this Calzada spills his guts, it means Ibarra knows there's someone after him, but he could figure that from what's been going down since nine o'clock last night. He's still short names and faces for at least a couple of us."

"Not if Hargis talks," the ex-cop from Miami said. "And, anyway, that's not the half of it."

HE PAUSED before plunging into it. He knew that confession was supposed to be good for the soul, but it was still embarrassing as hell. Doyle Mitchum felt a blush suffuse his cheeks as he described his own misadventure in Piedras Negras, the botanica ambush that ended in death, leaving no doubt that he was expected—and marked for murder—by someone in the squalid border town.

And if he had to make an educated guess as to that "someone's" identity, it would not take a genius to finger Fernando Martinez.

The *palero* had been waiting for him, playing Mitchum like a fish, feeding him line and then reeling him for the kill. Dumb luck and fair reflexes had saved his life, in the final analysis, and you could never count on luck a second time.

"It had to be Montoya, out of Ciudad Acuna," he concluded. "Christ, I should have known that weasel would go running to Martinez the first chance he got. Why settle for two hundred dollars, when he could turn around and sell me for five bills or a grand?"

Bolan sat in silence for a moment, thinking that one over before he spoke. "You had to start somewhere," he said at last. "You took a necessary chance, and here you are. It gives Martinez something else to think about, the fact his stooge screwed up."

"But not by much," said Mitchum, thinking of the blade, its whisper in the musty storeroom, slicing air that could as easily have been his flesh. "I caught a break. You want to know the truth, I don't feel all that lucky anymore."

"We make our own luck," said Bolan. "Now Martinez knows that someone's after him, not just Ibarra. It divides his concentration, makes him wonder if the two things are connected, keeps him thinking overtime to figure out a motive and a name."

"Just what I've always wanted," Mitchum said. "A voodoo psycho breathing down my neck."

"It has to shake him up," Bolan said. "Assuming that Martinez gave the word to take you down, it means he blew it. Now he's got a dead man on his hands and nothing to show for the effort. It has to piss him off."

"That's reassuring," Mitchum groused. "A pissed-off voodoo psycho."

"Pissed-off psychos make mistakes, sometimes. It may be helpful, throwing him off balance."

"Still, there's Hargis."

And that, Mitchum knew, was the problem. The blind spot in their calculations. Hargis was not dead or wounded, necessarily; they could have dealt with that and formulated strategy to take up the slack. The Ranger was a goddamned MIA, and that made all the difference in the world. If he was out of touch but working on his own, some kind of scam to ingratiate himself with Marcella Grant, then any move they made to find him could be lethal, blowing his cover and bringing Martinez down on his back like the wrath of God—or Chango, in this case.

On the flip side, if Hargis was in trouble, every second they delayed increased the likelihood that he would spill his guts and burn them all. Mitchum knew the Ranger well enough to recognize his courage, but he also knew that every man possessed a breaking point. It might be physical, emotional or mental—but there was a point of no return in any full-bore grilling, where the subject lost his grip and gave it up. Some kind of drugs, a certain kind of pain, a threat against his loved ones—something. And once the floodgates were opened, there was no closing them again, short of the grave.

An hour plus, since Hargis and Sanchez walked into the San Carlos ambush, and Mitchum realized it must have gone down right around the same time he was fighting for his life in the botanica. Coincidence? Forget it. Someone—Martinez, Ibarra, or a combination of both—had been shooting for a clean sweep. The fact that he—or they—had only scored one out of three, at best, would leave the hunters smarting, anxious for a re-match.

And if Hargis was in hostile hands, unloading everything he knew, their enemies would be better prepared the next time around.

Mitchum felt stupid and useless, sitting there with his elbows braced on his knees, staring at the faded motel wallpaper and wishing he was back in Miami, Atlanta—anywhere, in fact, except this dusty border town. The plan had been his brainchild, but it was twisting and growing beyond his control now, blossoming into some kind of freakish Frankenstein monster, bent on destroying them all.

He would have liked to take it back and start from scratch, but that was not an option in the real world. Once the cards were dealt, you played your hand and took your chances. Some games—like the present one, for instance—you were not allowed to simply fold and walk away.

Whatever happened to Brock Hargis and the others would be *his* fault, damn it, and the ex-cop from Miami was prepared to live with that fact for the rest of his days...however long that turned out to be. He was not prepared to compound his mistake with any more blunders, however, playing out of his league in a game he no longer understood, where the stakes had graduated from win or lose to life and death.

His mind made up, he turned to face the man from Justice—or whatever the hell he was—hoping he would have some kind of backup plan, a way to salvage something from their present state of chaos.

"So," Doyle Mitchum said, "what now?"

THE PLAN WAS relatively simple... or at least it sounded that way when he ran it down in words. The physical reality was something else, but Bolan did not have to tell these men that they were gambling with their lives. That much was obvious to every person in the room.

The ambush with Marcella Grant still made him nervous, thinking of the several different ways it could have been arranged. He had Sanchez's word about the disappearance of his captain, and assuming it was true, that still did nothing to insure that Sanchez was the honest *federale* he appeared to be.

Still, Bolan thought himself a fairly decent judge of character, whatever that entailed. In some ways, judging men was like appreciating art: the subject might defy description, but he still knew what he liked, and what he trusted, when it came to allies in his private war against the savages. If Sanchez was acting out a role, he had Bolan's vote for the Oscar... and the Executioner would pin the award on him personally, in the form of a marksman's medal. If his anger and concern were genuine, the only problem left would be the information spilled by Hargis or the missing *federale* officer to hostile ears.

It was conceivable, thought Bolan, that the Ranger might be holed up somewhere with Marcella Grant, chasing an unexpected advantage and worming his way closer to Fernando Martinez. Conceivable... but un-likely. The disappearance of Miguel Calzada, on the other hand, was pure bad news. Honest or otherwise, captains in the FJP simply did not vanish from the streets without a presumption of foul play, and Calzada's link with Sanchez was too strong to qualify as a coincidence in Bolan's book. By this time, the missing *federale* would have spilled everything he knew to a team of skilled in-terrogators. They had to assume that Sanchez was com-promised, at least. As for the rest...

No halfway measures were permissible in this kind of action. Their choices were simple: drop out of the game entirely, or press ahead, full-bore. In Bolan's case, the choice was obvious, but he had put it to a vote on behalf of the others.

And they had not let him down.

Sanchez would pursue his contact with Ricardo Ob-regon, playing on the dealer's sense of isolation and betrayal, milking him for information on Ibarra's oper-ation, the connection with Martinez, anything at all that might advance their cause. The methods he employed would be discretionary, just so long as they produced re-sults.

Doyle Mitchum would continue stalking the Martinez cult, taking advantage of his specialized knowledge in the field, but he would stay alert to any risk of capture or assassination while he was about it.

As for Bolan, there was only one course left.

Brock Hargis was beyond his reach, impossible to ap-proach without the risk of blowing his cover, which might, against all odds, still be intact. That left Ibarra's border operations open to attack, and Bolan knew from experience that turning up the heat would force his ad-versary's hand. Depending on the dealer's temperament, he might retreat or launch an all-out counteroffensive, but Bolan would be ready, come what may.

The battle had been joined, and there could be no turning back.

The Executioner was adding fuel to the fire, and it was time to watch his adversaries squirm.

Before they fried.

CHAPTER SEVENTEEN

The office complex in Piedras Negras was one of the newest buildings in town, a model of modern American architecture gone south. Burnished steel and smoked glass, stacked twelve stories high near the center of town. The building would have been a midget in Dallas or Houston, but Piedras Negras was less cosmopolitan, taking its time en route to the twenty-first century.

Bolan had considered a sniper attack, but the neighboring structures were too short to place him above his eleventh-floor target, and the smoked windows would have foiled his aim in any case. On top of that, he had no reason to believe Ramon Ibarra would be in this afternoon, with all the heat he had endured in the past few hours.

More than likely, he had gone to ground for the duration, putting soldiers on the street to do his fighting for him, while he kept an eye on strategy from the rear echelons. A clear shot at Ibarra would have been too much to hope for at the moment, and it would not have precisely suited Bolan's needs at this point.

Instead he had a different plan in mind.

The tailored suit he wore was cut with extra room beneath the left arm for his shoulder holster, and the hardware was invisible as Bolan left his rented car and moved across the parking lot, a briefcase in his hand. He was the very picture of a gringo businessman, in town to strike a bargain with his equals on some matter that could profit all concerned.

No obvious sentries in the lobby, but he saw a TV camera mounted near the elevators, catching Bolan's good side as he waited for the car. He smiled for the birdie, straightening his tie, nothing to put the hidden monitors on their guard.

Bolan had the elevator to himself, canned music all the way, disembarking on eleven with plush carpeting under foot. The suites were numbered consecutively, and he counted off the doors until he found Jalisco Enterprises, halfway down the air-conditioned corridor. Beyond the door was a small reception room, presided over by a secretary in her early twenties, with a face and curves to knock your eyes out, maybe put you in the mood to strike a bargain with the boss.

His eyes took in the office layout swiftly, missing nothing. Beyond the secretary's desk, behind a partition screening open cubicles, electric typewriters clacked away like mechanical jaws. He could not see the executive suite from where he stood, but that was fine. He didn't need to.

"Buenos dias, señor." A thousand-candlepower smile. "Can I help you?"

"Señor Ibarra, please?"

"I'm sorry, sir. Señor Ibarra is not in today. Perhaps, if you would care to speak with his assistant..."

Bolan frowned. "I was really hoping to see Señor Ibarra."

"I'm sorry," she repeated. "As I said..."

"Perhaps I could just leave a message."

The smile flashed again, bright enough to read by in the dark. "Of course, *señor.*"

"All right. Why don't you tell Ramon he's going out of business. Can you do that for me?"

Her smile faltered, fading in the stretch as she tried to decide whether this was some kind of bizarre gringo joke.

"Señor?"

"You heard me right."

As Bolan spoke, he placed his briefcase on the secretary's desk, springing the latches with his thumbs and opening the lid. Inside, two smoke grenades lay close beside a pair of tear-gas canisters. Before the secretary could react, he lifted out the first grenade, yanked the pin, and pitched it high across the partition at her back. The other three followed in swift succession, Bolan changing his angle a bit with each toss to scatter the cans, dropping one in the open hallway and three into separate cubicles.

"Remember," Bolan told the secretary, turning toward the door. "He's out of business, starting now."

Behind him as he left the office, he heard shouts and screams, employees scrambling for the exit, gagging and choking on the fumes that swirled around them. Bolan beat them to the elevator, stepped inside, and watched the doors slide shut before the first escapees overtook him in their clumsy flight.

That left the TV monitors and any kind of audio alarms Ibarra might have had installed. Bolan had one hand inside his jacket, wrapped around the sleek Beretta's pistol grip as the elevator doors slid open, bringing him back to the lobby.

Two shooters dressed as businessmen were moving out to intercept him, and he spotted them at once, their suits unequal to the task of making them appear respectable. He let them take the lead, hands disappearing in a dive for side arms, Bolan there ahead of them with his Beretta as they did their best.

Two shots at close to point-blank range was all it took, and Bolan had a clear path to the street. Behind him, stretched out on the marble floor, Ibarra's shooters lay like crumpled rag dolls in a spreading slick of blood. He could not smell the smoke or tear gas yet, but as he neared the tall glass doors, a smoke alarm began to shrill its warning through the spacious room.

The heat of afternoon was waiting for him on the sidewalk, bringing sweat to Bolan's brow.

He'd left a taste of things to come.

It was Ramon Ibarra's turn to sweat this time.

RICARDO OBREGON was hiding in a small house east of Piedras Negras, surrounded by a plot of arid farmland that had gone back to cacti and sagebrush years ago. No air-conditioning and precious little shade, but it had been the dealer's choice, coming out of the firefight in San Carlos, muddleheaded and still unclear on who had tried to kill him.

Sanchez had been reluctant to leave Obregon on his own, but there had seemed to be no option. He'd been already pressing his schedule for the meeting at the motel with the others, no outsiders invited, and he had to trust Obregon's instincts when the dealer told him where to go. At first, he had suspected that the whole thing might be one colossal setup, luring him off into the desert where he could be questioned and dissected at leisure, but he'd driven the rental with a pistol in his lap and let Ricardo know the first round through the barrel was reserved for him if anything went wrong.

And nothing had.

The "ranch" had been deserted when they got there, safe and silent. He'd left Obregon with specific instructions to keep out of sight and stay off the portable field telephone if he valued his life. The dealer had answered him in monosyllables, some grunts thrown in for punctuation, and Sanchez had taken him at his word, for what that was worth.

Returning to the desert house, Sanchez had a whole new set of risks to keep in mind. Brock Hargis was missing, maybe squealing to the enemy by now. His captain likewise, a more direct threat to his personal well-being. With hindsight, Sanchez thought he should have disabled the field radio, but at the time he had decided it would only spook his pigeon. Obregon was smart enough to recognize a set up when he saw one, but he did not strike the *federale* as an actor.

Obregon was frightened for his life, and no mistake.

The trick was taking hold of that emotion, turning it around and using it against the dealer, making Obregon suspect his friend Ibarra of the hit. It was a logical assumption, all things considered, and Sanchez did not think he would have any trouble selling it, once he let Obregon see his more persuasive side.

He was alert for any sign of treachery as he approached the ranch house, driving slowly, dust plumed out behind him in a smoke screen effect. His pistol was snug in its holster this time, a compact Heckler & Koch MP-5 K submachine gun resting on the seat beside him. The H&K was small enough to fire one-handed if he had to, even though it had a forward pistol grip for greater accuracy with sustained fire. Extra magazines were weighing down his pockets, making the jacket drag on his shoulders and spoiling its lines.

So much for fashion in the rough-and-tumble world of undercover operations.

He wished the others well with their respective tasks, then brought his mind back to the here and now, focus-

ing his full concentration on the silent house. It was a
perfect ambush site, dark windows staring inscrutably
out at the desert, any one of them a potential sniper's
nest. It would have been impossible to hide a car, but
dropping gunners off and driving back to town would
cover that, or they could use a four-wheel drive and park
it down in one of the arroyos that scarred the landscape.
That way, it would take an aerial survey to find them out,
and in the meantime, they could do their dirty work on
any unsuspecting *federale* who came knocking at their
door.

No point in beating it to death. He had a job to do, and
none of them were getting any younger while he sat there,
sweating in the rented car.

Emilio tucked the H&K underneath his jacket, tight
beneath his right arm, with the pistol grip facing forward where he could reach it easily with a cross-hand
draw. It wasn't the best way to go, but he had no swivel
rig available, and he was not about to make the walk between car and house with the weapon exposed. Obregon
would be watching, and if the dealer was still alone, the
hardware would spook him, perhaps put him to flight.

It was a strange sensation, half expecting to be killed
at any moment, dropped between one step and the next.
He could not force his muscles to relax, bunched up as if
some involuntary reflex were trying to make his body
bulletproof by sheer force of will.

He reached the door without incident, knowing he was
still at risk, and knocked with his left hand, leaving the
right arm clasped against his side, holding the stubby
automatic weapon in place. He did not hear the dealer's
footsteps approaching, but suddenly Obregon was there,
opening the door and staring past him, toward the dusty

car, as if expecting a platoon of gunmen to spring from the back seat and trunk.

"You are alone?" asked Obregon.

"Who else?"

He brushed past the dealer, smelling dust and dry rot in the house, a sign that it was rarely used. The smell of coffee took him by surprise. Somehow, he had not pictured Obregon possessing any kitchen skills. The kind of man who would burn water if he tried to boil an egg.

"I'll have a cup," he told the dealer, nodding toward the tiny kitchen. "Then we need to talk."

He sat on a swaybacked couch, pulled the little H&K from under his jacket, and placed it on the cushion beside him. Obregon went wide-eyed at that, taking a long step backward before Sanchez raised his hand and smiled in reassurance.

"For protection, Ricardo. If I wanted you dead, I could pour my own coffee."

Obregon seemed to relax a little at that, but his hands were trembling when he returned with two ceramic mugs, slopping coffee on the floor when he served Sanchez and retreated to a chair across the room.

"What is it that you want from me?" the dealer asked.

"The truth," Emilio said. "Somebody set you up today, along with me. I don't know what the game plan was supposed to be, but I can tell from looking at your face that they went out of bounds. I want it all. Begin at the beginning. Now."

"They said you were..."

"A *federale?*"

"*Sí.*"

"What difference does it make, if I can save your life?"

FERNANDO DE LEON MARTINEZ felt invigorated by the sacrifice. The Texas Ranger had been strong and proud, a worthy adversary, and his soul would do good work for its *palero* master on the other side. Meanwhile the information gained by questioning their captive was invaluable to Martinez on the earthly plane.

The slug called Sanchez had apparently escaped them. Still no word from Obregon, no indication whether he was dead or alive. It occurred to Martinez that he might be in hiding, afraid for his life after the cantina shootout, and he made a mental note to track the dealer down without delay.

The ambush in San Carlos might have been a bit extreme, but it had placed the Texan in their hands for questioning. In retrospect, Martinez thought it would have been a good idea to warn Obregon in advance, but he had been afraid of leaks, some slipup on the dealer's part if he was sitting there, expecting gunplay while he tried to talk business.

Besides, they had the other names now. They could go ahead without Ricardo, if he was among the dead.

And if he had betrayed them somehow, death would be the least of Obregon's concerns.

Martinez thought about the others. One, Doyle Mitchum, was an ex-policeman from Miami, Florida. Dismissed, retired...whatever. It would be a simple thing to make some phone calls, check him out, and find out his credentials. He was here, in Mexico, to find Martinez and his family, destroy them if he could. Some kind of a crusader, with enough connections on both sides of the border to put wheels in motion, not clever enough to watch from the sidelines. He had to involve himself, using his so-called expertise in *santeria* and *palo mayombe* to track his quarry one-on-one. It was a trait that might betray him, in the end.

The other man, this Mike Belasko, was an unknown quantity. They had a rough description, clear enough to match the gunman reported by some of Ibarra's survivors in Ciudad Acuna and Piedras Negras, and the Texan's dying word that this Belasko was supposed to be some kind of federal agent from El Norte.

Bullshit. Martinez knew the gringo *federales*—FBI and DEA, INS and ATF. He had bribed them on occasion, seen them work up close, and he was perfectly familiar with the rules by which they lived. No operations in a foreign land without an invitation and participation by native authorities. No violence, except in self-defense...and even then, the cocky Anglos were notoriously slow. Too slow to save themselves, in many cases.

No. This man Belasko was a different breed. If he was actually responsible for the attacks upon Ibarra, it could only mean...

Martinez caught himself. The CIA? Implausible. From what he knew about the Company, they dealt chiefly with political matters, focusing their spyglasses on the Communist threat wherever it reared its ugly head. More often than not, CIA spooks recruited hardworking, patriotic gangsters to assist them in defeating the Red scourge. It had been true in Italy, in France and Greece, Taiwan and Southeast Asia, in Japan, in Panama and Nicaragua...the list went on and on. At the height of America's war in Vietnam, Company agents helped "loyal" Vietnamese smugglers and right-wing Chinese Triads smuggle heroin into the United States, to help finance the South Vietnamese "democratic" regime. Years later, drug money financed the Contra rebels in Central

America, with blessings from the White House and the CIA.

Small wonder, thought Martinez, that the vaunted "War on Drugs" in the United States had never really moved beyond the skirmish stage. Money talked, regardless of its source, and bullshit walked. It was a kind of testimony to Fernando's faith—in the *orishas,* in himself, in cold, hard cash.

No, this Belasko must be something else, and solving his riddle was part of the challenge. Fernando was racing the clock, but he was not dismayed. He had a plan to draw the others out.

The Texas Ranger had served him well...and he would keep on serving, through eternity, as one of Fernando's spirit slaves. On the earthly plane, there was another task he could perform, revealed to Martinez in a flash of insight so brilliant that it almost struck him dumb.

He found his voice and started giving orders to Marcella, telling her exactly what to do. It would be difficult, but not impossible, and it was clearly worth the risks involved.

If he could pull this off, Martinez would have his enemies right where he wanted them, in the palm of his hand. And he would take his time at crushing them to death by slow degrees.

The better to make them scream.

THE SEX CLUB, situated on the outskirts of Piedras Negras, was an old converted warehouse, skylights painted over with an eye toward privacy, swamp coolers working overtime to beat the desert heat. It was a futile effort, but the patrons seldom noticed, and none had ever voiced a complaint.

What the hell, thought Bolan, as he parked out front. The patrons drove out here and laid their money down to break a sweat. Efficient air-conditioning would probably have spoiled the "atmosphere."

Still early for the show, with only two cars in the parking lot beside his own. The club had no external signs— no neon, posters, floods. No name, in fact. The taxi drivers in Piedras Negras knew exactly where to drop the fares who had a taste for certain hard-core action, and they did not need a map or beacon when it came to finding ready cash.

The door was open, and he let himself inside. A pungent barnyard smell came out to meet him, wrinkling Bolan's nose. In front of him, portable bleachers were arranged in a three-sided box, surrounding an expanse of open floor. Track lighting in the rafters lighted the floor up like a stage, but the bleachers were presently unoccupied.

Bolan moved to his left, around a plain plasterboard partition, following the barnyard smell with the Beretta 93-R in his hand, a heavy satchel slung over his shoulder. Two wooden stalls were lined with straw and occupied by donkeys. Farther down, a German shepherd curled its lip at Bolan, showing teeth behind a screen of chicken wire. No women yet in evidence, but Bolan knew they would be on their way, trucked in from sleazy cribs in Ciudad Acuna or Piedras Negras to complete the set.

Revulsion kept him going, picking up the sound of voices from an office up ahead, beyond the small menagerie. Three figures moved toward him in the shadows, wising up to their danger too late.

"*¿Quien es?*" From the tall one on the left.

"*No se.*"

Bolan showed them the Beretta, gave them time to start their moves before he shot the bookends, slack bodies dropping on either side of the man in the middle. The survivor stood frozen with shock, recovering in time to spread his jacket wide and show that he was unarmed.

"You run this zoo?"

"Sí, señor."

"I've got a message for the boss, *comprende?* For Ramon."

"A message?"

"Simple. Even you can understand it, champ. He's going out of business. Have you got that?"

"Sí."

"Now, hit the road, before I change my mind and leave you here."

The sleaze dealer wasted no time making himself scarce, leaving Bolan alone with the animals. He freed the shepherd first, keeping the wire gate between himself and the dog until it gave up its snarling and broke for the exit. The donkeys were tougher, each requiring a slap on the rump to make them clear their stalls. Bolan walked them to the entrance and herded them outside, letting instinct take over from there.

He set the timer on his satchel charge and left it under the bleachers. There was enough C-4 inside to do a fair amount of damage, even in the open spaces of a warehouse. Five minutes and counting on the digital clock as he jogged back to his waiting car, noting that one of the cars was missing, the red flecks of taillights vanishing back toward town.

He turned the rental's ignition key and set off in pursuit, passing two slow-walking donkeys en route.

Behind him, as he reached the outskirts of Piedras Negras, a fiery mushroom blossomed on the dark horizon.

"Gotcha."

CHAPTER EIGHTEEN

Doyle Mitchum had misgivings as he hit the street again that night. His close brush with death in the botanica had set his nerves on edge, reminding him that he was an American ex-cop on Mexican soil, without jurisdiction or authority of any kind. If he was killed, the case would rate no more than cursory examination by the *federales,* possibly by a protest to the State Department. Meanwhile, there was the threat of the local law connecting him with the death of his assailant.

Mitchum put the thought out of mind, refusing to contemplate the possibility of arrest, much less conviction and trial on a homicide charge. It was a whole different ball game south of the border, without the laundry list of civil rights that put so many American felons back on the street time after time.

In Mexico they locked you up and threw away the key, or stood you up before a firing squad.

The radio news was in Spanish, but that made no difference to Mitchum. He listened carefully as he circled downtown Piedras Negras, wrapping up his list of potential contact points. So far, there was no mention of a fatal shooting on the airwaves, and he wondered if the local cops were holding back the news for reasons of their own, perhaps to bait a trap.

A new possibility occurred to Mitchum. If his enemies were anxious enough to snare him, they might have followed up on the shooting themselves, disposed of the body without a report to police. Such things happened in Miami, and it certainly was not beyond the realm of possibility that it could happen in Piedras Negras, where a fair percentage of the law was bought and paid for with drug money.

The lull could work to his advantage, even so. Without police involvement, he would only have to watch his back for one set of enemies . . . or was it two?

He had no way of knowing whether Martinez and company were acting under direct orders from Ramon Ibarra or flying on their own, but he was taking no chances. He would have to keep both eyes open, just like the old days in Little Havana, prepared to respond with force to any challenge from his enemies.

The last botanica on Mitchum's list was a hole-in-the-wall several blocks from downtown, low-wattage bulbs pooling shadows in the corners as he entered, a brass bell jangling overhead. The proprietor was chunky, bearded, long hair tied back in a careless ponytail. He did not seem suspicious of the gringo entering his shop. If anything, the smile he offered Mitchum was relaxed, the next best thing to friendly.

They danced around the questions for a while, Mitchum starting with generalities and working up to the jackpot. He expected the proprietor to shine him on, perhaps plead ignorance, but the reverse was true. No sooner had he dropped Fernando's name than the longhair began to nod, a small, thoughtful frown on his face.

"I know this man," he said. "Know *of* him, I should say."

"If there's a chance that I could get in touch with him . . ."

"Such things are possible, *señor*. Unfortunately, I do not know where he lives."

"If it's a matter of *dinero* . . ."

"No, *señor*." The smile was back, ingratiating. "There is someone who can help you, I believe, but you will have to ask him for yourself."

"Of course. Where do I find him."

Curt, concise directions to a new apartment complex on the edge of town. Mitchum listened and memorized, relying on his brain instead of written notes. When he had it down pat, he thanked the man and left a twenty on the counter by the register.

Outside, he walked back toward his car, repeating the directions to himself once more for insurance. He had the ignition key in his hand when someone gripped his arm from behind, tightening a painful grip around his biceps. At the same instant, Mitchum felt the hard, unmistakable thrust of a gun's muzzle against his spine.

"No rush, *señor*," a gruff voice told him, almost whispering. "We take a ride together, *sí?*"

The odds were lousy, but he had to try it. He stepped backward, twisting on the axis of his body, driving with his elbow. The gunner anticipated his move, and the pistol drove into his lower back, setting off an explosion of pain from his kidney.

Mitchum felt his legs folding, knew he was about to fall, but he would not give up. His left hand whipped the jacket back, an awkward move, but he was almost to the pistol in its shoulder rigging when a second gunner caught his arm and held it fast.

He never saw the blackjack that swung against his skull, impacting on a point behind his ear, and then the lights went out.

THE SNATCH HAD GONE like clockwork, smooth enough that Marcella Grant was impressed with herself. Of

course, the plan had been Fernando's, but she had re-
fined it to suit herself, telling the gunmen to wait for their
mark outside the botanica, rather than charging in after
him and trashing the shop. It was cleaner that way, a relatively simple pickup with no affront to the shopkeeper
who was already helping them under duress, and now
they had their man in custody.

The alternative had been a long stalk, trailing Mitchum to the phony address he received from the proprietor
of the botanica, but there was too much risk that he
would spot a tail and break away. The second attempt on
his life had already failed that afternoon, and if they
fumbled with the new approach, she was prepared to
write him off. No man with half a brain would keep on
coming back for more, when all the odds were clearly
stacked against him.

There had been a risk that he had split already, given
up the game after his near miss in the afternoon, but
Fernando had judged the man correctly, as one who
hated giving up. At least one more attempt to do the job,
another chance for them to bag him.

She thought about Gregorio Ruiz, still trying to re-
deem himself by tracking down Ricardo Obregon and the
elusive *federale*. She might have felt some pity for Ruiz,
if he had not been such a pushy, jealous little prick.

The emphasis on "little," she recalled, from one time
when she walked into the bedroom unexpectedly and
found Ruiz servicing Fernando. Ruiz had scrambled for
the covers, flushing brilliant crimson with embarrassment, Fernando's laughter making him feel smaller than
he was already.

He would never lash out at Fernando, though. Who
would? Marcella had become his mortal enemy that day,
humiliation heaped on top of jealousy and envy, turning

Ruiz from a kind of petty snob into a devious, backbiting opponent. Neither one of them had bored Fernando with the details, though he had to recognize the tension between them. If anything, Marcella believed Fernando thrived on it, enjoying the sideshow as they tried to take each other down a peg at every given opportunity.

Before she learned the magic, came to need it in her life, Marcella Grant would never have tolerated such a bizarre, unhealthy relationship. She put up with it now because anything less meant losing Fernando, and that was as good as losing her life, her very soul. She could put up with Ruiz for as long as she had to, as long as Fernando needed him...but there was no rule against her enjoying her latest triumph at Gregorio's expense.

If anything, Ruiz was contributing to his own downfall with temper tantrums that destroyed his concentration, leaving him open to all manner of grievous mistakes. He was working overtime to correct one such mistake at the moment, and Marcella knew that he'd better not fail.

Fernando's anger had been real enough on learning that the *federale* Sanchez had escaped, Ricardo Obregon vanished without a trace in the confusion of the San Carlos ambush. A cunning ploy to divide and conquer had gone wrong on Gregorio's end of the game, and he had lost the enemy, along with his own player. Fernando had been angry enough to bar Ruiz from their ceremony with the Texas Ranger, an unprecedented step in Marcella's experience, and she had no doubt there would be a more severe penalty for continued failure.

She found part of herself hoping Gregorio would fail, that he would be removed once and for all from her life. It would amuse her, seeing Ruiz on the sacrificial altar, though she had no personal desire to taste his blood. She would leave that dubious pleasure to Fernando, since the two of them were fond of tasting each other.

Marcella caught herself turning bitchy and nipped it in the bud. Leading the snatch car back to Fernando's desert hideaway, she had every reason to be happy, well pleased with herself. Gregorio Ruiz made his own bad luck. All she had to do was stand back and wait for the little sissy to hang himself.

The way things were going, Marcella thought that she would not have long to wait.

Doyle Mitchum, this tired-looking ex-cop from Miami, could be the key to vanquishing their enemies. Fernando was disturbed by recent events, though he tried not to let it show. Misgivings were a sign of weakness in Fernando's mind, and he maintained a stone face for the world at large, but Marcella had learned to look behind the mask, find out what he was really thinking underneath.

He was not frightened yet—she wasn't absolutely sure that anything could scare Fernando—but he was concerned about their losses, not to mention how Ramon Ibarra might react if things kept going badly for the team. Ibarra relied on Fernando's magic for protection, a large percentage of his personal success, but he was somewhat unpredictable, a wild man when his fury took control of logical thought processes, propelling him toward violent, irrevocable action.

Marcella hoped it would not come to that. The family was small just now—perhaps a dozen guns if you removed Ibarra's soldiers—and she was not certain that Fernando's magic could prevail against an army if it came to war.

The doubt made her feel guilty, and she offered up a silent prayer of contrition to the *orishas*. By the time she saw the ranch ahead, she was already feeling better.

She had done her job. Fernando would be pleased. Tonight, in bed, he might reward her in the way that she enjoyed.

Until then, she was doing everything she could to help the family.

It was the most that anyone could ask.

THE ARGUMENT had taken something out of Sanchez. He had calculated different ways of conning Obregon at first, then finally decided that the truth, or at least a modification of it, would serve him better in the long run. Some judicious editing, and he had laid it out for Obregon in no uncertain terms.

As Sanchez ran it down, the dealer had a choice: He could cooperate, spill everything he knew about Ibarra's operation in a timely move to save himself, or he could cool his heels in jail while Sanchez spread the word that he was talking to the *federales*. By the time they had to cut him loose—if he was still alive—it would be much too late for patching up relations with Ibarra and his gang.

The shocker was that Obregon did not appear surprised when Sanchez dropped his mask and finally admitted his affiliation with the FJP. In fact, according to the dealer, he had been the target going into the fiasco at San Carlos. The surprise, for Obregon, had been four men with guns appearing out of nowhere, laying down a screen of automatic fire. He had been told to look for a diversion, but the dealer had not counted on machine guns in his face. He had begun to think Ramon considered him expendable, and that meant he was finished on the border. There could be no going back, not now, when he had wasted this much time without reporting back. Ibarra would assume that he was dead or switching sides, and either way, it came back to the grave.

Leaving the desert safehouse, driving back toward his next scheduled meeting with Mitchum and Belasko, Sanchez ran the details of their conversation through his mind. A search for clues, anything at all to help unravel the mystery of the Texas Ranger's disappearance, but the leads were all too vague to be of any use.

For starters, Obregon had been approached by Fernando Martinez, rather than Ibarra. Martinez did the talking, running down his plan to snare the *federale* and his gringo sidekick at San Carlos. Marcella Grant would accompany Obregon to the meeting, a more or less silent observer for Martinez and company. When the diversion split them up, Marcella would handle the gringo, while Obregon was supposed to drop the net on Sanchez.

But Martinez had not mentioned bullets flying, broken bodies on the floor, a gunman shrieking with his clothes in flames. Ricardo Obregon had visualized a bogus fire alarm, perhaps a raid by local lawmen who were bought and paid for. He had seen men die before, had been a target on occasion, but he felt Martinez had betrayed him with deliberate silence, leaving Obregon to fend for himself against anonymous assassins. If the guns had cut him down, Ricardo thought, Martinez would have shrugged it off and tried some other ploy the next time out.

So he would talk, but as it happened, there was little he could share with Sanchez that was any help. Before the meeting in San Carlos, he had barely spoken to Marcella Grant, and Obregon had no idea where she would take a captive if she had one. Likewise, while he knew Fer-

nando de Leon Martinez on the basis of his reputation
and by sight, Ricardo could not say where the *palero*
might be found at any given time. Such questions were
unhealthy in Coahuila, and a dealer who intended to keep
breathing—much less stay in business with Ibarra—did
not ask.

Sanchez finally made do with information on Ibarra,
scheduled shipments for the next two weeks, the kind of
leads that he could use to turn the heat up if their search
for Hargis came to nothing. On the side, he tried to tell
himself that there was still a chance the Ranger might be
safe and sound, but logic told him it was wishful thinking. They had walked into a trap at the cantina in San
Carlos, and Sanchez was alive because the man assigned
to snatch him had been taken off guard and frightened by
the violence of Fernando's diversion. Pure dumb luck
had saved his life, and he would have to work for everything he got from that point on.

Obregon had insisted on remaining at his private safehouse, and Sanchez could offer no serious argument for
moving. With Miguel Calzada missing and presumed
dead, the *federale* did not know which of his brother officers to trust, and delivering Obregon to the FJP for
protective custody was the same thing as signing his death
warrant. Ricardo might survive a day or two in jail, if he
was very lucky, but the long-term prospects were grim
indeed. More to the point, Obregon knew the odds
against him and preferred to take his chances in the desert, where at least he could see the killers coming and
decide if he should fight or flee.

Sanchez felt embarrassed, coming back to another
meeting with Mitchum and Belasko almost empty-
handed. Even his new information on Ibarra would not

help them find Brock Hargis or the blonde who had lured him to almost certain death.

But his self-recriminations were a foolish waste of time. The circumstances in San Carlos had prevented Sanchez from sticking with Hargis, and the chances were that they would both be dead now if they *had* remained together. It was strange, the way he missed Brock Hargis now, as if they were the best of friends before San Carlos.

The toll bridge on the Rio Grande slowed him down, but Sanchez had ten minutes to spare as he rolled into Eagle Pass, taking several extra turns and checking for a tail along the way.

He would present his information in as straightforward a manner as possible, leaving Mitchum and the gringo *federale* to decide how it would best be used. The others did not blame him for San Carlos, and he should not blame himself.

He concentrated on the street signs and his rearview mirror, moving toward the rendezvous and hoping there was no grim news in store.

HIS LAST HIT, on the outskirts of Piedras Negras, turned into a running firefight, a carload of gunmen surprising Bolan and reminding him that it was possible to push your luck too far. It was supposed to be a simple tag, one of Ibarra's street dealers down for the count, a couple of his watchdogs wasted in the process, and there seemed to be no problem with the first stage of the action.

Not until he tried to disengage.

The dealer—one Silvero Costa—operated from the back room of a strip joint in the downtown red-light district, sometimes hanging out from dusk to dawn if there were customers around to make it worth his time. Two shooters for support, the kind of no-name, no-neck button men who served as cannon fodder for the syndicates, regardless of their race or nationality. Gorillas long on muscle, short on brains.

The hit was streamlined, nearly perfect. Three for three, and only one of Costa's gunners got off a wild shot before he hit the floor. The Executioner was pulling back, had reached the street in fact, before he realized he had a problem.

Spotters, four of them emerging from a black sedan across the street and shouting at him, showing hardware, two more staying with the car. His own wheels one block down and well beyond his reach, considering the circumstances. Even if he beat them to the car, he stood a chance of taking hits before he got the vehicle in motion, and a spray of bullet holes would stop him short at Customs, when he tried to cross the Rio Grande.

A choice, then. Bolan made it on the move, a sharp left turn into the nearest alley, running for his life until he reached a rusty garbage receptacle. He crouched in its shadow, the Beretta ready in his hand and set for 3-round automatic bursts. Bracing the weapon in a firm two-handed grip, he waited, sighting down the slide toward neon afterglow.

Two figures came into view a heartbeat later, but he held off.

Two more gunners were close behind them, fanning out and moving forward when they saw no target in the alley. Bolan let them close the gap to fifteen yards before he stroked the 93-R's trigger twice. Six rounds away and two men down, the others flattening themselves before he had a chance to clear the board. Then he was up and running with the echoes still reverberating from the walls on either side, no wasted time to let his adversaries catch their breath or get their bearings.

Bolan reached the far end of the alley, made a right, and heard a pistol crack behind him. Impact on the nearest wall, a whine and puff of brick dust in the night. He kept on running, loping strides, calculating the Beretta's load.

He had expended eleven rounds altogether, with another ten remaining in the magazine. No need to ditch it yet, and he had two more in reserve. Enough to do the job, unless he got himself pinned down, or blundered into reinforcements he had not discovered yet.

The black sedan was there ahead of him, squealing into the side street with high beams in his eyes, a muzzle-flash winking at him from the passenger's side. Bolan hit a fighting crouch and squeezed off three quick bursts, rewarded with a sound of crashing glass, the hit car swerving with a dead man at the wheel. It struck a hydrant, sheared the fireplug off, and settled with its grille against the front door of a pawnshop, water shooting thirty feet into the air.

Bolan reloaded on the run, watching over his shoulder for any sign of life from the car, or his pursuers from the alley. There they were, a moment of surprise as they beheld the ruin of their crew wagon, then they broke after Bolan in an angry rush. No pedestrians between them to impede a shot, and one of them fired two quick rounds that missed him by a yard.

It would be now or never.

He swiveled in his tracks and triggered two more bursts at something close to twenty yards. The gunners seemed to stumble, jostling one another in an awkward little dance before they fell, all tangled arms and legs, their hardware clattering across the pavement, out of reach.

A little crowd of rubberneckers started to assemble as he put his piece away and merged with foot traffic on the main drag, working back to his car and rolling out of there with all deliberate speed. Police were nowhere in evidence, as if they had been warned to stay away.

He let himself unwind on the drive back to Eagle Pass, wondering if the others would be there ahead of him. There was a lesson to be learned from cutting it too fine, but Bolan had been living on the edge for years. He felt at home there, knowing that every step he took was a potential life-or-death decision.

Status quo in the hellgrounds.

Sanchez was there ahead of him, sitting in his car when Bolan pulled in and parked directly opposite the rented room. Something wrong here, he could feel it, but the warrior took it slow, scanning the lot for another ambush, finding none.

The *federale* met him on the sidewalk. "Mitchum's car," he said, jerking a thumb over his shoulder toward another dusty rental, "but there's no one in the room. I didn't have a key."

Bolan turned toward the third car in line, approaching it cautiously, peering through the driver's window at a parcel on the seat. Wrapped in newsprint, something dark and greasy leaking through.

He tried the door, convinced that there would be no trip wire, nothing in the way of booby traps. He used fingertips to peel the newsprint back and stood aside to let Sanchez check out the calling card.

A human heart, or part of one. The rough wounds looked like teeth marks, maybe human.

Pinned to the sad piece of gristle, a star-shaped badge, the kind that you could buy at any dime store in the Lone Star State. The cheap engraving was smeared with blood, but still legible.

It read: Texas Rangers.

CHAPTER NINETEEN

The plan was simple, vintage Bolan with a Latin twist. Once they had cleared the Eagle Pass motel, ten minutes' driving time guaranteed they had no tails. It only took a moment of discussion to agree.

Brock Hargis and Doyle Mitchum were missing, at least one of them dead.

Emilio's captain vanished, likewise.

Presumably there had been someone with the Rangers they could trust, but Bolan did not have the name, and he was not inclined to ask for help at this stage of the game. Too many plays had blown up in his face already, and he knew that it was time to take the gloves off, hitting back with everything they had.

Sanchez had secured fresh information from the nervous dealer he had tucked away, and they could use it now to launch a new offensive. If they took the dimestore badge to mean that it was Hargis who had died, his heart wrapped up in Mitchum's car, then there was still an outside chance of getting back the ex-cop from Miami. Slim, perhaps, but failing that, the sole alternative was blitzing on until they scored a lethal blow or died in the attempt.

No objection from Sanchez as he laid out the plan, and Bolan read the *federale*'s new determination in the hard line of his frown. It might have gone against the grain for Emilio, but he was playing by a whole new set of rules.

They drove both cars across the toll bridge into Mexico, dropping one at an all-night garage in Piedras Negras, paying extra for security. Riding together in Bolan's car, they made straight for the first target on Obregon's list. It was a small upholstery shop that catered to the tourist trade, specializing in leather seat covers, and more than a few of the cars went home with kilos of cocaine or heroin tucked between the springs. A new delivery of Colombian flake was scheduled for this evening, and Bolan was relieved to see lights burning in the shop when he pulled up across the street.

"You take the back," he said to Sanchez, checking the load on his mini-Uzi before he slipped the weapon underneath his jacket. Sanchez had an H&K MP-5 K, with extra clips protruding from his pockets, and he answered Bolan with a smile as grim as death.

He gave the *federale* sixty seconds to complete his run, before he crossed the street and moved directly to the front door of the shop with long, determined strides. If anyone was pulling lookout duty, they could use some lessons on alertness. There was no alarm as Bolan reached the door, reared back and hit it with a solid kick beside the knob.

His first kick did the job, and Bolan lunged across the threshold, leading with the Uzi as he swept through a reception area that smelled of dust and cigarettes. A side door stood open, granting access to the shop itself, and startled voices told him that his entry had not gone unnoticed.

A gorilla with an automatic in his hand beat Bolan to the doorway, bringing up his gun too late. A burst of parabellum manglers ripped across his chest and punched him backward, sprawling on the concrete floor among dusty-looking scraps of leather. The Executioner went through the door behind his first kill, counting heads and coming up with five around a folding table, gunners scattering and leaving plastic bags of crystal powder where they lay. Stacked up beside the product, green backs were bundled up for easy transport, a briefcase standing open, waiting to receive them.

A sprinter on his right was nearest to the exit, running hard. One hand was outstretched toward the knob when Bolan caught him with a burst between the shoulder blades and helped him get there, the impact carrying his weight across the gap and slamming him face-first against the door. He left streaks of crimson on the wood as he folded, slumping to the ground.

Wild pistol fire came back at Bolan, and he hit a flying shoulder roll, came up firing in a crouch some fifteen feet from his original position. Two gunners, surprised by the move, went down in a heap as he stitched them with the Uzi, left to right and back again to make it stick.

The back door toppled off its hinges as Sanchez charged through and fired from the hip. He caught one of the two survivors swiveling to meet him, shotgun raised, and cut his man off at the knees. The gunner fell across Emilio's line of fire, the parabellum rounds ripping through him, rolling him across the floor.

They had agreed to leave one man alive, if possible, and number five made it easy, cowering on his knees beside a vintage sports car minus seats, empty hands held high above his head. Tears were streaming down his face, and he babbled in rapid-fire Spanish until Sanchez slapped him with an open hand, rocking him back on his haunches.

Bolan didn't need a translator to understand the message. They had rehearsed it in advance, and Sanchez stuck to the script.

He had a warning for Ibarra. If the dealer wanted to survive the night, he should prevail upon Martinez and his cronies to release Doyle Mitchum. Failing that, they wanted an address for the *palero* and his family of ghouls. The terms were nonnegotiable, and time was running out.

Sanchez made the weasel repeat it, nodding when the recitation satisfied. In parting, Bolan filled the briefcase up with cash and dropped one of his incendiary sticks among the bags of cocaine, herding their reluctant messenger outside before it sizzled into life.

One down, and Bolan wondered to himself how many it would take before they got an answer, one way or the other.

He could only keep his fingers crossed for Mitchum's sake, but they were running in the fast lane either way, their destination Sudden Death.

IBARRA LISTENED to the telephone ring seven times before a gruff voice answered.

"*¿Sí?*"

"Martinez. Now."

"*¿Quien es?*"

"How many people have this number, idiot?"

There was a scraping sound on the line as Fernando's flunky laid the receiver down on some flat surface and the spiral phone cord tried to reel it in. Ibarra waited thirty seconds, forty, going on a minute when a voice he recognized came on the line.

"*Ola*, Ramon."

Ibarra bit his tongue to keep from shouting curses into the receiver. Damn Martinez for his flippant, cocksure attitude.

"I have been waiting for some news, Fernando."

"As have I, Ramon. You know about the Texan and the gringo from Miami."

"Yes."

"I left a calling card for his companions."

"So? Where are they now?"

"Ramon—"

"I'll *tell* you where they are, Fernando! Half an hour ago, they burned up my upholstery shop in Piedras Negras, killed six men, and torched almost a million dollar's worth of product from Colombia. They left a message with the foreman of the shop, Fernando. Shall I tell you what it was?"

"I'm listening."

"They told me I was out of fucking business! Do you hear that? *I've* been hearing it since last night, when this shit began."

"Ramon—"

"*Silencio!* I haven't finished yet. Ten minutes after the upholstery shop, they hit another tavern where I have an interest. Two men dead, another fire that ruined most of the cantina. And the message. I am out of business. *Now,* Fernando. Speak to me."

"I'm doing everything I can, Ramon."

"It obviously isn't good enough."

"What more—"

"You have this gringo from Miami?"

"Yes."

"And he is still alive?"

"Of course."

"Then make him tell you where they hide. Use the police, if necessary. Do your job, Fernando, or by God—"

"I do not fear your god, Ramon."

"It won't be God you need to fear, I promise you. These gringos think that they can put me out of business, eh? I promise you, Fernando, if it comes to that, I won't be going down alone. You understand me?"

"Perfectly." The cocksure tone erased at last.

"So do your job, or be prepared to pay the price!"

He slammed the telephone receiver down, heart pounding in his chest. It was the first time he really pulled rank on Martinez, threatening to punish him if he did not perform. Of course, there had been no cause in the past, but that in no way excused the proportions of the trouble facing them now.

Ibarra knew, as did Fernando, that a single punishment would fit the crime of failure in a case like this. That punishment was death, and for a moment, standing in his den, Ibarra wondered whether it was even possible to kill the young *palero*. Did he not boast that his magic made him bulletproof?

We'll see, Ibarra thought. If he should fail this time, we'll see.

And if it came to that, Ramon would rip the heart out of Fernando's chest, bare-handed.

The way he felt right now, it sounded like a fine idea.

EMILIO SANCHEZ had begun to get the feel of fighting back without the restraints imposed by laws or regulations governing the conduct of the FJP. Although such rules were relatively slack in Mexico, compared to the United States, there had been times when Sanchez longed to throw the book away and move against the dealers who

had smeared his badge with the presumption of dis-
honor.

It was a whole new way of dealing with the *narco-
trafficantes,* and he liked how it made him feel about
himself. No sucking up to killers, working with his eyes
closed to the obvious or turning his back when the heavy
hitters rolled past in their armored, air-conditioned limousines.

He liked the feel of kicking ass, and if it had a price tag
on the other end, Emilio Sanchez was prepared to pay.

They did not talk about Belasko's role in law enforcement, what the gringos would have called his "job description." There was no point prying into matters that
did not concern Emilio at the moment.

He was focused on the task at hand, and that included
coming out the other side alive, if possible.

If he wouldn't succeed, he would know that he had
made his mark.

Their current target was a person, rather than a place.
His name was Jaime Franco, and he worked the dog track
on the eastern outskirts of Piedras Negras, dealing drugs
and other contraband to players from his car. He was a
fixture at the track, ignored by the police and uniformed
security because he paid dues to Ramon Ibarra and received a promise of protection in return.

Another link in the unholy chain.

Jaime Franco had never been hassled within living
memory, but he traveled with muscle just the same. It was
part of the show, a driver who packed heat beneath his
arm and looked as if he could tear a phone book into
strips if he was so inclined. The customers expected
something of the sort, to heighten their excitement, add
an element of danger, and the driver let them have their

money's worth, all scowls and sneers, sunglasses after
dark, a long scar twisting down the left side of his face.

A pet gorilla, waiting for the chance to strut his stuff.

They went for the direct approach, no wasted time or
motion, moving toward the vintage Continental in lock-
step, Sanchez on the left, his eyes fixed on the hulking
driver in his shiny suit. The man looked like a caricature
from the movie *Scarface,* but that did not mean that he
was clumsy, much less harmless.

Belasko put the ball in play, a smooth draw with the
black Beretta that he carried, bulky-looking with its custom silencer attached. The driver saw it coming, made his
choice and tried to beat the odds. A sucker play.

The target had his left hand raised, held up before his
face in imitation of a shield, while going for his hardware with the right. If he was counting on the hand to
stop a parabellum round, his disappointment was immediate and terminal. The bullet pierced his hand dead
center, boring through the other side to drill a hole beneath one eye. The driver's head snapped back, a tiny
gasp escaping from his throat as crimson geysered from
the blowhole in his face. He made no further sound, as
he collapsed like so much dirty laundry on the Continental's bench seat.

Jaime Franco thought about resisting, for perhaps a
second and half. It may have been the streaks of fresh
blood dripping from the Lincoln's windshield that decided matters for him, or it could have been pure common sense. Whatever, he had both hands raised and
empty when Belasko slid inside the car to join him, Sanchez standing guard outside, eavesdropping on their
conversation.

"Would you like to see the sun come up tomorrow?"

"*Sí, señor.*"

"Try English."

"Yes."

"I've got a deal to offer you. Your life for ten or fifteen minutes of your time."

"Go on."

"I have a message for Ramon Ibarra."

"Ah."

"You let him know what happened to your buddy here. What could have happened just as easily to you. It's his turn coming up, unless he gives back what he stole tonight. You got that?"

"*Sí.* I mean, yes, sir."

"So, live."

Belasko climbed out, and the two of them retreated while a shaken Jaime Franco shoved and shouldered his deceased gorilla off the driver's seat, crowding in beside a corpse and firing up the Lincoln. Never mind that he was sitting in the driver's blood and staring through a windshield streaked with crimson as he drove away.

Another blow against Ibarra's armor, making Sanchez wonder if they even had a shot at getting Mitchum back alive.

Belasko responded to the question with a frown and shrug. "We'll do our best," he said. "We blow it, someone has to answer, all the same."

Sanchez was counting on it as they left the racetrack.

Someone had to answer for it, either way.

THE PAIN HAD FADED, over time, until it only bothered Mitchum when he made a move. He reckoned that his testicles would ache for several days, if he should last that long, but the horrendous, jolting agony of the electrodes had receded to the level of a nauseating memory. The rest of it was mostly superficial cuts and bruises, coupled with a pounding headache that would doubtless take some time to dissipate.

At that, thought Mitchum, he was lucky just to be alive. If he had been a stronger man, held out a little longer prior to breaking, they would probably have killed him. Not that he was safe, by any means, but life was hope. While he survived, there was a chance—however slim—to break away.

If only he could shake the guilt that gnawed his conscience like a hungry rodent.

Spilling to Fernandez was the furthest thing from Mitchum's mind when he was captured, but experience had taught him that every man had a breaking point. Some died before they talked, but that was more dumb luck or pure coincidence than inner strength. In Mitchum's case, the assholes asking questions had been careful, knew what they were dong, and he spilled.

In fairness to himself, Mitchum had revealed as little as possible, but anything was too much in the kind of game Ibarra played. A single name or address was enough to get a good man killed, the same way Mitchum had seen more than one important witness snuffed when he was working Metro-Dade.

The good news, first. Martinez knew Emilio Sanchez going in, and there was little Mitchum could append to the *palero*'s stock of information. Mike Belasko's name was known, but the Brognola team was so hush-hush that Mitchum knew his adversary would require top-secret clearance and computer codes on par with those the CIA maintained at Langley to unearth substantial background on the guy. No address for Belasko or the *federale* in the past few days, no place Martinez could prepare a trap.

The bad news, now. With the electrodes ringing Mitchum's chimes, he had disclosed the time and place of their next scheduled meeting. A death warrant for both men, if Martinez had the wherewithal to mount a sweep in Eagle Pass and make it stick.

Goddamn it!

Early in his stint with Metro-Dade, Doyle Mitchum had begun unloading the superfluous baggage of guilt most people lug around as standard equipment, learning that a cop assigned to narco is required to deal with scum on a regular basis, cutting unsavory deals from time to time. Reality had hardened him against the "normal" feelings working stiffs were heir to, but betrayal of his working comrades was another story altogether.

Sanchez and Belasko might be dead already, but the ex-cop from Miami would not let it go at that. If he could only reach Martinez, get his hands around the slick *palero*'s throat, he thought that he could do the job before they dragged him off or put a bullet in his brain.

It wasn't all that hard to kill a man if you knew how, and Mitchum did not buy Fernando's rap about invincibility bestowed by the *orishas*. Given half a chance, he knew exactly what he had to do.

A sound of footsteps in the corridor outside his door, a key turned in the lock, and one of Fernando's gunners entered first, covering Mitchum as Martinez stepped into the room. Another *pistolero* stood behind him, making it a perfect set.

"I hope you're feeling well," Martinez told him, with a mocking tone.

"Not bad. You want to go a few quick rounds?"

"Regrettably, we don't have time. We're leaving now. You will be coming with us to a safer place."

"Like hell. Don't hold your breath, *compadre*."

"I won't have to, Mr. Mitchum. You mistake my words for a request. In fact, you have no choice."

Two pistols stared back at Mitchum, with their muzzles like a pair of lifeless eyes. Martinez took no chances, relieving one gorilla of his piece and standing back while the shooter approached Mitchum, palming a set of shiny new handcuffs.

"You know the drill, I think."

"I've seen it done."

Mitchum rose from his cot, refusing to grimace at the flare of pain from his groin, turning his back to the gunner and waiting while the cuffs were tightened on his wrists. Handcuffs meant they needed him alive, at least for now, and that meant he could still expect another shot at the *palero* somewhere down the line.

"You want to tell me where we're going?" Mitchum asked.

"Would it serve any purpose?"

"Not offhand."

Martinez thought about it for a moment, smiling to himself. "Ah well, since you cannot communicate with your confederates . . . let's say we're taking a vacation in the mountains, and we'll let it go at that."

Communicate with his confederates?

That meant that Sanchez or Belasko—maybe both men, from the sound of things—were still alive! Martinez had not tagged them at the meet in Eagle Pass, and he was running now. A turnaround.

Mitchum smiled, the first time he had felt a surge of hope in days.

"I always liked vacations," he informed Martinez. "Shall we go?"

CHAPTER TWENTY

Ramon Ibarra's stronghold was a walled estate within the most exclusive section of Piedras Negras. Well removed from downtown's seedy sprawl, the neighborhood was clean and quiet, well patrolled by the police, secure against the kind of tourist-related disturbances that marked the standard border trade. Few of the homes were as stately as Ibarra's or surrounded by an equal tract of wooded ground, but all of them were well maintained, suggesting affluence beyond the grasp or wildest dreams of most Mexican nationals.

It was past midnight as the Executioner and Sanchez made their drive-by, checking out the neighborhood and noting guards on the perimeter of Ibarra's estate. They drove around the block and found an alleyway designed for trash collectors, so the upper class would not be forced to leave their trash cans on the street. As Bolan parked the car and shut the engine off, Sanchez had the MP-5 in his lap, already flicking off the safety, double-checking to make sure he had a live round in the firing chamber.

"Twenty, thirty men, you said."

"According to Ricardo, *sí.*"

Brognola had confirmed the dealer's address, but the information on his hardforce came entirely from Ricardo Obregon. The man had expressed misgivings, when it came to helping Sanchez mount a raid against *el jefe,* but he also seemed to recognize the fact that he would

have no chance whatsoever unless Ibarra was eliminated. It was all a gamble, strong odds favoring the
house, but Obregon had no alternative, unless he chose
to throw himself upon Ibarra's mercy.

And the dealer *had* no mercy.

"We'll go in through the back," said Bolan, scoping
out the long brick wall from where he sat. He made it
roughly seven feet in height, with razor wire along the
top, but every fortress had a weakness, if you just looked
long and hard enough.

In this case, Bolan's search was neither long nor hard.

Inside the wall, a giant oak stood tall and proud, thick
branches reaching out across the razor wire to cast deep
shadows in the alley. Wiser soldiers would have pruned
back the overhanging branches, but someone had allowed the tree to spread as nature planned. For beauty's
sake, perhaps, or maybe simple negligence, but it would
work to Bolan's benefit in either case.

"We'll have to scout for dogs and sentries," Bolan
said. "I don't want to be dropping in on hungry Dober-
mans."

Beside him, Sanchez smiled, the first time Bolan could
remember anything other than a frown or blank expression on his face. The *federale* played it close, but he was
coming around, as if their strikes against Ibarra had been
therapeutic, bringing Sanchez out of his shell.

"You have the rope?" he asked.

"Enough for this," said Bolan. "If that branch plays
out as sturdy as it looks, we're in."

He did not bother spelling out the grim alternative. A
case of dry rot, anything at all, and they could write off
their handy means of access. The noise alone would
probably draw any sentries from a radius of thirty yards
or more, and they would have to run to save themselves.

Then there would be no easy in—no in at all, more like it—and the only thing they would accomplish was to put Ibarra on his guard.

But he had no time to worry now. A life of slogging through the hellgrounds had convinced Mack Bolan that the only benefit from worry accrued to one's enemies, as a soldier undermined his own confidence and made eventual failure a self-fulfilling prophecy.

They left the car in unison, no dome light to betray them. Bolan took a coil of black nylon rope from the trunk, closing the lid softly and leaning his weight on the latch to avoid any telltale sound that would give them away. The climb would be a relatively simple matter, hand over hand, and he would have a chance to scan the grounds from a higher vantage point.

No sweat...unless a pack of guard dogs heard him coming and sounded the alarm. Unless a sentry spotted him first thing and hosed him off his perch with automatic fire.

Those were the immediate recognizable dangers, and they had no choice. They could not reach Ibarra from outside the walls, and that meant taking every necessary risk to put themselves inside.

A classic lasso would not do the job, too many leaves and smaller branches in the way, so Bolan simply tossed his line across the branch and caught it coming down. He rigged a slip knot, cinched it tight, and tried his weight against the rope to test the branch for strength. He felt no telling give and heard no cracking sounds from overhead.

"Wait until I'm topside and I have a chance to scope the yard," he said to Sanchez.

"*Sí.*"

"Okay, I'll see you on the other side." No point in tacking on *I hope.*

He gripped the rope in both hands and began to climb.

RAMON IBARRA lighted a fresh cigar and rocked back in his swivel chair, blowing a plume of aromatic smoke toward the ceiling fan that spun lazily overhead. His eyes were narrowed into angry slits, his mouth set in a hard, unyielding line. His anger was palpable, a living thing, as much a part of him as heart and lungs.

A little over twenty-four hours since his ordeal had begun, and Ibarra had already suffered stunning losses. Drug shipments, personnel, real estate, cash—it ran into the millions, but the greatest damage had been done to his machismo. His prestige.

Ibarra was a man who dealt in fear the same way that he dealt in drugs, and for the same result. Fear kept his customers in line, made sure they paid their bills on time, and kept Ramon from being troubled by the competition. Of course, there were sporadic rumbles on the border, white trash or pachucos born too dumb to realize what they were doing when they stuck their pointy little heads inside a lion's mouth. The narco trade would always be a world of violence, and Ibarra ruled Coahuila on the basis of his demonstrated ruthlessness.

It all worked until last night.

The raids against his property were bad for business, they were costly, and they were a personal insult against Ramon. The fact that he had lost a score of men and thirty kilos of cocaine was bad enough, but so far he had failed to punish those responsible, and that was ten times worse. It made the hungry border jackals think that they could steal a little piece of the Ibarra empire and slip away unnoticed in the chaos. Worse, they might begin to think of challenging Ibarra on their own, attacking when he had his hands full and his mind was elsewhere.

Twenty-seven hours, by the mantel clock, since the attacks had started. Time enough to win or lose a war, in his experience, and what had he achieved? Martinez had eliminated one man, snatched another, and allowed two more to slip away. He knew their names, believed they were connected to police in Mexico and the United States, but even that was wearing thin. Police did not bomb buildings or assassinate their prisoners unless you paid them very well indeed to do the job.

So, who was picking up the tab?

Who on earth despised Ramon enough for that? Too many suspects. Thin the herd by asking who among his enemies had cash enough to pull it off?

Ibarra thought at once of the Colombians, but that appeared to make no sense. He had been dealing with the Medellín cartel for years, without a problem, skimming just enough to make himself feel sly without alerting their accountants to the loss. Of course, some said the southern *Indios* were lunatics who turned their backs upon a friend and killed for reasons no sane man could understand.

He thought about it for a moment longer, then dismissed the notion out of hand. If the Colombians desired his death, they would have come for him directly, wild-eyed gunners bursting through the front door of his home or office, spraying automatic fire at everyone in sight. The last thing a Colombian would do was torch the very merchandise that he had shipped north to Ibarra in the first place.

There had to be another answer, if he only understood the clues, knew where to look. So far, he was drifting, waiting for Martinez to deliver on his promise of protection, and each minute it seemed that his losses mounted and his frustration grew.

The *palero*'s promises were crumbling like ash before Ibarra's eyes. Ramon had never really bought the line about his soldiers being bulletproof, much less invisible, but many of his *pistoleros* had a peasant's faith in magic. It discouraged them to find out that Martinez had been wrong on such a fundamental point. And if he was mistaken or had lied about the safety he could offer through his rituals... what else had been a lie?

Ibarra thought of all the money he had lavished on Martinez, keeping score each time a shipment crossed the border unopposed, recording the occasions when Fernando warned him of a raid and it had come to pass. Predictions of the future, sage advice on when and where to send his shipments north. A curse against his enemies from time to time, and celebrations when they died or disappeared.

Ibarra felt his heart and mind divided, even now. A part of him—the childlike peasant part—was willing to believe, at least to some extent. He had participated in a number of Fernando's ceremonies—screams and blood, all smoky darkness and oppressive heat, the raw flesh pressed against his lips—and he had come away from the experience a different man. He may have been invested with a demon spirit, or he may have simply learned that abstract evil, for its own sake, does exist. Whatever, there had been a kind of power in the ceremonies, in Martinez, that he still could not deny.

But it was power that had not assisted him in dealing with his present enemies.

The angry, chopping sound of automatic weapons startled him. Ibarra nearly dropped his fat cigar, recovered in a heartbeat, lurching from his chair. Another burst of gunfire came from the yard, immediately followed by a loud explosion in the night.

He thought about Colombians, wild-eyed, and shook the image off. Ibarra flicked his cigar into the cold, dead fireplace, moving toward a bookcase on the eastern wall. A subtle pressure on the spine of what appeared to be a *Don Juan* first edition swung aside the bookcase to put his real collection on display. Selected military weapons, dark and deadly, fully loaded where they hung on pegs, with extra magazines close by.

He lifted down a Browning double-action pistol, stuck it underneath his belt, and then went back to choose a Steyer AUG. The automatic rifle was a compact model in the bull-pup style, its magazine behind the pistol grip and trigger housing. Fiberglass shaved pounds off the weapon, and a vertical forward grip allowed Ibarra to compensate for recoil despite the relatively short barrel. A built-on telescopic sight was included as standard equipment, attached in the form of a carrying handle atop the AUG's receiver.

He was ready.

Ibarra had no clear idea who was raiding his home, and at the moment he was not concerned with individual identities. It was enough, right now, to have his enemies present themselves, allowing him to stand up for himself.

He jacked a round into the firing chamber of his rifle, moving out to join the party.

NO DOGS ON DUTY in Ibarra's yard, that they could see. The sentries were perpetually in motion, pausing only long enough to light a cigarette or tap a kidney when need called. Nobody was close enough to see or hear them as they scrambled down the thick trunk of the oak tree, dropping to the grass.

Their plans were laid before they ever left the meager sanctuary of the tree. It was agreed that they should separate and strike off toward Ibarra's mansion, trying to avoid the roving sentries, saving their firepower for the final assault on the house itself. It made good sense, in theory, but the fact was something else.

Emilio Sanchez hit the ground running, glancing backward once to see Belasko lost amid the shadows, concentrating on his own break toward the house from that point on. His H&K stuttergun was cocked and ready, the grenades Belasko had provided weighing heavy on his belt. Dressed all in black, he felt a little like a burglar or an assassin moving toward a crime scene.

True, he was about to break the law, there could be no denying that, but there was no one innocent among the targets he was seeking out. They might not find Doyle Mitchum here—in fact, the odds were slim—but there was still a chance that Ibarra or one of his stooges could finger Martinez, give them something to work with in their search if they got off Ibarra's property alive.

He kept waiting for the fear to strike him, but it never did. There was excitement, nervousness, a feeling of exhilaration, but Emilio did not feel the panic one expected from a man about to meet his death. He knew the odds were long and hard against him, but he trusted the American's judgment. More importantly, he saw a chance to strike back, make his mark, and he was not about to let it slip away.

His course across the wooded grounds took Sanchez south and east, circling the great house and approaching from the general direction of the tennis courts and swimming pool. When he had covered eighty yards,

Sanchez began to hope that he could make it. Once he reached the pool and patio, there would be no place left to hide, but having gone that far—

The sentry stepped in front of him, as if from nowhere, suddenly emerging from the cover of an ancient shade tree. Sanchez stopped dead in his tracks, his submachine gun locking into target acquisition in a swift, reflexive move. The sentry looked surprised, lurched back an awkward step, and fumbled at the riot shotgun he was carrying beneath one arm.

No time to waste.

Sanchez shot him in the chest, a 4-round burst at point-blank range that punched his target over backward in a lifeless sprawl. He was already moving as the voices of a dozen sentries started shouting questions, orders, curses in the night.

He ran as if his life depended on it, knowing that was no exaggeration of the facts. Two gunners near the swimming pool, another by the tennis courts, instinctively presented him with a defensive line. They had not seen him yet, or were not certain of their mark at least, and Sanchez knew that it would be a fatal error to allow them any breathing room.

The double-header, first. He dropped to one knee, elbows locked to hold his weapon steady as he raked them with a burst from left to right. He saw their shirts and jackets ripple with the impact of his parabellum rounds, a burst of crimson mist as one man toppled forward and the other went down on his side.

He swung his weapon toward the tennis courts and found the solitary runner having second thoughts about his move. Too late, as Sanchez caught him with a rising burst, the *pistolero* jerking through a spastic pirouette before he fell. A final shudder rippled through his slack muscles as he gave it up.

The big house stood before him, maybe fifty feet away. Sanchez palmed one of the American warrior's hand grenades and jerked the safety pin, followed by a high pitch through the broad glass doors that fronted the veranda and the swimming pool. He counted precious seconds, crouching, ready with his head down when the panels of remaining glass blew outward in a smoky thunderclap, drapes shredded, smoldering. A ragged scream from somewhere just across the threshold beckoned Sanchez on.

He took a firm grip on his H&K, stood up, and ran to meet the enemy.

THE FIRST SOUNDS of gunfire galvanized Ibarra's sentries, bringing gunners in from the perimeter at a dead run. Bolan froze in the shadow of a looming tree, counting to ten, marking time.

Two runners pounded past him, racing toward the house. He gave them a five-yard head start and then fell in behind them, running in their tracks, pacing the pointmen and keeping them covered with his mini-Uzi as he ran. Halfway to the house, one of them heard him— the guy on the left, glancing back over his shoulder on the run.

He gaped at the intruder and almost lost his balance in the first rush of surprise. His mouth dropped open, ready with a warning to his comrade, when the Uzi stuttered, taking off the left side of his face. The sound of gunfire on his flank brought number two around, tripping over his own feet in sudden panic, the Uzi helping him down with a 3-round burst to the chest.

Bolan sprinted past the bodies, putting on the speed now, as new firing erupted from the general direction of the pool and patio. Sanchez running into opposition, maybe getting through and maybe not. The sudden blast of a grenade was a good sign, anyway, and Bolan kept on running, making for the mansion's broad front porch.

Most likely the house would not be locked, with all these gunners on the grounds, men slipping in and out all night. A chance, at least, and he was not about to double up with Sanchez, risking both their lives to give the enemy a single target. Better to remain apart and thus increase their chances of survival, slim as those might be.

He encountered no immediate opposition on the porch as he got there, taking the marble steps two and three at a time. The tall, ornate doors swung open as he launched a flying kick, his boot impacting on a startled gunner's chest and driving him backward, across the entry hall. His shoulders struck the wall directly opposite, and Bolan pinned him with a 3-round burst, already past him, moving toward the sunken living room and spiral staircase.

A weasel with a Fu Manchu mustache came out to greet him, jabbering in rapid Spanish, tugging on a big revolver in his belt and getting some resistance from the blade sight, maybe snagging in his shorts. Bolan shot him in the face and left him twitching on the carpet. Now he had to make a split-second decision between the ground floor and the stairs.

Another grenade exploded, spewing smoke and plaster dust through a door on his right. His Uzi tracked that direction, finger tightening around the trigger, when Sanchez crossed the threshold in a fighting crouch.

"The stairs!"

He started up, with Sanchez close behind him, covering his back. Halfway up, he spotted a figure on the second-story landing, a man in motion, carrying an automatic weapon level with his waist. The ceiling fixture lighted his face, and Bolan recognized Ramon Ibarra from the photographs in Mitchum's file.

The dealer saw them coming up and fired a burst before he had the time to aim, his bullets chewing plaster over Bolan's head. The Executioner went down, the stairs sharp against his ribs despite a layer of carpeting, the mini-Uzi tracking. Sanchez flattened behind him, cursing volubly in Spanish.

"Don't kill him!" Bolan snapped.

"Goddamn it!"

Ibarra advanced like a gunslinger, bolt-upright, firing from the hip. Bolan's burst ripped into his legs between the knees and ankles, dropping him as if a snare had jerked his feet from under him. A cry of pain was ripped from Ibarra's throat and he lost his weapon, lunging for it too late as it slipped down the stairs toward the Executioner.

Bolan bounded past the gun and grabbed Ibarra by the hair, dragging him upright. The dealer gave a strangled cry as the shattered bones in his legs ground together. Sanchez joined them on the landing, standing guard.

"¿Habla Ingles?"

"I speak your language, gringo."

"You've got one chance to survive, ten seconds tops."

"I'm listening." A hiss between clenched teeth.

"Martinez and the Anglo. Where?"

Ibarra looked confused, as if the question were beyond his comprehension.

"What? That's all you want?"

"Time's up." The Uzi pressed against Ibarra's jaw.

"The mountains! South and east of here, above a village called Tres Lobos. *El padrino* goes there sometimes when he wants to get away."

No further time to waste, if they were going to retreat before Ibarra's yardmen cut them off. Bolan rose, stepped back a pace and aimed the Uzi at Ibarra's face. The dealer blanched.

"You said—"

"I lied."

CHAPTER TWENTY-ONE

Daylight overtook them on the highway, driving southwest from Piedras Negras toward the Sierra del Huacha. Bolan watched the sun rise in his rearview mirror, checking the empty road behind him for traffic, anything that might suggest a tail, but spotted nothing so far.

No reason in the world why anyone should be pursuing them. Ibarra was beyond revealing their intentions and no one else outside of the Martinez cult should theoretically have any knowledge of the mountain hideaway. As for Martinez, he was bound to think that he was safe, beyond the reach of mortal enemies.

The fallback from Ibarra's house had been a close thing, all the way. The darkness helped, together with the fire ignited by Sanchez's grenades. They had dropped three more gunners outside, on their run for the gate, but once beyond the wall they were home free.

On phase one, at least.

The village of Tres Lobos did not show up on the maps they had at hand, but Highway 63 was the only route available into the Sierra del Huacha, and Bolan trusted his instincts, along with the Mexican's working knowledge of the territory, to take them the rest of the way.

They barely spoke in transit, each man focused on his private thoughts, the price that they had paid to come this far. Brock Hargis dead. Doyle Mitchum hanging in the balance, maybe dead and maybe not. If he was still alive,

Bolan thought, it might still turn out to be more curse than blessing, in the end.

He thought about the photographs Mitchum had shown him back in Del Rio, the shots taken at Rancho Santa Maria after the raid. A bloody caldron, thick with swarming flies. A human spinal column lying in the dust. Wire markers lined up in the sand like spindly weeds.

He did not want to think about Doyle Mitchum in captivity, but he could not escape the images that came to mind unbidden, forcing him to dwell upon the endless possibilities of pain and death. Martinez would allow an enemy to live while he or she was useful to the "family." The moment that a pawn outlived that usefulness, it would be cast aside—or else converted into fodder for Fernando's morbid rituals.

Bolan tried the radio for some distraction, picked up music intercut with static, and finally gave up. He concentrated on the open road, easing off the accelerator to let a fox make its way across before his headlights. It was bright enough to do without them now, and Bolan switched them off. He estimated they were something over halfway to their destination, or at least the point where they would have to leave the car.

Before departing from Piedras Negras, they had changed to hiking clothes. Their hardware was concealed beneath a blanket in the back seat, easily within arm's reach. The highway stretched before them like a scar across the arid landscape, with the mountains looming closer, dark against a sky suffused with rose and gray.

Gradually, almost imperceptibly at first, the highway started gaining altitude, a slow curve from the desert floor to meet the Sierra del Huacha. The sparse vegetation of scattered cacti, mesquite, and Joshua trees gave

way to evergreens as they climbed. The changing landscape meant more cover when they had to walk, perhaps
a cooler temperature. Some shade at least, if nothing else.

The primary problem was that Bolan had no way to
calculate the hostile odds. Ricardo Obregon could tell
them nothing more about the cult than they already
knew, and there had been no time to grill him for the details. Bolan did not know if they were going up against a
handful of fanatics or an army braced for combat, how
Fernando's troops were armed or trained. He could not
even say with certainty if Mitchum was alive or dead, but
they would have to take a chance.

In either case, Martinez had already earned a spot on
Bolan's hit parade. Ramon Ibarra might be gone, but
other dealers would be vying for the services of *el
padrino,* seeking mystical protection from their enemies, unless the man was crushed, his twisted "family"
destroyed.

Even a clean sweep, Bolan realized, would not destroy
the link between drugs and black magic along the border—much less in the United States. The first hard lesson of his one-man war against the savages had been the
understanding that he could not actually change society,
or save man from himself. He did not have the time or
skills required to educate humanity from top to bottom,
so he did the best he could, removing predators where
they were visible—and sometimes not so visible—to give
the larger, peaceful tribe a chance. It would be someone
else's job to scrutinize the spread of cults, plan law-enforcement seminars and college courses on their role in
modern crime. As for the Executioner, his course was
clear.

Identify.

Isolate.

Destroy.

Identification was complete, at least for the top three leaders of Fernando's cult. As for the flunkies, gunners and disciples, he would take them as they came. Bolan was not empowered to hear confessions or grant absolution. That kind of justice remained for a higher court, beyond the reach of men with guns. For Bolan's purposes, it was enough to know his enemies by name or sight, facilitating their removal from one plane of existence to the next.

Isolation had, apparently, taken care of itself with Fernado's retreat to the mountains. Ibarra had been less than explicit, but his blurted directions made Bolan believe that the cult hideaway would be removed by some distance from the village of Tres Lobos. He could reasonably expect that the problem of civilians cluttering his line of fire would solve itself. With Doyle Mitchum on his mind as they continued their approach, Bolan had enough to think about without considering the prospect of a shoot-out in a crowded market square or a running battle through the village streets.

"We're getting close," said Sanchez. "Look for someplace we can hide the car."

There were more choices here than in the desert, with the trees for cover, turnouts, unpaved access roads irregularly spaced on either side. Bolan picked a copse of evergreens and pulled into their shadow, walking back to verify that no one driving by could see the car without a special detour.

"You have a fair idea where we're going?" he asked Sanchez.

"Fair," the *federale* answered with a cautious smile. He slipped his pack on, Bolan doing likewise, seeing to

their weapons and their other gear before they locked the
car.

Full light, and while the mountains made it cooler,
Bolan did not need a map to know there was a desert
close at hand.

"All set?"

"This way," Sanchez said, and struck off through the
trees.

SANCHEZ KNEW TRES LOBOS as he knew so many other
villages around Coahuila, from a combination of experience and word of mouth. That is to say, he knew *of*
them, having visited a tiny fraction of their number in the
course of his official duties. In a pinch, Sanchez thought
he could describe the village they were seeking, since so
many of them looked alike: a central area ringed with
dwellings, possibly a little store or blacksmith's shop,
perhaps a tiny church if there were residents enough to
make it pay. More often it would be just homes, the occupants scratching their living from the soil or finding
other ways to meet their needs.

This far above the flatland, there would not be many
farmers. More subsistence gardening, each family keeping up a tiny plot of corn and beans, some peppers on the
side. Maybe there was some work along the highway, for
able-bodied men and older boys, while others dealt in
handicrafts, selling their wares to jobbers from San Carlos or Piedras Negras. Either way, a living wage was hard
to come by, hunger a companion who was never far way.

Sanchez's mother had been born in such a village. He
had listened to her stories all through childhood, and he
understood the peasant life as well as anyone who has not
lived it for himself. The rural villagers of Mexico knew
poverty that few Americans would ever truly under-

stand, despite the endless string of documentaries and television appeals for funds to "foreign missions." Mexico, to the majority of Anglos, was either a vacation paradise or someplace where you shouldn't drink the water, Acapulco or Tijuana—sun or sex, with nothing in between. Few tourists had the time or interest to investigate the culture, meet the people one-on-one, and learn where they were coming from.

Stereotypes were so much easier and more convenient. Wetbacks slipping into the United States to swell the welfare rolls, smoke dope, pick lettuce, maybe join an L.A. street gang if they got the urge. Siesta time, with everybody knocking off from noon to four o'clock and sleeping underneath a giant cactus, swaddled in serapes. Donkeys pulling carts down Main Street, wearing straw hats, holes cut to accommodate their ears.

The American might not fully understand Sanchez's people, either, but at least he had the common sense to recognize that they were human beings, good and bad, some honest, some corrupt. He had a job to do, and he was doing it, though Sanchez still could not decide on whose behalf.

The *federale* led the way because he knew the territory, more or less, and if they met an obstacle along the way, it would be speaking in Spanish. Still, he had a feeling that the American warrior could have found his way alone, perhaps even dispose of the Martinez cult by himself. The man's ability to kill and simply walk away was awesome, something to be mourned or envied, all depending on your point of view.

He used a compass sparingly, to keep himself on track, but it was not much help without a more specific fix on the village itself. He thought Tres Lobos had a narrow wagon track connecting it to the highway, passable by car, but Sanchez and Bolan had agreed to make the hike in lieu of rolling into a potential ambush on the one route that Fernando's gunners would be sure to watch. This way, at least they had a shot clinging to the slim advantage of surprise.

Their course led generally north and west from where they left the car, Sanchez navigating by guesswork at first, feeling better about his decision once they met the rutted wagon track. Instead of following the unpaved road, however, they hiked parallel, some fifty yards due west, taking turns to sneak up on the road at fifteen-minute intervals and make sure that they had not strayed too far off-track.

If there were spotters on the mountain road, they seemed to be invisible, and Sanchez was beginning to feel foolish, hiking over rugged ground and dodging thorny shrubs, when they could easily have used the road to reach Tres Lobos. Even so, the guards might be there, watching, and he did not plan to die before he had a fair shot at Martinez.

The guards they met ten minutes later moved so silently they seemed like part of the surrounding forest, shadows come to life. One moment, Sanchez and Bolan had the wooded hillside to themselves; the next, three men had blocked their paths, two armed with rifles, the third aiming a shotgun at Sanchez's face.

The hikers froze in place, made no move to reach their automatic weapons. They were covered, and the first barrage would kill them, barring acts of God. If these were three Martinez soldiers, they could kiss it all goodbye.

The first step was to stall for time.

"We're looking for Tres Lobos," Sanchez informed the silent gunmen, meeting each pair of eyes in turn, from left to right.

"With those?" The tallest of them wagged his rifle back and forth, to indicate their weapons.

"Not the village, really," Sanchez answered, knowing that his next few words made all the difference in the world. Thumbs up, they had a chance. Thumbs down, at least he might distract the riflemen enough to get a few rounds off before he died.

"What, then?" the peasant with the shotgun asked.

Sanchez felt a tiny surge of hope. A peasant! Would three soldiers working for the likes of *el padrino* dress this way? Not even hiking clothes, but simple peasant garb. Of course, Martinez could be paying off selected villagers to do his dirty work, but it was still a shot.

"A man," Emilio said. "A group of men, in fact. Their leader is Fernando de Leon Martinez. A *palero.*"

Something flickered in the man's eyes that held his own.

"And you are friends with this Martinez?"

Sanchez shook his head. "I am a sergeant with the *federales,* back in Ciudad Acuna. My companion is a lawman from El Norte."

The gunmen whispered something back and forth, too softly for Sanchez to eavesdrop, their eyes and aim unwavering throughout. At last, one passed his shotgun to the man immediately on his left, approaching them with empty hands.

"We take your weapons now," he said, allowing no room for discussion. "You come back with us, to see the leader of our village."

"Yes," Emilio said. Why not?

And what choice did they have, in any case?

BESIDES a dull, persistent aching in his privates, Mitchum hardly thought about the pain at all. Instead he wondered where the hell he was, and what their hasty exit from the ranch outside Piedras Negras meant in terms of personal survival.

Any way he tried to scope it out, the ex-cop from Miami wound up dead.

There had been no discussion on the drive, Mitchum lying in the back of a van, biting his lip as the road got worse, jostling him back and forth, rousing his aches and pains from uneasy slumber. He had no fix on their destination, no clear idea why they had abandoned the last hideaway. Something had spooked Martinez, making him figure the time was ripe for a change of scene.

Sanchez? Belasko? Ibarra?

There were too many variables left in the equation for Mitchum to work it out. A threat, for sure, and since Martinez told him he had missed Doyle's comrades at the meet in Eagle Pass, he still had hopes that one or both of them would try to cut him loose.

For all the good that it would do.

Careers in law enforcement don't spawn optimists. Doyle Mitchum knew the bad guys won more often than they lost. Some skate without a hitch, while others bargain down and serve a tiny fraction of the time that they deserve. The ones who really crash and burn are flukes, especially in narcotics, where police seize barely ten percent of the imported product nationwide, arresting maybe five or six percent of those involved in smuggling, distribution, sales. The homicides that sprang from drugs were almost never solved, unless you had some kind of psycho loner on your hands, too dumb or too self-confident to cover up his tracks.

Even if he assumed that Belasko and the *federale* caught a lucky break and both of them were still alive, so what? They would be raising hell along the border somewhere, maybe giving Ramon Ibarra a headache, but that was a long way from tracing Martinez and Mitchum to their present location.

Mountains.

Mitchum knew that Martinez had been telling the truth about that from scoping out the wooded landscape on his short walk from the barn to his present quarters. Some kind of campsite, with crude wooden buildings scattered around a clearing, some of them butting against the trees. It was not large and didn't have to be, from what he saw. Twelve or fifteen members in the party, tops, if he counted Martinez and the woman. Eight or nine of those had weapons showing when he saw them, but you had to figure there were other guns around. Enough to do the job, at any rate.

What job was that?

Defense, for starters, but an order from Martinez could as easily produce a firing squad to rid the camp of one unnecessary prisoner.

Stay cool.

The up side: handcuffs off, his mind and body fairly functional, considering the punishment he had absorbed back in Piedras Negras. He could fight, if given half a chance, and if he managed to acquire a gun.

There was no furniture nor a fixture of any kind in his cell. His bed would be a mat of woven straw, if he was still alive come nightfall. Nothing to do except sleep after sundown, since he did not have a lamp or candle in the room. No windows, and the door was locked from outside, probably with a guard posted.

No escape on his own, short of ripping up floor-boards and tunneling out bare-handed through the soil beneath. The slightest noise would bring a sentry running, and a tunnel from his prison to the open ground outside would still leave him standing in the middle of the camp.

Case closed.

He needed hardware to escape, which meant he had to take a guard, disarm him, come out shooting. Maybe he could take the others by surprise and kill as many as he could before they cut him down. If he was very, very lucky, he'd reach the trees with breath and blood enough to try a wild run through the mountains . . . going where?

Dead end.

Still, suicide by means of an explosive grandstand play looked better than submission to his captors, leading up to Mitchum's sacrifice, his blood drained off for the *nganga*. Take some of the bastards with him, or at least make sure they had to kill him quick and clean.

It wasn't meant to end this way, he thought, but what the hell.

Doyle Mitchum flexed his hands, decided they were strong enough, and settled on his sleeping mat to wait.

TRES LOBOS WAS SMALLER than Bolan had expected; cleaner, too. He counted fifteen dwellings built around a central plaza, hard-packed soil beneath his boots. A smell of cooking hung over the village, as it would all day. Too late for breakfast, coming up on lunch. The rural peasants went to work at daybreak, when they had a job to do, and Bolan noted a preponderance of women, children here and there, the able-bodied men conspicuous by absence, whether at work or standing guard at other compass points to keep the village safe.

He wondered if armed guards were normal for Tres Lobos, but he kept the question to himself. Sanchez was doing fine so far, in terms of keeping them alive. The villagers who studied them with cautious curiosity did not strike Bolan as the wild-eyed types Martinez would recruit...or who would let themselves be drawn into his web. A hunch, but there it was.

The village headman met them in the central plaza, listened to his sentries for a moment, then conversed with Sanchez, shifting into English for Bolan's sake, once they had disposed of the amenities.

"You seek Martinez and the others?" he inquired.

"That's right. We have no wish to trespass in your village or alarm your people. If you know where we can find the men we seek—"

"What is your business with these men?"

Sanchez glanced at Bolan, silent agreement that a lie could get them killed. So might the truth, if Bolan was mistaken in his judgment of the villagers, but it was all they had right now.

"Martinez is an evil man," the *federale* said. "He deals in drugs, makes wicked magic, and converses with the dead. He has a friend of ours, a prisoner. We mean to get him back."

"Your friend is still alive?"

Sanchez shrugged. "Perhaps. If not, there is the matter of revenge."

"I know these men you seek," the headman said at last. "They are not far away, perhaps three hours' walk if you are strong."

"If you could show us where—"

"Not in daylight. You would surely die."

Again Sanchez glanced at Bolan. Waiting for the sun to set would mean a full day lost, perhaps Doyle Mitchum with it, but the Executioner was not inclined to spurn advice when it could save his life. Besides, going in for a rescue when they were sapped by the sun and open to detection could spell failure from the start.

He saw a woman, younger than the others, staring at him from the ring of faces that surrounded them. She tried a smile for size, stepped forward, whispered something in the headman's ear.

"We keep your weapons now," the leader of the village said, not offering the subject to debate. "Come dark, I show you where to find your enemies. First thing, you eat."

The Executioner allowed himself a smile.

"I don't mind if I do."

CHAPTER TWENTY-TWO

The food was simple but plentiful: rice and beans, homemade tortillas and tamales, fruit, and rich, dark coffee for a chaser. Somehow, by accident or design, Bolan found himself seated next to the woman he had noticed in the crowd. Sanchez was seated several yards away, in close conversation with the village headman, and Bolan left them to it, trusting the *federale* to ferret out any information they required.

Several men had returned to the village over the past half hour, eyeing the new arrivals suspiciously, speaking briefly to their chosen leader, but none appeared to be the woman's husband. She was on her own, a fact that Bolan found both interesting and suggestive in the circumstances.

"You are American," the woman said when both of them were seated in the shade, with full plates in their laps.

"That's right."

"From California?"

Bolan smiled at the assumption. Gringos came from Texas or from California, preferably from Hollywood. Case closed.

"Not quite," he told her, waiting for the disappointment to show, pleased when it did not.

"I am Inez Lozaro."

"Mike Belasko."

"You travel far to risk your life," she said.

"I have a job to do."

"This man you seek, Martinez, he is evil."

"I believe that's true."

"We hate him, but we cannot drive him out. He has the power."

"Maybe," Bolan answered. "Maybe not."

"You have not seen what he can do."

"I've seen enough."

She hesitated for a moment, glancing toward the headman of the village, huddled with Sanchez, clearly wondering if she should hold her tongue. At last she made her mind up, turning back toward Bolan with a frown.

"You see I have no man, no children."

Bolan shrugged, not quite embarrassed, still unable to decide what he should say.

"Before Martinez and the rest of his *paleros* came, our life was different here. I had a husband, Paco. We were ... how would gringos say it ... newlyweds?"

"That's how we say it," Bolan answered, smiling.

"Four months we were married," said Inez. "The first time, when Martinez and his people came to trade for food, they tried to buy a child and were refused. Maria Fuentes lost her son that night, a three-year-old. Nobody saw him go. We searched the forest, all around. Two days went by before we found the body...what was left."

"Martinez?"

Slowly, solemnly, she nodded. "There are predators, of course, but they do not remove a heart with knives, or..."

Choking up, she left the rest of it unspoken. Bolan waited, chalking up another reason why Martinez and his sick disciples had to pay the tab.

"My Paco and Maria's husband went to see the *federales*," said Inez, when she regained her voice. "They traveled to Piedras Negras, and the *commandante* promised them that he would see to justice. On their way back from the city, someone met them on the highway. Paco and Luis were shot."

"Martinez?"

"He came back to see us the next day, pretending that he mourned our loss. We are his friends, he says, and friends have his protection."

"Just as long as they stay friendly?"

Inez nodded slowly. "From that day, we knew the *federales* would not help us. We avoid all contact with Martinez and his people, when we can."

"Have there been any other...incidents?"

She shook her head, a grudging negative. "He proved his point, and now he lets us be. We still post guards, though. Just in case."

"You may not need the guards much longer," Bolan told her.

"Will you kill him?"

"Possibly."

"Martinez needs to die," she said, with sudden vehemence. "He is a curse upon the very air we breathe."

"You ever think of living somewhere else?"

She frowned and shook her head again. "This is my home. *Our* home. To leave and let the likes of these *paleros* win would be a shameful thing."

"If anything goes wrong tonight, there could be repercussions," Bolan said. "Martinez figures out your people helped us, he'll be looking for a way to pay you back."

"Then you must not let anything go wrong," she told him, turning on a cautious smile. "Besides, I think you are a man with power of your own."

"I don't know any magic spells," the Executioner replied.

"But there are many kinds of magic," said Inez. "The strength within a good man's heart is magic, of a kind."

He felt suddenly uncomfortable with the conversation and changed the subject. "Why Tres Lobos?"

"Ah, 'Three Wolves.'" Her smile was brighter now. "A story from the first days of the village, when it had no name. A pack of wolves lived in the forest, and they claimed it for their own. When people built their homes here, there was trouble. Raids by night and day, the wolves attempting to defend their territory. Finally a young man named Rodrigo went to find the pack alone. His people were afraid to join him in the hunt, and some were ready to desert the village they had built."

"What happened?"

"On the first night of the full moon in September, long ago, Rodrigo found the pack. His courage shamed the leader of the wolves, who chose a single champion to fight and kill the man. Instead it was the wolf who died, and two more after him. Rodrigo suffered grievous wounds, but he would not give up. The leader of the pack respected him, and there were no more raids against the village. So, Tres Lobos. All the wolves are gone today, of course."

"Not quite."

Her smile was thoughtful when she asked, "Are you our champion?"

He thought about it for a moment, watching Sanchez in the midst of his negotiations with the headman, and replied, "I guess we'll see."

"NO LUCK?"

Martinez turned to find Marcella watching him as he emerged from the communications hut. He frowned and shook his head, disturbed that there was still no contact with Ramon Ibarra in Piedras Negras.

"Nothing."

He had tried the two-way radio sporadically since their arrival at the camp last night, knowing Ibarra would be furious over his fleeing the city, prepared to deal with the problem from a distance, while Ibarra's troops destroyed their mutual enemies. He would consult the gods meanwhile, and use his strongest magic to ensure a proper victory.

When the smoke cleared, he would find some way to claim a measure of the credit for himself—assuming that the victory was his.

It crossed Fernando's mind that there was still an outside chance Ibarra might not win this latest battle for supremacy. All magic spells aside, he was a man of flesh and blood, with mortal weaknesses. Martinez had considered taking out the dealer on his own, a possibility still on his mind, but he was worried that he might not get the chance.

"Is something wrong, Fernando?"

"No."

She would accept the lie because she leaned upon Martinez for her strength, like all his followers. He was supposed to be omniscient and omnipotent, all things to each of them in turn. No matter what should happen in Piedras Negras, he would have to put a brave face on for those who followed him and trusted him to shape their lives.

The chosen few.

This afternoon, Martinez realized how few there really were. Some half a dozen for his inner circle, privileged to attend the sacrificial rites and help him work with the *nganga*. Twice that number in subordinate positions, all initiated with a taste of blood, expected to perform upon demand, no matter what the task.

Nineteen in all, now that they had none of Ibarra's gunmen to assist them. If Ramon could not defeat their enemies with all the soldiers he commanded, how—

Martinez caught himself and cut off the defeatist train of thought before it further undermined his confidence. He needed all his wits about him now if he was going to survive.

"You think that something's happened to Ramon."

It did not come out sounding like a question, but he answered anyway. "Twelve hours now, with nothing on the radio. He always leaves a man to handle messages."

"Some kind of interference?"

"No. The weather's clear. We've never had a problem getting through before. He simply does not answer."

"So?"

"So, either he has chosen to ignore us, or he cannot answer."

There was a momentary silence while Marcella took that in. If she was frightened by the prospect of Ibarra being taken out of action, she concealed it well. A true believer.

"If we lose him?"

"There are others," said Martinez, smiling to himself. "It may be time for us to do without the middleman."

"You think so?"

"Dear Marcella." As they walked, he slipped an arm around her shoulders, pulled her close. "We have the contacts and experience. We have the power. If Ramon should have an accident, who is there to deny us our reward?''

"You think of everything, Fernando."

"Someone has to."

"If Gregorio had found the *federale*—"

"Never mind." He recognized Marcella's jealousy, a point of pride in other times, potential weakness now. "If he survives Ibarra, we will hunt him down in time."

It crossed his mind that someone might be hunting *them,* but who could find their secret place? Ibarra knew about the camp, of course, from sending men to help with its construction, but Martinez did not fear Ramon just yet. If he was still alive, the dealer had his hands full with their adversaries, fighting to defend himself, recapture what was lost.

Despite the reassurances of common sense, Martinez could not shake a certain feeling of foreboding, like a shadow falling across his own and bringing on a chill. Someone was intent on running him to earth and trashing everything that he had fought for all these years. His dreams and aspirations balanced on a razor's edge.

He felt a sudden rush of vertigo, leaned on Marcella for an instant to prevent himself from falling while the surge of panic ebbed away.

"Fernando?"

"Danger, little one. We must prepare ourselves without delay."

IT WAS A SHORT WALK from the village proper to a mountain stream that flowed year-round despite the relative proximity of arid desert. As Inez explained, the stream and lake it fed, a half-mile distant, had been instrumental in the selection of the village building site, long years ago. Without a constant source of water, any settlement would be foredoomed to failure, bargain with the wolves or not.

They walked through shade, tall trees around them, following a path worn smooth by usage over time. A rustling in the undergrowth to Bolan's left betrayed the passage of an animal, but it did not alarm Inez. Though still unarmed, he felt no qualms about their distance from the village. If his reading of the situation was correct, Martinez and his cultists would be focused on their own defenses at the moment, and the last thing on their minds would be a side trip to Tres Lobos.

Several hours remained yet, till sundown, when a volunteer would lead them north and west to find their target. He would not be coming with them on the raid, of course, and that was fine. The pointer was enough, and Bolan frankly did not want an untrained, innocent civilian in the way.

For now, though, he had time.

It felt peculiar, verging on surrealism, to be walking in the forest with Inez this way, before a desperate battle. Calm before the storm, and then some.

"You are very quiet."

"Thinking," Bolan told her, as they paused beside the stream.

"About your enemies?"

"In part."

"What else?"

"The life you have," he said. "It can't be easy."

"What is easy? We have always lived this way."

"No urge to take a shot at something new? The city? Maybe the United States?"

"I tried El Norte once," Inez replied. "Coyotes take your money first, and the employers do their best to see that there will never be enough for independence on the other side.''

"You came back on your own?''

She smiled and shook her head. "The Immigration people found me working in a Dallas sweatshop, sewing labels on designer jeans. I might be there today, if someone had not...what is the expression...blown the whistle?''

Bolan matched her soft smile with his own. "You don't regret what happened?''

"No. I had to try, but I was also young and foolish. There is nothing for our people in El Norte but the kind of grief and heartbreak they cannot afford.''

"Some disagree.''

"And they are welcome to their choices. I will not go back. My life is here.''

"Despite—'' He caught himself, too late, and bit it off.

"What happened to my husband?''

"That was out of line. I'm sorry.''

"Never mind. It seems so long ago...and still, like yesterday.''

"I know the feeling,'' Bolan said.

"I see it in your face. You are a man who knows the pain of loss.''

"It's been a while.''

"No matter. You can understand. This is my home.''

"I hope it holds.''

"It will. You're here, now.''

"Don't put too much stock in that,'' he said. "I've played this game enough to know that things go wrong sometimes.''

"You should have faith.''

"I do my best, but anything can happen.''

"Even so.''

She took his hand and led him toward the lake, birds warbling in the trees around them. More small sounds greeted them along the way, but nothing sinister. He took the forest noise in stride, as he had learned to do in Vietnam, when any rustling leaf or cracking twig might signal the approach of enemies.

In front of them, mist from a waterfall rose from a drop of fifteen feet or so. The lake spread out before them, ripples swiftly fading into distance, with the surface like a dusky mirror.

"I believe this is my favorite place on earth."

"It's beautiful," he said, and meant it.

"Do you have a special place?"

He thought of Stony Man, the Blue Ridge Mountains of Virginia, far beyond his reach.

"Sometimes I think so. Other times, I'm just not sure."

"Then we can share this place."

"I'm only passing through," he told her, leaning on the obvious.

"No matter. You are here. Who knows when we shall meet again."

She did not add the "if," but then, she didn't have to. Bolan recognized it for himself.

"Who knows?"

She stepped into his arms and stood on tiptoe to be kissed.

You're here. Her voice inside his head.

And for the moment, it was all he had to know.

EMILIO SANCHEZ SAT ALONE and sipped a cup of steaming coffee, waiting for the sun to set. He had completed his discussions with the village headman, briefed Belasko on the plan, and then the Anglo had disappeared. The *federale* counted heads as best he could and found that the woman who had sat beside Belasko during lunch was also missing.

He passed no judgment on them, cared for nothing but the mission yet to come. If the Anglo found an opportunity to clear his mind, however briefly, more power to him. Sanchez was concerned, for just a moment, that the villagers might take offense, but they had either failed to notice, or they kept their personal opinions to themselves.

The *federale* checked his watch. An hour later, before official sundown, but the shadows had begun to lengthen, giving him a foretaste of the night to come.

It was appropriate, he thought, that they would do their work in darkness. Everything about Martinez and his followers was dark, obscure, still shrouded in a veil of mystery. How fitting that his end—or theirs—should come by night.

Sanchez was wise enough to know that it could still go either way. They had reduced the odds by neutralizing Ibarra's army, but they were still outnumbered, outgunned by the enemy. A part of him, however small, was still concerned about the thought of going up against Fernando's magic, but he pushed the doubts aside. There was no time for falling back on peasant superstition now, at this late date. If nothing else, their battle with Ibarra had confirmed what Sanchez knew already, that the strongest spells of a *palero* could not save their adversaries from a bullet fired at point-blank range.

Sanchez hoped he got the chance to met Martinez on his own, without Belasko standing by. One shot was all he asked for, just to prove beyond a shadow of a doubt that he was not infected by the *palero's* corruption. Sanchez felt he owed it to himself, and to the other *feder-*

ales, few and far between as they might be, who worked against the odds and the *mordida* day by day.

A little payback, from the heart.

His hands were steady as he set the coffee cup aside and flicked a fire ant from the cuff of his fatigue pants. Waiting was the hardest part, he thought. Compared to marking time, the heated rush of battle was a sweet relief.

They would begin at sunset, with a full two-hour hike ahead of them through darkness, to Fernando's camp. From there, they would be forced to improvise. Without a layout of the compound, they could not prepare a battle plan ahead of time, but they would find a way.

Or die in the attempt.

Sanchez did not understand the American warrior's motives, even now, but he had seen enough of him in action to convince himself that he could not have picked a better partner if he tried. The gringo might not be the federal officer he claimed to be, but he was clearly a professional in all respects.

He glanced across the clearing in the middle of the village, toward the hut where he had seen their weapons stored. Between them, they were carrying sufficient ammunition and explosives to destroy a hundred men, but it was still a gamble. If Fernando's men were not immune to death or injury, the same was true for Sanchez and Belasko. But none of their impressive hardware would be worth a damn if they were cut down in their tracks before they had a chance to use it.

Sanchez caught himself before the train of thought went any further, switching directions and concentrating on Doyle Mitchum. Was he still alive? Could they do anything to help him now, or would they only get him killed?

Whatever the odds, they had reached a point where nothing mattered more than bringing down Martinez and his followers. The ex-cop from Miami knew that, going in, and there was no way that he would have asked them to back off on his behalf. No way at all.

They would proceed because they had no choice.

Sanchez had not come this far to back out now. Whatever lay ahead of them, he was prepared to see it through.

A man could do no less.

CHAPTER TWENTY-THREE

They did not trust the dusk, but waited until full dark fell across the mountains, pooling midnight blackness in among the trees. Their guide was named Filipe, tall and lean, a vintage Winchester shotgun slung over his shoulder with knotted twine. He spoke when spoken to, and clearly liked it best when his companions kept their questions to themselves.

Inez Lozaro was not there to see them off when they departed from Tres Lobos. It had been agreed between them: no goodbyes or sadness at the end. It helped that they had only known each other half a day, and yet...

Some moments freeze forever in your mind, like specimens preserved in amber. You can take them out and hold them in your hands ten years from now and still remember every nuance of the moment. Fragrances and flavors. Sounds, sensations, silent messages that pass between two souls.

But he couldn't dwell on such things when there was work to do, and Bolan needed a distraction like he needed broken firing pins on all his guns. There would be time enough to think about Inez tomorrow or the next day...if he lived that long.

No guarantees, by any means. He understood that they were tackling a force of unknown size on unfamiliar ground, encumbered by the hope of bringing back a hostage safe and sound. If Mitchum was their driving motivation, he could also be a handicap, preventing them from launching any all-out blitz against the camp. Until his status was confirmed, alive or dead, they would be going in with one hand tied.

Maybe they had a small potential advantage, too.

By all accounts, the compound was not large, no more than fifty yards across, and damn near everything they did would be at point-blank range. Restricted target area would make it easier, at least in theory, for the two of them to sniff Doyle Mitchum out, assuming he was still alive.

It could go either way, Martinez feeling cocky now that he was tucked away securely in the mountains, thinking no one had the brains or contacts necessary to pursue him there. A critical mistake, and that was fine, but it could also make his hostage seem superfluous, a piece of excess baggage, prime for sacrifice. They might be too damned late to make a difference, more particularly if Martinez had disposed of Mitchum in Piedras Negras, prior to taking off.

The speculation took him nowhere, and he gladly cut it short. Fernando de Leon Martinez was the target, with his coterie of sick disciples. They were marked to die, and anything beyond achievement of that goal—the rescue of an ex-cop from Miami, for example, would be gravy on the side.

Dark trees and rustling undergrowth. More evergreens than anything, but even so the general atmosphere took Bolan back to other night patrols and other killing grounds, a world away.

Ahead of them, Filipe stopped dead on the trail, raising one hand in the darkness. They waited, Bolan shifting slightly to the left, his night eyes picking out the sinuous shape of a snake as it crossed the trail. A parting twitch of rattles as it disappeared into the undergrowth, then Filipe gave it a few more seconds before he dropped his hand and moved ahead.

All kinds of predators in darkness, Bolan thought.

But he had time for only one.

THERE WAS AN UNPAVED ROAD or wagon track between Tres Lobos and the camp, but they avoided it and took a game trail through the woods instead. For one thing, the established road would certainly be guarded day and night, affording them no cover, while their enemies had ample time to lay a trap and cut them down from ambush. Equally important, though, was pure geography. The road was more circuitous, adding better than a mile to their trek, while the game trail took a more direct approach.

Of course, the trail might just as easily be guarded, but Emilio Sanchez knew that they would have to risk it. There was nothing free in life, and they could not expect to penetrate an armed encampment of their enemies without some risks along the way.

The snake, for openers. Thick-bodied and dusty-looking, it still possessed a streamlined, almost-sensuous quality, flowing across the trail like dark liquid made flesh. It hardly spared a glance for the intruders on its hunting ground, one lidless eye regarding Sanchez and Filipe with the fine disdain inherent to an animal incapable of feeling fear. Emilio had the feeling that their guide allowed the rattlesnake to live as much from sheer respect as from a wish to keep quiet on the trail.

They spoke when words were absolutely necessary, but the silence did not trouble Sanchez. He was busy concentrating on the trail with one part of his mind, the rest considering the job ahead. More killing to be done.

Before he met the gringos—Mitchum, Hargis, and Belasko—Sanchez had two shootings on his record. One man dead, one wounded in a fight with bandits near Reynosa. Now, within the space of two days, he was losing count of all the bodies he had seen, the lives that he had taken. And the strangest part, the worst part, was he didn't mind.

Each time he squeezed the trigger, watched a target crumple to the ground, Emilio felt he was eliminating one more tiny piece of evil from the world. Not a crusader by nature, he still felt a powerful urge to destroy these parasites in human form. Consider it a piece of sanitation work, like taking out the trash.

More elevation now, a steeper slope, and he could feel it in the muscles of his thighs. Behind him, not a sound from Mike Belasko as they moved along the trail. It would have pleased him, made him more at ease perhaps, if he knew something of the Anglo's background, his connections with the government, but they were both committed now. The time for turning back was past. Surrender at this point in the game was infinitely worse than losing, even if the loss would mean his life.

The sky was clear, with moonlight to guide them as they climbed, with eerie shadows in among the trees. Wings whispered overhead, bats or night birds sweeping insects from the air. Emilio thought about the possibility of meeting a jaguar on the trail, deciding it would be the least of his concerns.

He pressed a button on his watch, illuminating the display, and found they had been walking for an hour. Halfway there, unless they met some obstacle along the way.

Martinez would be on his guard, but overconfidence could work against him, leading the *palero* to believe that he was safe, beyond the reach of any adversaries. Even if he posted guards, which he was almost sure to do, their chances were improved—in theory, anyway—by numbers. Two men had a better chance of slipping past Fernando's sentries than a larger team, and once they reached the camp...

He could proceed no further with his plans, until they saw the target for themselves. It was the greatest single weakness of their plan, this blank spot where the layout of the compound was concerned. Some of the villagers had done their best to sketch the place, from glimpses on clandestine visits, but their fear was obvious, the recollections taken with a grain of salt.

They had a fix on size, approximate descriptions of the buildings, but their witnesses could not provide an estimate of hostile strength, and they would not have recognized security devices, even mounted in plain sight. It seemed unlikely that Martinez would employ elaborate precautions, so far from a power source, and no one could recall a generator at the camp, but there was still a chance he might surprise them.

Emilio had considered all his options prior to setting out with Belasko from Piedras Negras. He could just as easily have stayed behind, without recriminations from the Anglo, but his own pride would not let him quit. Removal of Ramon Ibarra from the picture was a major victory, but while Martinez lived, there would be further sacrifices, new atrocities from one day to the next. And he would find another patron soon enough, if he did not decide to go in business for himself.

Either way, it was too great a risk. The cancer had to be eliminated, rooted out once and for all. If he could do that much, it would be worth a life.

His own included, if it came to that.

FULL DARK inside his cell, but Mitchum did not mind. The guards had brought a plastic flashlight with his dinner plate, and he had used it to prevent himself from spilling any of the food, but otherwise the darkness was a friend. It helped him concentrate, thoughts channeled toward escape or vengeance.

It occurred to Mitchum that he might not have a chance in hell of breaking out, escaping through the woods, but taking several of the bastards with him when he died was an entirely different matter. He would take the risk, and gladly, for a clear shot at Martinez, one-on-one.

Or ten-on-one, if that was what it took.

His fatalism came from years of working homicide and vice, instinctive recognition of a hopeless situation. There was no point getting misty-eyed and thinking of the things that he had left undone, the words unspoken to selected individuals who mattered in his life. When you were cornered, with your back against the wall and nothing in your future but a cold hole in the ground—or a protracted session on some psycho's operating table— it was best to come out swinging, fighting back with everything you had.

In Mitchum's case that wasn't much, but they had given him a metal plate, a spoon, the flashlight. If they tried to move him, they would have to come within arm's reach, and that was all he wanted now. One chance to grab a human shield, perhaps a gun, and let his captors sample life on the receiving end.

He thought about Belasko and Emilio Sanchez, wondering if either one of them was still alive. Assuming that Belasko kept in touch with Hal Brognola, would the man from Justice mount some kind of punitive assault against Martinez, after they were gone?

It didn't really matter now.

Lesson number two from working Metro-Dade: When you were dead, that spelled the end of hopes and aspirations, plans and dreams. There might be something on the other side, some kind of afterlife, reward or punishment, but no one Mitchum knew of had returned to settle up accounts on Planet Earth. You did a job with what you had, while there was time, and then you said goodbye.

He wondered whether anyone would mourn his passing, or even realize that he was gone, but that was futile thinking and a major waste of energy. The ex-cop from Miami had regrets, like any other mortal man, but there was nothing he could do about them now. The next few hours—maybe minutes—would be all the time he had, a final chance to get it right.

The spoon, reversed, became an awkward but effective blade. Its edge was blunt, but if he struck an eye, perhaps soft tissue underneath the jaw, he had a chance to penetrate.

The plastic flashlight had some heft, with batteries inside, and he could always try to blind his enemies, if all else failed. A crack against some *pistolero*'s skull, more likely, if he got that close.

A plastic bucket sat in the corner, Mitchum's rest room, waiting to be filled. A little something he could douse the gunners with, to blind them for a precious moment while he made his move.

As for the empty plate...well, he could always skim it in their faces like a Frisbee. Maybe slam it into someone's face and help him get that million-dollar smile you always hear about.

Futility came home to Mitchum like a weight dumped on his shoulders, but he shook it off. Assuming that survival was a no-go, then the simple act of fighting back became an end unto itself. No reason much beyond resistance for the hell of it, and damn the consequences. When they took you down, at least the sons of bitches knew they had been in a fight, and they remembered you when they were counting bruises or comparing scars.

Small consolation, in the scheme of things, but it was all he had.

The pain had more or less abandoned him by now, except for tenderness around his groin and the pervasive headache. Fond companions in the darkness, keeping him alert to every sound outside. Stray voices, or a sound of footsteps, faded into the distance. His appointed sentry, fighting boredom, yawned as he paced outside the shack.

It wouldn't help Mitchum if the sentry fell asleep, since breaking down the door or digging through the plywood wall would surely wake him up and bring him running. Anyway, the shack was only part of it. His obstacles extended past those walls, beyond the camp, incorporating trees and darkness, unfamiliar ground where he would quickly lose himself, provide the hunters with an easy chase.

Better to wait, bide his time, and let them think that he had given up, a broken man. When they came in to get him, hours or days from now, he would be waiting, dark rage bottled up inside him like a potent elemental force. Meanwhile, if they believed him beaten, so much the better.

One chance was all he asked. One clear shot at the man he had been chasing for a year, and it would be enough.

It had to be.

FILIPE LEFT THEM about two hundred yards from the Martinez compound, pointing them in the direction they should go. He did not shake their hands or wish them luck, but there was something in his eyes—almost a touch of envy—that spoke volumes to the Executioner.

Enough hate there to go around, and then some.

The strong emotions had their place, and it was true that hate or anger could work wonders on a battlefield, especially when the odds were all against you, but a soldier who depended on emotion to perform his basic tasks was riding for a fall. At some point, if you wanted to survive long-term, you had to separate your feelings from cause.

Not easy, but Mack Bolan had been practicing the trick for years.

They took their time on those last two hundred yards, Bolan leading now that they no longer needed someone with a knowledge of the Spanish language on the point. From now on, if they were challenged by their enemies, the only fitting answer had to be a bullet.

Bolan left the Uzi slung across his chest, palming the Beretta 93-R with its 20-round clip and customized suppressor. There was still a bit of game trail left, and the warrior planted each step carefully, avoiding any sound that might alert a hidden sentry. Sanchez followed in his wake, observing Bolan's moves and stepping in his footprints, taking care with springy limbs that had a tendency to snap back in his face.

If there were gunmen posted in the woods, they hid themselves extremely well and made no move to intercept the new arrivals. Spending forty minutes on the last two hundred yards, to get it right the first time, Bolan and the *federale* saw the light that emanated from their target as the clock struck half-past ten.

Not floodlights, Bolan noted. More like torches, with a bonfire for support. A few more yards confirmed his first impression, showing him a compound without fences or visible electric lines. The tell-tale racket that a generator makes was also absent from the scene, and Bolan realized that they were making do with batteries for anything that absolutely needed power. Sentries presently on duty in the compound carried automatic weapons, pistols and police-style flashlights on their belts. He counted four, and estimated one or two more on the road, beyond his line of sight.

No power meant no floodlights to pin Bolan and Emilio when they made their move, but it would also mean he could not throw a switch or blow a single hut to black the compound out. A number of the huts were dark already, or possessed no windows, but the others were aglow with lamplight, for an almost homey feel.

He thought of Christmas cards, over the river and through the woods to Grandmother's house, and then his mind flashed back to Mitchum, the *nganga,* and the reason he was here. They had a score to settle, possibly a life to save, but first they needed more intelligence about the target.

Turning back to Sanchez, speaking softly, Bolan told him, "Circle to the right. I'll take the left. We'll meet directly opposite this point. Remember everything you see, and we'll compare notes on the other side."

"Okay."

He let the *federale* move away before he started circling to his left, a slightly harder route, since he would have to cross the road at some point, risking observation by the guards. Still, Bolan felt he had a better chance than Sanchez, and he also had the only silenced weapon in their mini-arsenal, if he was forced to take a lookout down.

In fact, the road was no great obstacle. He spied Fernando's watchdog from a distance, homing in on the red glow of his cigarette, some forty feet downrange. That left a gap between the sentry and the camp, his back turned as the Executioner stepped out of cover, standing upright as he crossed the narrow, unpaved track.

And that made five guns standing guard. Assume an equal number resting up, twice that if they were working eight-hour shifts, and that made it fifteen or twenty, for a basic estimate.

That gave them odds of ten-to-one, or slightly less, and he had played that game before. It was not one that he preferred, but options were in short supply.

Bolan kept on moving past the road, his eyes recording every detail of the camp. Nine plywood buildings circled an open yard, a bonfire burning in the center of the camp. No concrete way of telling where Doyle Mitchum might be held, but Bolan started by assuming that a prison hut would have no windows and would likely be the smallest no-frills shack available.

That narrowed down the field to one, but it was only guesswork. They would have to watch their step with the grenades and automatic fire until they spotted Mitchum in the flesh . . . or satisfied themselves that he was dead.

And if they blew it, then what?

Nothing would change. In the last analysis, Doyle Mitchum was expendable. Their basic goal was the elimination of Martinez and his cultists, liberating Mitchum in the process if they could, but wiping out the compound either way. It was not always possible to compromise in battle, and you had to keep priorities in mind.

He met Sanchez on the far side of the clearing, carrying a mind-map of the compound in his head. He listened to the *federale* first describing what was basically a mirror-image of the camp as seen by Bolan on his rounds.

No trip wires visible. No motion sensors, infrared or video equipment in a camp without a generator. Eyes and ears to spot them coming in, and that was all.

If they were swift and slick about it, Bolan knew the sentries would not be enough.

"Okay," he said at last, "here's what we do...."

CHAPTER TWENTY-FOUR

Martinez stood in darkness, savoring the night and watching as his sentries walked their beats on the perimeter. He tried to tell himself that he was safe here for the time being, but the nagging doubts returned to haunt him, worrying his mind.

Ibarra's silence bothered him the most, though he had sought the refuge of the mountain camp partly to put himself beyond the dealer's reach if things went sour in Piedras Negras. Their relations had been strained of late, and he would not have put it past Ramon to try some kind of double cross, especially if the man had begun to doubt the magic.

Faith was everything, regardless of the sect or creed involved. If he did not inspire Ibarra's trust—and fear to some degree—Martinez had no hold upon the dealer's loyalty. He could be cast aside, eliminated, as so many of Ramon's late business partners had been done away with in the past. So far, his various predictions, spells and curses—backed up in the real world with intelligence from law-enforcement sources, a strategic bribe or execution here and there—had been enough to do the trick.

Before this week.

The magic seemed to work against him this time. When an ordinary smuggler ran afoul of enemies, he wrote it off to rotten luck and did his best to punish those responsible. Martinez, though, had built his reputation on predictions of the future. Any time an accident or ad-

versary took him by surprise, his reputation suffered with
the clients who depended on his second sight to keep their
business running smoothly, day by day.

There were two likely reason for Ibarra's silence, then.
One possibility, the better option from Fernando's point
of view, had some calamity befall Ramon at home. Their
common enemy, perhaps, grown confident enough to
move against Ibarra at his home. Continued silence on
the radio could only mean Ramon was on the run, or
worse. For all Fernando knew, he might be dead by now,
and that would be the end of it, once he allowed some
time to pass, his adversaries growing tired of the inter-
minable wait.

The other possible scenario had Ramon alive and well,
his enemies destroyed or put to rout. No longer trusting
in Martinez or respecting him, Ibarra would begin to
question all the payments he had made for counsel and
protection, feeling that he had been swindled and betrayed. There could be only one response to such an insult, and Ibarra knew exactly where to find Martinez, if
he cared to look.

His handful of disciples matched against an army, if it
came to that. Martinez could not count on armed assistance from the spirit world, but if his followers were
strong enough, if they believed and kept the faith...

A voice distracted him, Gregorio Ruiz approaching
from the shadows, striving for a look of confidence and
not quite making it.

"Gregorio."

"I've just been out to check the guards again, make
certain that they understand their orders."

Ever since he lost the *federale* and Ricardo Obregon,
Ruiz had been the very model of efficiency, assuming
duties in advance of being asked, trying every trick in the

book to regain Fernando's good graces. It amused Martinez to watch him—or would have, under other circumstances—but this evening he had too much on his mind.

"You may as well go on to bed, Gregorio."

"Will you—"

"I need some time to think."

"Of course." Ruiz delayed another moment, toeing at the earth, before he spoke again. "About the prisoner, Fernando..."

"Yes?"

"I thought, perhaps, if I could question him again—"

"He has already told us everything he knows," Martinez said.

"Can we be sure of that?"

"I'm sure."

"Of course, if you're convinced."

"Where is Marcella?"

Angry color rose in Gregorio's cheeks, almost enough to make Martinez smile.

"She's in her quarters."

"Ah."

"I wonder..."

"What, Gregorio?"

"If we can really trust her."

"She has never failed me." Fernando put enough emphasis on "she" to tell Ruiz that nothing was forgotten or forgiven yet.

"I've told you, it was not my fault, Fernando."

"So you say."

"If Obregon had followed his instructions—"

"But he didn't."

"No."

"Enough, for now. If we are followed here, it won't be Obregon."

"If there is anything I can do, you simply have to ask."

"Go on to bed, then, and I'll see you in the morning."

"As you wish."

Ruiz was turning back in the direction he had come from, shoulders slumped, dejected, when the sudden crack of an explosion rocked the camp. Directly opposite Fernando's cabin, flame erupted from a larger building where four of his disciples slept together. It was empty now, with all four on perimeter patrol. He saw the corrugated metal roof blown skyward, bright flames licking at the walls, before the sound of automatic weapons rocked the camp.

"Gregorio!"

"*Sí, jefe?*"

"Bring the Anglo. Now!"

"I will!"

Martinez ducked back through the open doorway of his cabin, snuffed the lantern's flame, and found his submachine gun in the dark, by touch. A place for everything, and everything in its place.

Outside, as he emerged, the night had changed from peaceful darkness to a firelit scene from hell itself.

It was appropriate, Martinez thought, that he should play the devil of the piece.

SIMPLICITY can have its drawbacks in preparing for a combat strike. The layout of the camp placed everything within their reach, but that meant everything was also neatly covered by the sentries on patrol, no doubt with dozing reinforcements close at hand. Emerging from the trees, they would have nothing but the plywood huts for cover. Any movement in the open left them vulnerable to hostile fire.

And yet, simplicity had benefits, as well.

The buildings were not fortified in any way that Bolan recognized. Four vehicles—a van, two Rovers and a pickup truck—were parked together on the south side of the compound, nearest to the unpaved access road, and they were under guard. Destroying them was not a top priority, as long as Bolan could prevent his enemies from getting to the vehicles and roaring out of camp.

He gave Sanchez time to reach his starting point, at roughly two o'clock if he described the compound as a clock face, with the road and vehicles at six. His own position would be nine o'clock, and he was counting down the numbers in his head now, glancing at his watch to mark the fleeting passage of time.

H-Hour.

Bolan palmed a thermite grenade, released the safety pin, eased forward to the near edge of the trees. In front of him stood one of the largest structures in the camp, some twenty feet by twelve. Too large for Mitchum by himself, and he had glimpsed an open window to the front, when he was circling the camp on his reconnaissance.

A barracks hut, perhaps, and Bolan had no way of knowing whether it was occupied. In fact, he did not care. They needed a diversion, and if some of the *palero*'s troops were caught up in the middle of it, then so much the better.

Bolan reached the edge of the trees, his limit of cover, and checked both directions for sentries before he pitched the grenade in a gentle underhand. It struck the ground about three feet on his side of the target, rolling out of sight into the crawl space that was standard with each building in the camp.

Five seconds, counting as he doubled back and circled to the north, toward ten o'clock. When he was almost there, the thermite can exploded, swallowing the plywood cabin in a ball of flame. The white-hot coals were not thrown far and wide, as if the blast had taken place on open ground, but they had done their job.

A burst of automatic fire across the compound, Sanchez wading in, and then the sentries answered, some of them firing at shadows, others winging hot rounds toward Emilio's muzzle-flash, at least one wasting bullets on the burning cabin. Chaos reigned in the compound, as the others came awake or were distracted from their private thoughts by sounds of combat, answering the call.

He chose his mark and moment, bursting from the tree line with his Uzi spitting death in rapid-fire. The nearest sentry had his back turned, but the basic rules of battle didn't allow for courteous behavior. Bolan cut him down, a burst from brain to buttocks, pitching his target facedown in the dust.

Moving on, he drew fire from a gunner on the far side of the compound, ducking under cover of another building as a burst of automatic rifle slugs fanned past him, rippling the humid air. He was out of range for a grenade, and accuracy with the stuttergun was problematical, so Bolan let it go, advancing in a new direction with the hut for cover, covering his flank in case the sentry made his way across and tried an end run.

There was no one on his track as Bolan cleared the building, running low and fast in the direction of a hut with lamplight spilling through its single window. He plucked a frag grenade from his webbing, yanked its pin on the run, and swerved toward the front of the cabin, pitching his lethal egg squarely through the small pane of glass.

He dodged back toward the cover of the trees with bullets swarming on his heels, making a headlong dive into the shadows as the frag grenade exploded. Then he was on his feet and running back the way he came, with shrapnel hissing through the air and smacking into tree trunks overhead. No time to waste.

The position change saved him, as two sentries charged through the dappled firelight, blasting as they came and riddling the undergrowth where he had gone to ground. The Executioner was already twenty feet away and waiting for them, sighting down the Uzi's barrel, tightening his finger on the trigger for a zigzag burst that caught them by surprise.

One shooter dropped to his knees, a stunned expression on his face, life fading as he tried to turn and face his enemy. His comrade fired another burst before he fell, blood spouting from his chest, but it was high and wide, no threat to Bolan crouching in a clump of ferns. The dead man's weapon kept on firing as he hit the ground, its last rounds wasted on the moon and stars.

Three down, at least, but they were still outnumbered, still outgunned. Without a pause to breathe, Bolan fed a fresh clip to his Uzi, charging back in the direction of the camp.

There would be time enough for resting in the grave.

Right now, the Executioner had work to do.

IT WAS A STROKE OF LUCK, Gregorio Ruiz decided, that he had the Browning automatic tucked inside his belt, beneath the loose hem of his shirt. He did not have to waste time running for his cabin, doubling back for Mitchum once he armed himself.

Preparedness. It cost him nothing, and with any luck at all, it just might save his life.

He had not seen the enemy, but from the sound of automatic weapons and explosions, they were everywhere. The camp appeared to be surrounded, but he would not give up hope yet.

Fernando trusted him to fetch the prisoner, and *el padrino* always had a plan for every situation that arose. Retreating to the mountain camp had seemed to be a good idea, but someone had pursued them here.

Fleetingly he wondered if Ibarra was responsible. But he couldn't contemplate the odds now, it would only slow him down. The last thing he needed was any greater fear to paralyze his muscles, when he relied on them the most.

The gringo's padlocked cell was on the far side of the compound, still another thirty yards to go. Ruiz could see the guard assigned to watch their prisoner, crouched down beside the hut in shadow, looking for a clear-cut target as the world went mad. A new explosion came from somewhere on Ruiz's flank, and he could almost feel the shock waves pushing him along, compelling him to greater speed.

"Gregorio!"

He skidded to a halt and swiveled toward the sharp sound of Marcella's voice. She huddled in the doorway of her simple cabin, staring at him, wide-eyed in the semidarkness.

"Ah, Marcella."

"What is happening?"

He heard her voice crack and smiled to himself. A glance behind him showed no sign of Fernando at the moment. He would never have a better opportunity.

"Get back," he told her, moving toward the open door. "It isn't safe outside."

"Who is it?" she demanded. "Is Fernando safe?"

"He is," Gregorio replied. "But you're not."

He fired from the hip at point-blank range. A blind man could have made the shot from where he stood. His bullet struck Marcella just below one breast and spun her toward the cot on which she slept. He let her fall, stepped forward and waited for another burst of automatic fire outside before he triggered two more rounds into her back.

When it was over, come what may, Fernando would assume the bitch was shot by one of their assailants. Perfect. He felt giddy for a moment, wishing he could shout and dance for joy, but he had other things to do. There would be time enough later to celebrate in private when he had a moment for himself.

Looking out from Marcella's room, he checked again for *el padrino* and saw him just emerging from his quarters with a submachine gun in his hands. Ruiz slipped out and sprinted toward the gringo's quarters, out of breath when he arrived, the sentry waiting nervously until he found his voice.

"Fernando wants the prisoner, right now."

"You have the key?"

Ruiz produced it from his pocket, almost dropping it before he got control. "You cover me."

He stepped out of the shadows, circling to the door, his shoulders braced for the explosive impact of a bullet. Any second now, he thought, imagining the pain and what would follow after. If Fernando was correct, about the life beyond—

Of course he was correct! The only sin was doubt, and nothing mattered more than faith, except for total loyalty.

He was at last so close to everything that he had always wanted, he could almost taste it. He had Fernando to himself, no bitch to come between them. All they had to do was beat this trap, survive to find themselves another hiding place and start again.

With *el padrino,* anything was possible.

He got the padlock open on his second try and dropped it at his feet. The hasp was stiff. He had to claw it open, peeling skin off his knuckles in the process.

He had it now, oblivious to fleeting pain as the door swung open on darkness, the reek of stale urine and worse. Ruiz wrinkled his nose at the smell, squinting into the shadows.

"Flashlight!" he snapped at the guard, extending his free hand, receiving the flash in return. He flicked it on and thrust it out in front of him, the Browning leading him across the threshold.

EVEN AS HE WAITED FOR IT, counting down the seconds, the explosion almost took Sanchez by surprise. White phosphorus, a brilliant flash and rolling flames to follow, took out what seemed to be a kind of barracks structure. Instant gunfire from the sentries, well before they had a target, and Belasko came back with short bursts of his own.

The *federale* broke from cover, cradling the H&K submachine gun, coming up behind a sentry who was carrying an M-16. He was about ten feet away when suddenly the lookout heard him coming, pivoting to drop the stranger in his tracks.

Emilio beat him to it, shooting him in the face, three parabellum rounds at close to point-blank range. The sentry's face imploded in a burst of crimson. Down and out, the nearly headless body was still twitching as he leapt across it, veering to his right.

The camp erupted in chaos, with half a dozen guns unloading all at once. He ducked behind a plywood building, pressed his ear against the wall, and picked up muffled voices, with the sound of scuffling feet. Two men, at least.

Doyle Mitchum?

Sanchez worked his way around the building, checked both ways before he showed himself. A new explosion on the far side of the compound added more confusion to the hectic scene. He chose his moment, mounted wooden steps in two quick strides, and kicked the flimsy door wide open on the run.

Inside, a lantern glowed brightly on a table in the corner. Radio equipment sat on a second, larger table, silent now. Two gunmen in the middle of the room, confused and plainly frightened, gaped at the apparition that had burst into their lives.

"The gringo!" Sanchez snapped. "Where is he? *Pronto!*"

One of them went crazy, groping for an automatic pistol on his hip. Flap holsters are a bitch for quick-draw situations, and he never made it, vaulting backward as Emilio shot him in the chest. His partner came unglued at that and swiveled toward the radio, scooping the heavy set up in his arms, half turning toward Sanchez as if he meant to throw the whole damned thing.

A burst of parabellum manglers ripped across his waistline, well below the radio that blocked a clear shot at his chest. He staggered, dropped it, slumping to his knees, and Sanchez shot him in the head to wrap it up.

Three down, and he was wasting time.

Outside, two huts were burning now, their light combining with that of the bonfire to drive back some of the forest shadows. In their place, flickering new shadows: giants running here and there, in groups and singly, sometimes sprawling in the dust.

He sought Martinez, but had no luck with faces in the firelight, and began to work his way around the camp. The vehicles were still intact, one guard in place, but no one was attempting to escape so far. A mix of anger and confusion had them running back and forth around the compound, squeezing off at targets when they could, or sometimes just at other shadows in the night.

He turned back arbitrarily, retracing his steps past the radio shack, no special mission ordered once he got inside the camp. Doyle Mitchum and Martinez were their two prime targets, one to kill, the other to remove if possible, and Sanchez reasoned that it could not take long to find one or the other in a place this small. Say fifty yards from one end to the other, maybe thirty-five or forty yards across. In daylight, he could easily have counted heads and picked the individuals he wanted, but the night and blasting weapons made it difficult.

Beyond the radio shack, another silent building, front door standing open, swinging gently on its hinges. Sanchez took the steps in a rush, shouldered through the doorway and flattened himself against the nearest wall in a crouch, out of sight. If someone was waiting for him, they should have fired as he entered, when he was a perfect silhouette against the firelight from outside.

He took a penlight from his pocket, held it well away from him, the H&K ready as he switched it on. The beam did not attract a swarm of bullets, so he left it on and swept the cabin, shoulder-high at first, then dipping toward the floor. A flash of blue and crimson, almost close enough to touch.

He recognized Marcella Grant from photographs in Mitchum's file, no longer quite the beauty she had been in life. A bullet in the chest and two more in the back had done a quick, efficient job of snuffing out her life. Ge-

ography and timing told him that Belasko had not been
here yet, which meant the rats had started turning on each
other.

He swore in his frustration. If they were killing one
another now, what chance did Mitchum have?

Emerging from the witch's quarters, Sanchez nearly
collided with a running sentry. Startled, the gunman lost
his balance, skidding on one knee, but kept a firm grip
on his AK-47, finger on the trigger, swiveling toward
target acquisition. Sanchez emptied out his magazine and
left the gunner stretched out where he fell, reloading on
the move as he went off in search of Mitchum.

They were running out of time, and he had not come
all this way to line Fernando's flunkies up like targets in
a shooting gallery.

They had to find their primary targets. But where was
the *palero?* Where was Mitchum?

CHAPTER TWENTY-FIVE

The first explosion brought Doyle Mitchum to his feet, the metal spoon in one hand, flashlight in the other. Standing rigid in the darkness, he felt shock waves from the blast brush up against his quarters, rattling the metal roof and sending tremors through the walls. A brief smiled played across his face—explosions had to mean bad trouble for Martinez—but he caught himself a heartbeat later, realizing that a raid against the camp would also put his own life on the line.

The blast was followed by all kinds of automatic-weapons fire outside, as if the posted sentries were confronting several dozen enemies. More likely, Mitchum thought, they would be squeezing off at shadows, but he kept his fingers crossed. No matter what went down, no matter who the raiders were, it helped to think about Martinez and his cronies scrambling for their lives, some of them blowing it and catching hell.

Another blast, and for an instant he saw firelight glimmering, a gap between two sheets of plywood on the eastward-facing wall. He visualized Martinez dead or badly wounded, squirming in the dust, and felt the cold smile coming back.

It was erased a moment later, when he thought about a raid against the camp with heavy weapons or grenades. Explosions ripping through the simple buildings, fire to follow, consuming the mess. Unless the raiders had some reason not to kill him—if they even had a clue that he was there—it stood to reason that his own shack might be hit.

Instead of the *palero,* now, he pictured shrapnel ripping through his own flesh, bright flames lapping at his clothes. No way to stop it, locked up in a cage. He was a sitting target, helpless to defend himself.

With all the shooting, Mitchum almost missed the sound of running footsteps, muffled voices close beside his hut. Two men, presumably his watchdog and a new arrival, hastily conferring on the battle's sidelines, maybe lying low to save themselves.

Of course, there was another possibility, as well.

He detected more movement, boot heels on the wooden steps outside his door. The ex-cop from Miami turned his flashlight on just long enough to guide his steps, two strides to reach the plastic bucket, pick it up, and take another long step toward the door. He clenched the spoon between his teeth, like some pathetic takeoff on a pirate from the Disney movies he had watched when he was just a kid.

The bucket needed both hands, if he meant to do it right, and there would only be one chance.

The padlock rattled, someone grappling with the key, and then he heard the hasp scrape open. The door swung back, providing Mitchum's first view of the courtyard since they had brought his food, but he had no time to look.

Coming in was a silhouette, no face to speak of. Mitchum saw a gun in one hand and a flashlight in the other, waited for the light to blaze before he swung the bucket in a firm two-handed grip and let the contents fly.

He was rewarded with a splash, a gasp of outrage and a pistol shot. The bullet missed him and drilled the back wall of his quarters, as Mitchum swung the bucket one-handed now, slamming it into the gunner's face. It was light plastic, but at least the impact knocked his man off balance, made him drop the flashlight as he brought the left hand up to guard his face.

The pistol swung toward Mitchum, but he dropped the plastic pail and seized the shooter's wrist, left-handed, palming the spoon in his right hand and striking by reflex, hoping to find soft tissue.

He jabbed an eye, and heard screams of pain from his assailant as he ripped the spoon free, coming back for more. Warm blood flowed across his knuckles, and the pistol fired a third time, close enough to singe his rib cage through the denim of his shirt.

It was a combination move that finally did the trick. He struck out with the spoon, put all his weight behind it, penetrating underneath the gunner's jawline on the left. This time there was a rush of blood, and Mitchum twisted on the wounded shooter's gun arm, putting pressure on the wrist and elbow, startled when the automatic clattered at his feet.

They scrambled for the weapon, Mitchum on his hands and knees in semidarkness, with the gunner right on top of him, blood spurting from his throat, weird gagging noises coming from his lips. The pistol was under Mitchum's hand, and then he had it, leaning into the gunner with a shoulder and twisting, forcing him back toward the door.

Mitchum rocked back on his haunches, squeezing off one round before he had a chance to aim. A gut shot, from the sound of it, and the reaction of his target. One more squarely in the chest blew his adversary backward through the door, and he had time to check the pistol, saw it was a Browning parabellum, meaning eight or nine rounds left, depending on the load.

He went through the door pistol-first, swinging to his right as a shadow lurched upright, cursing him in gutter Spanish, leveling an automatic rifle. Mitchum shot the gunner twice at something close to skin-touch range, the impact shearing off his target's forehead, flattening the guy without another sound.

He glanced around the compound, alive with leaping flames and jagged muzzle-flashes, then came back to check the first man he had shot.

It was Gregorio Ruiz. A good one to get.

"Tough luck, *compadre.*"

He was turning back to claim the second dead man's rifle when a soft voice froze him in his tracks.

"Doyle Mitchum?"

Slowly he faced the sound of the voice, needing some fix on his target prior to hazarding a shot.

"Sanchez?"

The *federale* ran to meet him, dressed in olive drab, with camo war paint on his face. He had a submachine gun, with grenades and shit all over him like something from an army training film.

"Are you all right?"

"I'm getting there," the ex-cop from Miami said.

"You killed these two?"

"Seems like."

"Belasko's here, as well."

Doyle Mitchum smiled. "Then I suggest we find the boy," he said, "and help him kick some ass."

HIS THIRD GRENADE caught three men just emerging from their quarters, two of them without their shirts, the third in Jockey shorts and nothing else. Body armor might have helped them with the shrapnel, but the flash fire and concussion would have been the same in any case.

Three up, three down.

He watched their bodies scatter, ready with the Uzi if they needed any help to die, but they were managing without him. Bolan met another sentry, coming up behind them, startled by the sight of mutilated flesh, recovering in time to fire a burst that came in high and wide.

He was given no second chance as Bolan caught him with a rising figure eight, the parabellum shockers spinning him around and dumping him beside the others in an awkward, lifeless sprawl.

How many left?

It seemed like dozens, in the chaos of the moment, but he knew the crowd was thinning out. By any reasonable estimate, Martinez had no more than half his soldiers left, but that could still mean six or seven guns, at least. Perhaps eight or ten, if he had underestimated the contingent's strength to start with.

Either way, poor odds.

A rifleman was firing from the doorway of the next building down, his target uncertain, but no question about his determination. Even, measured bursts of automatic fire, as regular as clockwork, as if the guy had no concern about his stock of ammunition. If he let the shooter go, there was a chance that he would wind up taking out some of his own comrades, but Bolan still had to think about Sanchez, maybe Mitchum in the huts and shadows that were taking fire.

He came up on the shooter's blind side, palming a grenade and working out the safety pin as he advanced. The angle wasn't good, there was a swinging door in Bolan's way, but he could use that to his own advantage, if he watched his step.

A window in the plywood wall, beside the door, invited him to take his shot.

He moved lightly, conscious of the fact that he was totally exposed. Stray bullets kicked up spurts of dust across the compound, and it only took one gunner, sighting from the shadows on the far side of the camp, to bring him down. Confusion was his ally, bodies scattered in the open, no one sure exactly where to point their weapons from one moment to the next.

It almost took him back to Nam, the kind of crazy firefights that would blow up in the jungle on patrol, but Bolan concentrated on the present, knowing that a heartbeat of distraction was enough to cost his life. When he was close enough, he made the pitch, a little something extra just in case they had a screen. The grenade hit dead center on the glass and fell inside, making a muffled plop on impact with the floor.

He scuttled backward, crouching, ready for the blast. Somebody shouted in the cabin, lunging headlong for the door and out, a swan dive into dirt. Behind the diver, hell broke loose, the door and windows blooming flame. One of the plywood walls split down a seam and buckled outward, bringing down a portion of the corrugated metal roof. A scream like nothing human came from the midst of the inferno, quickly swallowed by the hungry fire.

The lone survivor struggled to his feet and was bending to retrieve his weapon when the Uzi spat a string of bullets from a range of twenty feet. His body seemed to ripple, shuddering as it absorbed the burst then toppled over backward with no hint of a graceful dive this time, his limbs all slack and rubbery in death.

The warrior was about to move, when he heard someone coming on his flank. Two runners by the sound, a fact confirmed as Bolan swiveled back to meet them, tracking with the submachine gun, tightening into the squeeze.

"Don't shoot, for God's sake!"

It was Mitchum, with Sanchez close behind him. Bolan took a heartbeat to assess the captive's physical condition, noting that he had a pistol in his belt, an AK-47 in his hands.

"Are you all right?"

"Been better," Mitchum told him, "but I guess I can't complain."

"Martinez?"

Mitchum shook his head. "I haven't seen the fucker for a while," he answered, "but I got Ruiz."

"The woman, Grant, is also dead," Sanchez told them.

"How?"

"Somebody shot her. One of theirs, unless . . ."

"I never got the chance," said Bolan. "Anyway, that still leaves a few."

"What say we clean these bastards up," Doyle Mitchum said with a grin, "and take it on the road?"

MARTINEZ GAVE UP WAITING for Gregorio to bring the Anglo back. His plans had fallen through somehow, and he could not afford to linger in the shadows any longer, waiting for a bullet or grenade to find him out.

If they were dead, then that was that. Otherwise, Ruiz could have the gringo to himself and find his own way out. Every man for himself.

And woman, *sí*. He thought about Marcella, wondered where she was, but there was nothing close to pity in Fernando's heart. A perfect egotist, he was concerned for number one and no one else. If his disciples could not save themselves, it was unfortunate, the price of playing in a game where you were hopelessly outmatched.

He still had no clue who was battering the camp, Ibarra's men or someone else, but it would make no difference if they gunned him down. Once he was safe, there would be ample time to study his mistakes, consider options, tap his secret bank accounts if running seemed the smartest way to go.

There was a chance that he could salvage something from the chaos, even now. If this was all Ibarra's work, he could negotiate—albeit from a distance—making some concessions here and there, perhaps refunding his most recent payment from the dealer's war chest.

He discarded the idea. Returning money was against his principles. Ibarra would consider it a sign of weakness, and besides, Ramon would not have sent an army for Martinez if the cash was all he had in mind.

He had to escape first, then decide.

It might just be a blessing in disguise, the unknown fate that had apparently befallen both Marcella and Ruiz. Martinez traveled faster on his own, no one to slow him down or place his life in jeopardy. If he could only reach the vehicles....

They left the keys in the ignition switches as a matter of routine. Martinez only had to get there, pick his wheels and drive away, but it was not as simple as it sounded.

First, the compound had become an open shooting gallery. His surviving men were blasting aimlessly at shadows, sometimes firing at each other when they took the nearest muzzle-flashes for an enemy. As for the raiders, he had no idea how many there might be or where they were around the camp. It took only one bullet to defeat his plan, and it would matter little whether it exploded from a hostile gun or came as friendly fire.

For all the risks involved, Martinez knew his chances of survival were reduced each moment he remained in place, a sitting target. If he meant to go, it should be now, while there was still a chance.

He swallowed hard, worked up his nerve, and took off running from the shadows, breaking for the vehicles. They seemed undamaged yet, despite the concentrated firing, and he only needed one. A guard was still on duty, squatting under cover near the pickup truck, and he was waiting when Martinez slid in beside him, like a ball player stealing third base.

"Padrino!"

"I am leaving in the van," Martinez told him, dusting off his pants from force of habit as he shifted to a crouch.

"Bien," the gunner said, "we go together."

"No. I need someone to watch my back."

"Jefe—"

No more time to waste on arguments. Martinez waddled back a yard or so, to keep from messing up his clothes, and shot his startled follower between the eyes. He would not have a guard behind him now, but neither would he have some jealous bastard shooting at him as he drove away.

A trade-off, and he felt that he had made the right decision in the circumstances. It was done now, come what may.

He reached the van, stretched up and got the driver's door open, climbing awkwardly into the seat. The key was waiting for him, safe and sound. In front of him, no more than fifty feet away, the dark road beckoned like an escape tunnel, offering safety and freedom.

Martinez hesitated, one hand on the key. Suppose the raiders had crept in beforehand, planting booby traps among the vehicles? Explosives wired to the ignition, ready to explode if someone tried to drive away?

He had no choice.

Martinez held his breath, closed his eyes and twisted the ignition key. The engine grumbled once, caught hold and roared to life. No blast to send his mangled body sailing off across the camp.

He felt a wild, almost-hysterical sensation of relief as he put the van in gear, twisted the steering wheel and pressed the accelerator pedal to the floor. Sand spat out behind him as he rolled away.

No one could stop him now!

With the *orishas* on his side, he meant to have the last laugh, after all.

BOLAN HEARD the van's engine turning over, a growl beneath the sharper sound of gunfire, and he saw his plan begin to crumble. Someone was slipping out, and while it could be any member of the cult, a gut reaction told him he should stop the vehicle at any cost.

Mitchum and Sanchez followed as he broke from cover, running toward the makeshift parking area. A scrape of tires and spitting gravel, rubber digging for a grip and finding it a heartbeat later, brake lights winking briefly as the unseen driver made his way around the next two cars in line. He'd have a clear shot at the access road in two or three more seconds, and there would be nothing they could do.

Bolan had an instant choice to make. The van was pulling out of range for submachine-gun fire, but Mitchum tried his captured AK-47, missing by an easy yard and losing it among the trees. The other vehicles were waiting, if they found a way to get one started, but pursuit would mean abandoning the camp with cultists still alive...and any one of them could be Martinez, hanging back and lying low.

There was no real choice, then.

Since they could not split their forces, they would have to finish up the job they came to do. And if Fernando de Leon Martinez was the one who got away, then they would have to start from scratch.

Angry shouts and random firing brought their full attention back to the surviving enemies in camp. Sanchez crouched behind the pickup truck, while Bolan and Mitchum sought the cover of a dark sedan. Poor choices, when he thought about the risk of fuel tanks detonating with a lucky shot, but they were too far from the nearest building to attempt the move.

From Bolan's vantage point, he counted half a dozen separate muzzle-flashes, mostly concentrated on the east side of the compound. They were playing leapfrog, two or three men firing while the others bypassed their position, moving in to close the ring. It was a more or less effective tactic, if your prey was cornered, but Bolan and his allies had the whole dark forest at their backs, a custom-made escape hatch.

But they could not slip away. Not yet.

Retrieving Mitchum had been part of their objective, but a secondary part. Until they saw Martinez dead or knew that he had managed to escape, they still had work to do.

A rifle bullet smacked against the fender, next to Bolan's face, and he immediately swiveled to protect his flank. A gunner moved in from the direction of the road, no doubt a sentry who was stationed there to warn the camp if anyone approached from the direction of Tres

Lobos. He was lining up another shot when Bolan let the Uzi rip and dropped him on his backside.

That left six that he was sure of.

All three vehicles were taking hits now, windows shattering, the bodywork echoing with sounds like rapid hammer strokes. A tire blew on the pickup, then another, and the steady drip of water from a punctured radiator worked on Bolan's nerves. The Mexican water torture. Under other circumstances, Bolan would have smiled, but he was concentrating on survival at the moment, and his sense of humor had to wait in line.

In retrospect, he never knew exactly what made the *paleros* dump their leapfrog tactic for an all-out frontal charge. It could have been impatience, or perhaps they really did think they were bulletproof, protected by Fernando's magic somehow.

A shout rang out across the compound, and the gunners broke from cover in a rush, all firing as they ran, six automatic weapons chewing up the cars and raising spouts of dust on impact with the earth. The starting distance measured close to thirty yards, but they had cut it down by half when Bolan tossed his first grenade, immediately followed by another.

Fire and thunder wreaked havoc in the clearing. Sanchez was winding up to pitch another frag bomb, and Bolan watched two men disappear, a third *palero* lifted off his feet and somersaulting through the air. Survivors of the chain-reaction blasts were reeling in the smoke, disoriented and firing blindly, burning up their ammo in a panic.

Bolan jumped in with his Uzi, spotting targets in the cordite haze and milking out abrupt precision bursts. Supporting fire came from Sanchez, with Mitchum late but getting there with his Kalashnikov until the magazine ran dry.

And it was done.

They spent another moment under cover, waiting for the other shoe to drop, but there were no more hostile gunners in the camp or the surrounding forest.

"Martinez," Bolan said, already on his feet. "We need to find him, if he's here."

They spent a quarter hour kicking doors and peering under the surviving buildings, rolling bodies over for a glimpse of lifeless faces. All in vain. Fernando de Leon Martinez was not found among the dead.

Three buildings were still engulfed by flame, and Bolan recognized a possibility that the *palero* might be roasted to the bone in any one of them, but he could not afford to make that leap of faith. His gut was churning, bringing home bad news.

"The van," said Mitchum.

"Probably."

"Well, shit."

"What now?" Sanchez asked.

A quick scan of the vehicles showed two with engine damage, all three sitting on their rims with shredded rubber.

"Now," the Executioner replied, "we walk."

CHAPTER TWENTY-SIX

Dawn was breaking by the time they reached Tres Lobos, three men coming back instead of two, and Sanchez gave the villagers a brief account of what had happened. With Bolan's blessing, he included a description of Martinez's escape, in case the self-styled warlock started hatching plans to get revenge against his erstwhile neighbors on the mountain.

Anything was possible, once ego tinged with madness took control, and Bolan again urged Inez Lozaro to think about a change of residence.

"He may have soldiers we don't know about, some trick left up his sleeve. I wouldn't want to be here, if he got it in his head your people were responsible for what went down."

"I think you would," she told him, putting on a gentle smile. "You would not run away, and I can't, either. This is still my home."

There was no arguing with roots, and Bolan understood the kind of pride, mixed up with pure, unselfish love, that made her stay. It was a choice each man and woman had to make alone, at some point in their lives, and he admired her courage, even as he clung to his concern.

They made another hike, once they had eaten, and the car was waiting where they left it. Nothing seemed out of place, no signs of tampering while they were gone. It started on the second try, and Bolan took them out of there, remembering Tres Lobos and its people as he drove, already looking forward to the next phase of their task.

"The little shit's long gone," said Mitchum from the back seat, sounding angry and dejected.

"Even so, he had to leave a trail," the Executioner replied. "If we can pick it up, he's ours."

"Good luck. You think he's advertising? Guy like that, he's bound to have some ready cash laid by where he can pick it up, regardless of the time. Once he finds out Ibarra's gone, he'll burrow down so deep they'll have to pipe the sunlight in."

"He can't just disappear," said Bolan, trying not to share the ex-cop's pessimistic mood despite the odds against them. "He's already tried the mountains, and he blew it. Cash or not, he'll need a helping hand to make the fade. Some kind of transportation when he dumps the van. A place to stay. If he's afraid to show his face, somebody has to do his shopping for him, maybe even patch him up if he was hit."

"You're saying someone has to be clued in on where he's going."

"Right."

"Terrific. How are we supposed to find out who *that* is? I would have voted for Ibarra, but you knocked him off. Ruiz and Grant are dead. If he's got more disciples out there, *I* can't tell you who they are."

"You may not have to," Sanchez said. He had not spoken since they started driving, and the *federale*'s tone was muted now, as if he were reluctant to proceed.

"Explain."

Emilio shook his head. "Not yet. I may be wrong. In fact, I *hope* I'm wrong, but there's a way to check. I need a telephone, as soon as possible."

They drove in silence for another twenty miles, until they reached La Babia and found a service station with a public telephone that worked. While Bolan filled the tank, Sanchez shut himself inside the booth and dialed a number, feeding coins into the slot. The *federale's* back was turned to Bolan as he spoke into the mouthpiece, shoulders hunched, his free hand buried in the pocket of his jeans.

"What's going on, you think?" asked Mitchum.

"We'll just have to wait and see."

Emilio was stone-faced as he left the booth and walked back to the car. The station was a quarter mile behind them when he spoke, eyes focused on the foothills easing into desert as they drove.

"I told you my immediate superior had disappeared," the *federale* said.

"Cabeza, was it?" Mitchum asked.

"Calzada. *Capitán* Miguel Calzada. Other than myself, he was the only member of the FJP who knew about our plan . . . until the day he vanished."

"Say again?"

"I called his secretary, at her home," Sanchez said. "She was devoted to Calzada, and his disappearance has affected her the same as if a relative had died. I think she loved him, secretly. It makes no difference, now."

"Go on."

"The morning of his disappearance, he was summoned to a meeting at the *commandante's* office. He did not return directly, but he telephoned to say he had important work to do. The next word came that afternoon, when the police in Ciudad Acuna found his car abandoned."

"Let's make sure I've got this straight," said Mitchum. "You believe this *commandante*—"

"Salvador Fragosa."

"You think this Fragosa sold your captain out?"

"Who else? Calzada had no other pressing cases at the moment, just some minor smuggling here and there. The urgent meeting with Fragosa came immediately prior to the attack where Hargis was abducted and I narrowly escaped with Obregon. It would explain the ambush in San Carlos, anyway."

"You have some reason for believing this Fragosa's dirty?"

Sanchez frowned. "He lives above his means. I know Calzada was reluctant to discuss our mission with him, even though department guidelines called for him to clear any undercover operation with superiors."

"So, now what?" Mitchum asked.

"I say we drive to Ciudad Acuna. Make Fragosa tell us what we need to know."

"He may not have a fix on where Martinez went to ground."

"It's all we have."

"And once he talks?" asked Bolan.

"*Muerto.*"

Death.

"We've got a problem here," the warrior said.

"Which is?" Doyle Mitchum asked, watching in the rearview mirror.

"Bottom line, I've never killed a lawman," Bolan said. "I don't much feel like starting now."

"Don't worry," Sanchez told them both. "Fragosa's mine."

TEQUILA WAS the best thing for a case of nerves, in normal circumstances, but today, thought Salvador Vidal Fragosa, things were far from normal. Working on his second glass of liquid fire, he felt no more relaxed than when his telephone had started ringing off the hook, two nights ago.

Ramon Ibarra was dead, with something like a dozen of his men. The massacre was making news across the border, in El Norte, where the gringo DEA was celebrating, maybe breaking out champagne for all Fragosa knew. Ibarra had evaded their best-laid plans for years on end, with the cooperation of his friends inside the FJP, and nothing short of death seemed likely to prevent him from continuing his reign.

Now, death had done its work, and there was chaos in the local underworld, a scramble for the spoils, with half a dozen upstart dealers claiming credit for Ibarra's murder, working overtime to build their reputations on a pipe dream. None of them had been responsible, Fragosa knew, because the strike was too efficient, almost military. None of the attackers had been killed or wounded— at least, no bodies were left behind. The only dead had been Ibarra and his men, cut down with automatic weapons and explosives, the estate resembling a war zone rather than the most expensive mansion in Piedras Negras.

Therefore Fragosa's first concern was that if none of the pretenders were responsible for taking out Ibarra and his troops, who *was?* A partial answer dogged him, gnawing at the corners of his mind, but he would not allow himself to think it through. It seemed impossible, and yet . . .

The next event was Martinez, a frantic collect call at 2 a.m., as if a man so wealthy could not find a pocketful of coins to feed a public telephone. His caller verged on hysteria until Fragosa calmed him down, then Martinez ran down the details of a raid against his mountain campsite, his lieutenants dead, the camp in flames. He had managed to escape, but he was being hunted. He would have to run. He needed help.

Fragosa had always known this day would come, when he began his dealings with Martinez, but the pay was excellent and he was not required to soil his hands with dirty work. A piece of information here and there was all that was asked, a warning in advance of raids against Ibarra's merchandise or dealers. It was nothing other *commandantes* didn't do for wealthy narco traffickers around the country every day. Why should Fragosa be the only one to play it straight and be impoverished by adherence to a vague ideal of honesty?

But there had been a flip side to the coin. In selling information to Martinez, he had forged a bond. Fragosa did not quite buy Fernando's magic act, but there was still enough peasant blood in his veins to leave some room for doubt. A fool played fast and loose with the unknown, defying forces that he did not fully understand, but Salvador Fragosa was no fool.

He had allowed Martinez to divine his future, gratified when wealth kept cropping up in the predictions. Life was sweet ... as long as he cooperated with Martinez and the rest.

Of course, Fragosa never *really* thought Fernando had the power to curse him with disease or strike him dead with magic from afar. Martinez could pick up a telephone, however, and report their dealings to Fragosa's own superior—or worse, the gutter press—with critical results for his career. It might seem self-destructive, but he reckoned that Martinez would have ways of riding out the storm, new guardians inside the FJP and in the courts by then, before he made a move.

One thing about Fernando, he was always looking out for number one.

A born survivor, he always landed on his feet. But this time Martinez needed a helping hand . . . from Salvador Fragosa.

Perhaps, the *commandante* thought, one more tequila might just do the trick. Perhaps two or three.

Fragosa had all day.

FRAGOSA'S HOME was situated in the western part of Ciudad Acuna, not a neighborhood of millionaires, by any means, but more extravagant than any lawman living on his basic salary could readily afford. The garden was a riot of pastels, surrounded by a wall that seemed more suitable for decoration than security. A wrought-iron gate was set into the wall, no padlock readily apparent on their drive-by, but Sanchez saw a uniform beyond the gate and estimated that there would be more inside.

"He's called the troops out," the American warrior said, cruising past the house and driving on until he found a place to park, beyond view of Fragosa's grounds.

"Unusual, I grant you," Sanchez said, "but not unheard of. Sometimes, when a major case is breaking here—as in Colombia—the principals react with violence aimed at the authorities."

"You think Fragosa's frightened of the cult?" Bolan asked.

"A possibility. More likely, he is worried that the men who killed Ibarra may be trying for a—what is the expression?—a clean sweep."

Doyle Mitchum chuckled to himself. "Ain't that a shame?"

"Five minutes going in, and then the time required for questioning Fragosa," Sanchez said, rehearsing every movement in his mind. They had to make allowances for unexpected obstacles, resistance by the guards, but if they moved decisively it should be possible to overcome the sentries with a minimum of violence.

Sanchez did not wish to kill the men outside, but if it came to that, he was prepared to use all necessary force. Nothing short of death would keep him from Fragosa now, and if the uniforms should try, it was *their* tough luck.

Besides the automatic pistol in his shoulder holster, Sanchez had a blackjack and a stun gun in the pockets of his sport coat, ready to deliver something less than lethal force if given half a chance. Doyle Mitchum had the bindings—two pairs of handcuffs and several plastic strips favored by police for mass arrests in riot situations—for immobilizing guards.

"Let's go."

He glanced back at Bolan, staying with the car, and recognized the warrior's ambivalence. He was a soldier with ideals, however abstract, and Sanchez sympathized. In other circumstances, Sanchez doubtless would have felt the same, but in the past few days his sense of absolutes had come unhinged, a new perspective on his world demanding fresh priorities.

"We'll be back soon."

Bolan nodded, watching as they moved along the sidewalk. Drawing closer to Fragosa's property, they circled to the rear and found an alley, Sanchez watching out for guards before he nimbly scaled the fence. Behind him, Mitchum dragged himself across.

"I'm getting too damn old for this," the ex-cop from Miami whispered.

"Shh."

They met the first guard moments later, Sanchez creeping up behind him on tiptoe, the stun gun ready in his fist. No chance for an alarm as he poked the electrodes against his target's spine and held the trigger down, stepping back as the *federale* convulsed and collapsed to the garden path. Doyle Mitchum snapped the handcuffs on, made sure their man was breathing on his own, without apparent difficulty, and then knotted a handkerchief around his face as a gag.

Next stop, the garden out in front, where Sanchez found the sentry they had spotted on their drive-by. From appearances, unless he had another man inside the house, Fragosa felt secure with only two guards on the property.

This guard was concentrating on the street, where no traffic showed at the moment, and he stood at ease, hands clasped behind his back. The pistol on his belt was nickel-plated, shiny grips fashioned from mother-of-pearl. His boots were spit-shined to a mirror gloss. The very image of military discipline.

Sanchez approached from the lookout's blind side, stun gun in hand, his mind so focused that he missed the gravel underfoot. His boots made a scraping sound, completely insignificant, except that it betrayed him to the *federale* at the gate. His man was turning, curious at first, then startled, when Sanchez leapt to close the gap.

He thrust the stun gun out, connecting with his target's jaw before the officer could focus on his face. No sound whatever came from the weapon as it fired a blast of voltage into flesh and muscle. With a gasp, the second guard slumped backward, rolling into decorative cacti as he fell.

After checking the man's pulse and respiration, Sanchez lifted him away from the prickly thorns before Mitchum snapped his second set of handcuffs onto unresisting wrists. They rolled the *federale* over on his side to keep him from swallowing his tongue, knotting another crude gag in place to silence him if he revived before their work was done inside the house.

They had made it this far.

With guards on station, Fragosa had not locked the door. Sanchez smelled tobacco as he crossed the threshold, followed his nose along a corridor that led him past the living room and kitchen, toward an open den. Doyle Mitchum was on his heels, both men with automatic pistols in their hands.

They found Fragosa in his study, seated in a chair upholstered in leather and sipping a glass of tequila. The half-empty bottle stood beside him on a smallish table. Beside the bottle, an expensive cigar smoldered in a ceramic ashtray, adding its aroma to the smell of wood and leather in the room.

Fragosa saw them as they entered, blinking in surprise. Their pistols kept him from trying anything foolish. Instead of rising from his chair, the *commandante* finished his tequila in a single gulp and forced a smile.

"Emilio Sanchez, I presume?"

A scowl from Sanchez banished any thought of fond amenities. "We need to have a talk," he said.

WAITING IN THE CAR, the mini-Uzi resting in his lap beneath an open magazine, Mack Bolan had the time to question his beliefs and attitudes. It felt unnatural for him to sit a mission out, and yet he felt he had no choice.

Interrogating crooked cops was one thing, but Sanchez had made no secret of his plan to kill Fragosa, and the Executioner could hardly blame him. It still bothered him.

His private ban on killing cops went back to Pittsfield
and the start of Bolan's one-man war against the Mafia.
It really *was* a one-man war, in those days, and he quickly
learned that honest lawmen were committed to arresting
any vigilantes who went looking for their own rough justice on the streets. He understood their jobs, their oath
of office, and he made a private vow that he would never
maim or kill a cop. They were soldiers of the same side,
standing up against the evil in society, and they were not
allowed to pick and choose which laws they would en-
force. Attempting to arrest or kill the Executioner was
part of it, and Bolan recognized his outlaw status from
day one.

The crooked cops were something else, of course. They
sold their badges, dropped their honor in the nearest
trash can when they started taking bribes from pimps and
hookers, narco dealers, mafiosi and the like. Bolan knew
his history, and he was not naive enough to think that all
policemen were—or ever would be—straight, but those
who broke the law themselves, including forays into
murder on occasion, posed a dilemma for his personal
value system.

In combat, traitors and deserters were subject to summary execution, for the good of the unit at large. A dirty
cop betrayed his loyal, hardworking comrades and his
oath of office, taking money underneath the table to ignore specific crimes. When dirty cops were compromised enough, their outlaw masters had been known to
send them out on muscle missions, even contract murders, and the cops in question had no choice but to com-
ply, unless they wanted their illegal dealings aired before
the brass, grand juries and the media.

It was a tough call, but the Executioner had finally
decided crooked cops deserved the same protection as

their honest colleagues from his ban on plugging badges. It was difficult for him to spell the reasons out in words, but Bolan felt the dirty officers had once been clean, perhaps idealistic when they started out, and some of them, at least, might have a shot at personal redemption, somewhere down the line. It happened—rarely, granted—but he could recall a case or two from personal experience. The only men immune to inner change were psychopaths and dead men, two groups which the Executioner had done his level best to merge.

Of course, there was another kind of cop, as well. Aside from those who came on clean and stayed that way, or those who lost their dreams along the way and made an ill-considered compromise, there were a few who sought the job with the deliberate intention of perverting everything it stood for, looking for a way to break the law with absolute impunity. Miami's so-called ''river cops'' had been a case in point, a few years back: recruited during a manpower shortage and without sufficient background checks to reveal their criminal inclinations, their goal from the beginning was to shake down dealers, rob them blind, and sell their confiscated merchandise to larger syndicates. When dealers made an effort to resist the muscle, they were killed.

A syndicate in uniform.

In military terms, it was the same as if an agent from the KGB should join the U.S. Army or the CIA, intent on sabotaging everything they stood for. There was no validity to any oath he took, no personal desire to serve the country or its people. He was an alien, an outsider, a saboteur. It wasn't even treason, since his allegiance lay elsewhere. Instead it was an act of war. And if they were caught red-handed . . .

Bolan stopped himself. He knew the argument by heart, and it would always come down to the same choices. Any attack on sworn servants of the law, no matter how they compromised themselves, would be an insult to the thousands who performed their duties honorably, day by day. It set a precedent for future violence where the bluesuits were concerned, and—worse, in Bolan's estimation—there would always be the possibility of a mistake. A bent cop's honest partner stepping in the line of fire. Mistaken identity. A false lead off the streets.

It was a choice that he would have to live or die with, but each man had to make his decision for himself.

He saw them coming back, Sanchez leading, Mitchum bringing up the rear. Another moment put them in the car, and Bolan noted flecks of blood around the right cuff of Emilio's jacket.

"So?"

The *federale* did not seem elated or relieved. If anything, he looked worn out, a man exhausted . . . and perhaps depressed.

"We have it," Sanchez said.

"I'm listening."

"The last place anyone would think to look," the *federale* told him.

Mitchum, leaning over from the back seat with a tight grin on his face, stole the punch line for himself. "It's Dallas, damn it! Ten, eleven hours if we drive straight through."

CHAPTER TWENTY-SEVEN

Emilio Sanchez chose to stay behind. He spoke of problems still to be resolved in Mexico, and Bolan could not fault him for his choice. Across the border, he was doubling his risks if anything went wrong, and he did not seem quite the same since dealing with Fragosa. It was not as if his fighting spirit had been drained away, exactly, but he had the look that every veteran combat soldier recognizes. He looked like a man about to reach his limits of endurance.

So they parted friends, or close enough. Doyle Mitchum wore a grim expression of his own, but kept his comments to himself until they got back in the car and left Sanchez standing on the curb, a figure dwindling in the rearview mirror.

"I've been following this trail for better than a year," the ex-cop from Miami said. "And now, just when we've almost got it hacked, I start to ask myself if it was worth it. Christ, Brock Hargis dead—and what a lousy way to die. God only knows how many men we killed, between us."

Not enough, thought Bolan. Not just yet. They still had one to go.

"Get past it," he suggested. "When you take a job, you think about the consequences going in. Martinez and Ibarra made the rules in this game. One of them has paid the tab already, but it isn't over till we bag Martinez. Anything less than a clean sweep, and we lose."

"I keep asking myself if it really makes a difference," Mitchum said. "By now, some other dealer has Ibarra's outlets covered, status quo. If anything, the chances are we raised the bastard's prices for him. He'll be tickled pink we came to town."

"Could be," the Executioner replied, "but you can only fight one battle at a time. If nothing else, the PR on Ibarra may rejuvenate the drive against cocaine along the border."

"For a month or so, if that."

"I'll take a decent month, if I can get it. When we started, no one had a firm line on Ibarra. He was home free, making it up as he went along. At least his new replacement has to start from scratch, and that should give the FJP and DEA a chance to do some good."

"It's funny," Mitchum said. "I never took you for an optimist."

The Executioner responded with a weary smile. "I have my moments," he replied. "Just keep it to yourself."

"Will do."

It was a long drive north and east from Ciudad Acuna. They were edgy at the border crossing to Del Rio, with automatic weapons in the car, but Bolan caught a break and Customs passed them through with perfunctory questions and a casual glance at the empty black seat. They picked up Highway 90, eastbound from Del Rio, with 150 miles of flatland stretching out in front of them to San Antonio, home of the Alamo and a mecca for last-ditch stands.

From San Antonio they went north on Highway 35, through Austin and Temple, stopping off to eat and stretch their legs in Waco, then at last rolled into Dallas after nightfall. Bolan stopped for gas and bought a city map to double-check the address Sanchez had supplied. According to their information from Fragosa, Martinez had a condominium just off Jefferson Street, in suburban Cockrell Hill. Bolan skirted Red Bird Airport on Highway 12, picked up Westmoreland Road northbound, and started checking street numbers after he turned west on Jefferson.

"There," Mitchum told him, pointing, when they had covered a half-dozen blocks.

"Okay."

The building was a monolith with smoked-glass windows and an underground garage. A drive-by told the Executioner that he would need a key or ID car to enter the garage, and so he wrote it off. The neighborhood was high-rise residential for the most part, but they found a shopping mall two blocks downrange and parked the car.

"So, what's the drill?" asked Mitchum.

Bolan thought about it for a moment, watching foot traffic around the mall. "He's running anyway. We can't rule out some kind of contacts in the city, but I don't see anyone throwing major weight behind him with what's happened in the past three days."

"You want the hardware from the trunk?"

"Not this time."

"Right. Let's hit it, then."

"I thought you might prefer to sit it out."

"Get real. You think I came this far to punk out on the two-year line?"

"You've still got law-enforcement ties," said Bolan. "I won't be arresting anybody here today."

"Suits me. They couldn't give this prick the kind of time he needs to put things right."

"You're sure?"

"Damn right."

"Okay, let's do it."

Bolan locked the car, and Mitchum followed him across the street, mercury-vapor lamps overhead and stylish pedestrians passing by on the sidewalk. Bolan tried to picture Fernando Martinez walking those streets, dressed in his finery, passing for an upwardly mobile Hispanic businessman. No one was searching for him here, as far as Martinez knew, and he would have no need for a disguise.

Security was something else, of course. The doorman on the block of condos took a look at Bolan's laminated ID card from Justice, frowned, and passed them through without complaint. They did not state their business or inquire about Martinez, since they had the condo's number going in. He had no reason to believe the doorman would alert Martinez to their presence if he knew where they were going, but the Executioner did not see fit to take the risk.

"Sixth floor," said Mitchum, almost whispering. "You want the elevator?"

"Service stairs," said Bolan, suiting words to action as they reached the access door. "If he's got watchdogs, I'd prefer to take them by surprise."

"Your call."

The door clicked shut behind them, and they started up the stairs.

FERNANDO DE LEON MARTINEZ was exhausted from his flight. He had switched vehicles twice in the past twelve hours, ditching the van in Ciudad Acuna and driving a sports car across the border into Texas, delayed by an overzealous Customs officer who insisted on checking his trunk and poking underneath the bucket seats. In Austin, he ditched the sportster on a side street, walking four blocks to a used-car lot where he purchased a year-old sedan with cash. The salesman was delighted, rambling on with small talk till Martinez cut him of with an excuse of business to the north that would not wait.

The Dallas condo was a fall-back option, purchased under a pseudonym twelve months earlier. None of his disciples knew about the hideout, and they could not finger him for enemies, assuming they were still alive. The landlord knew him as Miguel De Soto, whose expansive bank account made up for any latent prejudice against Hispanics in the neighborhood.

One person knew where he had gone. It had been necessary to alert Fragosa, thus preserving crucial ties, eliminating any danger that the *commandante* might suspect that he was dead and go in search of other patrons in the underworld.

It was one link between his present status and the power he intended to regain without delay.

Fatigue was catching up with him, but he could not relax enough to sleep. It seemed preposterous: three days to ruin everything that he had worked for through the years. It still appalled Martinez that he could be taken by surprise that way, manipulated by his enemies as if he had no link to the *orishas* and the psychic world beyond.

He had been robbed of his *nganga* once again, the second time within a month, but he could always start again. The sooner the better, in fact. But he would have to let the heat die down before he made a move. It would not only be counterproductive but actually potentially disastrous to attempt such rituals in the United States, before he had a chance to gather new disciples for the cause.

In one respect, it would have been a challenge that he relished, starting fresh . . . but not this way. The sudden, crushing blows he had endured, and his ineffectual response, had shaken the *palero*'s confidence. More to the point, his clients and potential clients would inevitably learn about his troubles, if they did not know already. It would make him seem weak.

But that would change, and quickly, once Martinez satisfied himself that there was no more danger from his enemies. Rebuilding would take time, but he had ample money stashed away to live for months—a year or two, if it came down to that. Perhaps a rest was what he needed, after all.

But what Martinez really needed in the short term was something to help him relax. A woman, perhaps, except that he could not risk calling any of the "escort services" that advertised throughout Dallas, and he did not feel like doing business with a pimp tonight. Unlike some practicing magicians, he avoided using drugs on the assumption that they cloud the mind and set up interference to communications from the spirit world.

But he could use a glass of wine, most definitely. Maybe two. Enough to take the edge off his anxiety and bring the calming sort of warmth he knew so well. In better times, he would have gotten that sensation from his work with the *nganga*, but his tools had all been captured by the vandals who had sacked his mountain compound.

They hadn't vanquished him, though. He would surprise them all with his return, stronger than ever, no mercy for those who conspired to destroy him. One way or another, he would learn their names and send his demons out to track them down. His enemies would have a taste of hell on earth before they died . . . and everlasting fire was waiting for them on the other side.

A fitting punishment, indeed, for those who trifled with a master of his craft.

No one could touch him now, and by the time they found out where he was—if anyone was even looking for him—it would be too late. Martinez would have rallied new disciples to his banner, found more donors for a fresh *nganga,* and his power would be multiplied by virtue of the losses he had suffered. All experience was beneficial, but the kind that toughened spirits was the best of all.

He crossed the room and poured himself a glass of wine, was sipping it with pleasure. Catching sight of his own image in an ornate mirror mounted on the wall, he grinned and lifted his glass in a toast to himself.

His head bent, he filled up his glass again, starting to feel a little soothed by the fine bloodred wine coursing through his veins. But there was something else in the mirror, something unbelievable, and Martinez whirled around in shock.

A strange voice broke the silence.

"Fernando de Leon Martinez, I presume?"

DOYLE MITCHUM was nervous climbing the stairs, painfully conscious of the sound their footsteps made inside the claustrophobic stairwell. Beside him, Belasko had not drawn his weapon, but the ex-cop from Miami kept one hand inside his jacket, wrapped around the Browning automatic he had lifted from Gregorio Ruiz in Mexico.

His good-luck piece.

If there was shooting, he would try to let Belasko take the lead. The warrior's weapon had a silencer, and they were trying to avoid a three-ring circus in the building, if they could. This kind of neighborhood, the tenants would be quick to ring up 911 the first time guns went off, and the police or sheriff's deputies would probably respond without delay.

Despite that, the thought of turning back had never entered Mitchum's mind. If he could help erase Martinez, it was worth a bust, derision in the public eye, and time in prison. Screw the stories he had heard about what happened to a cop inside. He wasn't known in Texas, but if word came down and someone tried to rough him up... well, he would cope with that one when he had to. At the moment, Mitchum had his plate full, concentrating on the job at hand.

Six floors meant twelve flights of stairs. No sweat in the old days, when he was working out a couple times a week at the department's gym, but Mitchum's thigh muscles were burning by the time they reached their destination, and he felt a little winded by the climb. Belasko seemed to notice, but he kept it to himself.

There was no window in the metal door that opened onto six. Belasko had to check the corridor beyond by opening the door and slowly, cautiously peering around the jamb, ready to jerk his head back at the first sign of danger. He seemed to take forever, scoping out the hall, while Mitchum held his breath and kept his fingers crossed. At last, Belasko pulled his head back, and the ex-cop let his breath out.

"No guards," Belasko said.

"That's good, right?"

"If he doesn't have men in the condo with him, then it's good."

They stepped into the hallway, carpeting beneath their feet now, checking numbers on the doors and moving to the left, toward the Martinez condo. A different name here in the States, of course, but that made no difference to Mitchum. He would never forget the bastard's face, his evil smile as the electrodes were applied.

It had been something special, taking out Gregorio Ruiz, but nothing to the pleasure he would feel at standing over the *palero*'s lifeless body, maybe quick enough to watch the spark of life fade out behind his eyes.

No slick plea bargains with the D.A.'s office. Nothing in the way of "rehabilitation" or parole. Scratch off the country-club asylums where the courts warehoused the worst of psychopathic misfits, waiting for some egghead with a Ph.D. behind his name to claim they were "no danger to society."

That was pure bullshit. The only cure for a maniac like that was death, and all the liberal jargon in the world would never change that basic fact. A psychopathic killer likes his work—better than sex, better than anything— and he will never stop as long as he can find another victim. Many of them kept on killing after they were sent to prison, never mind the sentence, whether it was twenty years, two hundred, or two thousand. Guards and other inmates were their prey from that point on; some hellbent psychos even took a shot at visitors, if institutional security was lax enough.

Tonight, if all went well, Martinez would be cured, and the world could rest a little easier. At least, thought Mitchum, maybe *I* can rest.

They stood outside the door and listened for a moment, knowing they could blow it if they simply kicked it in and tried to take the place by storm. For one thing, they would spook the neighbors well before they got a clear shot at Martinez, and they had no way of knowing whether he was even home. A safe bet, possibly, but if he felt secure enough in Dallas, he might want to stretch his legs and strut his stuff. If that was the case and they were forced to wait for him inside, a shattered door would tip their quarry off on his return and blow the whole damned thing.

Another problem to consider was the possibility that Martinez had some kind of backup with him. Crashing in would put them up against the sentries, possibly outnumbered, in a firefight that would waste their precious time . . . or maybe get them killed.

"I'll have to pick it," Belasko whispered. "Watch out for neighbors."

"Right."

The condos were arranged so no two doors directly faced each other. You would never poke your head out in the morning, bleary-eyed, unshaved, and find a neighbor blinking at you in his bathrobe. Distance with a touch of class, but anyone could still emerge from one of the adjoining flats at any time and find them standing there, Belasko on his knees and fiddling with a set of picks to beat the knob lock and the dead bolt.

Doyle Mitchum offered up a silent prayer that there would be no noise to tip off Martinez or the gunmen he might have inside. He pictured some gorilla sitting on the far side of the door, a sawed-off shotgun in his lap, just waiting for the knob to turn so he could blow them both away. A dumb, shit-eating grin the last thing Mitchum would ever see before the lights went out for good.

Another moment, and Belasko beat the locks, a sharp click from the dead bolt, but he couldn't help it, given the construction of the piece. They stood and waited for another few seconds, one on each side of the door, in case somebody opened up before they tried to step inside.

No shots. No sounds of any kind to indicate the flat was even occupied.

Belasko drew his gun and Mitchum followed suit. He watched the door ease open, felt the tension in Belasko's body, knowing that a bullet could be waiting for them on the other side. Maybe Fernando's watchdog wanted something better than a door to shoot at when he opened fire. It made more sense to get a living, breathing body in your sights and make the first shot count.

They were inside now, and they could hear soft music, so muted that it barely carried to the foyer. Something classical and smooth, like bedroom music. Mitchum could not place the artist or composer, and he didn't give a damn. The only thing that mattered now was that the tune had covered up whatever sounds they made on entering the condo.

A blank wall in front of them, with artificial flowers on a decorative table, Mitchum trailed Belasko to the left, around a corner, following the music to a nicely furnished sitting room.

Martinez was standing with his back turned, sipping at a glass of wine. He lifted his head, as if he were following a stray thought, when his eye fell on an ornate mirror mounted on the wall. Three faces stared back at him, when it should have been only one.

His blank expression was everything that Mitchum could have hoped for. Turning on his heel, Martinez gaped at them, clearly recognizing Mitchum from their last encounter.

Belasko said, "Fernando de Leon Martinez, I presume."

Shocked, Martinez took in the tall dark man with tombstone eyes, then stared right past him, facing Mitchum with an expression stuck between shock and fury.

"You."

"I didn't have a chance to say goodbye before you split," said Mitchum. "Anyway, I didn't want you thinking I was rude."

When the *palero* made his move, it came so suddenly that Mitchum almost missed it, even staring at Martinez as he was. Fernando dropped his wineglass, leaping headlong for the cover of a sofa standing with its back toward Mitchum and Belasko, dropping out of sight before Belasko had a chance to aim and fire.

"Goddamn it!"

Mitchum barely got it out before a hand slid into view, wrapped tightly around an automatic pistol, and the weapon's muzzle flared directly at his face.

So MUCH FOR SUBTLETY. The Executioner sprang one way, Mitchum automatically recoiling in the opposite direction as a bullet hissed between them. The *palero*'s weapon had a silencer attached, which might be clever planning or a matter of coincidence, but either way it helped to buy some time. If Mitchum held his fire, they still might pull it off before a nervous neighbor spooked and called the riot squad.

Bolan was ready when the hand appeared again, returning fire, but he was off by something like an inch, his bullet disappearing into the upholstery and spitting cotton stuffing out the other side. Martinez, by comparison, blew up a decorative vase and scattered jagged shards of china on the floor.

No cover where he lay, and Bolan shifted further to his left, squeezed in behind a bulky armchair. It was close and awkward there, but he could trust the chair to stop a bullet, maybe more than one, unless Martinez found his mark and ripped a pattern through the cushions.

Take advantage of the lull, thought Bolan. Now, before Martinez shows himself and Mitchum can't resist a shot.

As luck would have it, Bolan burst from cover just as the *palero* fired another round. It was coincidence, perhaps, but Bolan felt the slug breeze past his face as he lunged forward, squeezing off a quick round of his own. Martinez was up and moving, firing as he ran in the direction of a nearby bedroom, nearly stumbling once, but he was on the threshold when a round from Bolan's 93-R caught him in the side and spun him off his feet.

Up and moving as the target wriggled out of sight, Doyle Mitchum closed on the open doorway, leading with his Browning automatic, tension written on his face. Bolan circled wide, still no view of Martinez from where he stood, but from the visible layout of the room there seemed a limited range of possibilities.

He would not settle for a standoff now, when they had come this far. He scanned the wedge of bedroom he could see and timed his move, making a restraining gesture to Mitchum before he launched himself forward.

Bolan cleared the bedroom doorway in flight, accompanied by a rapid spitting sound from the weapon somewhere on his right, and Bolan felt a line of fire across one thigh before he tumbled out of sight behind the bed. A shoulder roll helped to recover his balance in a heartbeat, and he came up in a crouch with the Beretta braced in a two-handed grip.

He knew the risk before he surfaced, but he couldn't accurately hit a target that he couldn't see. The warrior came up firing, wasting two rounds off the top before he found Martinez, crouching by a vanity and firing back, brass leaping from the ejection port of his weapon.

Bolan squeezed off four more rounds in rapid-fire, the impact lifting Martinez off his feet and slamming him against a closet door. He hung there, seeming suspended for several seconds, and finally slipped to the carpet, trailing crimson in his wake.

They had come to the end.

Doyle Mitchum stood in the doorway, staring at Martinez, shoulders slumped, the automatic dangling at his side. To Bolan, he resembled nothing quite so much as a sports fan who has waited all year long for a championship game, only to have the crucial play carried off while he was glancing elsewhere.

"Damn."

Bolan moved across the room to stand before Martinez, fishing in the pocket of his sport coat for a small metallic object. Bending down, he pinned the dime-store Texas Rangers badge to the *palero*'s leaking shirt.

"Okay," he said. "We're finished now."

New morning light found them in Houston, far enough removed from the previous night's action that they heard no mention of Martinez on the local news and felt no danger from authorities investigating his demise. The diner where they met for breakfast was a simple place with 1950s atmosphere and 1990s prices. Bolan ordered eggs and bacon, Mitchum going for link sausage wrapped in buttermilk pancakes, advertised on the menu as "pigs in a blanket."

"What now?" the ex-cop from Miami asked when the waitress had left them alone.

"Now, you go back to doing what you do," said Bolan. "Something tells me when the smoke clears, you'll be talking to a more respectful audience."

"I hope so," Mitchum told him. "God knows, as bad as Martinez was, he was only a part of the problem. We've got guys just like him—some worse—in southern Florida and all along the border, moving into California, New York City, you name it."

"Try the bright side," Bolan said. "You've made a start. The evidence the FJP turned up in Mexico will go a long way toward convincing skeptics in the States."

"I'm counting on it. What about yourself?"

"Same story, different players. This time tomorrow...who knows?"

"No time for yourself?"

Bolan frowned, thinking of Inez Lozaro in Tres Lobos. He still had a satchel of Ramon Ibarra's money in the trunk of his rental car, but he would find another way to make delivery. His war had already impinged on the lady's life enough, for good or ill, and there were other fronts already waiting for a visit from the Executioner.

"I'll give it some thought," Bolan said, his thoughts moving on to the Blue Ridge Mountains of Virginia, Stony Man the closest thing he had to a home these days.

But there would be another serpent waiting for him in the garden. Bolan took that much for granted, and he had no qualms about tomorrow. It was what he lived for, after all.

BATTLE FOR THE FUTURE IN A WASTELAND OF DESPAIR

AURORA QUEST

by JAMES AXLER

The popular author of DEATHLANDS® brings you the gripping conclusion of the Earthblood trilogy with AURORA QUEST. The crew of the U.S. space vessel *Aquila* returns from a deep-space mission to find that a devastating plant blight has stripped away all civilization.

In what's left of the world, the astronauts grimly cling to a glimmer of promise for a new start.

Available in July at your favorite retail outlet.

A new warrior breed blazes a trail
to an uncertain future in

JAMES AXLER

DEATH LANDS®

Twilight Children

Ryan Cawdor and his band of warrior-survivalists are transported
from one Valley of the Shadow of Death to another, where they
find out that the quest for Paradise carries a steep price.

In the Deathlands, the future looks terminally brief.

Don't miss out on the action in these titles featuring
THE EXECUTIONER®, ABLE TEAM® and PHOENIX FORCE®!

SuperBolan

#61431   ONSLAUGHT $4.99   ☐
With his cover blown by a leak traceable to the highest levels of Russian
security, Mack Bolan is forced to go solo, with Mafia hit men and cartel killers
burning a trail of bullets and blood from Moscow to the Black Sea coast.

#61433   RAMPAGE $4.99   ☐
Rampant terrorism is sweeping through Europe as a fearless new force with
a gruesome agenda turns the French Riviera into a killing ground.

Stony Man™

#61889   STONY MAN V $4.99   ☐
When an international drug machine declares war, Stony Man—Mack Bolan,
Able Team and Phoenix Force—jumps into the heat of battle.

#61891   STONY MAN VII $4.99   ☐
Stony Man: America's most classified weapon—action-ready and lethal.

#61892   STONY MAN VIII $4.99   ☐
A power-hungry industrialist fuels anarchy in South America.

(limited quantities available on certain titles)

TOTAL AMOUNT	$
POSTAGE & HANDLING	$
($1.00 for one book, 50¢ for each additional)	
APPLICABLE TAXES*	$ _____
TOTAL PAYABLE	$ _____
(check or money order—please do not send cash)	

To order, complete this form and send it, along with a check or money order for the
total above, payable to Gold Eagle Books, to: **In the U.S.:** 3010 Walden Avenue,
P.O. Box 9077, Buffalo, NY 14269-9077; **In Canada:** P.O. Box 636, Fort Erie, Ontario,
L2A 5X3.

Name: _____
Address: _____ City: _____
State/Prov.: _____ Zip/Postal Code: _____

*New York residents remit applicable sales taxes.
 Canadian residents remit applicable GST and provincial taxes.

GEBACK6A